Susanna Strom

SECRETS
—OF—
SHOOTING STAR
LAKE

BLACK
ROCK
GUARDIANS

SUSANNA STROM

Visit my website at https://susannastrom.com/
https://www.facebook.com/susannastromauthor/
https://www.facebook.com/groups/1572291033136914

Developmental Editor: Christina Trevaskis
www.bookmatchmaker.com

Interior Designer: Jovana Shirley
Unforeseeen Editing, www.unforeseenediting.com

Proofreader: Brittany Meyer-Strom
brittanym.edits@gmail.com

Editor: Julia Fortune
https://www.fortuneliteraryservices.com

Cover Designer: Lori Jackson Designer
www.lorijacksondesign.com

Photography: Wander Aguiar Photography
www.wanderbookclub.com

ISBN ebook: 978-1-960382-05-4
ISBN paperback: 978-1-960382-06-1

Published by Cougar Creek Publishing LLC

DEDICATION

*This book celebrates the close bond between cousins, a relationship
inspired by real life. I grew up in a large Scandinavian-American family.
More than a hundred Torland family members showed up at our
Christmas Eve and Fourth of July celebrations. I lucked out when it
came to cousins. Mine were the best. The happiest memories of my
childhood are bound up with my cousins. They were my playmates, my
closest friends, my confidants, and occasionally my partners in mischief. If
I listed them all, their names would fill the page, but a special shout out
to Barbee, Joanne, Jan, Becky, Don, Craig, and Steve.*

CHAPTER ONE

MARIT

An orange ball of fur barreled out from between parked
cars. I slammed on the brakes. The car skittered to an
abrupt stop. I hadn't felt a telltale bump—thank God—but
that didn't mean the dog had escaped unscathed. Heart
pounding, I scanned the quiet residential street.

Buttercup Mittelmann trotted out from behind a bush and
nonchalantly plopped down onto his haunches in the middle
of the road, to all appearances unfazed by his narrow escape.
His tail thumped against the pavement. His tongue lolled from
his mouth. If I didn't know better, I'd swear the unrepentant
Pomeranian was smiling at me.

The knot in my stomach eased. I lowered the driver's-side
window. "Dude, do you have a death wish?"

He yipped, as happy and chatty as ever.

Sighing, I cut the engine and unfastened my seat belt.
"Does your mama know you got out?" I demanded, stepping
from the car.

As if on cue, Dorrie Mittelmann scurried down the front
walk of her blue Craftsman bungalow, a fluttering hand
pressed against her chest. Despite her seventy-odd years, not a

single gray strand stood out in her tousled pixie cut, her hair the same vivid reddish-orange as the dog's fur. Of the two, I bet only Buttercup sported a natural hue. Mrs. Mittelmann's hair color might have been suspect, but the relieved smile that crossed her face when she spotted her dog was one hundred percent genuine.

She scooped up her wayward pooch, kissed him on the nose, then turned to me. "The girls and I are having our weekly coffee klatch, and Janine left the back door open. I've warned her that Buttercup is an escape artist, but does she listen?" She sniffed. "No."

I scritched Buttercup between the ears. "At least he's safe now."

"Yes, he is, the naughty boy." The old woman's eyes lit up, and she touched my arm. "Your wedding is just around the corner, isn't it, Marit?"

"Yes, ma'am. In eleven days."

She sighed and shook her head. "It's too bad dear Freya couldn't be here to watch you get married."

My chest tightened. Grandma had passed away early last September—almost a year ago—but unexpected reminders of her death still choked me up. "Grandma is here in spirit."

"Yes, I'm sure she is." Mrs. M. squeezed my arm, her brown eyes warm with sympathy. "And I bet you girls will be using one of her wonderful recipes for your wedding cake."

I laughed, back on safe ground. Baking was my happy place, a passion I'd shared with Grandma. After her death, my cousins Annika, Liv, and I borrowed money against our inheritance and bought a failing florist shop from its bankrupt owner. We sunk all of our cash into renovating the building. Now, Freya's Bake Shop occupies a place of honor in Belle Reve's quaint downtown district.

"We're making Grandma's famous pink champagne cake," I said. "With Bavarian cream filling."

"Yummy," she cried. "I'm so looking forward to the wedding. I'll be there with bells on."

I dropped a kiss onto her cheek. "I'm counting on it."

She gestured toward the house. "Why don't you come inside and have coffee with the girls and me? We'd love to hear all about your wedding plans."

"Can't." I offered a regret-filled shake of my head. "Bryce has been putting in long hours, trying to catch up on work before we go on our honeymoon. I thought I'd surprise him with some coconut curry soup from our favorite Thai restaurant. He's working from home today. I'm on my way to drop it off."

"You're a sweetheart, just like Freya."

Grandma had been many things—fiercely loving, loyal, headstrong—but a sweetheart wasn't one of them.

My lips twitched. "If you say so."

"I do. Of all the cousins, you're the most like her, you know."

If only. "I *look* the most like her," I agreed.

Her expression sobered. Grandma's oldest friend touched my cheek. "I see Freya every time I look into your face, but it's more than that, Marit. You have her spirit."

I swallowed, deeply touched. "Best compliment ever, Mrs. M."

Buttercup barked and Mrs. Mittelmann shifted the wriggling dog from one arm to the other. "You get along now. And tell your handsome fiancé I'm counting on him to save a dance for me at the reception."

"Will do." I gave Buttercup a final pat, raised a hand in farewell, then slid back behind the steering wheel. I peeked into the paper bag seat-belted onto the passenger side. The to-go container of soup had survived the sudden stop without popping the lid or springing a leak. I blew out a relieved breath. The last thing I wanted was to clean red curry off the seat cushion. First Buttercup and now the soup. "I'm dodging bullets left and right today," I muttered, pulling away from the curb.

Three minutes later, I turned onto a tree-lined street and brought the car to a stop in front of Bryce's tidy rental house.

Two cars occupied the driveway, Bryce's flame-red roadster and a familiar, white luxury SUV.

"Great," I said under my breath. "Just great."

Bryce had insisted that we hire his old friend Courtney as our wedding planner. Courtney was a big-deal event planner in Seattle. Her father was one of his father's closest friends. The fact that she'd consider taking a job in the sticks of central Washington was a huge favor, Bryce said. Moreover, the whole family would consider it a slap in the face if we hired anyone else.

Okay. For the sake of getting along with my future in-laws, I could make a concession.

Our first meeting went well enough. I was no bridezilla determined to micromanage every aspect of the wedding.

Salmon or halibut?

Prime rib or tenderloin?

As long as there was a vegetarian option for my cousin Annika, I really didn't care.

Bryce had his heart set on a jazz quartet for the reception. Not my first choice for music, but fine. It was his wedding, too, and I wanted him to enjoy it.

See? Not a bridezilla.

Courtney and I didn't butt heads until she suggested a naked wedding cake from a trendy bakery in Seattle. I put my foot down. My cousins and I would bake the cake using one of Grandma's recipes. Courtney frowned, clearly aghast. From her expression, you'd think I'd suggested sewing my own wedding dress.

Speaking of dresses… when I told Courtney that I didn't want matchy-matchy bridesmaid dresses—that I'd told Annika and Liv to wear whatever made them feel happy and pretty—Courtney's right eye actually twitched.

Tradition be damned, I added. I'd have two maids of honor, not one. She tossed Bryce a pitying look, as if she couldn't believe her old friend was marrying such a yokel.

I piled on. No, I didn't want to fly to San Francisco to meet with her favorite wedding dress designer at his atelier. "I always thought I'd wear one of Grandma's vintage dresses when I got married," I explained. "You know, a late-1960s flowy, boho style."

"With flowers in your hair, I suppose? And barefoot?" Courtney blinked rapidly. "Like a hippie?"

Give me a break. I didn't want a '60s-themed wedding. I simply wanted to wear a dress that meant something to me. Still, I'd admit that the knowledge I was getting under the snobby wedding planner's skin gave me a mean-spirited thrill.

I lifted my shoulders in a wordless shrug.

"Bryce will be wearing Armani," she said through clenched teeth. "Not tie-dye and bell-bottoms."

Tie-dye and bell-bottoms? Really? I thought wedding planners were supposed to make things easier for the couple, not cop an attitude or pummel the bride with snark. What was the woman's problem with me?

"Bryce can wear whatever makes him happy." I smiled.

She smiled back, a humorless flash of teeth that didn't touch her eyes. No doubt about it, I was on Courtney's shit list.

Now, at the sight of Courtney's white SUV, I heaved another sigh. Was I supposed to meet them at the house for some last-minute wedding preparations? If Bryce had told me she was coming to town, I totally forgot.

I cut the engine, grabbed the bag from the Thai restaurant, and let myself in through the front door. Glancing into the living room, I expected to see Bryce and Courtney sitting on the sofa, the coffee table in front of them strewn with paperwork. No sign of the two, but Loki, the adorable mixed-breed mutt we'd adopted a few months ago, lifted his head from his bed on the hearth. He stood, trotted over to me, and bumped against my leg. I dropped to my knees and gave him a one-armed hug.

"Where's Daddy?" I asked.

He whined.

"Still haven't warmed up to him, huh?" I sighed. Loki loved me from the start. Bryce tried to win him over—throwing tennis balls and offering him treats—but the dog kept a wary distance.

"Do you need to go potty?" I led the way toward the patio door that opened onto the back yard. Loki slipped outside and bounded toward his designated corner of the lawn. I glanced at the gazebo in the opposite corner of the yard, but Bryce and Courtney weren't there either. Rocking back on my heels, I waited for Loki to finish his business.

Muffled laughter punctuated the quiet. Holding my breath, I cocked my head to one side. A moment of silence, then the sound of hushed voices drifted from the other side of the house. I padded through the kitchen and down a hall toward Bryce's home office, pausing outside the room. I cracked the door open and peeked inside. Empty. Another low laugh. I frowned and swung my head toward the source of the sound.

I made my way toward the guest room at the end of the hall. Behind the closed door, Courtney giggled. Bryce groaned, an unmistakable sound of pleasure that I knew too well. I stood stock-still, my heart pummeling my ribs. Goose bumps erupted across my shoulders. A tsunami of conflicting thoughts slammed through my mind.

What the hell, Bryce?

He swore he loved me, that I was his one and only, his dream come true, his gift from fate.

Another groan. Another body blow. Everything inside me stilled.

The easiest thing in the world would be to slink away, to pretend I hadn't heard a thing, and to bury the memory. Bryce and I hadn't formally exchanged vows. Maybe this was a last hurrah, a farewell to bachelorhood. My brain clutched at that idea for a good three seconds before I kicked the notion to the curb. Nobody with a shred of self-respect could be that desperate.

Sucking in a breath, I twisted the knob, pushed open the door, and stepped inside.

My gaze fell on the long line of Courtney's naked back as she straddled Bryce, riding him like an overeager cowgirl. Her shiny dark hair slid against her bouncing shoulders. Bryce bucked beneath her, his fingers pressing divots into her pale thighs. I took it all in, speechless.

Eleven days. We're supposed to get married in eleven days. And then…

How do you cancel a wedding at the last minute?

Courtney must have sensed my presence. She turned her head and glanced my way. Her lips curved up in a triumphant smile. Malicious cheer sparkled in her eyes.

"What?" Bryce grumbled. He tilted his head to the side, peering around Courtney. Spying me, he pushed up on his elbows. "Oh, fuck."

"Yeah," I agreed, my voice surprisingly flat and uninflected. "Oh, fuck."

Bryce shoved a hand through sweat-drenched hair, then gestured at Courtney. "Marit, baby, this isn't what you think."

Despite my shock, the absurdity of his words struck like flint against stone. Anger sparked in my chest and rolled through my veins, burning away the numbness that had settled over me.

My fiancé was buried balls deep in another woman, but it wasn't what I thought?

Clearly I was gullible, taken in by all his sweet talk about love and forever, but did he actually think I was stupid enough to buy his, *this isn't what you think?*

I barked out a harsh laugh, and my fingers tightened on the paper bag.

"My lying eyes are deceiving me; is that what you're saying?"

Bryce sat up, pushing Courtney off his hips. She landed on her ass, then crab-walked backward until she bumped against the padded headboard. Drawing her knees up to her chest, she watched me with eager eyes, all the while flashing her cooch. She bit her lower lip, and her shoulders shook with barely suppressed laughter. Dammit, she actually loved this.

Bryce ignored her. He stretched out a hand, an infuriatingly patient expression painted across his handsome face, like he was trying to reason with a stubborn child. "C'mon, baby. We can fix this. Just listen—"

"Just listen?"

Something inside me snapped. I *should* have listened. When Annika gently warned me that Bryce might be too good to be true. When Liv—bitter after a breakup with yet another "loser fuckboy"—urged me to put the brakes on. When that little voice inside my head insisted that we were moving too fast, that I was getting carried away by how picture-perfect Bryce was.

"Just listen," Bryce said?

I almost choked on anger and regret. Tearing my gaze away from a face that oozed false sincerity, I looked down at the paper bag I still clutched in a death grip. With trembling hands, I opened the bag and pulled out the container of soup. Balancing the disposable container on the palm of my hand, I hefted its weight. I raised my eyes to Bryce and Courtney, naked on rumpled white sheets, their skin shiny with sweat from their exertions.

Before I could think twice about it, I peeled the plastic lid off the soup container. Shrimp and cubes of bell pepper floated in a pungent red curry broth that glistened with melted coconut fat. I smiled and turned my gaze back to Bryce and Courtney.

Eyes wide, Courtney leaned against the ivory upholstered headboard. She held out a warning finger. "Don't you dare."

I hurled the container of soup against the wall over her head. It exploded, raining red curry down over her glossy dark hair and creamy shoulders, staining the linen headboard, and splattering Bryce and the sheets.

"Bitch," Courtney sputtered, wiping soup from her cheeks.

Who me? A bitch?

Maybe.

I couldn't deny the petty glee that shot through me at the sight of the red soup sliding down their shocked faces.

"You okay?" Bryce touched Courtney's cheek.

At the tender gesture, my pleasure sputtered out and died. A knot formed in the pit of my stomach. I hadn't walked in on a spur-of-the-moment hookup. Bryce cared about Courtney. So what the hell was he doing with me?

Stupid. I'd been so damned stupid to believe this man loved me. I staggered backward, suddenly desperate to be anywhere else, to be with people who truly cared about me, to be with Annika and Liv. At the thought of my cousins, I whirled and dashed down the hall, then cut through the kitchen toward the front door. I flung open the door and stumbled outside, blinking into the bright late-July sunshine. Pressing my fist against my stomach, I gulped in air.

Bryce appeared in the doorway, breathless and butt-naked. "Come back inside. We can work this out."

Un-freaking-believable.

After the way he comforted Courtney, he expected me to buy that he really wanted to work this out? Shaking my head, I backed away. "If you want Courtney, be with Courtney. We're done."

"No, Marit. We aren't done." A slow smile crawled across his handsome face. Instead of making me weak in the knees— like it always had before—it filled me with the urge to do violence. "I messed up, sweetheart. It won't happen again."

"I don't care if it happens again. Just… just leave me alone." Turning my back on my cheating ex, I ran to my car.

Chapter Two

Adam

A teenage girl wandered into my path, forcing me to stop short to avoid bumping into her. In a chain reaction, the people behind me on the crowded sidewalk came to a halt, too. The girl looked up from her cell phone, caught my eye, and froze. Her lips twitched in a small uneasy smile.

"Sorry."

I dipped my chin, acknowledging the apology, then sidestepped the girl. Regaining my stride, I made a beeline toward the city parking lot where I'd left my truck.

During the summer tourist season, downtown Belle Reve was the last place I wanted to be. A crowd of milling strangers made me wary and hypervigilant. Smells assailed my nostrils, and I automatically sorted them into categories. Friend or enemy. Predator or prey. Was that aggression I tasted on the air, or fear? Unfamiliar voices might call out, and my head would whip to one side, tracking the sound. Someone might dart in front of me, hurrying down the sidewalk, and I'd fight the instinct to give chase. All the while, my agitated wolf stirred uneasily beneath my skin.

It was fucking exhausting. That's why I took the thronging mass in small doses.

A block from the parking lot, my cell phone chirped with an incoming text. I stepped into the shelter of a recessed doorway and pulled the phone from my pocket.

You picked up the cupcakes, right?

I groaned, grinding the heel of my hand against an eye.

On my way out of pack headquarters this morning, Rolf, the senior sentry, had pulled me aside. His daughter—pregnant with his first grandchild—had ordered cupcakes from a fancy new bakery downtown for her baby shower this evening. Since I was already driving the thirty miles into town, would I be willing to pick them up? Of course, I said yes. Unfortunately, after I finished at the county courthouse, I'd been in such a hurry to get out of town that I totally forgot to stop.

A promise was a promise.

On my way, I typed. I wheeled around and headed back the direction I'd come from, shouldering my way through the bustling crowd.

Two blocks from the bakery, a woman rushed past me. She stumbled as she ran, her gait unsteady. Hair the color of dark honey tumbled around her shoulders. She jostled a pair of ice-cream-eating tourists who had planted themselves in the middle of the sidewalk. Halting, she tossed an apologetic smile over her shoulder.

"Sorry. Sorry."

I stopped dead in my tracks.

My head jerked back and my nostrils flared.

An imaginary Mack truck slammed into my chest, knocking me off-balance.

As if pulled by a magnet, her gaze moved from the tourists to me. Our eyes locked. Her forehead furrowed and her brows drew down. Her feet were planted firmly on the sidewalk, but her body swayed toward mine. Had the imaginary truck hit her, too? Sadness, anger, and confusion poured off her, as well as a heady whiff of something... unexpected... something indefinable.

What was that?

Drawing in a long, slow breath, I sampled and discarded the scents that blew past me. My lips parted and I tasted the air as I honed my senses on the woman.

There.

I captured her essence. Sweetness exploded on my tongue—sugar, vanilla, butter—as well as her own unique natural perfume. Cupcakes, I realized with a start. She smelled like the cupcakes I'd promised to pick up for Rolf.

Already that scent was imprinted in my memory, never to be forgotten or mistaken for another. I fought the urge to stalk forward, to close the distance between us, to bury my nose in the crook of her neck and to breathe her fragrance in.

Get a fucking grip.

No way could I saunter up to a strange woman, grab her, and sniff her neck. I'd be arrested for assault. The pack alpha—my grandfather Matthew—would have to send somebody to bail me out, shooting to shit our policy of staying off the humans' radar. Wouldn't Grandpa just love that? Not a smart move for one of the pack's sentries.

I balled my fists and watched the woman shake herself like a forest animal emerging from chill lake waters. The confused expression slid from her face, and her eyes widened in obvious alarm. Whirling, she took flight.

Run, my wolf snarled, yanking on the restraints I'd imposed on my beast. His overwhelming need to soothe her hurt, to protect her from pain, flooded my veins.

No. I reined in the impulse, refusing to yield to my wolf. Chasing a stranger down the sidewalk? Rolf taught me better.

Not a stranger, the wolf hissed. *Ours.*

My wolf had never tugged so hard on the leash, his desperation in danger of overriding both common sense and years of training. Shifters who lost control of their animals didn't last long. They were either put down by their pack, or they went rogue and fled. Eventually, trackers hunted them down and dispatched them. I knew all about hunting rogues. I put in four long years as a tracker before Grandpa promoted me to sentry.

Follow her, the wolf urged.

As if they had a mind of their own, my feet moved forward. I couldn't cede control to my shadow brother, but neither would I ignore him when he was so intent on a goal. A delicate balance—a carefully constructed harmony—existed between the two halves of my soul. The man must reign supreme over the wolf, but never as a despot. Give and take was essential to prevent the wolf from being reduced to snarling discontent, a beast lying in wait for a moment of weakness on my part that would allow the animal to seize control.

Ours, the wolf repeated, writhing against his confinement beneath my skin.

Primal instinct and rational thought were the two sometimes conflicting drivers of a shifter's existence. Both must be in accord when selecting a mate. I'd never be as impetuous as the wolf. "There, she's the one," wouldn't work for my logical human half. But only a fool ran roughshod over their wolf when he alerted to a potential mate. The wolf called her ours. I felt the attraction, too.

Dammit.

While I hesitated, she disappeared from view. No matter. I could track her by scent. I wove between the humans crowding the sidewalk, stepping around a toddler throwing a tantrum in front of a candy store.

I caught up with the woman at the end of the block where she waited for traffic to clear at a crosswalk. She hunched over, her arms wrapped protectively around her waist. Her distress cut through me like a knife. Once again I wrestled with the urge to reach out to her, to offer the comfort of skin-to-skin contact. Jaw clenched, my back ramrod straight, I forced my feet to stop a good ten feet behind her. The wolf might not know better than to touch a woman uninvited, but the man sure as hell did.

The car blocking the crosswalk inched forward and turned the corner. She darted across the street. I shadowed her, a dozen paces behind. Halfway down the block, she came to a stop in front of a storefront. Pink-and-white striped awnings covered the doorway and windows. A few small tables with chairs dotted the sidewalk under the window awnings. A mother and little girl sat at a table sharing a giant cookie. Smiling, the mother nodded while the girl chatted excitedly about a princess and a unicorn.

The woman I stalked sucked in a breath, squared her shoulders, then pushed open the door. An old-fashioned shopkeeper's bell signaled her arrival. As the door swung shut, someone called out, "Marit, what's wrong?"

"Marit." I tested the unfamiliar name on my lips and found it to my liking. Marit had turned to a friend for comfort. She had her own sort of pack. Whatever was wrong in her world, she wouldn't face it by herself. Good. My tight muscles relaxed.

The wolf whined a protest, as if he suspected I might walk away now that I knew she wasn't alone in the world. If I was smart, I would walk away. No danger of that.

Patience, brother. I soothed my other half. Reassured, the wolf settled.

Instead of immediately following Marit inside, I paused outside the bookstore next door, pretending to study the books displayed in the shop window while I slowly counted to one hundred. Then I turned and stalked toward the shop where Marit had taken refuge.

The little girl fell silent and tracked me with wide eyes as I strode past the cafe tables. Sometimes human children—still open to the supernatural world—took note of a shifter's otherness.

I stilled and offered the girl a reassuring, tooth-free smile. The big bad wolf won't eat you, that smile promised. Her frown disappeared and she returned my grin, waving her cookie at me.

"Want a bite?" she offered.

I shook my head. "Nah, gonna get my own, but thanks."

I glanced away before I made the mother uneasy. My gaze fell on the window, where gold letters spelled out the words

Freya's Bake Shop. My head snapped back. A chill ticked down my spine. What were the odds that Marit's destination was the same as mine?

Told you. The wolf huffed triumphantly. *It's fate. She's ours.*

CHAPTER THREE

MARIT

I pushed open the door to Freya's Bake Shop, and the shopkeeper's bell jingled over my head. From behind the counter, my cousins swung their eyes my way. This time of day the shop was usually hopping, but there were no customers in sight. Good. My stiff upper lip was starting to fail me, and I didn't want to lose it in front of strangers.

"Marit, what's wrong?" Annika's pretty face puckered with concern.

Liv slid a tray of Nanaimo bars onto a shelf in the glass-front display cabinet. Straightening to her full height, she examined me. Her dark eyebrows slashed down.

"Who do I have to kill?" she demanded.

I'd been holding on to my composure by a thread. Now that I was face-to-face with my cousins—my favorite people in the whole wide world—my self-control unraveled. Hysterical laughter bubbled up from my throat, and I pressed my fingers against my mouth.

"Bryce—" I choked out.

"What did that shitass do?" Liv rounded the counter and stomped toward me.

Grandma used to tell us stories about our Scandinavian ancestors. Liv especially loved hearing tales of the shield maidens, the women warriors of the Viking age. Now, with her flashing eyes and clenched jaw, her long, lean body humming with barely suppressed rage, Liv looked like nothing more than a shield maiden ready to do battle on my behalf.

Annika scampered after her twin, less fierce than her sister, but equally loyal and supportive. "What happened?" She gently brushed a strand of hair back from my face.

I swallowed the lump in my throat. "I found Bryce in bed with the wedding planner."

A moment of stunned silence when the only sound was the *tick-tick-tick* of the cookie-shaped wall clock, then Liv erupted, throwing her hands in the air. "I'm going to kill the fucker."

"Sweetheart, I'm so sorry," Annika murmured, pulling me into her arms.

Sniffling, I buried my head against her shoulder. One minute. I'd give myself one minute to soak up her warmth and wallow in self-pity before I pulled up my big girl panties and made a plan.

The shopkeeper's bell clanged again. Out of the corner of my eye, I saw a man step into the shop.

"We're closed," Liv snapped.

"Sign on the door says open." His deep voice pierced right through my pity party.

I turned my head and looked at him. Familiar gold eyes locked onto mine, and a shiver slithered down my spine. The stranger from the sidewalk, the one who caught my gaze and wouldn't let go. What was he doing here? Had he followed me?

"Well, the sign's wrong," Liv countered. She pointed at me, huddled against Annika's shoulder. "Read the room."

"I'm sorry to intrude." He shoved a hand through shoulder-length dark-brown hair. "But Rolf Brandt sent me. I'm supposed to pick up ten dozen cupcakes for his daughter's baby shower."

The Brandt cupcakes, only our biggest special order since the grand opening last autumn. Annika and I had come in two hours early this morning to decorate the hundred and twenty cupcakes. Word of mouth could destroy our fledgling business if we failed to make good on a custom order.

I extracted myself from Annika's arms. "I'm fine."

"You sure?" Liv asked. If I said no, my cousin would kick him out and damn the consequences. I couldn't allow that.

"One hundred percent sure," I assured her.

"Your order is ready." Annika turned to the stranger. "It'll take just a few minutes for my sister and me to bag up the boxes. If you like, you can have a cookie or pastry while you wait. On the house."

The man dipped his head. "Thanks. I appreciate it."

Liv flipped over the open sign on the shop door, then she and Annika retreated to the back of the shop. The stranger's gaze followed me as I stepped behind the counter and gestured at the display case. "Anything you want. Your choice."

Did I imagine the heat that flared in his eyes?

"Anything I want?" he repeated. "What would you pick if you were me?"

The warmth that crept up my cheeks made absolutely no sense. I scanned the display case, feeling uncharacteristically awkward. "I don't know you well enough to make that call. But me? I'd go for a bear claw." I held up my right hand and curved my fingers into a claw. "Grrr."

The blush returned.

Oh dear lord. Why do I act like such a dork when I'm nervous?

His lips tipped up and he tilted his head to one side. "Grrr," he growled right back at me, his fingers shaping a claw that slashed through the air. "So you're in the mood for something wild?"

Was he flirting with me? I narrowed my eyes, ready to lift my left hand and wave my engagement ring under his nose. Then I remembered. The two carat, emerald-cut ring still glittered on my finger, but the engagement was over. My chest tightened and I blinked back tears. I yanked the ring off my finger and shoved it deep into my pocket.

"Shit." The word escaped before I could think better of it. I swallowed hard, rallying my wits. Business 101. No swearing in front of customers. "I apologize. That was uncalled for."

"Can I do anything to help?"

The unexpected question cut me to the quick. I wobbled, unsteady on my feet, and swayed toward him for the second time that day. The compassion in his golden eyes drew me in, and the sympathy in his expression undid me.

My lips parted, but I couldn't find any words.

"You're hurt. I want to help if I can."

I'd lied through my teeth when I told Liv that I was fine. It was a little white lie, totally justifiable under the circumstances. Somehow I couldn't make myself tell an untruth to this man.

"It's been a rough day," I conceded. "Somebody I trusted betrayed me. It hurts, but I'll get over it."

"Who?" he demanded in a low voice. I swear to god his eyes changed, each golden iris shattering into glittering shards of amber.

Absurd, illogical, absolutely preposterous impulses seized me. I longed to lean closer to him, to seek comfort in his arms, to breathe in his scent. What *was* that? Pine and woodsmoke? I gripped the edge of the counter and gaped at his eyes.

"Whoa," I breathed. Was that some trick of the light? Nobody's eyes could sparkle like that.

Shuddering, he blinked and glanced down at his feet. He swallowed, the corded muscles in his thick neck working. When he lifted his eyes, his irises once again looked normal.

"How about that bear claw?" he said with obvious effort.

I bobbed my head, grabbed a bakery tissue sheet, selected the biggest almond pastry from the display, and held it out to him. He reached for his wallet.

"It's on the house, remember?"

He pulled a five from his wallet, shoved it into the tip jar, then took the bear claw. "Thanks."

Annika and Liv emerged from the back room, each carrying a jumbo pink paper bag with Freya's Bake Shop emblazoned on the side. "Here you go," Annika said brightly.

When he hesitated, Liv marched to the shop door and held it open, a not-so-subtle hint that he needed to leave. He took the bags and nodded his thanks. Glancing at me once again, he looked like he wanted to say something.

"Have a nice day." I smiled, my professional demeanor in ascendance.

"You, too." He turned on his heel and strode through the open door.

Liv switched off the overhead lights, took my arm, and pulled me toward the break room in the back of the shop. The three of us sat around our small lunch table. Annika reached out and clasped my hand, her skin warm against my cold fingers. Liv followed her sister's example, and for a long minute the three of us held hands across the table. I settled back in the chair, grounded by my cousins' unwavering love and support.

"So spill." Liv released our hands and tucked a strand of chin-length brown hair behind her ear. "What happened?"

I told them the whole sorry story, from the instant I spied Courtney's luxury SUV in the driveway until the moment I flung red curry soup on the cheating lovers.

"That'll leave a stain," Liv said with satisfaction, then cut her eyes toward me. "You're done with the asshole, right?"

I bobbed my head. "Bryce tried to make excuses, to tell me that he messed up and it won't happen again, but yeah, I'm done."

Liv smiled grimly. "Once a cheater, always a cheater."

"What can we do to help?" Annika asked.

My shoulders sagged at the thought of everything I needed to do. "I have to cancel the wedding. Call Dad and Mom and tell them not to fly in. Contact all the vendors. Reach out to everybody we invited and let them know it's off." I groaned, overwhelmed. "Dorrie Mittelmann told me she's looking forward to Grandma's pink champagne cake and that she wants to dance with Bryce at the reception."

"When Dorrie Mittelmann finds out what Bryce, did she'll round up her garden club and they'll chase after him with pruning shears," Liv said.

I smiled at the mental image of Bryce fleeing from a gaggle of outraged senior citizens.

"Don't worry about canceling the wedding." Annika squeezed my fingers. "We'll take care of everything."

Liv nodded. "We're your girls. We got you."

Gratitude for my cousins swamped me, and my eyes grew soggy. "I really don't want to face anybody or explain what happened. It's all so freaking embarrassing. I feel like a fool for believing him."

"This is on Bryce, not you," Liv said. "You've got nothing to be embarrassed about."

"Except crap judgment when it comes to men. And by the way, Liv, I appreciate you not saying 'I told you so.'" I scrubbed my hands over my cheeks. "But other folks are going to talk, and I don't feel like dealing with all the gossip or people looking at me with pity."

"So why don't you get out of town for a while?" Annika suggested.

"Run away and lick my wounds like some kind of wuss?"

"Shut up." Liv made a face. "Annika's right. Get out of Dodge for a while. Call it a strategic retreat if that makes it easier."

I considered the suggestion. The more I thought about it, the more I liked it. "I could go to Grandma's lake cabin."

As soon as she found out she was sick, Grandma had transferred ownership of her two-bedroom bungalow in town to Annika and Liv. She willed me the lease to her cottage on the lake, a place filled to the rafters with memories of time spent there with Grandma. It was only an hour away, but I hadn't been able to bring myself to visit it since Grandma died last September. Now felt like the right time.

"Perfect," Annika said. "And don't worry about the shop. Julia has been asking if she can pick up some extra shifts. We'll have to hustle, but Liv and I can handle everything."

"Are you sure?" My conscience protested at the thought of dumping so many responsibilities on my cousins.

"We'll do anything to help you get through this." Annika's eyes—a deeper brown than her fraternal twins—glowed with love. Mrs. Mittelmann called *me* a sweetheart? Without a doubt, Annika possessed the family's sweetest soul.

"I don't know what I'd do without you guys," I confessed.

"You'll never have to find out," she said.

Liv mimed sticking a finger down her throat and made a gagging noise. "Enough of this sappy stuff. Let's talk revenge." A brilliant smile wreathed her face. "I vote for slashing the tires on Bryce's fancy roadster."

Liv's snarky retort worked. Laughter bubbled up from my throat. "I think the red curry soup took care of any need for revenge."

Liv snorted. "Not even close." Deep in thought, she tapped a finger against her mouth. "I got it. Bryce is vain. Whaddaya say we sneak a depilatory into his shampoo? And write bad Yelp reviews about Courtney's event planning business? Something like, 'I found a dead mouse floating in the punch bowl.'"

"Behave yourself." Annika batted her sister's arm then turned to me. "We need to pack every indulgent treat we can think of for you. Chocolate. Brie. Your favorite wine. That expensive tequila you like." She bounced in her chair, warming to the topic. "Load up your e-reader with books. And we can make a playlist of songs about good women done wrong by bad men. You know, Taylor Swift and Rihanna and Alanis Morissette."

"You're in charge of the chocolate and the playlist," Liv said. "I'll pick up the booze."

"It's a plan." Annika bumped fists with her sister.

"Bryce wants to make up, and he knows about the cabin," I mused aloud. "I hope it doesn't occur to him to follow me out there."

"Slash his tires and he won't be going anywhere." Liv lifted one slim shoulder. "Just sayin'."

"Hard pass," I said. "It would be bad for business if you got arrested for criminal mischief."

"Spoilsport." She stuck out her tongue.

I ignored the mocking gesture. "I love you, too."

Liv slapped the table. "Enough chitchat. We have things to do." She turned to Annika. "Call Julia and see if she can cover the counter for the rest of the day."

"Will do." Annika hopped to her feet.

"Your clothes are all at Bryce's place, right?" Liv asked.

I winced. I'd emptied out my small apartment and shifted my belongings to Bryce's house a month ago. It had seemed like a smart idea at the time. "Yeah, unfortunately."

"No problem." She waved a hand. "You can borrow everything you need from Annika and me. Or—" Her expression grew thoughtful. "Give me your keys. I'll be happy to fetch your clothes and toiletries from the creep's place. There's nothing I'd like better than to have a few choice words with old Bryce."

"No." Bad enough I was hightailing it out of town, leaving Annika and Liv to handle my mess. I'd face down my ex and reclaim my belongings myself. "I'll get my stuff later when I'm back in town."

She shrugged. "Suit yourself. What about Loki?"

"Shit." I groaned. In my haste to get away from Bryce, I'd totally forgotten our new dog. Bryce loved Loki, or at least I thought he did. Maybe his affection for the dog was as bogus as his commitment to me. Loki hadn't really taken to Bryce, despite Bryce's efforts. Maybe the dog was a better judge of character than me. Who knows. I huffed out a deep breath, my cheeks puffing. No help for it. Bryce was the very last person I wanted to see, but I couldn't abandon the pup.

As soon as I'd driven away from the house, my phone started blowing up with calls and texts from Bryce. I'd pulled to the curb and turned my phone off. Now, I dug it out of my pocket and pressed the power button. Ignoring the many messages from Bryce, I typed, *On my way to pick up Loki. I don't want to talk.*

I glanced at Liv. "I'm going to go get Loki. Quick in and out. I'll grab his leash, his bed, some food, and go."

"Want me to come along as backup?"

"No." I laid a hand on my cousin's arm. "I got this. How about I meet you guys at your house in an hour?"

"If you're sure..." Liv looked doubtful.

"I am." My voice was firm. "And if I remember correctly, you promised to pick up the booze."

"Okay." She hesitated, then hauled me in for a hug, a gesture so unlike my unsentimental cousin that it brought fresh tears to my eyes.

I patted her shoulders and pulled away, clearing my throat to banish any telltale quiver from my voice. "See you guys soon."

I waved at Annika on my way out of the shop and dashed the three blocks to my car. Ten minutes later, I parked in my ex's driveway. Both Courtney's SUV and Bryce's roadster were gone. A relieved burst of air escaped my lungs. Coming face-to-face with Bryce was the last thing I wanted. With any luck I'd be out of here well before he returned.

Loki usually rushed me whenever I let myself in. This time, only silence greeted my arrival. I whistled, cocked my head, and waited. There was no welcoming yelp. No sound of claws clicking over the hardwood floor. No eager pooch nuzzling my leg.

Maybe Bryce had left him in the backyard. I crossed to the patio door and peered outside. No sign of the boy. Frowning, I walked through the kitchen. A piece of paper propped up on the kitchen table caught my eye, a note scrawled with a bright-red Sharpie.

After that display of violence, it's clear that you're too emotional and irrational to take proper care of a dog. He's safer with me. You can see him after you calm down and agree to talk things over in a civilized manner.

Oh, he did not.

"What the ever-loving hell, Bryce?" I sputtered.

There was a lot to unpack in those few sentences, none of it flattering, all of it infuriating. If Bryce thought he could win me back by insulting me—by holding my dog hostage until I consented to a "civilized" conversation—he was dead wrong. I leaned against the edge of the table, anger turning my legs to jelly.

"You're hurt. I want to help if I can." The stranger's words echoed in my head.

Why couldn't Bryce show the same quiet strength and compassion as my mystery man? For a handful of seconds, I indulged in a daydream of taking the stranger up on his offer, of pouring out my tale of woe, of siccing the big guy on my asshole ex. I bet he could make Bryce turn over my dog.

Crap. Where did that damsel in distress fantasy come from?

That wasn't like me. I was a grown-ass woman. I didn't need a knight in shining armor to set my world right again. I pulled out my phone and punched in Liv's number.

"Wassup?" she rasped.

"You know that divorce attorney who stops in every morning?"

"The one who always gets a chocolate croissant? Monica Navarro? Yeah. Cool woman. We've met up for karaoke a couple of times."

"Do you have her contact info?" I asked.

"Why?"

"I might have to sue Bryce for custody of Loki."

A moment of silence, then, "Are you shitting me?"

"Nope."

I explained what I found when I showed up to retrieve Loki.

"Too emotional and irrational?" Liv's voice rose. "The gall of the man boggles my mind."

"I'm surprised you didn't ask if you could slash his tires now," I observed wryly.

"Yeah, well, context is everything, and I figure I shouldn't talk about tire slashing when he's accusing you of being an out-of-control she-devil. I'll reach out to Monica and set up a call."

"Maybe I should stay in town—" I started.

"No way," Liv interjected. "You've got cell coverage at the cabin. You can take a meeting with Monica from there. In the meantime, leave the house keys with me. I'll do welfare checks on Loki every day. And if anything looks off, Loki might just go on a little ride with Auntie Liv."

My hand tightened around the phone. "You're the best."

She chuckled. "Remember what Grandma always used to say, 'Hell hath no fury like a pissed off Hagen woman.' We've got your back, cousin. Always."

Chapter Four

Adam

Somebody I trusted betrayed me.

As soon as the words escaped Marit's lips, my wolf went apeshit. Her pain triggered a visceral reaction in the beast, a primitive need to protect her and eviscerate whoever hurt her. Images flashed through my mind, visions that made clear the wolf's intent.

Track the enemy. Savage his body. Taste his blood.

Took everything I had to wrestle him back under control and to answer her with anything other than the promise of death in my voice. The harmony between my two halves had never felt so fragile, so liable to fracture. The wolf had fixated on a woman I barely knew. I felt the attraction—I really did—but I knew better than to act on it.

The survival of the pack came first. Rules were rules. I might be the alpha's grandson, but I wasn't above the law.

I jogged back to my truck, careful not to thwack the pink bags of cupcakes against any of the people I pushed past. Rolf wouldn't appreciate it if I smashed his daughter's party treats. After securing the bags in the back seat, I threw the truck into gear and headed out of town.

I followed the river toward the forestland and isolated lake that my pack called home. All the while, I tried and failed to keep thoughts of the enticing Marit from intruding in my mind. Twenty miles from town, I turned off the two-lane state highway onto a private road that curved through heavy stands of larch and pine trees. The closer I got to Shooting Star Lake, the narrower and bumpier the road got.

Once upon a time, before the pack purchased the land in the 1960s, the road had been well maintained, a conduit for tourists who boated and fished on the pristine alpine waters. No more. Under our guise as an environmental conservancy, the pack had banned boating, fishing, and swimming on the lake. We let the road degrade, all the better for keeping strangers away from pack land.

Two dozen cabins dotted the southern shore of Shooting Star Lake. The cottages had once been a hot property, with folks vying to secure ninety-nine-year leases to the lakefront cabins. Once the pack took over, the value of the cabins tanked. Who wanted to spend time at a lake where it was forbidden to stick a toe in the water?

One by one, we bought up the leases, until only a single, stubborn leaseholder remained. The woman had burrowed in like a tick. For decades she'd refused every offer to buy her out. Old lady Hagen had passed from cancer last September. Grandpa Matthew had tasked me with identifying her heir and persuading them to sell. I'd gone to the county courthouse today to view a copy of her will. Unfortunately, the will hadn't finished going through probate, so I'd been shit outta luck. I'd have to venture back to the courthouse in a month, when the resort town was packed to the gills with Labor Day revelers.

"Won't that be fun," I muttered, parking my truck in front of pack headquarters, an immense rustic lodge a wealthy lumber baron built on the north shore of the lake in the 1920s. The sixty-two guest rooms had been converted into pack lodgings. My top-floor room had a fireplace, a view of the lake, and plenty of wall space for my bookshelves. A spacious suite was one of the perks of being a sentry.

I took the bags of cupcakes out of the back seat and started up the wide stone steps. The front door to the lodge swung open. Grandpa hovered in the entryway. He stumbled, then caught himself on the doorjamb. I dropped the bags and rushed to his side.

"Can you give me a minute, sir?" I pitched my voice loud enough to be overheard by the half-dozen teenagers sprawled on Adirondack chairs on the porch. Stepping sideways, I positioned myself between my alpha and the curious adolescents.

"Sure." Grandpa leaned heavily against the doorframe. Despite his obvious discomfort, a small smile lifted the corners of his mouth as he played along with my ruse. Nothing got past the sharp old man.

I studied Grandpa's face, frowning at the clenched jaw and the eyes narrowed in pain. Around his neck he wore a leather cord with a wire-wrapped chunk of black rock resting against the base of his throat.

The alpha stone.

The symbol of his rank.

Above the stone, his pulse tapped a rapid staccato against his skin. I sucked in a calming breath then cast out my senses.

There. I felt the echo of Grandpa's pulse in my own chest, a hectic, irregular drumbeat. Shifters didn't catch human contagions, but our hearts were vulnerable to disease. Something was terribly wrong with the alpha's heart. Shit, he even smelled wrong. An acrid tang betrayed his condition. It was subtle, but as a sentry, my heightened senses allowed me to detect the change before the rest of the pack.

Grandpa swayed. I reached out to steady him. He shot me a warning glance, and I pulled my hand back. The alpha must not appear frail, not with war looming on the horizon. He sucked in a ragged breath then slowly straightened to his full height, an impressive feat for a man whose body grew weaker by the day.

My guts twisted. It killed me to see my grandfather suffer. I admired the hell out of the alpha, a strong leader who had never failed in his duty to the pack. What would happen when he grew too weak to continue and handed the mantle of power to his successor? Could any of us take his place?

"What can I do for you, Adam?" he asked.

Don't die. The plea flashed through my mind before I could come up with a more appropriate response.

"Matthew!"

The shrill exclamation spared me from making up a reply. Groaning inwardly, I composed my face before turning toward the familiar voice.

Olga scuttled up the porch steps. Her gray-streaked hair was pulled back in a bun that did nothing to soften her harsh features. Nudging me aside, she planted herself in front of the alpha. She was his second wife—a poor replacement for his beloved mate, Katia, if you asked me. She didn't much like me or any of Katia's other grandsons. The feeling was mutual although I always treated her with the respect she was due as the alpha's wife.

"Matthew, are you all right?" She pressed her palm to his forehead and cheeks and made unhappy clucking sounds. "Your color isn't good and your skin feels clammy."

The teenagers seated behind me fell silent, all ears. Without a doubt, word of this exchange would make the rounds within the pack. They say no shifters gossip more than the chatty bears. Hah. Wolves could give bears a run for their money any day.

In a couple of weeks, Grandpa intended to announce his retirement and name his successor at the Pack Circle, held annually during the height of the Perseid meteor shower. His sentries hoped to keep his deteriorating health a secret until then, a prospect that was beginning to look less and less likely.

"Don't fuss, Olga." Grandpa sighed.

I didn't want to embarrass Grandpa by witnessing the interaction, so I stared down at my boots.

"I'm not fussing, silly man," Olga protested. "Isn't it a wife's job to take care of her husband?" When he didn't reply, she shouted, "Xander!"

Her grandson Xander, at seventeen the youngest of my three cousins—well, I guess, technically a step-cousin—appeared behind Grandpa in the doorway. "Yeah, Grandma?"

"The alpha needs to rest. Help him to his room."

I suppressed a groan. Help him to his room? Why not tell Xander to tuck him into bed and bring him a warm cup of milk? The last thing the pack needed was for anyone to raise doubts about the alpha's health or ability to lead.

Xander hesitated, a confused expression on his face. No doubt he suspected that he'd been dragged into an argument he wanted no part of. "Um... sir?"

Grandpa placed a reassuring hand on the young man's shoulder. "I'm fine, son. Your grandmother is worried for nothing."

"Hardly nothing." Olga planted her hands on her hips. "You're not well. There's no shame in letting Xander help you."

Frowning, Xander shifted his weight from foot to foot. I shot the kid a sympathetic look. Olga was not a subtle woman. In a couple of weeks, the alpha would appoint the new leader of the pack. Olga clearly intended it to be Xander. Never mind the fact that he was young—totally untested—and related to Matthew by marriage, not blood.

"You heard me." When he didn't move, Olga wagged a finger at her grandson.

"Enough, Olga," Grandpa ordered.

Her husband's uncharacteristic harshness must have startled Olga into shutting her mouth. Tension crackled between the two elders. The air shifted.

People sometimes described an alpha's power as a force of nature, a tangible expression of will that tugged like an unseen thread at something in the lower-ranking members of the pack. That power struck me hard now, raising goose bumps across my flesh.

Acting on instinct, I lowered my head and angled it to the side, exposing my throat. Seconds ticked by. My breath came in shallow gasps. Then the alpha power withdrew, like a wave retreating from a sandy beach. I wasn't sure if Grandpa pulled it back as an act of will, or if he was too weak to sustain it. Shit. I hope he did it on purpose.

"Have it your way." Olga whirled around and retreated down the steps, her shoulders stiff with indignation.

"You *can* do something for me," Grandpa called after her.

Olga turned back, her face a study in wounded pride. "Yes?"

"I've had a craving for your meatloaf, sweetheart. Best in the world. Do you think you could make it for me tonight?"

Her expression softened. "Of course. Mashed potatoes, too. Dinner will be ready at seven. Don't be late." A playful light sparkled in her eyes, her good humor restored at his praise.

"Yes, ma'am." He touched two fingers to his brow in a salute. He smiled at her retreating form as Olga hustled off. "She means well," he said under his breath.

The alpha didn't expect a response to that comment, did he?

My cell phone vibrated. I tugged it from my pocket and read the incoming text.

ALERT. Security breach on eastern perimeter.

I glanced at my grandfather. "We have visitors."

He nodded, his expression grim. "Remy is repairing a broken security camera on the northern perimeter, but Rolf, Zane, and Kyra are close."

Four sentries to deal with the interlopers.

"Hey, Xander." I pointed at the bags from Freya's Bake Shop. "Give those bags to Rolf's mate, will you?"

"Sure thing." He reached for the cupcakes. Xander was a good kid despite his grandmother's machinations.

Zane ran outside jerking a T-shirt down over his chest. My cousin must have been drying off after a shower when the alert came in to all the sentries. Water dripped from his blond hair. The shirt clung to his damp skin. One of the teenage girls on the porch let out a long admiring sigh. Girls always went wild over my cousin's muscles. He ignored her.

"Grandpa." Zane dipped his head, awaiting orders from the alpha.

"Report back as soon as you've secured the perimeter."

"Yes, sir." Anticipation gleamed in Zane's eyes. My cousin loved nothing more than a good brawl.

Side-by-side, we jogged down the porch steps. Zane's Harley was parked next to my truck.

"I am not riding on the back of your bike," I said. "We'll take my truck and follow the old logging road till we get close. Then we can shift and run the rest of the way."

"Don't want to ride bitch?" Zane growled and threw open the passenger door. "I'm crushed."

Sliding behind the wheel, I grinned. My cousin was trying to get my goat. "Ride bitch? Try saying that in front of Kyra. She'll kick your ass."

He cracked his neck. "She could try."

"Yeah, right," I drawled. Zane might be the biggest grouch on two legs. He might live to poke the hornet's nest, but he was one of the most loyal men I knew. He'd die in a heartbeat for a fellow sentry.

Zane hated chitchat, so we rode in silence. A mile from the eastern perimeter, a downed tree blocked our way forward. I made a mental note to report the downed tree to our maintenance crew. I killed the engine and we climbed out of the truck. Tilting my head back, I sniffed the air then shot a glance at Zane.

His nostrils flared. "I smell it, too."

"Coyotes." My mouth twisted into a scowl.

The goddamned coyotes had breached security again. Didn't matter that they always lost in a one-on-one with the larger and more powerful wolves. Unlike wolf shifters, coyotes were easy breeders. Their greater numbers allowed their shit-for-brains alpha to use his soldiers as cannon fodder. It defied sense. Undeterred by the loss, no matter how many times we pushed them back, no matter how many we killed, they kept coming.

Zane rolled his shoulders, loosening his muscles in preparation for the fight. "Let's go."

CHAPTER FIVE

MARIT

Holding my breath, I flipped the light switch inside the cabin's front door, half-afraid that the conservancy had finally disconnected the cabin from the electrical grid. The overhead incandescent light flickered to life, its reassuring glow scattering the darkness.

"Thank God," I breathed.

Grandma's lease predated the conservancy's purchase of the land. In a bid to raise some capitol, the property's original owner—struggling under heavy debt—sold ninety-nine-year leases for the cabins. Those leases were grandfathered into the conservancy's purchase of the property. As long as a single leaseholder occupied a cabin, they weren't supposed to cut off the power, but they might have seized on Grandma's death as a pretext for doing just that.

I dropped my suitcase onto the wide plank floor and surveyed the place. Grandma had loved color. Both the chairs surrounding her kitchen table and the china hutch were painted a vivid coral. Blue-and-white dishes filled the hutch. Cheerful apple-green-and-white striped slipcovers covered the comfy sofa and overstuffed chair. Pillows in a riot of colors were tucked into the corners of the sofa and chair. Whimsical paintings of local flora and fauna—Grandma's celebrated artwork—covered the walls. A vintage Little Red Riding Hood cookie jar sat on the kitchen counter. The sight made me catch my breath.

"Grandma," I whispered as memories of standing at that counter making cookies with her flooded my mind. I crossed the room, lifted the lid to the jar, and peered inside. When Grandma was alive, it was always full to the top. It was empty now, of course.

I'd hired a cleaner to tidy up the cabin after Grandma died. The fridge had been emptied and scrubbed, the perishables disposed of, the dishes washed and put away in the cupboards, the sheets stripped off the bed and laundered. A fine layer of dust now covered everything. I'd throw open all the windows and air out the place tomorrow.

"I'm home," I announced to the empty cottage, then switched on all the lamps, casting pools of light on the wood floor and the rag rugs.

The quiet room unnerved me and gave me too much time to think. Grandma and I used to blast music through the cabin, dancing around the rooms to her favorite '60s bands. On impulse, I knelt in front of an old cabinet and thumbed through Grandma's collection of vinyl records, finally settling on Janis Joplin's *Pearl*. I slid the record from the sleeve and placed it on the turntable on top of the cabinet.

"Perfect." I smiled as the first track began to play.

Singing along to "Me and Bobby McGee" and "Mercedes Benz," I hauled box after box in from the car. I couldn't carry a tune to save my life, but there was nobody around to complain, so I belted out the songs as I worked.

Annika and Liv had packed so many supplies that you'd think I was preparing for the apocalypse. Liv had purchased *two* bottles of my favorite tequila. Did she think I planned to drink myself into a stupor?

After emptying out the car and putting away all the food, I turned my attention to the bedroom. Sliding into bed over fresh, crisp cotton sheets had to be one of my favorite sensual pleasures. I put clean sheets on the big brass bed, fluffed the pillows, and took one of Grandma's hand-sewn quilts out of the carved trunk at the foot of the bed.

While the claw-foot bathtub filled with water, I rolled up the blind covering the east-facing bedroom window. Strings of crystal suncatchers dangled from the top of the frame. When I visited the cabin when I was little, I'd lie in bed in the early morning and watch sunlight stream through the window, sending rainbow-colored sparkles dancing across the walls and ceiling. It would soothe my soul to see it again.

I dropped a gardenia-scented bath bomb into the tub, poured a glass of pinot noir, stripped, and slid into blissfully fragrant water. I sipped the velvety wine, my muscles unknotting and tension leaching from my body. I refused to let myself think about Bryce. Instead, I studied the old poster hanging on the wall over the tub.

Bright bands of color—pink, yellow, and lime green— splashed across a poster promoting the Woodstock Music and Art Fair in August, 1969. "Arlo Guthrie, the Grateful Dead, Jimi Hendrix, Joe Cocker." I read aloud the names of some of the artists who performed at the famous event. "Jefferson Airplane. Santana." I smiled. "Janis Joplin."

Grandma and her best friend Dorrie had driven Dorrie's bright-blue Buick Skylark all the way from Washington state to New York for the three-day music festival. A month after they returned home, Grandma discovered she was pregnant. Her twin sons—Nicholas and Michael—were born the following spring. If Grandma knew who their father was, she never told. Dad and Uncle Mike called themselves "Woodstock babies," their mysterious origin part of family lore.

I sunk down into the water until it covered my chin. "You kept your secrets, didn't you, Grandma?" I mused aloud.

Unbidden, Bryce's face intruded into my thoughts. In my mind's eye, he smiled, showing perfect white teeth and flawlessly handsome features, a sort of human Ken doll.

I held my breath waiting for misery to strike, waiting to feel gutted because the man I loved had betrayed me. It didn't happen. Instead of heartbreak, I felt only bewilderment and anger.

What was up with that?

I blew out the air I was holding. Oily residue from the bath bomb swirled on the water's surface. Repressing grief wasn't healthy, so I goosed the emotional floodgates, deliberately recalling the day I met my dream man.

For months after Grandma died—once a week like clockwork—I brought flowers to the cemetery. On a cold, drizzly Wednesday in early November, I placed a single white lily on her marble headstone. A rain-drenched man clutching a bouquet of red carnations threaded his way between the grave markers. Coming to a stop at a grave five over from Grandma's, he bent and deposited the flowers.

He straightened, then swiped water from his cheeks. His hair was so wet that it was impossible to tell the color. His fleece jacket was soaked through. Our eyes met. He flashed a smile. "Guess I'm not the only one who forgot to bring an umbrella."

I laughed, mostly dry under my waterproof coat and hood. "I didn't forget my umbrella. I don't own one."

Shoulders hunched against the rain, he walked toward me, stopping a dozen feet away. I appreciated that he kept his distance. No woman in a lonely location wanted a stranger breathing down her neck.

He smiled. "So you're a card-carrying member of the anti-umbrella brigade?"

"What can I tell you? I'm a Pacific Northwest native. We scoff at rain."

It was his turn to laugh. "I'm originally from Arizona, and I think umbrellas are the best invention ever." He glanced around the sodden landscape. "Especially on a day like today. Looks like you and I are the only ones crazy enough to brave the elements."

"It's a small town," I said. "Rain or not, the place is usually quiet in the middle of the week."

"So it's providential that we ran into each other." He hesitated. "Listen, I don't want to be pushy, but I just moved to town and haven't met many people. There's a new bakery downtown that's supposed to serve good coffee and great pastries."

"Freya's Bake Shop?" I asked, delighted by the praise for our new venture.

"That's the one." He shivered and his teeth started clacking together. "I'm feeling like a drowned rat here. How about I buy you a cup of coffee and a pastry, and we warm up somewhere out of the rain?"

"You're on," I said. "And I can guarantee us the best table in the joint."

"Oh, yeah? You've got pull at the bakery?"

"I'd better. I'm one of the owners."

His blue eyes sparkled. "We meet in a cemetery in the middle of a rainstorm. It turns out you own the bakery I invite you to. Shoot, it's got to be fate that we met like this."

It turned out that Bryce and I had so much in common, so many shared interests, that every step along the way of our budding relationship he declared that fate must have brought us together. We both loved the Thin Man detective movies from the 1930s. Thai drunken noodles were our favorite food. What were the odds that we'd be so perfect for each other? It had to be fate.

"Fate." I snorted and dunked my head, staying under for a good thirty seconds. Sputtering, I emerged from the water. I shook my head to get the water out of my ears, then opened the drain and carefully climbed out of the slippery tub. My hand was on the towel when a chorus of howls splintered the silence of the night.

Wolves. There were wolves nearby. I shivered.

For some reason, I visualized the hauntingly beautiful gold eyes of my mystery man.

CHAPTER SIX

ADAM

Ready to rip the intruders to shreds, our four wolves confronted the six coyotes who'd breached our territory. The dumb-ass coyotes often stood their ground and fought to the death. This time they showed some smarts. They yipped and snarled then retreated, tails literally between their legs.

We shifted back to our human forms.

"Why'd they bother?" Kyra asked, tugging her jeans up over her slim hips. "I mean if all they planned to do was cut and run?"

"Probably looking for weak spots in our defenses." Rolf yanked a tee down over his chest. The senior sentry was in his fifties, but only the silver streaks in his hair and the lines in the corners of his eyes gave away his age. That and the fact that he was about to become a grandfather.

"They won't find any weak spots." Butt naked, Zane arched his back and stretched his arms over his head.

Shifting hurt.

It took a few minutes to loosen up and shake off the kinks.

"You coming to the baby shower tonight?" Kyra asked him, her green eyes wide and innocent, as if it was a serious question. The pack celebrated the arrival of every new member in a big way, but nobody expected the notoriously grumpy Zane to put in an appearance at a noisy, crowded baby shower. The commotion, the balloons and cutesy decorations, would set his teeth on edge.

Zane made a face. "I'm not coming to the damned baby shower." His gaze sliced to Rolf. "No offense."

"None taken." Rolf's lips twitched.

"You sure?" Kyra batted her lashes and poked the bear, so to speak. "They'll be games—guess the baby food and a blindfolded diaper-changing challenge."

I snickered at the mental image of a blindfolded Zane changing a baby doll's diaper or trying to distinguish between pureed peaches and pureed apricots.

"And cupcakes," Kyra continued. "Don't forget the cupcakes."

Cupcakes. Just like that, my thoughts turned again to the pretty woman with the sad eyes. Marit.

Find her, my wolf begged, still close to the surface after the shift.

Sorry, buddy, I shot back. *We can't.*

Zane growled. Kyra lifted both hands in defeat. She turned to me. "How about you? Are you coming to the baby shower, Adam?"

"Can't. Zane and I are running patrols tonight, but save me a cupcake, will you?"

"You bet."

Zane and I drove back to headquarters. After reporting to Matthew, we spent a few hours training a group of teenagers in hand-to-hand combat. We ate dinner at the communal dining hall, then ambled toward my truck. We planned to drive to a trailhead, then split up. I'd run the western perimeter of pack lands, Zane the north.

"Lights are on at the Hagen place." Zane pointed across the lake to the opposite shore.

Humans occasionally broke into the old cabins. Sometimes they came looking for things to steal. We caught a man a few months ago stripping a cabin of its copper pipes, no doubt planning to sell the metal for scrap. Once, a group of intrepid college kids hauled in beer, lit a bonfire on the beach, and partied till we ran 'em off.

The cabins were rumored to be haunted, a rumor we did nothing to discourage. Last year, we confronted an amateur ghost-hunting team holding a midnight séance. When faced with a dozen growling wolves, they bolted, leaving behind their EMF meters and digital thermometers.

The day when the pack—excuse me, the *conservancy*—was legally allowed to put gates across all the access roads and close the hiking trails couldn't come soon enough.

Whoever was in the Hagen cabin wasn't trying to hide their presence. The porch light glowed like a beacon, and light shone through all the windows.

"Better check it out," I said.

"You want to drive up and make ourselves known, or sneak up on the place?" Zane asked.

I thought about it. "Let's make a covert approach. Figure out what's going on before we reveal ourselves. That way, we'll have a chance to call for backup if the situation warrants it."

"Agreed."

We drove around the lake, parked half a mile from the Hagen cabin, then ran the rest of the way.

"What the fuck is that?" Zane hissed as we drew close.

I stopped in my tracks, my head cocked to one side.

A female voice warbled the lyrics to "Bobby McGee." With my hypersensitive shifter hearing, the shrill, off-key singing was ear-piercingly unpleasant. Or it should have been. My wolf perked up, happy and excited.

A now-familiar scent drifted toward me.

"Marit," I said in a low voice. My pulse jacked up, hammering against my throat. A rushing sound filled my ears as the wolf fought to emerge.

"Marit?" Zane turned to me, a single eyebrow raised. "You know her?"

Ignoring the question, I kept my gaze focused on the cabin. Marit leaned over the open hatch of a sporty blue sedan. She lifted out a box full of foodstuffs. Her singing faltered as she staggered under the weight. I had to stop myself from racing forward and taking the heavy box from her. She blew a strand of hair off her face and shifted the box in her arms. The song started again as she trudged up the steps and into the cabin.

Zane elbowed my side. "You know her?" he repeated.

"I met her in town today."

"Saw the wolf in your eyes," he said slowly. My cousin knew exactly what that meant.

No way was I ready to talk about my wolf's forbidden fixation on the woman, not even with my closest friend. I pivoted the conversation. "She let herself in with a key. Isn't trying to hide her presence—"

Zane snorted, cutting me off. "Not with that god-awful caterwauling she isn't."

Marit skipped down the steps and lifted another box from the trunk. She trilled a song about a Mercedes Benz.

I continued, ignoring Zane's interruption. "She turned on all the lights. Looks to be making herself at home."

"Like she owns the place." Zane scrubbed a hand over his chin. "What do you think? Old lady Hagen's heir?"

Mrs. Hagen was a fixture of my childhood—a distant fixture—the woman across the lake. Grandpa had ordered the pack to keep away from her. We mostly did, although curious children sometimes couldn't resist creeping close and spying on the human who lived on pack land. I did it myself. One time she caught me peeking at her from behind a blackberry bush. Instead of getting mad, she offered me a chocolate chip cookie. Best cookie I ever ate. Other kids told similar tales.

I stilled, putting two and two together.

The cabins were never intended to be permanent homes. Since the 1960s, Mrs. Hagen spent two weeks at the lake almost every month, the maximum the lease allowed. She stopped visiting when her sons were small. Maybe the boys were too rowdy and rambunctious to be allowed near the water. Within a few years, she was back. Decades later, the pack spied three little girls playing outside the Hagen cabin.

Three little girls who now would be young women.

Marit had fled in distress to Freya's Bake Shop, to the comfort of close friends. Or maybe they were family. Cousins.

"Bet she's one of Mrs. Hagen's granddaughters," I muttered, my heart sinking.

"Could be," Zane said. "We should radio in a report, then finish our patrol."

"Yeah," I agreed, my mind reeling. How was I supposed to keep my distance from Marit when she had just moved onto pack land? When every time I'd look through the window in my quarters, I'd see the cabin where she was staying across the lake? When I was under orders from my alpha to talk her into selling the pack her lease?

You aren't supposed to keep your distance, the wolf cried triumphantly. *It's fate. She's ours.*

I ran my patrol along the western border of pack land. Instead of showering and heading to bed, I asked Zane to drive my truck back to the lodge. Told him my restless wolf needed to run.

He did. Straight back to Marit. I prowled around the structure, making sure no predators lurked nearby, then settled down to watch over the cabin while she slept. Joy filled my shadow brother. He threw back his head and howled.

Chapter Seven

Marit

The sharp crack of a snapping branch followed by muffled voices startled me out of my drowsy stupor. I opened my eyes and lifted my head, blinking into the late afternoon sunlight. A flicker of movement in my peripheral vision caught my eye. I hadn't seen a soul since fleeing the city three days ago, but now two men stood under the canopy of trees at the edge of the property.

Great. Just great. Strangers caught me sunbathing barebreasted. At least I was lying on my stomach.

Who were they?

Not neighbors. Thanks to the Black Rock Environmental Conservancy's aggressive carrot-and-stick tactics, all of the other cabins stood empty, sad and derelict shells of their former selves. Maybe they were hikers? No. Most hikers would slip discreetly back into the woods if they stumbled on a half-naked woman. Maybe they worked for the conservancy. I considered and rejected that idea. Grandma called the environmental group a major pain in the ass, always pestering her to sell her lease, but the few members I'd encountered had been unfailingly polite, not likely to alienate the last leaseholder by gawking at her.

So who were they? Why were they just standing there watching me?

Grandma always said to trust your intuition, and my intuition was shrieking danger.

Pressing my bare breasts against the quilt, I snaked out a hand and snatched my bikini top. I slipped my arms into the sleeves and raised my chest an inch from the quilt, just enough space to allow my fingers to fasten the bikini's front clasp. I reached for my nearby T-shirt and jerked it down over my head. At least now I wouldn't flash the strangers when I stood. I gripped one edge of the quilt, rolled onto my side, and wrapped it around my body as I rose to my feet. Pretty nifty trick, if I said so myself.

I glanced toward the trees again. The two men had disappeared, thank God. I whirled around, intending to dash to the cabin and bolt the door. My limbs locked. The strangers stood between me and the cabin, a palpable sense of menace emanating from their still figures.

Shit. Nobody could move that quickly. I stumbled backward, clutching the quilt to my chest, my heart pounding.

My eyes darted from one man to the other. They had to be related, brothers maybe. Both of middling height with wiry builds, they had narrow faces, high cheekbones, and straight reddish-brown hair that hung to their shoulders. One man stood a few feet closer to me than the other. Lifting my chin defiantly, I addressed my question to him.

"What do you want?"

It must have been sunlight reflecting off the surface of the lake that made his eyes appear to glimmer.

Barefoot and weaponless, I blustered. "My boyfriend is out hunting, but he should be back any minute." As soon as the words passed my lips, I stifled a groan. Lamest most transparently bogus lie ever.

The presumed leader smirked. Yeah. No armed and dangerous man was rushing to my rescue. I was on my own.

Some people go numb when confronted with danger. Their muscles constrict and their brains turn to sludge. Fear shuts them down. It was an instinctive survival mechanism. Become so small and still that the big, bad predator looks the other way.

I wasn't like some people. If anything, my senses sharpened when I was scared. My thought processes grew crystal clear, icy cold, and swift, like spring runoff.

I couldn't dash through the men to the relative safety of the cabin. Even if I made it around them to my car, I didn't have my keys. The lake lay behind me, blocking my retreat. My gaze fell on an old canoe, long disused since the lake was off-limits.

No way could I move quickly, cocooned in a quilt. Modesty be damned. I dropped the quilt and sprang at the canoe, snatching up the oar and brandishing it like a sword. It was a flimsy weapon, but if I struck hard and fast maybe I could take out one guy with a blow to the side of the head, then turn on the other one... and... and...

Crap. I was spinning a fantasy and I knew it. The odds were not on my side, but at least I would go down fighting. My gaze flicked from one man to the other.

"Back off," I warned.

They were in no hurry. Confidence and contempt stamped their faces as they sauntered toward me. They stopped a few steps in front of me. Mocking smiles twisting their lips.

I tightened my grip on the oar. "Which one of you assholes am I going to hit first?"

"She's a spunky little thing." The leader cast a backward glance at his companion, then dug a finger into a nostril. He examined what he found before flicking it onto the ground.

"I like a little fight in my prey," the second man drawled. His eyes were beadier than Booger's, giving him the look of a rat. "What fun is it if they don't resist?"

Prey? Resist?

"You want to run, sweetheart?" Booger asked, wiping his fingers on his shirt. "We'll give you a head start."

"Yeah, we'll give you a head start." A cheerful grin split Rat Face's countenance. He cackled, his eyes bright with glee.

The manic laughter raised goose bumps across my shoulders. "What... what—" I faltered, searching for the words to make sense of this. "You're saying you want to... to *hunt* me?"

Booger snapped his teeth and growled like a wild animal. "Chasing little bunnies through the woods is our favorite game."

"And fear—" Rat Face shivered. "There's nothing like the smell of fear in the air, so thick and heavy you can taste it." He threw back his head, sniffed, and smacked his lips.

"You can't hide, little bunny." Booger added. "Your fear will lead us straight to you."

I blinked, stunned.

A few years ago, I watched an old black-and-white movie about an eccentric millionaire who lured people to his country estate and hunted them for sport. A crazy notion, right? Except, Booger and Rat Face were proposing a similar chase.

And what would happen if they caught me?

Would they kill me? Mount my head on the wall of their trophy room, like in the movie?

I glanced over their shoulders, half expecting a camera crew to pop up and for someone to shout, "You've been pranked."

But no. Booger and Rat Face danced sideways, circling me like a pair of rabid dogs, yipping and gnashing their teeth.

I swallowed back bile. "How much?" I demanded.

"How much what?" Booger smiled, revealing stained incisors.

"How much of a head start?"

If they rushed me now with my back to the lake, I'd likely go down within a few minutes. If I took the head start and ran from the two men, well, I had only a thin chance of getting away, but it was better than nothing. I jogged four mornings each week. My strength and stamina were above average. Even if I couldn't outrun these asshats, I might be able to find a place to hide or climb a tree.

They couldn't really track me by smell, could they?

Booger turned to his companion. "Whaddaya think? Ten minutes?"

Rat Face shrugged. "Why not?"

A mirthless smile twisted Booger's lips. "Scat," he barked, gesturing for me to run.

He didn't have to tell me twice. Skirting the men, I ran toward the dense forest land surrounding the lake. Just as I ducked under the first low branch, a piercing howl erupted behind me. I glanced over my shoulder.

Booger and Rat Face had thrown back their heads, and an inhuman yowl burst from their throats.

I tripped, sprawling on the forest floor. Scrambling to my feet, I plunged into the undergrowth. No time to cover my trail. I leapt over ferns and fallen branches, trying to put as much distance as possible between me and that horrible cry.

Unreal. What gods had I pissed off to deserve this nightmare? I was supposed to be getting married in a few days, packing for my honeymoon in Bora Bora, not stumbling through the woods with repulsive strangers in hot pursuit.

Damn Bryce, the cheating asshole.

My eyes caught a flash of light between the trees, a stream flowing toward the lake. In movies people sometimes eluded pursuers by walking in flowing water. Hope gave my feet wings, and I flew toward the creek. Maybe I could make Booger and Rat Face lose my trail.

I waded into the middle of the stream. The water lapped at my knees. We'd had a drier-than-normal spring. The water level was low, so I didn't have to fight the current, but the moss-slicked rocks made for slow progress. It took all my concentration not to slip.

"This isn't working," I muttered, frantically scanning the forest for any sign of my pursuers. Should I abandon the stream and risk leaving a trail any kindergartner could follow, or should I stick with the water?

Come on, think.

Up ahead the stream cut under a rocky outcropping. I splashed toward it. Ducking my head, I peered into the dark recess where rock sloped down to meet the water, creating a small hollow, not quite a cave, but I could hide there.

I wriggled into the space and lay on my side, knees drawn up to my chest. My skimpy bathing suit offered no protection from the cold and wet. Wedged into the muddy hole, I shivered. The stream tumbled past mere feet from my hiding place.

I held my breath, trying to sort out the sounds I could hear over the splashing water. The hair-raising howling had stopped, but that realization brought no comfort. The ten-minute head start must be over. Booger and Rat Face were in the woods.

I strained my ears, listening for any sound of their approach, snapping branches, footsteps, or shouts. Nothing, except the whine of a mosquito that landed on my arm. Not daring to move, I tried to blow it off, but the bugger bit me. I ignored the itch and squinted at the narrow strip of stream and forest visible from my position under the rocks.

A loud splash.

Someone jumped into the stream directly across from my hiding place.

Maybe the bastards really *could* track me by smell. I recoiled, smacking my head against the rocks. "Shit," I mouthed.

A pair of denim-clad legs kicked through the water. I wriggled back further into the dark recess, holding my breath.

"Come out, come out wherever you are," a voice singsonged.

He was toying with me. I clenched my jaw to keep my teeth from chattering.

The stranger dropped into a crouch and peered under the rocks. Rat Face. "There you are," he said cheerfully. "Caught you fair and square. Now come on out." He cupped his fingers and beckoned me.

What was it Liv had said? *Hell hath no fury like a pissed-off Hagen woman.*

"Damned straight," I whispered.

Pretending to cooperate, I slipped off the rock shelf and into the water. I climbed out from under the rocky outcropping. Adrenaline pumped through my chilled body, lending me a burst of energy.

Eye to eye with Rat Face, I pivoted and shot my leg out in a roundhouse kick that clapped hard against his chin.

Thank you, Master Lee. My childhood tae kwon do lessons hadn't been wasted.

Rat Face's head spun sideways. He stumbled backward into the water, sputtering with fury.

I scrambled across the stream and clawed my way onto the opposite bank. A hand seized my ankle and dragged me back into the water. I kicked again, driving my heel into his face. Blood spurted from Rat Face's nose.

Booger jumped into the water. Hands on hips, he smirked at his bloody and battered friend. "You having fun? Has your prey resisted enough?"

Rat Face wiped his hand across his nose, studied his bloodstained fingers, then glared at me. "Oh, sweetheart. You're gonna pay for that."

CHAPTER EIGHT

ADAM

My phone rang with an incoming call. Had to be either the alpha or my cousin Remy. Grandpa knew how to text— I'd taught him myself—but he didn't like it. He didn't see the point of tapping letters onto a keyboard when he could simply talk. "I'm old school and set in my ways," he said when I'd argued in favor of texting instead of calling.

Remy had no such excuse. He was a techie, for chrissakes. Kept the pack computers functioning in tip-top condition. Designed the security grid. You'd think he'd scoff at the notion of placing an actual phone call, but no. I swore he took a perverse delight in defying expectations, in being contrary.

I pulled the phone from my pocket and swiped my thumb across the screen.

"Where are you?" Remy demanded without preamble.

"Just left a meeting with the alpha and now I'm heading toward the gym," I said.

"We've got another perimeter breach."

I sighed and shoved a hand through my hair. "Where?"

"An hour ago a camera caught a pair of coyotes trotting across the southern boundary line."

"And you're just getting around to reporting it *now*?" I said, stunned by the delay.

"You know the cameras can't distinguish between natural coyotes and shifters in coyote form. We live in a damned forest. We can't respond every time an animal walks past a camera."

True and this was the first time I'd heard of coyote shifters coming only two at a time. "Where are they now?"

"The next time they showed up on camera they were in human form and fully dressed. Somehow, somebody must have stashed clothes and boots for them. Means this was a planned incursion."

"Where are they?" I repeated, a pit forming in my stomach.

"They were running through the woods half a mile from the Hagen cabin."

Fuck.

Marit.

My wolf growled.

"I'm on it." Shoving the phone back into my pocket, I sprinted for my truck.

CHAPTER NINE

MARIT

R at Face's threat galvanized me into action. I rolled into a crouch. With a loud cry, I sprang at the injured man, knocking him backward into the water. His head went under and his arms flailed. I vaulted over him, hurling toward the opposite bank. Maybe I stood little chance of escaping the men, but I'd be damned if I'd go down without giving it my best shot.

Booger snaked out an arm, grabbed me around my waist, and hauled me back against his hard chest. He moved with super human speed and surprising strength, the same unnatural speed I'd witnessed at the cabin. Struggling to escape his grasp, I stomped with all my might, but my bare feet didn't even dent his heavy boots. Fear and fury washed over me.

Booger laughed in my ear. "I like spunky. I don't like stupid."

"Let me go," I gritted out, twisting in his hold. I dug my nails into his forearm, ripping gouges into his skin.

He hissed, then his free hand clamped around my neck.

He tightened his fingers, cutting off my breath.

I clawed at his hand but couldn't loosen his grip.

My ears rang and spots flickered across my field of vision. Darkness rushed toward me and I stilled, abandoning the struggle.

"Good girl," Booger whispered, releasing my neck.

I slumped forward, dragging in air.

Rat Face scrambled to his feet, his eyes alight with glee. He touched his leaking nose and stretched out bloody fingers. I held my breath and pressed my lips together when he smeared his blood over my cheek.

"Payback, bitch," he murmured.

The smell of fresh blood turned my stomach, and I gagged, squeezing my eyes shut as he leaned closer.

"Nope. You look at me." His voice dripped with malice.

I opened my eyes and glowered at Rat Face. Up close, he more than earned the moniker. Large, slightly pointed ears poked out from his lank hair. His beady eyes sparkled with animosity. The yellow stain on his teeth betrayed a serious lack of dental hygiene.

"Remember our orders," Booger cautioned. "Don't kill her. Don't break any bones. No permanent damage."

Did he say orders?

Commotion exploded from the nearby trees. As one, my assailants' heads snapped back, and their nostrils flared, ears twitching as they reacted to the sound. A shadow fell across the water. I lifted my eyes to the opposite bank.

A huge gray wolf stood on a large boulder, his golden eyes fierce with bone-chilling aggression. Teeth bared, hackles raised, his white-tipped tail stiff, he slowly stalked forward. The promise of death hung heavy in the air.

Instinct made me shrink back against Booger. He shoved me away. I fell onto my hands and knees, banging my elbow on a sharp rock.

The wolf locked his eyes on my assailants. He swayed from side to side, mirroring the motion of the two men as they shifted from foot to foot.

A deep growl rumbled from his chest. Muscles bunched in his powerful haunches. Dear God, he was about to attack, to sink those sharp fangs and monstrous claws into flesh.

Hide.

Moving slowly, I scooted sideways under the overhanging rocks. I squeezed into the dark recess, my eyes fixed on Booger and Rat Face's boots as they stood in the water, facing the wolf. Maybe they'd break and run, leading the wolf away from my hiding place.

"C'mon guys," I breathed, willing them to flee.

I squinted as the light bouncing off the flowing water began to shimmer. Stream and forest disappeared, obscured by a field of sparkling lights. The lights swirled and danced before the image resolved and once again, I saw trees and water. Now, instead of four booted feet, I spied eight legs covered with reddish fur.

I blinked.

Booger and Rat Face must have run away.

Low growls rose from the animals' throats. They yipped, then bolted, kicking up water as they ran.

The wolf leapt into the stream in pursuit. I covered my ears but couldn't block the sounds when he caught up to his prey. Howls filled the air, then yelps of pain when flesh tore and bones snapped. The sickening smell of blood flooded my nostrils, and I covered my mouth.

Go away. Go away. Go away.

Heart galloping, I listened for the wolf's return.

The silence stretched on for several minutes, and hope unfurled in my chest. Despite their fierce appearance, wolves weren't especially aggressive creatures. I had no reason to expect the animal to come back for me. Maybe the angry wolf had ambled off in the opposite direction, his appetite for violence sated after he tore into whatever those animals were. And maybe the creeps who'd chased and threatened me had turned tail at the sight of the wolf. Maybe… maybe I was okay.

A pair of boots splashed through the water and paused outside the gap between rock and stream. Had Booger or Rat

Face returned? The man dropped down into a squat, and I braced myself for another fight.

His large body and broad shoulders filled the opening to my hidey-hole, blocking out most of the light and turning him into a dark, imposing silhouette.

"You all right in there?"

I sagged with relief, recognizing the deep voice. The mystery man from the bakery. A stranger, but not a malevolent one. Whoever he was, he wouldn't hurt me. I knew that with a certainty that bordered on religious conviction.

I swallowed. "Yes. I'm all right."

"You're safe now. I promise."

A handful of words, simple and straightforward, but they held a significance beyond their superficial meaning. No matter what happened, this man meant to keep me safe.

I shook my head. Talk about an irrational reaction. I was reading waaay too much into a few simple words. "This is bonkers," I whispered under my breath.

"What's bonkers?"

He heard me. How had he heard me?

"Who are you?" I asked, ignoring his question.

"I work for the environmental conservancy that owns this land. I was testing soil samples nearby and heard you shout. I ran over to help and chased off the men who were attacking you."

"So... so they're still out there?" I faltered, my lungs seizing. Shit. If Booger and Rat Face had escaped they might come back.

"No." Unlike mine, his voice was firm and steady. "I called for backup. By now, I bet the bastards are in custody."

I released the deep breath I'd been holding. "What about the wolf?"

"The wolf?"

"I saw a big gray wolf. I think it chased the men off, then it attacked some animals. It sounded like it ripped them apart."

"If you saw a wolf, it's long gone by now. It's safe to come out." When I hesitated, he held out a hand. "You're cold and wet, probably in shock. Please, let me help you."

Cold and stress had drained every ounce of my strength.

"Come on," he urged, stepping backward into the stream to make room.

I slithered out of the hollow, slid into the water, and crawled out from under the overhanging rocks. My trembling legs threatened to collapse beneath me when I tried to stand. Shivers racked my body.

"Whoa." He caught my elbows.

After a moment, I found my footing. "I got it. Thanks."

"You're freezing." He pulled his black T-shirt over his head and held it out to me.

I slipped it over my head. At five-foot-eight, I was hardly petite, but the tee fell almost to my knees.

Craning my neck, I studied my shirtless rescuer. He was powerfully built, his tawny skin stretched taut over deeply incised muscles. He would have dwarfed Booger and Rat Face, but the menace that oozed from their pores was entirely absent from this man. Angling his head down, he returned my scrutiny, a shock of dark hair falling across his brow.

His eyes, dear lord, his eyes. Golden yellow, flecked with amber, they radiated both strength and compassion.

Despite Grandma's experiences with the conservancy, maybe some good people worked for the group.

An odd sensation tugged at the back of my mind, a recognition that went far beyond our chance encounter downtown. Bryce's betrayal had kicked the crap out of my self-confidence, but something told me I could trust this man. I closed my eyes and shook my head. My reaction didn't make a bit of sense. Maybe my traumatized mind was latching onto a kind stranger, projecting a connection where none could logically exist.

Doesn't explain what happened the first time I saw him, how he stopped me in my tracks with a single glance.

"Who *are* you?" I asked again.

"I told you, I work for the Black Rock Environmental Conservancy. One of our board members ordered cupcakes for his daughter's party, and I picked them up."

"So it's just a coincidence that we crossed paths twice?"

He hesitated, then gave a clipped nod. "Looks like it."

Cold water lapped around my knees. My teeth started to chatter.

"Let's get you out of there," the stranger said gently.

We waded across the stream. He offered a hand and helped me climb up the bank. After a few steps, pain stopped me in my tracks. Wincing, I hopped over to a fallen log, sat down, and lifted my left foot.

"What's wrong?" he asked.

"Something hurts." I examined the bottom of my foot. Scratches crisscrossed my sole and a small thorn was embedded in my arch. The forest floor really did a number on my feet when I ran. "How could I not notice this till now?"

He hunkered down next to me. "When you're running scared, the only thing you focus on is getting away."

I got away.

Thanks to the wolf and this man I barely knew, I survived my ordeal relatively unscathed.

The reality of that narrow escape—of all of the horrifying things that could have happened, but didn't—crashed down on me. Wrapping my arms around my waist, I shuddered. I lifted watery eyes to my rescuer.

"They said they wanted to *hunt* me. They called me *prey*."

A shaft of late afternoon sunlight pierced the forest canopy and fell across his face, illuminating a clenched jaw and the rage that flitted across his features.

Staring into the distance as if at some unseen foe, his beautiful eyes darkened. I swore his chest rumbled. Danger radiated from him. Without thinking, I shrank back. His eyes snapped to mine, and his expression shifted from menacing to harmless so quickly that my head spun.

His generous mouth curved up in a small, reassuring smile. "Lemme check out your injuries." He carefully lifted my foot onto his thigh, cradling it in the palm of his hand.

At his touch, the tension eased from my body. That inexplicable feeling of connection, the certainty that this man would shield me from harm, warmed my blood.

I've always been a sucker for what Liv called arm porn. Watching the corded muscles in a man's forearm jump and twitch got to me every time. Now, my gaze naturally fell on the man's arms. Strong and beautifully shaped, they promised protection in a dangerous world.

Confusion heated my cheeks. I shook myself, fighting the urge to burrow into the stranger's arms.

Trauma. The impulse had to be a byproduct of trauma.

Unable to meet his eyes, I stared at the three strands of leather twined around his wrist. A wire-wrapped shiny black stone was affixed to the bracelet.

I pointed. "You work for the Black Rock Environmental Conservancy and you're wearing a black stone on your bracelet. Another coincidence?"

He offered a small shrug. "You believe in coincidences?"

I welcomed the change of topic. "More than I do in fate." Bitterness tainted my voice as I remembered Bryce prattling on about destiny and providence.

His head jerked back. "You don't believe in fate?"

It was my turn to shrug. "I don't believe in fate, ghosts, guardian angels, the Easter Bunny, or most things that go bump in the night." I paused, tilting my head to one side. "Although I reserve judgment on aliens."

"You're a skeptic?"

"I'm more of an empiricist. Show me a ghost or a guardian angel, and I'm willing to change my mind."

"So you have to see something, touch it, smell it, hear it, in order to believe it's real. If that's the case, I guess you never will believe in fate. Or friendship. Or love. Or loyalty."

He turned his attention back to my foot. Strong, calloused fingers brushed over my skin while he waited for my reply.

I frowned. "Love? Loyalty? Friendship? I believe in all those things."

"Then why won't you consider the possibility of fate?"

I pressed my lips together, unwilling to admit I was having a wee bit of a knee-jerk reaction to my cheating fiancé's declarations about destiny.

He deftly plucked the thorn out of my arch and held it up. "There you go."

I massaged the spot. "That's better. Thank you."

He still cradled my foot, his hand warm and comforting against my chilled skin.

"My name is Marit, by the way. Marit Hagen."

"Nice to meet you, Marit Hagen." His low voice lingered over the syllables of my name, sending shivers up and down my arms. "I'm Adam Landry."

"Nice to meet you, too, Adam Landry."

"And now I'd like to carry you back to the Hagen cabin so we can tend to your cuts." He stood, apparently waiting for my permission.

Jagged rocks, blackberry brambles, and dry pine needles had chewed up the soles of my feet. Walking barefoot over the same surface was just plain silly. Why not take Adam up on his offer?

"All right."

Adam swept me into his arms. His long strides made short work of the distance to the cabin. He carried me inside and deposited me on the old sofa. Rummaging through the kitchen cupboards, he found a wide, deep ceramic bowl. He filled the bowl with warm water and set it on the braided rug in front of the sofa.

"Soak your feet while I look for antiseptic cream to put on your cuts."

I did as instructed, moaning with pleasure when the warm water touched my skin. I pointed toward the bathroom. "There's a first aid kit under the sink."

A minute later, he crouched down on the rug beside the bowl, a towel slung over his shoulder, and the first aid kit in hand. "Let 'em soak for a few more minutes." He lapsed into silence. I followed his gaze as it traveled around the cabin, then settled on the Little Red Riding Hood cookie jar. He grinned.

"That was my first wolf," I said more to break the quiet than anything else.

His eyes cut to mine, curious.

"Not the cookie jar, the real wolf. I mean, I've heard wolves howling at night, but that was the first time I've come face-to-face with one."

"What'd you think?" he asked.

"That he was huge, pissed off, and terrifying."

He glanced at the cookie jar again. "A real-life big bad wolf, huh?"

"I guess so." I made a face. "But I'm glad he showed up when he did."

"Me, too."

One by one, Adam lifted my feet from the water, gently dried them off, then daubed ointment on all the cuts. He wrapped gauze around both feet.

"Socks?"

"Top dresser drawer. Left side."

He retreated to the bedroom and returned with a pair of fluffy socks and the quilt. Kneeling, he slipped the socks onto my feet and draped the quilt across my lap.

"Better?" he asked.

"Much. I appreciate you taking such good care of me."

"It's my..." He hesitated, as if searching for the right word. "It's my pleasure. Glad I could help."

Looking down at the basin of water, I smiled. In my mind's eye, I saw Grandma standing at the counter, kneading bread, then sliding the oiled dough into this very bowl to rise.

"What is it?" Adam settled next to me, his muscular arms stretched across the sofa back.

"Grandma would roll over in her grave if she knew I'd soaked my feet in her dough bowl."

Just like that, memory sliced through me. Grandma loved this homey cabin beyond reason. Never mind that she couldn't swim in the lake. Never mind that she would have pocketed a small fortune if she'd agreed to sell out to the conservancy. Nothing made her waiver in her resolve to hold onto the lease. When cancer was eating away at her bones, leaving her bedridden and glassy-eyed with pain, she made me promise not to let it go. I had no idea why the cabin was so important to her. The question nagged at me, but I put it away for later, when there wasn't a far-too-distracting man sitting on my sofa.

"Your grandma baked bread?" Adam's question pulled me from my thoughts.

Grateful for the small talk, I nodded. "The best bread ever. And pies and cakes and cookies. My cousins and I learned to love baking from her. She's why we opened Freya's Bake Shop."

"I was sorry to hear about her passing," he said. "I met her a few times. She was a nice lady."

"I miss her every day," I confessed.

"This is the first time you've visited the cabin since her passing, isn't it?" He shifted his weight on the sofa cushion, as if he couldn't find a comfortable position.

I need to tip over the couch and see if I can tie down that loose spring.
"Marit?"

"Sorry. Lately, my mind wanders a lot." I shook the cobwebs away. "Um... the cabin... Grandma left it to me in her will. I paid somebody to clean up the place after Grandma died, but I couldn't bring myself to visit until now. It hurts. Too many memories, you know?"

He frowned. "If the cabin brings only painful memories, why don't you sell the lease?" he asked slowly.

I opened my mouth to reply. The words froze in my throat.
Why don't I sell the lease?

My heart sank and acid roiled in my stomach. My crap taste in men—my absolute lack of good judgment—had struck again. Adam worked for the conservancy. Of course he was nice to me. He had an agenda. First I'd trusted Bryce, then I'd trusted Adam, the white knight whose easy charm belied his true intentions. That mysterious connection I felt was all in my head. How could I be so stupid, so blind? Why did I always believe the wrong man? Squaring my shoulders, I turned to Adam.

"Why don't I sell the lease?" I repeated.

"It's a logical question."

"No. It's a self-serving question," I snapped. "You work for the conservancy, the same group that pestered my grandma for years to give up her lease. The same people who did everything in their power to drive her from her home."

"What are you talking about?" he demanded. "We offered to buy her out, but we never pestered her. We never tried to drive her from the cabin."

"That's not what Grandma told me."

"Oh yeah?" He leaned forward, planting his elbows on his knees. "What did your grandmother tell you we did besides offering her a small fortune to sell the lease?"

"You made her dismantle her dock and pay a crew to remove the wood from the lake. That cost her a pretty penny."

He grimaced, acknowledging the truth. "Yeah, we did that. What else?"

I threw my hands in the air. "A lot of petty, mean-spirited stuff over the years. Somebody kept letting the air out of her car's tires. Grandma fenced in a small garden. Her tomato plants all died overnight, like somebody had dumped herbicide on them. Every rosebush she planted died, too. Her clotheslines were cut. Her bird feeders kept disappearing. Once, when Grandma was gone, somebody jimmied open the door and locked a skunk inside the cabin."

"What the hell?" Adam sputtered.

He was either a good actor or his shock was genuine.

I held up a finger. "There's more. Overnight, one of the porch steps mysteriously came unscrewed, and Grandma fell when it slid out from under her."

Adam sat back, his expression incredulous. "You think we're the kind of people who would hurt a little old lady?"

"If not you guys, then who did all those things? Who else had motive and opportunity?"

He frowned. "I don't know, but it wasn't us."

He looked sincere—but of course, Bryce had looked sincere when he lied to my face for months. Unraveling the truth might be beyond my pathetic powers of observation.

I threw him a bone. "Maybe you don't know everything about the people you work for. Maybe the harassment campaign was on a need-to-know basis." A horrible thought occurred to me. Booger and Rat Face said they were following orders. Somebody sicced them on me, and the list of possible suspects was damned short.

"Maybe you work for the kind of people who'd hire thugs to scare me off the property and force me to sell."

"Are you fucking kidding me?" Adam burst out, obviously affronted. "My people would *never* do that."

My shoulders sagged as all the events of the past week caught up with me. I felt wrung out, emotionally depleted, and bone-tired. Dropping my face into my hands, I rubbed my temples.

"Are you okay?"

I clenched my fists to keep my hands from trembling. "It's a little late for your nice guy act. Time to go."

Adam slowly rose to his feet. Towering over me, he opened his mouth to speak, then apparently thought better of it. He whirled and strode to the door. With one hand on the knob, he turned back to me.

"Will you be all right here alone?" he asked.

Was he trying to scare me, to remind me that I was by myself and vulnerable?

Disappointment tasted like bitter ashes. "Take your phony concern and shove it up your ass."

He nodded once, his expression stony, then he left, shutting the door quietly behind him.

I stood carefully on my bandaged and stockinged feet, hobbled across the room, and locked the door. When I peeked through the window, he was out of sight.

My cell phone rang and I glanced at the screen. Another call from Bryce. What made him think I'd pick up this time when I'd ignored the dozens of calls and texts he'd sent since I caught him with Courtney?

"Nope." I declined the call, dropped the phone back on the kitchen counter, and heaved a deep, defeated sigh.

It was time to think about dinner, but I had no appetite. If I tried to eat, I'd choke on every mouthful. I was beyond ready to be done with the day. Sleep—and the promise of oblivion—beckoned like a siren, but before I turned in, I needed to clean up.

I limped to the bathroom and filled the old tub. Generous handfuls of lavender bath salts filled the room with a calming scent. I stripped out of my damp clothes, then glanced down at the fluffy socks my so-called hero had tenderly slid onto my feet.

Adam.

Tears stung my eyes again. I furiously dashed them away.

"Nope," I repeated, refusing to waste any more time thinking about the men who'd let me down or my own stupidity.

Instead, I focused on the problem at hand: keeping my bandaged feet dry while I bathed. I sat on the edge of the tub. My feet dangled over the bath mat. Catching my weight on my hands, I slid ass-first into the steaming water, coming to a stop when my heels hit the porcelain edge. I swung my legs around into a more-or-less comfortable position, then relaxed into the fragrant warmth. I lingered until the water cooled and the skin on my fingers puckered. I toweled off and slipped into my favorite pair of cotton pajamas, the ones with zebras and antelopes cavorting against a red background.

Before clambering into my bed, I made the rounds of the cabin, double-checking the door lock and the window latches. I'd sleep better knowing the cabin was locked up tight.

I parted the curtains and took one last look at the lake. The landscape was painted in shades of black and white, a silver moon reflected on the still surface of the water. Trees loomed like silhouettes against the darkening sky. Far away from the city lights that obscured its beauty, the sky twinkled with stars. A shooting star streaked the heavens.

Make a wish before it disappears.

Grandma's voice. I flashed back to childhood, to sitting on the porch with Grandma, wrapped in a quilt against the cold, watching the night sky.

Quickly, I murmured the words, casting my wish out to the universe before the last glints of the shooting star faded from the sky.

"Love. True love."

Shaking my head, I laughed softly. Was it really that simple? Was that what I wanted?

My gaze followed the path traced by the shooting star, across the sky and over the trees on the opposite side of the lake. I squinted, pressed closer to the glass, and spied a dark form at the water's edge. Leaning sideways, I reached into a drawer and pulled out Grandma's old bird-watching binoculars. I spun the ring, adjusting the focus until the image sharpened. Standing tall on his four legs, a large wolf faced the cabin from across the lake.

The wolf from this afternoon? The one who scared off Booger and Rat Face? Impossible to know for sure, but somehow I sensed it was him. Not a snarling beast, but the hero who saved the day. And now he stood sentry, watching over the cabin, keeping me safe.

I dropped the curtain, padded across the floor, and crawled into bed. A minute later—when the wolf's howl split the night—I smiled to myself and snuggled down into the sheets.

"I'm okay," I whispered into the darkness.

CHAPTER TEN

ADAM

A *little late for your nice guy act.*

My boots pounded against the ground as I ran, venting some of the anger that had grabbed me by the balls and refused to let go. The injustice of Marit's accusations filled me with so much rage that I thought my head would explode.

Nice guy act, my ass.

I'd never forget the condemnation in Marit's eyes, the unhappy twist to her lips, and most of all, the pain that accompanied her anger. My stride lengthened as I raced across the forest floor, covering ground as if I couldn't get far enough away from that infuriating woman.

Hire thugs to scare me off.

That accusation cut to the bone. What kind of asshats did she think we were? Hardwired by nature to protect, the very last thing we'd ever do was to sic coyote scum on a woman. The very notion turned my stomach.

My pace quickened till my feet skimmed over the ground, and I jumped easily over boulders and fallen trees. I bounded over the stream and landed on the other side.

Take your phony concern and shove it up your ass.

Nice. She learned that language from her grandma?

Maybe. A reluctant smile quirked my lips as I remembered the old woman. Sweet as the huckleberry pie she served me, until I showed her the very generous check the conservancy offered in exchange for her lease. Then the same sweet old lady—with the ready smile and the butter-wouldn't-melt-in-her-mouth expression—told me to take the check and stick it where the sun don't shine.

Physical exertion coupled with the memory of the spunky old woman calmed me. I stopped running, planted my hands on my hips, and caught my breath. The anger seeped from my blood, allowing me to think straight. Much as I hated to admit it, Marit's words stung because they contained a kernel of truth. The pack needed her lease, and they were counting on me to persuade her to sell.

Shit.

My phone rang and I fished it from my pocket.

"Yeah?" The clipped monosyllable ensured that my cousin wouldn't hear the emotion that still pumped through me.

"Remy told me about the intruders," Zane said. "You track them down?"

"I did. Send a cleanup crew to the stream, a mile northwest of the Hagen cabin."

"Will do. Dammit." Zane's voice shook, his frustration palpable. "How many coyotes do we have to kill before they stop poking their damned snouts into our territory?"

I touched the chunk of meteorite the leather cords secured around my wrist. "You know they're not gonna stop, not as long as we have the Black Rock."

"Nothing but the truth there." Zane sighed, then, "How the hell did they find out about it?"

"That's the million-dollar question."

The Black Rock—a boulder-sized meteorite my people had discovered in Alaska in the mid-1920s—was my pack's greatest treasure, guarding it, our sacred duty. We'd hauled the Black Rock out of Alaska when it became clear that we were losing the Great War. Now, only the alpha and Rolf knew where on pack land it was hidden.

I ran a hand through my sweat-dampened hair. "There was a complication. The coyotes went after Marit Hagen. Chased her into the forest. They were roughing her up when I caught up with them."

"Fuck," Zane groaned. "What did she see?"

I bristled but held on to my temper. "She told me a wolf ran off the men who attacked her. Far as I know, she didn't see anything we need to worry about."

"She'd better not have."

At his indifference to Marit's well-being, my hackles rose. "She's okay. Thanks for asking." My voice dripped with sarcasm. "Scared, but unhurt."

"Good. Last thing we need is the human authorities searching pack lands for a missing woman."

Sometimes I swore that Zane gave zero fucks about anybody outside the pack.

"Seriously, man," I protested. "You don't care if a woman gets attacked on our land?"

Zane huffed out a breath. "Of course I don't want a woman to get hurt, but protecting the pack comes first. And that woman's presence is a threat to the pack."

I couldn't argue with that. The Hagen lease predated our purchase of the lake and surrounding forest for a so-called nature preserve. As long as a single leaseholder held title, the roads leading to the lake couldn't be closed. Hikers and other visitors to the forest land couldn't be banned until our control was absolute. For a security-driven pack, this was intolerable.

"We lost too much in the Great War," Zane continued. "Our numbers are a small fraction of what they were before the grizzlies drove us out of Alaska."

"You're right," I said, the truth of his words like a heavy weight in my chest.

"We can't afford to be sentimental about humans," Zane piled on.

Yeah, but what if your wolf insists that a human is your mate?

I couldn't say the words aloud, not even to my closest friend. Until our depleted numbers were restored, pack law forbade mating with a human. Any child born of such a union would stay locked forever in human form. Only those with more than fifty percent shifter DNA could turn into wolves. The pack needed wolves.

"Uh... Adam?" Zane interrupted my thoughts.

"I'm here."

"What are you going to do? About the Hagen woman, I mean."

Good question. My fists clenched at the memory of the coyote scum pawing at her. The best thing for the pack—the safest thing for Marit—would be for her to sell the lease and return to the city.

"I'm her hero, remember? I rescued her from the creeps who attacked her. Already got a foot in the door. I'll keep an eye on her and encourage her to sell."

It was only half of the truth, but a partial truth would buy me time to figure out what to do. My wolf paced back and forth inside my skin. Soon my shadow brother would be clawing to get out, demanding to be heard. My two sides were rarely at odds, man and beast usually living in peaceful coexistence, ceding control to each other when the need arose. But now my wolf was snarling, demanding that I pay heed.

"What about the police?" Zane asked.

I was so preoccupied that it took a moment for his question to sink in. "The police?" I repeated. Then it hit me.

Shit.

Marit might be in shock now, but sooner or later it would occur to her to contact the cops and report the assault. No way would my lie that the conservancy had taken her attackers into custody stand up to scrutiny. Not when my wolf had ripped them apart.

"Adam?" Zane persisted.

"I'll stop by the cabin tomorrow and tell her some cock-and-bull story about what happened to the men. Something that makes it clear she doesn't need to bring in the cops."

"Do whatever you have to do to keep the police out of it," Zane said.

Neither my wolf nor I liked the sound of that. "I'll figure it out. I gotta run." I hung up without giving Zane a chance to reply.

Now what?

I looked up at the sky. The sun had slipped below the horizon, and the temperature had dropped. My metabolism ran hot in both wolf and human form. Despite the cool air touching my bare chest, I felt warm and comfortable. Was Marit warm and comfortable tonight? I peered through the darkening forest, as if my gaze could pierce the trees and cover the miles to her cabin.

Get a grip, man.

Marit had made her feelings perfectly clear. I'd saved her ass and the woman had kicked me out, hurling insults.

The wolf scrabbled against my skin, desperate to break free.

"Ours."

I said the word aloud, then shook my head, rejecting the pointless notion. The wolf stilled, waiting for my human side to catch up to the knowledge that already gripped the beast's heart.

Ours.

What the fuck was I doing? The wolf edged closer and closer to the surface.

"She is ours." I blinked, then stared unseeing into the distance. "Well... hell."

Claws sliced through my fingertips as I ceded power to my other half. I hissed, my body racked with spasms from the pain of muscle, bone, and skin reshaping themselves into their animal counterparts. Now a wolf, I stretched and shook my limbs, exalting at the transmutation. I wheeled around and charged through the trees. With every step closer to the cabin, Marit's scent grew stronger. I thundered across the forest floor, ignoring the branches that slapped against my fur as I ran.

Rational thought splintered. Human intellect was subsumed into animal instinct. The wolf broke through the tree line on the shore opposite the cabin and paused, gazing at the dark structure.

A curtain twitched in a window, and Marit's face appeared behind the glass. The wolf whined and pawed the ground. She startled. A moment later, she raised a pair of binoculars to her eyes. The binoculars swept across the lake shore, freezing when they pointed directly at the wolf.

I stood tall and proud, her guardian, her sentinel. Tomorrow the man would speak to the woman. Tonight, no harm would come to our mate while the wolf stood watch.

CHAPTER ELEVEN

MARIT

I jerked awake and opened my eyes. Bright sunbeams flooded the room with light. A glance at the clock on the nightstand confirmed it was past two in the afternoon. How had I slept so long? I sat up.

"Ow." The pain that greeted the movement dashed the cobwebs from my brain and banished my confusion. My joints ached and a dull pain pulsed at the base of my skull. A mottled bruise and bloody scab covered my right elbow. I swung my legs out of bed and wobbled to a stand. Even the soles of my feet hurt.

Memories of yesterday's ordeal flitted through my mind. Chased through the forest by strangers. Cornered like a trapped animal. Threatened. It was all so incredible, so unreal, that if I didn't bear physical signs of the ordeal, I'd think it had all been a nightmare.

And the wolf, my unlikely hero, was he still standing guard? I hobbled to the window and pressed my face against the glass, scanning the opposite shore. Of course he wasn't there. A wolf was a wild animal, a creature with no agenda beyond survival. He was no guardian angel. That notion was nothing more than a fantasy, a comforting delusion that had allowed my exhausted mind and body to drift into sleep untroubled by fear. Still, a pang of disappointment shot through me.

And Adam? Was he an illusion, too?

Nope. Not an illusion, just another in a long line of dickheads.

Stepping gingerly on my abraded feet, I shuffled into the bathroom. I brushed my teeth and splashed water on my face. My reflection in the mirror startled me. Overnight my tan had faded, leaving my cheeks pale and drawn. Purple half-moons discolored the skin under my eyes. I'd slept for seventeen hours, yet I looked a wreck. I took a bottle of ibuprofen from the medicine cabinet and dry-swallowed two pills.

I'm okay.

I'm okay.

I am okay!

My new mantra. Sucking in a breath, I said it out loud, but the hitch in my voice gave the lie to the words. Truth be told, I wanted to crawl back into bed and hide under a blanket. Or better yet, throw everything into my car and skedaddle back to Belle Reve and my cousins.

I stared at my face with dismay. The image wavered as tears filled my eyes. For a moment, I saw Rat Face's stained teeth, smelled his fetid breath, cringed from the sensation of rough hand squeezing my neck. I furiously blinked back the tears.

They're gone. They can't hurt me. I'm a grown woman and I won't run away like a scared little girl.

I slid my feet into a pair of plush, cushioned slippers and strode to the kitchen. I filled the coffee grinder with my favorite Sumatran beans. While the water heated, I checked my phone. Four more missed calls from Bryce. He'd called two more times last night, once this morning, and again an hour ago.

Dammit. Why couldn't my persistent ex take a hint and get lost?

I filled the French press, poured a mug of coffee, then walked outside to the deck overlooking the lake. Settling back into an Adirondack chair, I took my first grateful sip of the heavenly brew. My gaze fell on the quilt and oar I'd dropped when I fled from Booger and Rat Face. Panic constricted my chest. With a trembling hand, I set the mug down on the wide arm of the wooden chair.

Get a hold of yourself.

I picked up the mug and forced myself to take measured swallows. Maybe it was the need for distraction. Maybe it was the well-loved cabin working its old magic. Whatever the reason, I knew what to do.

"Muffins," I said out loud. "Grandma Freya's orange honey muffins." Suddenly I felt ravenous and my mouth watered. I fetched the recipe box from the kitchen and shuffled through the note cards until I found *Orange Honey Muffins* written in Grandma's stylized cursive handwriting.

I heated the oven and assembled the ingredients. Once the muffins were baking, I poured a second mug of coffee and pulled a chair up to the kitchen table. Acting on impulse, I turned over the recipe card. Across the top Grandma had scrawled, *Aleks loves these!*

Who the heck was Aleks?

The timer went off at the same instant my phone rang. I glanced at the screen. Bryce again. Ignoring the call, I took the muffins from the oven and set the pan on a rack to cool. I picked up the card again and studied the puzzling note. I'd bet good money that neither Liv nor Annika had heard about the mysterious Aleks. Maybe I should ask Dorrie Mittelmann.

A loud rapping on the cabin door made me jump. I turned toward the sound, frowning. First Bryce had kept calling and now I had an uninvited visitor. I was so not in the mood for company. With an unhappy sigh, I answered the door.

CHAPTER TWELVE

ADAM

Now that I was standing on Marit's doorstep, a bouquet of pink lilies from the pack garden clutched in my hands, I started to have second thoughts about the gesture. Would she see the flowers as a cheap attempt to curry favor? I was about to toss the bouquet over the porch rail when she answered the door.

"You," Marit said, her voice flat and unwelcoming. "What do you want?"

Her fingers twitched on the doorframe, as if she was fighting the impulse to slam it in my face. Lines of fatigue etched her face, and she was far too pale. My wolf stirred, alarmed by her appearance.

No choice but to make the best of it now. Ignoring the unfriendly greeting, I held out the flowers. "A peace offering."

She frowned at the lilies then lifted her gaze to my face. Her beautiful gray eyes betrayed both weariness and caution. My guts twisted. I'd put that wariness in her eyes, hadn't I?

Marit sighed. "I'm not going to sell the lease, so there's no point in making nice."

Making nice.

A phony, insincere attempt to win her over, to get her to do what I wanted. I couldn't take offense, not when her suspicions held a sliver of truth. But the whole picture was a lot bigger than that small piece.

"We got off to a bad start, and I'm sorry for that. I wanted to check in on you, to see how you're doing after the incident yesterday."

"I'm fine." She shook her head and a strand of hair fell across her cheek. "Listen, I'm grateful for your help yesterday, but you're wasting your time."

The compulsion to reach out and touch her hair, to run the heavy silk between my fingers was almost irresistible. My fingers clenched around the flower stems as I wrestled myself under control.

"Not a word about the lease. I promise." She looked unconvinced. How to keep her talking? A sweet scent wafted through the open door. I sniffed. "Do I smell honey?"

Hospitality warred with reluctance on her face, but after a moment, good manners won. "Orange honey muffins. Would you like one?"

"Yes, please."

Marit accepted the flowers, stepped aside, and gestured for me to enter the cabin. I took a chair at the kitchen table and planted both elbows against its battered surface. Marit laid the blossoms on the counter.

"Coffee?" she asked without enthusiasm.

I gave my best smile. "Yeah. That'd be nice. Black, please."

She plated a muffin and poured coffee into a mug, then set both on the table in front of me. Instead of taking a seat, she turned her back to me and reached into a cupboard for a blue-and-white pitcher. She busied herself filling the pitcher, trimming the lily stems, and arranging the bouquet. Her shoulders were tight with stress.

"You gonna sit with me?" I asked.

Marit jerked, nearly upsetting the pitcher of flowers before she set it down in the middle of the table. She inhaled, then let out a slow breath. When she lifted her eyes to meet mine, her expression was blank, as if she'd schooled her features into a polite mask.

Apex predators scent fear. I could almost taste the sour wave of anxiety that rolled off her. A knife to the gut; that's what her uneasiness in my presence felt like. She didn't really think we'd set the coyotes on her, did she?

I patted the chair next to mine. "C'mon, sit with me."

"Fine." Marit topped off her coffee and took the chair opposite mine.

"I don't bite," I said, trying to lighten the mood. I broke off a piece of muffin and popped it in my mouth. "Least not till I know you better."

"What are you doing?" Her polite mask gave way to exasperation. "I'm not going to fall for your charm offensive. I told you to get lost, so why did you come back?"

I abandoned the playful banter. No way could I confess to the truth—that my wolf wouldn't give me a moment's peace until I made sure she was all right. She'd think I was nuts. And I sure as hell couldn't admit to the other, less savory truth, that the pack needed to stay on good terms with her until they could buy her lease.

I leaned across the table. "Less than twenty-four hours ago, two men chased you through the woods. You were hunted down, cornered, and attacked. I saw how it traumatized you, and I'm concerned about how you're doing. Jeez. What happened to make you so damned suspicious?"

Marit slammed her mug down on the table. Coffee sloshed over the side. Color touched her cheeks and her eyes flashed. "Don't you dare make this about me. Don't act like I'm being... like I'm being too emotional and irrational just because I question your motives."

Marit had spirit. Both man and wolf approved of a woman who stood up for herself. I leaned back and raised both palms into the air. "I apologize. Your skepticism makes sense. We want to buy your lease. You don't want to sell. That's an undeniable conflict of interests, but it doesn't mean we have to be enemies."

Marit scrubbed both hands over her face then dropped them to her lap. "Am I supposed to just pretend that you don't have an agenda?"

"No. I'm not asking you to do that. Acknowledge it, but look beyond it."

"How about the vandalism?" she asked. "Am I supposed to ignore that, too?"

No way would our alpha tolerate criminal mischief, of that I was one hundred percent certain. "Our board of directors would never sanction theft or the destruction of property," I said firmly. "That's not how we do business."

"If it wasn't the conservancy, then who?"

"I'm looking into that. I promise."

"All right." She frowned, unconvinced, but she held her peace.

A long moment of silence, then I spoke again. "Did your grandma tell you about that big wind storm seven years ago? The one where a branch crashed through her roof?"

Marit bobbed her head.

"My cousin Remy and I spent a day repairing the damage and putting on new shingles. She insisted on fixing us dinner. Beef stew with dumplings and huckleberry pie." I smiled at the memory. "Would we have helped her, and would she have fed us, if we were enemies?"

"I remember Grandma telling me about that," she conceded. "You and your cousin were the 'nice young men' who showed up on her doorstep the morning after the storm?"

I nodded. "Yeah. We all looked beyond our conflict of interests and acted like decent people."

Marit pondered my words for a few minutes, then swung suspicious eyes my way. "I don't want to be played."

The word *again* hung unspoken in the air between us. Her chin trembled and she stared down at her empty hands. Somebody she trusted had betrayed her. She'd told me as much the first time we spoke.

The wolf surged forward and tried to break free. His wrath, his primal need to protect and extract revenge heated my blood. My hand tightened on the mug. I felt the same need to protect and avenge—to reach out and offer comfort—but I was a less impulsive creature than my wolf.

"Hey." I waited for Marit to focus her attention on me. I needed her to see the sincerity on my face, to hear the conviction in my voice. "I'm no player."

Brow furrowed, Marit studied me. "I don't know what to believe. Maybe my asshole radar is messed up. Maybe you really are a good man. I don't know how to tell anymore." She sighed, looking confused and defeated. Tears welled in her eyes. When the first one slipped down her cheek, she furiously brushed it away, looking embarrassed by the show of emotion. "Dammit. I hate being pathetic."

My chest tightened, my determination to keep my distance cracking in the face of her distress. Closing the distance between us, I crouched down beside her chair. "You aren't pathetic."

She rolled her eyes, rejecting my reassurance. Why was the woman so hard on herself?

I tried again. "Trauma doesn't disappear overnight. It's gonna take time to get over what you went through yesterday."

"I know that." She let out an unsteady breath. "It's been a shit week, and my stress levels have maxed out."

That reminded me. "Listen, I have news about the men who assaulted you."

She groaned and clutched her head. "Oh, God. Where's my brain? I need to go to Belle Reve and make a statement to the police, don't I?"

"No," I said. "There's no need. The men who attacked you... they're dead."

"What?" Her jaw dropped. "How?"

"My people called the police, then set out to track down the attackers. When my people got close, the men tried to cross the stream over rough water. They slipped, hit their heads, and drowned. The cops recovered the bodies. The case is closed."

Marit blinked.

Fingers crossed she'd accept the story at face value. If she knew anything about police procedure, my fiction wouldn't pass the sniff test.

Her head fell back. She closed her eyes for a moment, then opened them to meet mine. "I really don't have to make a statement to the police?"

"That's right."

"Thank God."

The relief on her face took some of the sting out of the fact that I'd told her a bald-faced lie.

"You don't have to talk to the cops, and I won't say a word about the lease." I repeated my earlier promise. "How about I pour you a fresh cup of coffee and you tell me how you're doing? And if you decide I'm still an asshole, you can kick me out again."

Marit opened her mouth, but her voice seemed to catch in her throat. She stared into my face. And there it was again, that sense of connection that hit me hard the first time we spoke. I hardly knew her, any emotional tie between us should be a fragile and tentative thing, but instead the bond felt heavy, almost palpable. My rational mind—my human mind—questioned it, but my wolf recognized the truth. In her eyes I saw the promise of love, of children, of lives and souls intertwined.

God help me.

Duty to the pack had been drilled into me since birth. Even if I wasn't a potential alpha—charged with maintaining the pack's laws and traditions—I couldn't mate with a human. The pack had come within spitting distance of extinction during the Great War seventy years ago. Our numbers were creeping up, but we were still vulnerable. How could I ever choose personal happiness over the good of the pack?

Torn between duty and primal instinct, I silently returned Marit's gaze.

Did she feel the bond? Did she sense my ambivalence? She groaned and dropped her face into her hands.

Her pain cut me to the quick and silenced any thoughts of duty. I caught her chin and tilted her face up. She dropped her hands and met my eyes again. A shaky breath, then she pressed her cheek against my palm. Without warning, she leaned forward and slipped from the chair.

Shocked the hell out of me, but I caught her and pulled her pliant form against my chest. Cradling her in my arms, I rocked back and forth.

"You're safe." It was both a declaration and a promise. Whatever the future held, I wouldn't allow harm to come to this woman. What that meant, I'd figure out later.

Marit clung to me, wrapping her fingers around my bare bicep. The skin-to-skin contact sent a shock of pleasure throughout my blood. Her racing pulse slowed as tension melted from her body. Back and forth we rocked in a rhythm that echoed her heartbeat.

She turned her head, nuzzled my throat, and slowly inhaled. "Mmm…" The tip of her tongue fluttered against my skin, a sensation that went straight to my cock.

I drew in a sharp breath, and my arms tightened around her.

She sat up straight, blushing. "Honest to God. I have no idea why I did that."

I tucked a strand of hair behind her ear and offered a lazy, satisfied smile. "You don't?"

"No." She shook her head for emphasis. "I don't do things like that."

A pained expression crossed her face. "I don't… lick strangers." She groaned, clearly mortified. "It must be a reaction to trauma, some kind of PTSD symptom. My inhibitions and impulses are shot to hell, and you were here, and you were being nice, and…" Her voice trailed off.

I nodded, more to appease her anxiety than in agreement with what she said. Despite all the turmoil of our brief acquaintance, Marit had sought comfort in *my* arms. She reacted to my scent by tasting my skin, an impulse every shifter understood. As a human she probably questioned her reaction to me—the sudden change in her behavior—but it made sense to the wolf. When I took a mate, I'd seal the bond with a claiming bite, branding her with my scent and a faint scar that would forever mark her as mine.

My wolf bristled with pride, nudging me as if to say, *See, I told you she's the one.*

I stood, still holding Marit in my arms, then I gently set her on her feet. Last thing I wanted was to let go of her, but I sensed that she needed distance to regain her composure. Unable to resist one final touch, I fingered a lock of her hair, sliding the glossy honey-colored silk between my thumb and forefinger.

"Beautiful."

Thunderous pounding on the cabin's front door broke the spell. Both Marit and I whirled toward the sound. A man peered through the small window in the door, his face flushed with anger while his fist thumped against the wood.

I thrust Marit behind me, my instincts on high alert. I clenched my jaw, disgusted with myself. How could I have been too distracted to hear an intruder approach the cabin?

"Marit, open the door," the man bellowed.

I glanced over my shoulder. "You know him?"

"Yes." She frowned. "His name is Bryce Toobin. He's my ex-fiancé."

Fiancé? Oh, hell no. My wolf growled in possessive rage. "Were you expecting him?"

She shook her head. "No. I came to the cabin to get away after we split up. He's been calling and texting, but I haven't picked up."

"Let. Me. In." A booming thump punctuated each word.

"He's the one who betrayed your trust?" I asked.

Marit bit her lower lip, then after a moment, "Yes. Slept with our wedding planner."

All I needed to hear. The unwanted interloper would be sent packing. If Bryce thought I'd allow him to bother Marit or to stake any claim to her, I'd set him straight. A positively feral smile curled my lips.

Marit caught my arm. "Let me handle this, Adam. Bryce is probably just worried because I haven't answered his calls or texts. He'll go away once he sees I'm okay and that I don't want him here."

A shifter is a protector to his core, and a possessive protector at that. Every fiber of my body protested her words. But Marit was a human, and a human couldn't understand the impulses that drove my kind. Besides, she was in no real danger. If Bryce posed any threat to her, I'd take him down.

"Your call." I stepped aside.

Marit squared her shoulders and marched to the door.

As soon as she unlocked it, Bryce shoved the door open and stormed inside. "I've been out of my mind with worry. Why didn't you have the decency to pick up?"

Everything about this asshole made me see red. I stepped up next to Marit.

"And who the fuck is that?" Bryce glared at me.

My eyes widened. "You gotta be kidding me."

I drew back my fist, then let it fly right into Bryce's face.

CHAPTER THIRTEEN

MARIT

Adam leapt at Bryce and smashed a fist into his cheek. The force of the blow slammed Bryce backward against the wall. His head struck with a loud *crack*, and he slid to the floor.

Stunned, I gaped at Adam. Where did this violence come from? Five minutes ago, he'd rocked me in his arms and comforted me. He'd talked about recovering from trauma and the importance of acting like a decent person. Now he was beating on Bryce. How could he do such a one-eighty? Did he think... did he think he was protecting me?

Adam seized Bryce's shoulders and hauled him to his feet. Bryce hung limp as a rag doll, his feet dangling inches above the floor while Adam pinned him to the wall.

"What did you do?" Adam spat out, his face a mask of fury.

Huh? Adam knew exactly what Bryce had done. I'd told him.

Bryce squinted, a dazed expression on his face. He moaned and lifted a hand to his cheek, staring bemusedly at the blood on his fingertips.

"I'm bleeding." He sounded surprised. Bryce lifted puppy dog eyes to Adam, looking for all the world like a little boy who didn't understand why he was being punished. "Why'd you hit me? I... I was just worried about Marit. I came to make sure she's okay."

"Liar." Adam dug his fingers into Bryce's shoulders, jerked his body forward, then slammed him against the wall. *Thwack.* His skull bounded against the wall with a sickening thud. *Thwack.* Adam did it again.

Whimpering, Bryce turned pleading eyes my way. "Marit." His trembling lips shaped my name. He waved a weak hand in my direction. As I watched, his eyes rolled back in his head.

Holy hell. Bryce didn't stand a chance against Adam. Common decency demanded that I intervene.

"Adam, stop it," I shrieked.

He growled, a low rumble that rose from his chest and swelled until it filled the air. The hair on my arms stood to attention. Adam growled? No time to wonder at that now.

I wrapped my hand around his bicep. "Let him go."

He ignored me, his laser-like focus on Bryce. "What did you do?" he repeated through gritted teeth.

Bryce's eyelids fluttered open. "Marit, help me," he begged. His cheek was turning purple and his eyelid swelling shut.

Adam's lips curled in contempt. Gone was the gentle man who'd held me so tenderly. Every instinct urged me to shrink back from the anger I saw in his eyes—from his out-of-left-field violence—but I couldn't abandon Bryce to his rage. He might be a cheating rat bastard, but he didn't deserve to be beaten to a bloody pulp.

"Adam, please stop." I tried to speak calmly, but my voice quavered.

The tremor must have caught his attention. He released Bryce, who slid down the wall and collapsed on the floor, gasping for air.

With an obvious effort, Adam turned away from Bryce and toward me. He touched my cheek, his fingers gentle.

I flinched.

"I frightened you." Regret colored his voice.

"Of course you frightened her, you animal," Bryce wheezed from the floor.

"Shut up." Adam didn't spare him a backward glance, but I couldn't tear my eyes away from the injured man.

Bryce looked like hell. Bruises bloomed on his ashen skin. His chest rose and fell as he struggled for breath. Groaning, he touched his head. His fingers gently probed the surface as if making sure his skull was intact. Blood smeared the spot where his head had impacted the wall.

And... oh dear God... was that *hair* stuck in the blood?

My stomach lurched.

Too much.

It was all too much.

After yesterday, the violence hit too close to home. What was the difference between Adam and the men who'd attacked me? Neither assault made sense. I'd done nothing to provoke Booger and Rat Face. Adam had no valid reason to pulverize Bryce.

Was his good-guy persona all an act? Had I been a fool? Again? How much of a chump was I?

"Marit." Adam touched my cheek again.

Furious, I jerked away and stumbled backward out of his reach. "You could have killed him. And for what? Cheating doesn't warrant a death sentence. Or do you just get off on beating people up?"

Before Adam could answer, Bryce moaned again and lifted a limp hand. "I don't feel so good." The words slurred. "Something is wrong with my head."

Dammit. Cheater or not, I couldn't let him suffer brain damage. "I need to get you to a hospital."

"No. No hospital." Bryce shook his head, then hissed, as if the back and forth motion hurt. "Just take me home. A painkiller, a good night's sleep, and I'll be okay. Besides, somebody's got to feed and walk Loki."

Bryce was usually a bit of a hypochondriac. How many times had we canceled plans with Annika and Liv because he had a headache or an upset tummy? But now, when he was really hurt, he didn't want to go to the hospital? The man was being ridiculous. Or maybe the knock to the noggin left him unable to think clearly.

I swallowed my impatience "You could have a fractured skull or a concussion. You can't go home without seeing a doctor. I'll take you to the ER and get you checked in. Then I'll go to the house and take care of Loki."

By "take care of Loki" I meant pack up his stuff and bring him home with me. It was past time to take custody of my boy. If Bryce protested, I'd echo his words and tell him he was in no condition to take care of a dog. A little tit for tat was more than fair.

"I don't know." Bryce frowned, clutching his head. "I'm dizzy and I feel nauseated. How will I get home if you drop me off? What if I have trouble walking? What if the doctors want somebody to keep an eye on me?"

"Drama queen," Adam muttered.

I glanced again at the bloody smear and the strands of Bryce's hair embedded in it. How hard must his head have hit the wall to leave that mess behind? I shot Adam a dirty look, pointed at the bloodstained wall, then turned back to Bryce.

"Can't Courtney take care of you?" I couldn't keep the bitterness out of my voice when I mentioned the stunning brunette's name.

"No." He sucked in a ragged breath. "We're finished. She's gone back to Seattle. I'm alone. It's just me and Loki." His chest heaved. "I think you're right about going to the ER. My vision is blurry and something feels really wrong with my head."

"Oh, for fuck's sake." Derision filled Adam's voice and I could almost hear him roll his eyes.

Massaging my forehead, I took stock of the situation. Nausea, blurred vision, and dizziness were bad signs. Bryce needed to get to the ER. Adam didn't take Bryce's symptoms seriously. Which meant it was on me to step up and do the right thing. My cheeks puffed as I blew out a deep sigh. The damned men created this mess, and I had to clean it up.

"Okay," I said, all business. "Here's the plan. I'll drive you to the hospital and stick around until they release you. Then I'll take you back to the house, and I'll feed Loki and take him for his walk."

"And if the doctor says I shouldn't be alone overnight, will you stay?" Bryce whined.

"There's nobody else you can call?"

"No."

Dammit. I hated that Bryce put me in this position. "If the doctor says somebody needs to keep an eye on you, I'll spend the night."

Adam made an unhappy noise. I ignored him.

Bryce turned a wary eye on Adam. "Thanks, Marit. I appreciate the help. Loki will be happy to see you. He's missed you almost as much as I have."

And who had kept Loki from me? Rather than point out the obvious, I bit my tongue. Loki wouldn't be missing me much longer. As soon as I finished with Bryce, the dog was coming home with me.

"I... I'll need help getting to the car," Bryce faltered.

"Of course."

I took a step toward Bryce, but Adam blocked my path, lifting a hand to halt my progress. "Marit, he's not as badly hurt as you think. He's hamming it up for your benefit. Trust me."

Hamming it up? Didn't Adam see the blood and the bruises?

"Trust you?" Astonishment made my voice shrill. "I'm done giving you the benefit of the doubt. I've seen the real you, and it isn't pretty."

"I'm not going to leave you alone with him." Adam's voice was low, his tone urgent. "You have to listen to me. He's dangerous."

"Oh, *he's* dangerous? That's rich, coming from you." I threw both hands in the air, then glowered at him. "Out of my way, or I'll call the cops and have you charged with assault."

After yesterday, I couldn't deal with a man who flies off the handle at the least provocation.

"No." Bryce waved a weak hand. "No cops. Just get my head checked out, then take me home."

Adam didn't budge. Instead he lowered his chin. "I mean it. You're not safe with him."

Really? He was trying to maintain the fiction that bloody and battered Bryce—a man who could barely lift his head—posed a danger to me?

I jabbed a finger into his chest. "Get out of my way."

Another jab. "Get out of my cabin."

A final jab. "And get out of my life."

Frowning, he backed toward the door, opened it, and stepped onto the porch. Good enough. As long as he was out of my way and out of the cabin, he could stand on the porch till he rotted. I stuffed my phone into my purse, grabbed my keys, then knelt next to Bryce.

"Let's get you out of here." I slid an arm around his waist and helped him to his feet. He shuffled through the door, took a few halting steps, then collapsed against the porch railing.

"Give me a minute." He bent over, bracing his hands on his knees. From his expression he looked like he was about to puke or pass out. I kept a wary eye on him while I locked the cabin door.

"Proud of yourself?" I asked Adam, who hadn't moved.

Without waiting for his reply, I wrapped an arm around Bryce's waist. Staggering under his weight, I helped him down the stairs and toward my car.

"Thanks," he croaked.

"Just a few more steps." Balancing Bryce's weight, I fumbled for the latch on the car door. With a groan, he crawled onto the passenger seat. I jogged around to the driver's side and slid in behind the wheel. Bryce's head lolled weakly against the seat back.

He offered me a small, apologetic smile. "Sorry to be so much trouble."

"You're still an asshole. Both of you are," I said, my eyes drawn to the still figure on the porch. Adam stood with his hands on his hips, watching intently while I started the engine.

Why? Why did you turn out to be such a jerk?

I blinked furiously against the tears that filled my eyes.

Nope.

Prince Charming fantasies were for suckers. Locking eyes with a handsome stranger and feeling any kind of connection was nothing more than a delusion, a flight of fancy. Time to face reality. With a dismissive shake of my head, I put the car into gear and headed back to town.

Chapter Fourteen

Adam

As soon as the car disappeared from view, I dug my phone out of my pocket and punched in Zane's number.

"C'mon. C'mon." Impatience tore at me while I waited for my fellow sentry to pick up. There was no time to waste, not with Marit heading back to town with that dickhead.

On the fourth ring, Zane's surly voice sounded in my ear. "Yeah?"

"Need you to call an emergency meeting of all the sentries. I'll fill everybody in when I get there."

"Will do," Zane drawled. "What's going on?"

"I'm at the Hagen cabin. Marit Hagen just headed back to the city with her ex-fiancé."

"So what's the problem? You wanted her out of harm's way, right?"

"The problem—" It was hard to speak through clenched teeth. I forced my jaw to relax before I continued. "The problem is that the man she was planning to marry, the man who just showed up and maneuvered her into going back to the city with him… He's a coyote."

Gravel flew as my truck skidded to a stop. I jumped out and sprinted up the steps to the small building marked Black Rock Environmental Conservancy Administrative Office.

Olga sat behind the reception desk. She hopped to her feet when I stormed into the lobby and shook a finger at me.

"I have a bone to pick with you, Adam."

No surprise there. She looked for every opportunity to make Zane, Remy, and me look bad, to promote her grandson Xander at our expense. Luckily, Olga wasn't the shrewd Machiavellian schemer she fancied herself to be.

I paused next to her desk and spoke with as much patience as I could muster. "Yes, ma'am?"

"Matthew was lying down trying to get some rest when you stormed into our home this morning."

"You mean when I knocked on the door at 11 a.m. and Grandpa called out for me to come in?"

Olga harrumphed. "Your grandfather isn't well and the last thing his poor heart needs is for you to come to him with old stories about vandalism at the Hagen cabin. As if it makes a lick of difference now. Freya Hagen is dead and buried. Matthew has more than enough on his plate without worrying about ancient history." She shook her finger again. "Let it go."

I didn't have time to hash this out with Olga, not with Marit in the clutches of a coyote.

"Can't let it go," I said. "I made a promise."

Olga's mouth puckered. Experience told me she was winding up for a tongue-lashing. Before she let loose with her tirade, I brushed past her and strode down the back hall to the conference room.

I paused in the doorway, my gaze sweeping over the people assembled around the long table. Despite the haste with which the emergency meeting was called, Zane had managed to pull together all the key members of the security team.

Grandpa sat at the head of the table. He *was* pale, his complexion almost gray. Dammit. Maybe Olga was right that I shouldn't be piling on when his heart was failing. As if reading my mind he gave me a curt nod, his eyes as sharp as ever. Failing health be damned, the alpha's duty to the pack came first. That's what that nod told me.

To Grandpa's right sat Rolf, the old-timer of the bunch. Next to him, Kyra. Zane must have pulled our youngest sentry off patrol for the meeting. Zane and Remy sat across the table from them.

Grandpa gestured for me to take a seat. "What do you have to report?"

I leaned forward in my chair, too full of nervous energy to recline. "The coyotes are up to something new."

That got everyone's attention. Rolf put down his coffee cup, and Kyra turned toward me, her green eyes alight with curiosity.

"Explain," Grandpa ordered.

"Coyotes breached our southern perimeter yesterday and they targeted Marit Hagen. Chased her into the woods, cornered her, and scared the crap outta her."

"Is she all right?" Kyra asked, sounding both shocked and concerned. Clearly, this was the first she heard of the attack.

I shot her a grateful look. Her sympathetic reaction was a helluva lot better than Zane's indifference.

"I got there in time. She was shaken up, but not badly hurt. I took her back to her cabin," I explained to the young sentry. "When I stopped by to check on her this afternoon, her former fiancé, a guy named Bryce Toobin showed up." I paused, reliving the colossal clusterfuck. Would it have been less of a disaster if I'd managed to keep my cool? How could I not react violently to the presence of a man who posed such a threat to Marit?

"And?" the alpha asked.

"And it turns out Bryce is a coyote." I let that bombshell simmer for a moment before continuing. "It can't be a coincidence, a coyote who was engaged to marry the last leaseholder."

"No," Grandpa agreed. "Not likely. Sounds like the coyote alpha put one of his men in a position to persuade Marit Hagen never to sell us her lease."

"Making it that much harder for us to secure our borders." Rolf drummed his fingers against the table. "Smart play."

"The coyotes don't need to twist Marit's arm," I said. "She's determined to hold onto the lease."

"Then what do they want?" Kyra asked.

My stomach churned and I tasted bile in the back of my throat. "Think about it. If Bryce married her, he'd be first in line to inherit the lease if she died."

The coyote alpha wouldn't think twice about arranging the "accidental death" of a human woman.

Zane groaned. "And we could kiss goodbye any chance of getting our hands on the lease before it expires."

"Wait." Kyra spoke up. "You called Bryce her ex. So Marit broke off the engagement—and what—she came to the cabin to get away?"

"Yeah. She ended it," I said. "Apparently he's been reaching out, but she wants nothing to do with him."

"She told him to get lost, and the coyotes escalated," Remy guessed. "Sent pack members to scare her into running back to the city."

Grandpa nodded. "Where Bryce could work his wiles on her and win her back."

"Makes sense," Rolf concurred. "What happened when Bryce showed up at the cabin?"

Hard to admit that I'd lost control, but there was no lying to the senior sentry. "He shoved through the door, yelling at Marit for ignoring his calls. I saw what he was, and I snapped. I punched him."

Grandpa studied me, concern stamped across his face. Yeah. I'd blown it, big-time. I never had issues with self-control. Kyra jokingly called me the Ice Man. Until now, I kept my cool during every crisis. The fact that I'd lost control must have raised red flags for my alpha.

"What happened next?" Rolf asked.

"He played her. The fucker carried on like he was dying—" I cut off abruptly. Dammit. I knew better than to swear in front of the alpha. If Grandpa was concerned before, he'd be doubly worried now.

"Continue," Grandpa ordered in a low voice.

"Marit has no idea how strong shifters are, how quickly we heal." I chose my words carefully. "She saw him hit the floor, saw the bruises, and assumed he was badly hurt. He hammed it up for her benefit." I shook my head at the memory. "Moaned and carried on like he was at death's door. But every time she looked away, he sneered at me. Rolled his eyes. Even stuck out his tongue."

"And then?" the alpha asked.

"And then, she insisted on taking him to the hospital. He whined about taking care of their dog, and she offered to go home with him to help." I threw my hands in the air. "He's trying to reel her back in."

And I played right into his hands by losing control.

"We can't let that happen," Zane said in a low voice.

"Sir." Kyra looked to the alpha. "If coyotes targeted Marit in order to hurt the pack, then the pack owes her its protection."

"I agree." I deliberately kept my tone calm and dispassionate. I couldn't allow my wolf's agitation to color my words, not under the nose of my eagle-eyed alpha. "We can't allow an innocent woman to get hurt because of our war with the coyotes. And we need to find out exactly what he's planning."

"What do you propose?" Grandpa asked.

"I go to Belle Reve. Set up surveillance, both to protect Marit and to keep an eye on Bryce and the coyotes."

"Isn't she angry at you?" Rolf raised a brow.

"Yeah." I conceded the point. "But I'm still the logical one to send. She knows me. I rescued her from the coyotes who attacked her. If something happens, I'll be able to intervene better than someone who's a complete stranger to her."

Zane shot me a suspicious look.

Get out of my way. Get out of my cabin. Get out of my life.

Marit's angry words still rang in my ears, but nothing good could come from confessing the depth of our estrangement to the pack. The alpha *had* to send me to watch over Marit. If he didn't... I'd never disobeyed an order. The very idea was inconceivable. But if the man refused to disobey his alpha, would the beast declare war on his human half? Could he? I never wanted to find out what would happen if my two sides were at odds. The best solution—the only solution—was for the alpha to consent to my plan.

I held my breath waiting for Grandpa to respond.

"Rolf, your thoughts?" Grandpa asked.

Every eye turned toward the senior sentry, whose pensive gaze drilled a hole in my head. I resisted the urge to shift position in my chair, a nervous tell my former trainer would recognize as a sign of strong emotion. Couldn't let Rolf declare me too personally invested to maintain my objectivity.

"I agree with Adam," Rolf finally said. He shot me a slight, knowing smile. "There's no one better positioned for the job."

"All right." Grandpa slapped the table. "Adam, you're going to Belle Reve. Remy, start a deep dive into Bryce Toobin and his role in the coyote pack. Find his address in town and investigate the cover story he used when he moved there. Zane, be ready to move quickly. If things go south, I'll send you to back up Adam." He turned to me. "Anything else you need?"

"No, sir. I'll pack a bag and be out of here in ten."

"Very good." Grandpa glanced at his sentries. "Anyone have anything to add?"

"No, sir." Their responses echoed around the table.

"Dismissed."

Ignoring the curious glances from my fellow sentries, I walked briskly from the room. Rolf caught up with me on the porch. He dropped a hand on my shoulder, bringing me to a halt.

"You sure you know what you're doing?" he asked. "No... um... personal issues are clouding your judgment?"

"I'm solid," I said. "I know my duty."

"I'm sure you do, son," Rolf said. "But sometimes what you know here—" he tapped his head—"and what you know here—" he touched his chest—"can be very different things."

What does a man say when confronted with that truth bomb? Rolf could smell a lie, so I kept my mouth shut.

"We count on you to do the right thing," Rolf continued. He squeezed my shoulder, a fatherly gesture that only compounded my sense of guilt.

I cleared my throat. "I always try to do the right thing." Nothing but the truth there. So why was my wolf pacing unhappily beneath my skin?

"I know you do." Rolf gave my shoulder a final squeeze. "If you need to talk, call me."

Frowning, I watched Rolf's back as he walked away.

Do the right thing, Rolf had said.

Yeah? But the right thing for who?

Was that my voice speaking in my head, or the wolf's?

With a shrug, I jumped into my truck and drove to the lodge to grab my things. I counted the minutes it would take to drive to Belle Reve. Better call Remy to see if he'd tracked down Bryce's address. No way would I leave Marit alone with the damned coyote.

CHAPTER FIFTEEN

MARIT

I threw open the passenger door and helped Bryce climb out of the front seat. He swayed, then sagged against the side of the car. He looked like crap, his face a mess of bruises already turning from purple to yellow and green. At least the swelling around his eye had gone down. A cervical collar stabilized his neck. He clutched the bottle of pain pills prescribed by the emergency room doc.

"You ready?" I asked.

"Yeah." He flashed me a weak smile. "As long as you're here to help me, I'm good."

I mentally calculated the number of steps from the curb to the front door. Bryce's injuries were worse than I feared. Not only had he suffered a concussion, but he also had damage to the soft tissues in his neck. Even the ER doctor seemed surprised by how much pain Bryce was in following the assault. The meds they'd administered at the hospital left Bryce loopy and uncoordinated. He couldn't walk unassisted and I wasn't at all sure that I could support his weight.

"Let's do this," I muttered under my breath.

Bryce slung an arm across my shoulders. We took a step. He leaned heavily against me, and I staggered. Gritting my teeth, I summoned all my strength as we shambled up the sidewalk and to the front door. He fumbled in his pocket for the house key. I took it from him and unlocked the door. We lurched into the foyer. A brown-and-white dog hurtled himself against my legs.

"Loki, my love," I cried.

The dog danced back and forth, barking excitedly while I helped Bryce to the living room and settled him on the sofa. Dropping to my knees, I opened my arms to the dog. Loki threw himself into my arms, and his exuberant welcome knocked me on my ass. I laughed, burying my face in his neck.

"I've missed you, handsome boy," I said.

"Did you miss me, too?"

Bryce's petulant tone grated like nails on a chalkboard. Why did he have to begrudge me my happy reunion with Loki? Frowning, I glanced at him. Bryce slumped against the sofa cushions, pressing a hand to the side of his head. My conscience pinged. Maybe getting smacked around had made him peevish. Maybe he was high from the pain pills. Who wouldn't sound pissy under the circumstances? Instead of answering, I flashed a noncommittal smile.

"Can I get you something to eat before you head to bed?"

"I don't feel up to eating, but if you're hungry, you can throw a frozen dinner in the microwave. Not as good as your home cooking, of course, but it's that or takeout."

Was I imagining it, or was a reproach hiding behind the innocuous words? *See what I have to eat when you're not around to cook?*

I bristled. I loved to cook. Bryce, not so much. Whose fault was it that I wasn't around to prepare meals anymore? And couldn't a grown man fend for himself?

"Marit?"

Good grief. I shook my head. I was projecting, carrying on an imaginary argument when all he had done was compliment my cooking. Bryce wasn't the only one reeling from the events of the day.

"I'm fine. I'll get something later if I'm hungry. You're supposed to be resting. Can you make it up the stairs to your bedroom, or do you want to sleep in the guest room?"

Was I going to have to change the damned sheets in the room where he'd had sex with Courtney?

"I probably shouldn't try the stairs. You take the master and I'll take the guest bed. Unless you want to stay with me, you know, in case I need help in the middle of the night."

I nipped that suggestion in the bud. "I'll sleep upstairs. Stay here for a few minutes while I get your pajamas and toothbrush."

I jogged up the stairs, Loki at my heels, then paused for a moment outside Bryce's bedroom, steeling my nerves. I pushed open the door. My gaze traveled over the room. Nothing had changed since our split. A framed photo of us taken right after he proposed still sat on the dresser. Propped up next to it stood an embossed wedding invitation.

I pulled open a dresser drawer and peered inside. There were my sleep shorts, tee shirts, socks, and panties. Bryce hadn't reclaimed the space yet. In another drawer, I found a pair of his pajamas. In the bathroom, I grabbed his toothbrush and toothpaste, then glanced at the hook on the backside of the door. My pink terry cloth robe still hung next to Bryce's navy-blue one.

It was disquieting to see how little the room had changed, like walking into a snapshot of my life that was over and done. Shouldn't Bryce have packed up my stuff by now? Was he holding on to hope that he could win me back?

Not going to happen.

"Marit?" Bryce's voice carried up from the first floor.

My teeth ground together. "On my way."

Loki trotted behind me as I made my way back to the living room. Bryce had collapsed against the leather cushion. He lifted his head and smiled listlessly at me.

"You need to be in bed," I said.

He nodded, then winced as if regretting the gesture. I offered a hand to help him stand, then wrapped an arm around his waist when he wobbled. We shuffled across the foyer and down the hall. I hesitated outside the guest bathroom. Would I have to help him put on his PJs?

"I got this," he said.

When he closed the bathroom door, I raced into the guest room. Somebody had stripped off the dirty sheets and comforter and remade the bed. Only the dark-red stain on the ivory linen headboard gave evidence of our ugly breakup scene.

I threw back the blankets, fluffed the pillows, and then raced to the kitchen for a glass of water. Bryce emerged from the bathroom. He had managed to put on his pajamas by himself, thank God. He rested a heavy hand on my shoulder as we lumbered to the bed.

"You got your pain pills." I pointed at the bottle on the nightstand. "Here's water. Can you think of anything else you need?"

His eyes flashed and I mentally kicked myself. I'd walked into that one, hadn't I?

Don't say me.

"Yeah. Would you stay for a few minutes? Sit with me until I fall asleep?"

Relief coursed through me. "Sure."

I perched on the edge of the bed. An awkward silence filled the space between us, expanding with each wordless moment that passed. Toying with a loose thread on the hem of a blanket, I cast a furtive glance at Bryce's face. Did he really just want company, or was he about to launch into another attempt to get me back? I was in no mood to deal with that.

"That guy, you know he's bad news, don't you?"

A safer subject than another attempt at reconciliation. "He was way out of line when he attacked you," I conceded.

"I'm not talking about what he did to me. I'm worried about you. How do you know him? What was he doing at your cabin?"

Telling Bryce about the assault would only agitate him when he needed to rest and recover. "He works for the Black Rock Environmental Conservancy. He stopped by to say hello."

"Yeah? So why did he go all caveman when I showed up?"

"Who knows."

"Damned tree huggers," Bryce snarled. "He probably thought I'd keep you from agreeing to sell them the lease."

Annoyance flashed through me. My ex had a mighty high opinion of himself and his influence, didn't he?

Hold on... My eyes narrowed. To the best of my recollection, I'd never mentioned the conservancy's attempts to get their hands on Grandma's lease. Why tell him about the small fortune they were willing to pay if I had no intention of selling? So how did he know? Had Annika or Liv mentioned it? Not likely.

"That was it?" Bryce pressed. "He dropped by to butter you up for another sales pitch? Nothing else was going on?"

"Listen," I said, keeping a tight rein on my temper. "We're not together anymore. You don't need to concern yourself with what's going on in my life. What you need to do is sleep and heal."

He opened his mouth and looked like he wanted to argue, but instead, he sighed and nodded. "Okay." He settled back against the pillow and closed his eyes.

Loki poked his head into the room. I patted my leg. He crossed over to me and pressed his head against my thigh. I stroked his silky fur while I waited for sleep to claim Bryce.

A few minutes later, Bryce's steady breathing told me he'd drifted off. I dropped a kiss on Loki's head and whispered in his ear, "Let's go."

He padded behind me as I made my way to the kitchen. I examined the refrigerator's bleak contents. Bryce hadn't been kidding. Leftover deli food—at least a week old and dried up— didn't tempt my appetite. The pizza and low-calorie dinners I found in the freezer were little better. Slamming the door shut, I looked around the kitchen.

Everything was painfully familiar, but I no longer belonged here. The expensive espresso machine Bryce and I bought to celebrate our engagement sat on the counter. My favorite rolling pin and wooden spoons filled the crock by the stove. I'd pack those up before I left, along with all of my clothes and toiletries.

A shiver ran down my spine. Familiarity bred not contempt but an odd disassociation, a conviction that I was in the wrong place. If not here, where did I belong?

"Let's go to bed," I said to Loki, leading the way upstairs.

In the morning, I'd reach out to Annika and Liv and let them know I was back in town and why. I had to decide if I'd go back to the cabin once Bryce regained his feet, or if I'd look for a new place to live and pick up the pieces of my old life.

"I'll think about that tomorrow," I told Loki. "But no matter what, you're coming with me."

I brushed my teeth, washed my face, and was changing into sleep shorts and a tee when something occurred to me. I groaned and turned to Loki.

"I forgot your evening walk."

His ears perked up at the familiar word.

"Gimme a minute." I pulled my leggings back on and jammed my feet into sneakers. "We have to be quiet. Bryce is sleeping."

We descended the stairs and I tiptoed to the door of the guest room. Bryce's even breathing assured me he slept undisturbed.

"We're going out the back way," I whispered to Loki. Luckily, his leash still hung on a hook inside the pantry. I attached it to his collar, then followed the eager dog toward the patio door. The heavy glass door squeaked as it ran over the track, so I left it open and slid the lighter screen door shut to keep out bugs.

We followed our familiar evening route, walking along sidewalks bathed in the cold blue light from overhead streetlamps. Loki paused hopefully at the entrance to Brenner Park.

I glanced into the shadowy trees.

A sudden chill racked my body.

I flashed back to my mad dash into the woods, ducking under tree branches in my vain attempt to get away from Booger and Rat Face.

"Sorry, Loki. Not tonight, boy."

We walked for several more blocks, then turned around at the corner by the gas station and headed home. As we stepped onto the patio, I paused, hearing a voice inside the house. I dropped to my knees and whispered in Loki's ear.

"Quiet, boy. Stay."

I cautiously approached the open patio door and looked inside. Bryce was in the kitchen. He'd discarded the cervical collar and dropped it on the counter. His head was angled sharply to one side, his cell phone nestled between his ear and shoulder as he used both hands to open the cupboard above the refrigerator. Stretching up on his tiptoes, he pulled a bag of potato chips from the back of the cupboard.

Bryce had experienced a miraculous recovery in the hour since he went to bed.

"I'm more than ready for the meeting, sir," he said, ripping open the bag.

Sir? Was Bryce talking to his boss? Hardly likely. From what I could remember, his boss at the firm was more of a buddy than an authority figure.

I reached for the screen, preparing to slide the door open and enter the kitchen. Some inner voice stilled my hand. Instead of announcing my presence, I took a step backward and retreated into the shadows, my eyes fixed on Bryce.

"I won't let you down, sir. Not like the Moseley brothers did. Morons."

He paused, listening to the voice on the other end of the line. He dropped the bag of chips onto the counter and shifted the phone to his hand.

"Yeah. Yeah." Reluctant concession colored his voice. "But it was a straightforward mission, and they haven't reported back. We know what that means. They're dead." A long silence. He pulled a pad of paper from a drawer and scribbled a note. "Yes, sir. I understand." He straightened as if standing at attention. Chin up, chest out, shoulders back. A soldier's posture. "You won't regret making me your second-in-command. I promise. And please assure our ally that I'm one hundred percent ready to do my part."

What the hell was going on? I'd always believed that Bryce's ambitions went no further than moving up the waiting list at the country club. And now I discover that he was a mysterious somebody's second-in-command and that they had an ally.

"Marit?" Bryce snorted. My ears perked up. "No worries. I have her wrapped around my little finger."

What did he say?

I stumbled backward.

A hand clamped over my mouth.

Chapter Sixteen

Adam

If she felt threatened, I knew for certain that the woman who bashed in a coyote's nose would put up a fight. Couldn't risk the sound of a scuffle alerting Bryce, so I pressed my lips against Marit's ear while covering her mouth.

"It's Adam."

Her pulse jackhammering, she bucked against my hand, then calmed down as recognition sunk in. I removed my fingers from her mouth and cocked my thumb, pointing behind us. She nodded. We slipped deeper into the shadows and away from Bryce.

Marit grabbed the leash of a big brown-and-white dog that stood at the edge of the patio. Hackles raised, tail high, body stiff, everything about him telegraphed his unhappiness. If he barked, it would be game over. We couldn't afford a pissing match over dominance. I had to put him in his place pronto.

Domestic dogs and cats recognized shifters as something other than human. Dropping down on my haunches next to the dog, I bared my teeth and riveted my eyes on his, allowing my wolf to rise close to the surface. The dog yielded at once, lowering his head and tucking his tail between his legs.

"Good boy," I breathed, then patted his shoulder, rewarding him for his submission. When I jumped to my feet, he pressed against my legs, ready to follow my lead.

I held out a hand to Marit. After a moment's hesitation, she took it. Sticking to the shadow of the house, we walked on silent feet toward the street. Bryce wasn't likely to look out his front window and spy us, but there was no point in taking chances. Soon as we hit the sidewalk, I broke into a jog, leading Marit and the dog away from the house.

Thirty seconds later, Marit tugged on my hand and planted her feet on the sidewalk, refusing to continue. The branches of a neighbor's tree hid us from the overhead streetlights. "What's going on?" she demanded.

I pointed up the street. "My truck's parked two blocks away. We can talk there."

She glanced at the dog, who'd dropped onto his haunches by my feet. He yawned, then nudged me with his nose. I laid my free hand on his head. If he had tried, the dog couldn't have looked more relaxed, more at ease. One hundred percent team wolf shifter.

Watching my interaction with the dog, Marit frowned in confusion. "Who are you?"

"I'm not the bad guy here. I'll tell you everything I can once we get to the truck."

It was a big ask, expecting a woman to climb into the vehicle of a man she barely knew, a man whose motives she distrusted. On my best day, I'd never pull off looking harmless, but I filled my words and expression with sincerity. Marit *could* trust me, could trust the connection between us. Surely the woman who turned to me for comfort, who nuzzled my neck, could sense that. I held my breath while she weighed my words.

"Okay," she said at last.

I offered my most reassuring smile, then led the way to my truck. Opening the rear door, I whistled. The dog hopped onto the seat and stretched out like he was home.

Marit's eyes cut to mine. "Loki likes you."

I lifted a shoulder. "Like I said, I'm not the bad guy. Loki knows it."

"Loki doesn't like Bryce," she said. "Even though Bryce tried hard to win him over."

Of course the dog didn't like Bryce. Dogs were intelligent creatures, and coyote shifters set them on edge.

I opened the front passenger door. She climbed onto the seat while I jogged around to the driver's side, then slid behind the wheel.

Marit turned to me, her arms folded across her chest. "You said you'd tell me everything. So spill."

I said I'd tell her everything *I could*, but nothing good would come from pointing out that distinction. My wolf wouldn't allow me to tell Marit an out-and-out lie—shit, I hated lies as much as my shadow brother—but pack law prevented me from revealing the whole truth. With a few exceptions, humans knew nothing about the supernatural beings who shared their world. Duty required me to keep our existence a secret.

Not from our mate, the wolf protested.

Shut up, I shot back.

"Adam?"

"Sorry." I sucked in a breath, searching for the right words. "My people are committed to protecting the land under our care. For us, being good stewards of the lake, the forest, and the animals who live there is a sacred trust."

Marit raised an eyebrow. "So far that sounds like more of a sales pitch for the conservancy than an explanation of what's going on."

The woman was *not* going to cut me any slack, was she?

"I'm getting there," I said. "Did you know that a hundred years ago, the gray wolf population of Washington state had been wiped out?"

She shook her head. "No, I didn't know that."

"Over the past twenty years, wolves have slowly been moving back into the state, mostly from Canada and Idaho." *Mostly* was right. Our pack came from Alaska, but we were wolf shifters and not natural gray wolves. "Only a few hundred gray wolves live in Washington today, most of them in the northeastern part of the state."

"I've read news stories about ranchers upset by wolves killing livestock," she said.

"Yeah." I sighed. "Doesn't happen often, but it's a contentious issue." I waved a hand. "My point is, a few wolf packs have made their homes here in the Cascade Mountains. One of those packs lives on our land."

No lie there. A small pack of gray wolves—naturally submissive to their shifter counterparts—roamed our land.

"The wolf who chased off the men who attacked me was part of that pack," Marit guessed, a logical but wrong conclusion.

Inside my skin, my wolf snarled at the reminder of that assault.

She's safe, I reminded him. He quieted.

"Apex predators like wolves play an important role in the ecosystem," I continued without addressing Marit's statement. "They keep the deer, elk, and coyote populations in check. It's a crime to kill a wolf. State law lists them as an endangered species."

"Okay." She nodded. "But what does this have to do with Bryce and why you hit him?"

"I'm almost there," I said. "Five years ago, a poacher came on our land and killed a gray wolf, a breeding female."

Fucker walked in on a hiking trail, shot the wolf, and left the corpse. We reported the crime to local law enforcement, one of the rare cases where bringing in outsiders was a good thing. A wildlife group offered a $10,000 reward for information that led to the arrest of the perpetrator. He was never identified, officially that is. Zane, Remy, and I tracked him down and administered our own form of justice. A few months later, Grandpa sent me off to hunt down rogues.

"That's a tragedy, but I still don't see the connection to Bryce."

120

"Our land is valuable. The lake. The lodge. The timber. A syndicate of investors has been trying to get their hands on our land for years—"

"Oh no. You're being pestered to sell?" Marit pressed a palm against her chest, her voice heavy with mock sympathy. "They didn't go away and leave you alone the first time you said no?"

I shot her a reproachful look. "Anyway, we've researched the group. They have big plans to develop the property around the lake." Moving in hundreds of coyote shifters was a big plan, right? "We think they intend to clear-cut swathes of timber." That one was a stretch, but they would need lumber for all the houses they'd build, and they'd likely harvest the trees for it. "And they've demonstrated an absolute hostility to the reintroduction of wolves into the state. They want to end the protections and declare open season on wolves." That part was one hundred percent true.

"So, they're not environmentalists, and you don't want to sell the land to them," Marit said. "I still don't see how Bryce fits into all of this."

"Bryce works for them."

Marit blinked, then shook her head, as if dislodging something from her ears. "What did you say?"

"Bryce works for the syndicate."

Marit's spine snapped straight. "No. That can't be true. I told him I was going to inherit the lease to Grandma's cabin. If his company was trying to buy the land the cabin sits on, why wouldn't he mention it?"

I let that question hang in the air, hoping she'd put two and two together.

"Hold on." She raised both hands. "Are you saying he kept that information from me *on purpose?*"

"Look at the facts," I said. "He cheated on you, which suggests he wasn't all that committed to your relationship. You saw through the patio door that he's faking how badly he's injured. And you heard what he said on the phone, 'I have her wrapped around my little finger.' Who do you think he was talking to? What do you think all that means?"

Frowning, Marit pressed her fingers against her mouth and stared off into the distance. I could almost see the cogs turning in her head. After a long moment, she dropped her hand and met my eyes.

"I don't get it. What does he want?"

I cut to the chase. "Your lease."

"Why?" She looked baffled. "Why go to so much trouble when the cabin will revert back to the conservancy once the ninety-nine-year lease is over?"

"It's a foot in the door. It buys them time," I said. "We can't lock down our land until we get our hands on the last lease. If Bryce's people control it, they can legally occupy the cabin two weeks out of every month. Imagine, our enemies parked across the lake, watching every move we make. And they have deep pockets. They could try to sue to reopen the lake. Keep us tied up in court. They could make themselves a real pain in the ass."

She shook her head, still deep in denial. "You're forgetting that even if we got married, I'm the leaseholder, not Bryce."

"Unless…" I hesitated. Beneath my skin, the wolf whined at the prospect of frightening her.

"Adam?"

"We've researched how the syndicate does business," I said slowly. "They cover their tracks, but people who stand in their way sometimes die under mysterious circumstances."

Zane and Remy's younger sister—by blood a potential alpha—was killed in a hit-and-run accident in downtown Belle Reve a year ago, shortly after the coyotes started their incursions onto our land. A coincidence? Maybe, but the timing was more than suspicious. Not long afterward, Grandpa called me back home to beef up security.

Even under the low light cast by the streetlamps, I saw Marit's face grow pale. "You think… you think they'd kill me so Bryce could inherit my lease?"

"Not gonna happen. I promise." I balled my hands into fists. Wolf shifters were a tactile people. I fought the instinctive need to reach out and offer comfort, to pull her into my arms.

"A few weeks ago, I thought he loved me." She buried her face in her hands. Her hair fell forward, hiding her features, but I could taste her distress. "And now you're telling me that it was all fake?"

"Marit, look at me, please."

After a moment, she lifted her head and fixed watery eyes on me. "I feel like such a fool."

"No," I said, my voice firm. "This isn't on you. They targeted you. I'm sure they researched you before Bryce made his first move."

"Oh, my God." She jerked upright, her back stiff. "I did it. I gave them everything they needed."

"What do you mean?"

"Bryce kept talking about all the things we have in common, about how we were perfect together. All he had to do was look at my Instagram." She choked out a disgusted laugh. "Everything was there. Dinners from my favorite Thai restaurant. Waiting in line to binge Thin Man movies at a classic film festival. The grand opening of Freya's Bake Shop." She faltered, staring off into the distance. "I even posted pictures of the flowers I left on Grandma's grave every Wednesday afternoon." She fell silent, then pounded a fist on the dashboard. "What's that phrase? I'm 'the architect of my own misfortune.' I might as well have handed him the keys to my house."

"Bryce is the bad guy here," I reminded her. "Not you."

"I bet Courtney was in on it from the start," she continued, wide-eyed. "I thought he cheated on *me* with her. Now it looks like he cheated on *her* with me." She threw her hands in the air. "*I'm* the other woman."

"Hey." I gripped her shoulder. "Bryce is a manipulative bastard who took advantage of your trust. Courtney was his partner in crime."

She sucked in a deep breath, visibly calming herself. "So what now?"

"You heard him. He told his... his boss he has you wrapped around his little finger. He must think he has a shot at reconciling with you."

She snorted. "Never going to happen."

"Amen to that," I muttered.

She cut me a sideways glance. "How long have you known what Bryce was up to?"

"I didn't put the pieces together until he barged into the cabin and you told me he was the man who'd betrayed you. I recognized his name from our research on the syndicate." I shook my head. "I figured out what he must be up to, and I lost it."

"I understand the anger," she said. "I really do. I'm angry, too. But that doesn't excuse the violence."

Taking down a coyote intruder was second nature to me, but doing it in front of a human was just plain irresponsible. "I'm sorry I hit him. My temper got away from me."

Marit touched a finger-shaped bruise on her neck. "I've got no room in my life for a man who can't control his temper, no matter how sorry he feels afterward."

My stomach clenched at both the sight of the injury the coyote had inflicted on her and at her suggestion that I posed any kind of danger to her. "You've been lied to by a man you trusted. I get why you might not believe me, but I swear by all I hold holy that I'd never turn that violence on you."

She tilted her head to one side, studying me while she weighed my words. I knew she wouldn't accept my promise at face value. Best I could hope for was that she wouldn't reject me outright and that she'd give me the opportunity to earn her confidence.

"I want to trust you," she said, "but I'm not even sure that I can trust myself."

The knot in my stomach pulled tighter. Damn the coyotes for making a bright young woman question her judgment.

"Give me a chance, Marit, and I'll prove to you that I'm a man of my word."

Shuddering, she inhaled a deep breath. "I was ready to think you were the bad guy, but maybe it was Bryce the whole time." She hesitated, then reached out and touched the back of my hand.

I flipped it over and wrapped my fingers around hers, half-afraid she'd retreat from the contact. Instead of pulling away, she clung to me as if my hand was a lifeline. If my touch gave her comfort, I'd hold on forever. I sat very still, reluctant to do anything to shatter the connection.

Did she feel it, too? The electricity that sparked across my skin, shooting bolts of lightning straight toward my cock?

"Marit," I breathed.

She pressed her lips together, deep in thought. "Screw it. I'm just going to come right out and ask." She waved her free hand back and forth between her chest and mine. "Am I imagining it, or is there some kind of... some kind of intense vibe between us?"

"You're not imagining it." I spoke before I could second-guess my response.

"What does it mean?" she asked. "Am I rebounding from Bryce?"

Honesty—not wisdom—compelled me to answer. "If you were simply on the rebound, I wouldn't feel it, too."

"Huh." She fell back against the seat cushion, then lifted one shoulder, frowning. "Honestly, I have no idea what to do about it."

Me neither.

I stood at a crossroads. For a wolf, their mate comes first, but Marit wasn't my mate. And if I followed pack law—if I mercilessly beat down my wolf's urgings—she never would be. Somehow I didn't have the strength to end our budding relationship. Instead, I hovered at the crossroads, turning neither right nor left, liable to get mowed down by oncoming traffic.

Fuck.

"We don't have to do anything about it today," I said. "Just keep an open mind and an open heart, and we'll see what happens. Okay?"

After a moment, the grooves in her forehead smoothed out. "Okay."

The tension in my stomach eased. "For now, would you like me to drive you to your cousins' place or out to the lake cabin?"

"No, I'm going back to Bryce's."

What? My wolf snarled and I bit back a protest. "Why go back to a man who means you harm?"

"Unless we're married, he has nothing to gain by hurting me," she said.

"That might be true, but what's the point?" I persisted.

"It would feel good to tell him off, to let him know I'm on to him, but I think it would be smarter to string him along. To play him the way he played me."

"What do you mean?" I asked.

She turned in the seat and leaned toward me. "Think about it. As long as Bryce believes he has a chance at reconciling with me, he'll make nice. God knows how things would escalate if he thought that marrying me was a lost cause. And if I stay cordial, maybe I can help you find out what the syndicate is up to."

"I don't like it." My wolf huffed in agreement.

"You don't have to like it. It's my call." She touched my hand again and heat shot up my arm. "Listen, tomorrow morning I'll pack up my things and leave Bryce on friendly terms. I'll let him think I'm considering forgiving him and getting back together."

Stubborn and strong-willed, wasn't she?

"And then what?" I asked.

"Meet me at Freya's Bake Shop at nine," she suggested. "I'll let my cousins know what's going on, and we'll make a plan."

CHAPTER SEVENTEEN

MARIT

"Nancy Drew's got nothing on me," I muttered, looking down with satisfaction at the notepad I'd pulled from a drawer, the same notepad Bryce had scribbled on last night. He'd torn off the top sheet, but when I dragged the flat side of a pencil lead over the indentations on the second sheet, letters appeared, ghostly white against slate gray.

Score one for old-school detective work.

Alpha 10 BP gz, the pencil revealed.

"Alpha?" I whispered. Wasn't that military speak for the letter A? Alpha, Bravo, Charlie, etc? But if that was what he meant, why wouldn't Bryce simply write the letter A? Scrunching up my face, I dimly recalled a reference to alpha particles in a physics class back in high school. But that couldn't be right either.

Alpha 10 BP gz?

From the far side of the house, a door creaked open, then slammed shut. I tore off the cryptic note, slid it into my pocket, and slipped the notepad back into the drawer.

Bryce shuffled into the room and heaved a deep sigh, as if the effort of trudging from the guest room to the kitchen was almost too much for his poor battered body to take. Once again, the cervical collar he'd carelessly tossed aside last night encircled his neck. He leaned heavily against a counter, making a show of catching his breath.

Ignoring his theatrics, I threw him a bright smile. "I made waffles and squeezed fresh orange juice."

"Waffles," he moaned. "I've really missed your home cooking, Marit."

Eat up, buddy. This is the very last time you'll ever taste my home cooking.

"Sit down." I gestured to the small kitchen table, where a single purple dahlia sat in a bud vase next to his glass of juice.

His gaze took in the table set with nice china and the flower from the backyard garden. A wide, complacent smile curved his lips. "It looks beautiful, babe."

"Coffee?" I offered.

"Yes, please." He nodded, then winced, pretending the head bob hurt his neck.

He'd really committed to playing the part of the walking wounded, hadn't he? Almost as well as he'd committed to his role as an adoring fiancé. If only I'd seen through *that* act as easily as I could see through this one.

I poured two cups of coffee, added a big splash of cinnamon-flavored creamer to Bryce's, and set it next to his juice. While he carefully lowered himself onto a chair—the act punctuated by an exaggerated *oof*—I plated a waffle for Bryce, then sat down opposite him.

"You aren't eating?" he asked.

"I've been up since before six. I ate hours ago."

I'd rolled out of bed early, leaving a snoring Loki sprawled across the mattress. After packing my clothes and toiletries, I carried my suitcase to the car, then turned my attention to the kitchen.

Bryce's taste ran toward shiny and new, while I preferred quirky and vintage. Luckily, most of my household things were still stored in Annika and Liv's garage. Only my absolute favorites were here: my wooden spoons and rolling pins, a hundred-year-old Mason Cash mixing bowl, rainbow-colored potholders crocheted by Grandma, and the embroidered dish towels she'd adorned with dancing vegetables. Bryce thought the towels were stupid, but I smiled every time I saw a potato doing the Charleston or a pair of waltzing carrots. I'd quietly packed up all my treasures and hauled the box to the car.

"Why did you get up so early?" Bryce frowned, pouring syrup on his waffle. "Did Loki bother you?"

"Loki never bothers me." I smiled serenely.

The dog was coming with me. I'd never again make the mistake of leaving him behind. Loki's food, bowls, toys, and bed were all secured in my trunk. If Bryce tried to stop me, he'd have a fight on his hands.

Hearing his name, Loki ambled into the kitchen and rested his chin on my thigh. I patted his head, drawing comfort from his presence.

"So why did you get up early, other than to make me this fabulous breakfast?" Bryce asked, brandishing his fork at the table.

I pointed to his face. "Your bruises have already faded. The swelling around your eye has gone down. You can walk unassisted. I think it's safe to leave you on your own."

"What?" He dropped his fork onto the plate. "I was counting on you to stay with me while I recover."

"Don't worry." I flashed my teeth. "I'm not abandoning you. I'll check in later."

"But... I thought... I mean... I hoped you were reconsidering the breakup." Jutting out his lower lip, he offered a hangdog expression so patently manipulative that I wanted to smack him. Instead, I laid my hand on top of his and gave a reassuring squeeze.

To think that only a week ago, I actually liked touching Bryce. Now, the skin-on-skin contact gave me the creeps. I had to force myself not to jerk my hand away, the exact opposite of what happened last night when I'd spontaneously reached out and taken Adam's hand. When Adam's fingers had closed around mine, a shocking desire had spiraled through me.

Desire accompanied by an odd sense of safety, of coming home after a long absence. I'd held on for dear life, stunned by my reaction to the man.

"I'm thinking about getting back together," I lied. "But I need time. I don't want to be rushed."

Bryce blinked. His throat bobbed as he visibly swallowed any objections.

Pressing my advantage, I took a sip of coffee, then, "And I'm taking Loki."

"What?" He frowned. "Where are you going?"

"I might stay with Annika and Liv for a while." Or I might not. I hadn't decided.

His brows lowered. "Well, at least you're keeping your distance from the thug who beat me up."

The insult to Adam made me bristle. Adam had more honor in his little finger than Bryce did in his entire body. His perfectly coiffed, painstakingly manscaped, and gym-honed body. Shit. It was like a veil had been pulled from my eyes. What had I ever seen in the dickhead?

Bowing my head and hiding my face, I took a long sip of my coffee. Loki lifted his head and looked into my eyes, his expression one of pure doggy trust and devotion. My fingers clenched around the mug. The sooner I got him safely away from Bryce's schemes, the better. A glance at the kitchen clock confirmed my need for haste.

"It's time for Loki and me to take off." I stood and carried my mug to the sink.

"Already?" Bryce sputtered and jumped to his feet.

What's the old expression? Give a man enough rope to hang himself? In my case, I'd give Bryce enough *hope* to hang himself. He had to believe he still had a shot at winning me back. While I kept him dangling, Adam and I would figure out exactly what he and the syndicate were up to.

I plastered a fake smile on my face and crossed to him. Rising up on my tiptoes, I kissed his cheek, then fought the urge to swipe my hand over my lips.

"I'll call you later," I said airily, then turned to my dog. "Loki, you want to go for a ride?" He knew that word. His ears perked up. He gave an agreeable *woof* and trotted to the front door. I snatched up my purse and followed him, calling over my shoulder to Bryce, "See ya."

Forcing myself to walk rather than run, I strode to my car and opened the door. Loki hopped in. I jogged to the driver's side and slid behind the wheel, then turned to him.

"Do you want to go see Adam?"

Loki's entire body wiggled with happiness.

I laughed softly, anticipation humming in my veins. At the prospect of seeing Adam, the tension that had tied my stomach in knots all morning unraveled, replaced by giddy excitement.

"Me, too, baby. Me, too."

Chapter Eighteen

Adam

Arms crossed over my chest, I leaned against the wall outside Freya's Bake Shop. A steady stream of customers came and went while I waited for Marit to show up. A few shot me anxious sideways glances, but most were undeterred by the presence of a scowling man loitering outside the bakery.

After checking in with Remy this morning, I'd come straight here from the apartment the pack owned on the outskirts of Belle Reve. Every time the door to the shop opened, I got a fresh hit of the tempting smell of coffee and pastries. My stomach growled. Strong black coffee and another bear claw or three sounded damned good, almost as good as getting off this crowded walkway.

At precisely two minutes before nine, Marit and Loki rounded the corner of the block. On his leash, Loki made straight toward me, zigzagging between people who swarmed the sidewalk. He reached my side, lowered his tail, and flashed a toothy, submissive smile.

"Good boy." I hunkered down and ruffled the fur on his neck, then stood and faced Marit.

She wore a bemused expression. "If I didn't know better, I'd swear you cast a spell on my dog."

Close, but not quite. I grinned. "Loki and I have reached an understanding."

"Uh-huh." She sounded suspicious, but returned my smile. Her head jerked back and her eyes lit up. "I almost forgot." She dug in her pocket, pulled out a piece of paper, and handed it to me.

"What is it?" I asked.

"When he was talking on the phone last night, Bryce wrote a note. I made a copy of it," she said proudly. "It says 'Alpha 10 BP gz.' I have no idea what that means. Do you?"

I unfolded the paper and stared down at the letters. Yeah. I had a pretty good idea of the note's meaning, but I couldn't share it with Marit. I scratched my head and gave a vague, but not untruthful reply. "That's a tough one all right."

"It was worth a shot," she said.

"That it was. Thank you." I tilted my head toward the shop. "I'd kill for some coffee and a bear claw."

"Follow me." Marit pushed open the door and led the way inside.

Behind the counter, her cousins glanced our way. Marit had told me they were twins, but nobody was likely to confuse the two women. The tall, lean cousin with short brown hair—the gruff one who almost chewed off my head the first time I saw her—frowned when she spied me. In stark contrast, a happy expression crossed the face of her sister, a sweet-looking woman with long light-brown hair.

"Marit, you're back," she cried.

"What's he doing here?" The taller one pointed at me.

"Julia," Marit called out to the third person working in the shop. "Can you watch the counter while I talk to my cousins?"

"Sure thing," the teenager said.

I followed Marit and Loki around the counter to a round table at the back of the shop.

"I'll be just a minute," she said after the rest of us took our seats and the dog sprawled belly up at my feet. Marit dashed to the front of the shop, then returned a minute later carrying a steaming cup of coffee and a plate of pastries. She set the food in front of me. "No bear claws today, but I brought you a couple of ham-and-cheese stuffed croissants and a maple bar." She paused. "I should have asked. You're not a vegetarian, are you?"

I suppressed a smile at the notion of a vegetarian wolf shifter. "Nope. I'm a meat eater." I picked up a croissant as if to prove the point. "Thanks."

Marit took a seat, then pointed to her cousins. "Adam, meet Annika and Liv."

"What gives?" Liv demanded, ignoring the pleasantries. "Why are you back in town, and what are you doing with the guy from the conservancy?"

Blunt, no-nonsense, and fiercely protective of Marit, wasn't she? Admiration for the loyal, tough-talking woman shot through me.

Annika rolled her eyes. "Play nice," she chided her sister before turning to Marit. "Is everything okay?"

Marit planted her elbows on the table and leaned toward her cousins. "This won't be easy to hear, but I need to tell you what's going on."

Liv and Annika listened with wide-eyed attention while Marit recounted all the events of the past week. Annika paled, and Liv swore when they heard how two men had chased and manhandled Marit. With a halting voice, she told them who Bryce worked for and why he had pursued her. Liv sputtered with outrage and her expression grew murderous. Shuddering, Annika buried her face in her hands. Marit didn't sugarcoat her description of my violent attack on Bryce. Liv met my eyes and held out her hand for a fist bump. When Marit wrapped up her story, the table fell silent for a long moment.

"What do you need?" Annika asked quietly.

"Can Loki and I stay with you for a couple of days?" Marit asked.

"For chrissake, you don't need to ask if you can stay with us." Liv burst out, anger still riding her hard. She relaxed the hands she'd balled into fists. "I'm sorry. I'm mad, but not at you. Never at you. If I thought I could get away with it, I'd eviscerate Bryce."

Recognizing a kindred spirit, my wolf nodded in agreement.

Marit reached across the table, and the three cousins clasped hands. No matter what happened between her and me, Marit had a pack—a family—who would stand with her till the end. Instead of warming my heart, that knowledge only made me feel bereft.

Our mate, the wolf insisted. *Our pack.*

I couldn't summon the will to argue with my shadow brother. In this moment, I felt it, too, the certainty that my life was inextricably bound up with hers.

And what the hell was I going to do about it?

Her brow wrinkled—as if she wasn't sure it was a good idea or how I'd respond. Marit turned to me and held out her free hand. Without hesitation, I tangled my fingers in hers. Smiling, she tugged. I took the hint and laid my palm on top of the clasped hands in the middle of the table.

Through my eyes, the wolf looked his fill at Marit, reveling in her touch. He turned his eyes to Annika and Liv, committing their faces and scents to memory. His resolve filled my chest. Marit was his mate, and because she loved her kin, they, too, fell under his protection.

I groaned inwardly. *What are we doing, brother?*

He snorted, the answer to my question painfully obvious to the wolf.

CHAPTER NINETEEN

MARIT

I clipped the leash onto Loki's collar, shrugged on my pink hoodie, and slid the house key into a pocket.

"You sure you don't want company?" Liv asked from the sofa.

I glanced over at my cousin. Clad in ratty old sweats with her feet up on the coffee table, she balanced a full bowl of jalapeno popcorn on her lap. Liv might spend her days working at a bakery, but she liked to snack on something salty. My cousin had clearly settled in for the night, but if I didn't want to be alone, she'd forgo her late evening routine and accompany me on Loki's walk.

My heart warmed.

"And drag you away from your *Real Housewives* marathon? No way."

Liv shrugged and returned her eyes to the screen.

"Good night, Annika." I cried out in a voice that would carry to the back of the house, where Annika was soaking in a bubble bath. "Loki and I'll be back in a little while."

A splashing sound—I imagined her sitting up in the tub—then, "Do you want company?"

I laughed. My cousins were the best. "Nope. Stay put."

"You have your pepper spray?" Liv asked, tearing her eyes away from the show.

I patted the left pocket of my hoodie. "Yes, Mom."

"Go for the eyes," she added, tossing another handful of the spicy popcorn into her mouth.

"You know that Belle Reve has a super-low crime rate, don't you?"

"Uh-huh," she mumbled around the popcorn. While she chewed and swallowed, I opened the door and made my escape.

Loki and I headed east toward the popular riverfront district. It was a few minutes past ten p.m., but folks were still out and about. A couple of teenagers played basketball in a driveway. A woman watering pots of flowers on her front porch called out a friendly greeting. We passed three other people walking their dogs.

As we passed the entrance to Brenner Park, Loki tugged on the leash and barked once. We'd visited the popular recreation area a number of times, but always during the daylight hours when we shared it with joggers, picnickers, and families. Brenner Park closed at ten. If we headed into it now, the benches and playground equipment would stand empty and quiet. Loki and I would walk alone under the tall red cedar trees.

A cool breeze blew toward us from the river that bordered the opposite side of the park. Shivering from more than the chill air, I pulled up my hood.

"Sorry, dude," I said, feeling anything but. "Park's closed." I knelt down, gave him a conciliatory pat, then noticed that one of the white shoelaces on my Chucks had come undone. I pushed the leash handle up my wrist, freeing my fingers to tie a bow.

Loki gave a sudden jerk, and the leash slid off my hand. With an eager *wuff*, he cannonballed into the park, disappearing into the shadows beneath the trees.

"Son of a bitch." I scrambled to my feet and hesitated for only a second before dashing after him. Loki was no untrained puppy. He was a well-behaved three-year-old—turned over to the humane society after his previous owner died. He'd never before even *tried* to break away while on his leash.

"Loki," I hissed, for some reason reluctant to shatter the silence in the deserted park. Up ahead, Loki barked frantically. Crap. Had he cornered another skunk? I sniffed, testing the air for the telltale smell, but caught nothing, not until a clamor of voices rang out. I ran faster. A dozen yards later, I rounded a corner, and skidded to a stop.

The crown jewel of the park, an elegant Victorian-style gazebo, lay straight ahead. White fairy lights strung along the gazebo's roof beams bathed the surrounding area in gentle light. Three men stood inside the octagonal structure. I squinted. Was that... was that Bryce? And the tall figure looming outside the gazebo—the man whose waist Loki was excitedly pawing—was that Adam?

Acting on instinct, I slipped behind a cedar tree and pressed against the bark. I held my breath and peeked around the trunk.

In the golden glow cast by the fairy lights, the air surrounding the gazebo shimmered, just like it had before Booger and Rat Face had run away. Power sparked, charging the atmosphere with so much electricity that the hair on my arms stood at attention. Bryce grabbed one of his companions by the arm and dragged the man away from the gazebo. Only Adam and the final stranger remained, their forms silhouetted against the glimmering light. Whining, Loki dropped to the ground and pressed his belly against the earth. Adam and the stranger swayed. At the same instant, their bodies contorted into sharp, unlikely angles, like marionettes jerked on a cruel puppet master's strings.

"Adam?" I whispered, horrified.

His head twisted toward the sound. No way, no way could he actually have heard me.

Brilliant sparkles coalesced and dazzled my eyes. Seconds ticked by. The shimmering field of light grew wisp thin and porous, the barrier no longer capable of hiding the world from view. Once again, I could see my surroundings. Adam and the stranger had disappeared.

Outside the gazebo, a huge, snarling gray wolf posed in an attack position, his white-tipped tail stiff with undisguised aggression. I blinked. His white-tipped tail? Like the wolf who had saved me from my attackers? Impossible for the same wolf to suddenly appear in a city park. It had to be a coincidence.

As if reading my thoughts, the wolf looked over his shoulder, gazing directly at me. If I didn't know better, I'd swear he recognized me, too. My lungs constricted and I struggled to drag in a breath.

Movement drew my eyes. Another wolf stood on the steps to the gazebo. No, on closer examination, not a wolf. This animal was smaller and scrawnier, with a tawny cast to his fur. His narrow, pointed nose and short bushy tail looked nothing like the wolf's, yet he emanated a similar, undeniable wildness. Not a wolf. Not a dog. A coyote, maybe?

The wolf lunged at the coyote. The beasts clashed in a tangle of fur and fang. The coyote screamed—no other words could describe the hair-raising sound that ripped through the night. Thankfully, the battle was short-lived. The wolf quickly dispatched the coyote, then turned his head to look at Loki, who cringed flat on his belly on the ground.

Loki. I let go of the tree and lurched toward them, the need to protect my dog overriding any survival instincts.

"Good boy." Holding out a placating hand to the wolf, I moved closer to the pair. I dropped down on my knees next to Loki.

Wolves rarely attacked humans. The big bad wolf was the stuff of fairy tales. I *knew* that, but still, my heart thumped, and my eyes grew wide as the wolf stalked toward us, blood dripping from his muzzle.

"Good boy," I repeated weakly.

He sidled up next to me and opened his mouth. Hot, copper-scented breath fanned my face.

What big teeth you have! The line from "Little Red Riding Hood" flashed through my mind. Followed by the wolf's response: *The better to eat you with.*

With trembling fingers, I reached for the pepper spray in my hoodie's left pocket. Before I tugged on the zipper, my hand stilled. Who was I kidding? Pepper spray wouldn't stop the beast if he chose to attack us. If anything, the caustic chemicals would likely send him into a violent frenzy.

"Nice wolf," I crooned, my voice shaking.

As if distressed by my fear, the wolf whimpered, then licked my cheek.

I had to be hallucinating. There was no other explanation for the shimmering lights that suddenly surrounded us, capturing me inside the same swirling vortex I'd witnessed a few minutes ago. The air grew thick and I struggled to draw a breath. The glittering mass gradually broke apart and dissolved. Next to me, a naked Adam Landry crouched on the ground. I fell on my ass and scuttled backward. Over Adam's shoulder, the dead coyote morphed into human form, the same man who'd stood next to Bryce in the gazebo.

"What the actual fuck?" I choked out.

Loki jumped to his feet and ambled over to Adam. Gazing adoringly at the wolf-man, he nuzzled Adam's face.

"Good boy." Adam laid a hand on Loki's shoulder, then turned his eyes to me. "There are more things in Heaven and Earth, Horatio, than are dreamt of in your philosophy." In a deep, resonant voice, he recited a line from *Hamlet.*

My brain glitched and shock robbed me of the power of speech. There was no denying what I witnessed. In an instant, my understanding of the world and how it worked had flipped on its head. Supernatural creatures existed. They walked among us.

Adam was a freaking werewolf, a werewolf who quoted Shakespeare.

He tilted his head, his glittering golden eyes fixed on me. When I continued to silently gape at him, he slowly rose to his feet, appearing utterly at ease with his nudity. Under other circumstances, I'd ogle his powerful body, but now I just stared, my thoughts a jumble.

His cast-off jeans and shirt lay on the ground next to the boots he'd kicked off when he... when he... transformed... into the wolf. He tugged the pants up over muscular thighs and shrugged the shirt over his sculpted chest. From the pocket of his jeans, he extracted his leather-and-stone bracelet and fastened it to his wrist. He was shoving his feet into his boots when his head snapped around, and he looked in the direction of the street.

"Shit. Cops are coming. Somebody must have heard the fight and called it in." Shaking his head with obvious aggravation, he glanced at the bloody body lying on the ground. "We need to get gone."

In the distance, a police siren wailed. Cops. I latched onto the word like a lifeline. The police would protect Loki and me, wouldn't they?

"C'mon." Adam held out a hand, offering to pull me to my feet.

"No." I swung my head back and forth.

He dropped into a squat and bent his head toward mine, the expression in his eyes deadly serious. "The police won't understand what happened here, and you can't tell them."

"Are you threatening me?" I sputtered.

"No. Fuck." He pushed both hands through his hair. "The world knows nothing about shifters, and that's the way it has to stay." He stood and waited for a beat. When I hesitated, he wrapped his hands around my biceps and hauled me to my feet, his grip both gentle and unrelenting. "Marit, we gotta go." He carefully enunciated each word as if speaking to a small child.

From the street, brakes squealed. Strobing blue-and-red police lights pierced the darkness. A siren yelped, then died when the car's engine cut. Doors slammed and flashlight beams swept along the path.

Adam was done reasoning with me. Bending forward, he tossed me over his shoulder and sprinted toward the river, Loki hard on his heels.

CHAPTER TWENTY

ADAM

What an absolute clusterfuck.

Marit hung limply over my shoulder, too stunned to struggle against my hold. Human brains tended to go on the fritz when they first realized that shifters were real. Took 'em a while to come around; at least it did for the trusted ones who survived the discovery.

Loki ran behind me, happy and oblivious to the fact that he'd alerted the coyotes to my presence.

When Marit showed me her ex's note—Alpha 10 BP gz— I'd immediately guessed its meaning. Bryce planned to meet his shit-ass alpha in the gazebo at Brenner Park when the place shut down for the night at ten. I arrived half an hour early and positioned myself to spy on the meeting. Luckily, the wind blowing up from the river hid my scent from the coyotes.

Bryce, his alpha, and a bodyguard gathered in a circle in the middle of the wooden structure. Shoulders slumped, Marit's ex bowed, scraped, and bobbed his head, kissing his alpha's ass in a way guaranteed to turn the stomach of any wolf. Wolves respected the chain of command and followed protocol, but we never groveled.

"Medved," Bryce murmured, a few minutes into their meeting.

My ears perked up at the mention of the name. Maxim Medved was the alpha of the grizzly pack, the son of the man who drove my people from Alaska during the Great War. Could Medved be in cahoots with the coyotes? Was he the ally Bryce mentioned?

I'd cocked my head, eager to hear the coyote alpha's response, when Loki barreled up the path, dragging his leash behind him. The same breeze that carried my scent away from the coyotes must have blown it straight at the dog. He hurtled toward my hiding place, barking like crazy. Finding me, he pawed at my chest, beside himself with joy. Good dog, shit timing. And just like that, my intelligence-gathering mission went tits up.

The cherry on top? A minute later, Marit ran up the path in pursuit of Loki.

That's all she wrote, as Grandpa liked to say. Bryce and his alpha slunk away. I killed the bodyguard. Now I was carrying a shell-shocked Marit away from the park and the police. I should've moved the coyote's body before the cops showed up, but I had to choose between him and Marit. No contest there. I jogged along the river, then jumped the aluminum fence on the north side of the park. I'd left my truck on a quiet residential street only three blocks away.

Carrying a limp woman over my shoulder on a dark sidewalk? Nothing suspicious looking about that. Before a concerned passerby or snoopy neighbor could dial 911, I settled Marit on her feet, gripping her shoulders in case she was still wobbly.

"We need to walk to my truck, okay?"

Stunned confusion was stamped across her features. "You're a werewolf." Her lips barely moved when she spoke.

"Wolf shifter," I corrected. "Werewolves aren't a thing."

That got her attention. Her gaze sharpened. "You mean you aren't allergic to silver, and you don't change into a wolf when the moon is full?"

"If silver hurt me, I couldn't wear this." I touched the silver wire-wrapped chip of black rock secured to my wrist by leather cords. "And I can shift any time I want, not just when the moon is full."

Thanks to the power of the same black rock, I failed to add. Assuming our animal form took a lot out of shifters. Change back and forth once, and it took days for most shifters to recover the strength to do it again. Not for members of my pack. Not as long as we wore Black Rock next to our skin. Just one of the many advantages the meteorite gave my people.

"Did a werewolf—I mean a wolf shifter—bite you? Is that how you became one?"

"Shifters are born, not made." Once again, I skimped on the details. No point in explaining the complicated intersection of pack law and shifter DNA, at least not yet.

"So if you bit me, I wouldn't turn into a wolf?" she persisted.

My lips twitched. "If I bit you, Marit, it would be for an entirely different reason."

Her eyes widened and I caught a whiff of fear. "You mean shifters eat people?"

"No," I said firmly. "Hunting and eating humans is against the law of every shifter pack in the world."

"Wait." Her voice rose. "There are other shifters? Not just wolves?"

Over her shoulder, I spied a young couple walking toward us.

"Listen, we need to have this conversation in private. Let's go to my truck and talk more there."

She frowned. Once again, the scent of her fear floated in the air. Her misgivings cut me to the quick. I pressed my fist over my heart, the sign of a sacred vow among my people. "On my honor, as a sentry of the Guardians of the Black Rock pack, I swear you're safe with me."

She bit her lower lip, weighing my words, then glanced at Loki, who leaned contentedly against my legs. His ease in my presence seemed to tip the scales in my favor.

"All right," she agreed.

Going all in, I offered my hand. I held my breath. Seconds ticked by while she made up her mind. Finally, she slipped her palm into mine. My hand closed over hers. Her fingers felt cold, colder than the evening air warranted.

We can warm her up, my shadow brother suggested. Beneath my skin, the wolf pranced, joy and pride making his steps light.

I strode sedately next to Marit, my gait revealing none of the wolf's triumph.

I'd parked the truck under a maple tree whose leafy branches blocked the glow from the overhead streetlight and threw shadows into the truck's interior.

"Hop in," I told the dog.

Loki jumped, settling onto the back bench. Marit and I climbed into the front bucket seats, then turned to face each other.

"What do you want to know?" I asked, allowing her curiosity to direct the conversation.

She considered her first question, then asked, "How long have shifters existed?"

I lifted a shoulder. "How long have humans existed? Our history tells us we've been here from the start."

"How about your pack? You haven't always lived in Washington, have you?"

"No." I sighed. How could I reduce a long and complicated history to a few sentences? "My people came to Pennsylvania from Germany in the early 1800s. The New World wasn't kind to wolves, natural gray wolves or shifters in our animal form. Kill on sight was the order of the day. State governments put bounties on wolves. Wolves were shot, hunted down, trapped, poisoned."

"What did you guys do?" Marit asked.

"Moved west to the Washington Territory in the 1870s. We settled first in the Puget Sound area, then later, we moved inland and worked in the lumber industry. The same war on wolves followed us there."

"You told me that gray wolves were wiped out in Washington state by the early 1900s," Marit said.

"Yeah." I let out a deep sigh. "When we heard that gold was discovered in the Klondike in 1896, we packed up and headed to Alaska. We were lucky. We made a fortune in the gold fields. We banked most of it and used the rest to buy some isolated property. Until the 1950s, we were sitting pretty."

Our elders called the decades before the Great War the golden years. The pack had land and money in the bank. We'd stumbled across a large meteorite half-buried in our forest, the Black Rock, whose powers made us stronger and faster than other shifters. Life was good.

"What happened in the 1950s?" Marit asked.

"Everything went to shit." I closed my eyes and my lips twisted into a sorrowful line. "The pack alpha and his two top lieutenants were killed in a logging accident. The alpha's son, my grandfather Matthew, was just fifteen years old. By blood, he was the new alpha, but he wasn't ready to lead, and the sentries who could best advise him were dead, too." I paused.

Marit touched my arm, sympathy clouding her pretty gray eyes. "How bad did it get?"

"Real bad. The worst. A grizzly pack took advantage of the power vacuum. Out of the blue—without a declaration of war—they attacked. They didn't just want our land and property. They wanted to exterminate us."

I balled my fists, remembering the stories of the Great War I'd heard from the old-timers. Even with our enhanced speed and strength, in a one-on-one battle, wolves fought at a disadvantage against the powerful grizzlies. Our best bet was to attack as a group, but the bears winnowed down our numbers. They waged war without honor, savaging soldiers and civilians alike. By the time the pack fled our home in Alaska, eighty percent of us had been killed.

"So you lost the war?" Marit guessed.

"Yeah. We lost the war and most of our people. The survivors grabbed what they could and ran."

When Zane, Remy, and I were kids, we'd sit slack-jawed while Grandpa told stories about the pack's narrow escape from Alaska. About the herculean effort required to pull the Black Rock from the ground and transport it to safety. About the caravan of cars and sturdy Dodge Power Wagon trucks that carried the pack back to the Lower 48.

"Where did your people go?" Marit asked.

"Moved around and laid low till the mid-1960s, when a big track of private timber land came up for sale in Washington state. By that time, Matthew had grown up and was ready to lead. He was happily mated to my grandmother Katia."

"Mated?" Marit's brow creased. "Is that the same as married?"

My wolf stirred. This was important.

"No, it's more than marriage." I turned my palm up and wrapped my fingers around hers. "A wolf mates only once, when they find their soulmate. Their missing half. The person they'll share eternal and unconditional love with. We believe that fate brings two souls together—"

"Fate?" Marit scoffed and pulled her hand away from mine. "Bryce was always yammering on about fate, about how we were destined to be together."

My jaw tightened. While trying to win over Marit, Bryce defaulted to language familiar to every shifter. He reduced a sacred bond to nothing more than a tool he used to manipulate his quarry. "Bryce was a damned liar, but don't be too quick to discount the notion of fate bringing you to your mate."

Marit sat up ramrod straight, then swung her eyes my way. "Bryce was in the park tonight."

I figured that once the shock wore off, she'd eventually get around to putting two and two together. "Bryce is a coyote. The syndicate he works for—the people trying to get a hold of your lease—they're all coyotes, and enemies of my pack."

"Shit," she exclaimed. "Does that mean that the men who attacked me in the woods... Are you saying that they were coyotes, too?"

"You didn't realize it at the time, but you probably saw them shift," I said. "Then my wolf chased them downstream and killed them."

"Shit," she repeated. "And later you attacked Bryce when he showed up at my cabin—"

"Because he's a coyote and my enemy." I finished the sentence for her.

"Wow." She scrubbed both hands over her face. "Just... wow." She lifted her head and looked at me, frowning. "Back in the park, you told me that I can't tell the police what I saw."

I waited for a beat. When she didn't keep talking, I responded. "That's right."

"What happens to people who find out the secret?" she asked slowly.

"That depends. Over the years, some trusted humans have become friends and allies. We've even welcomed a few into our pack."

Mates. We used to welcome human mates into the pack, but no more.

"What about the people you decide you can't trust?"

I hesitated, searching for the right words. Once again, the sour scent of her fear wafted toward me. "Adam?"

"We usually can reach an understanding with people who discover our secret." Bribes, threats, and intimidation could work wonders. So could dousing somebody with booze and persuading them that what they saw was an alcohol-induced hallucination. So could memory-inhibiting drugs. On rare occasions—when we had absolutely no other option and where a human was determined to blab—sterner measures were required.

"Are you going to tell your alpha what happened in the park?"

"Yes." I reached out and took her hand. "I have to. I killed a coyote and left his body for the police to find. And I overheard Bryce say something that suggests that the coyotes have made an alliance with the same grizzlies who drove my people out of Alaska. I owe a duty to the pack to report all that."

"And what about me?" Marit's fingers tightened on mine. "Do you owe a duty to the pack to tell them that I saw you shift?"

Without a doubt, I one hundred percent did.

My wolf growled a low warning.

My grandfather was a good man, but with the war heating up and the potential for grizzly involvement, a talkative human was the very last thing he'd want to deal with. The last time my pack resorted to extreme measures was back in Alaska, when a trapper tried to blackmail us. Marit posed no such threat. Grandpa was unlikely to do harm to a human woman. Still, even the possibility of such a thing had my wolf scrambling to emerge.

Easy, brother, I told him.

He stilled, head cocked to one side while he waited for me to untangle my thoughts.

What would I do if the worst happened, if my alpha declared Marit a danger to the pack? Not so long ago, the answer would be a no-brainer. I'd follow orders and do what was necessary. And now? If Grandpa decided we needed to play it safe, to confine her at pack headquarters, or something more... more *extreme?* Would I comply with my alpha's command?

Our mate, the wolf insisted. *Protect our mate.*

My heart sank. Understanding buried claws deep in my chest. I hunched forward, my lungs refusing to draw in air.

"Adam?" Marit laid a hand on my shoulder, a tentative touch that sent electricity jolting throughout my body. "Are you okay?"

I turned my head. Through my eyes, the wolf gazed at the woman who already possessed his heart.

"Yes." The wolf's guttural rasp clogged my voice. No matter what it cost me, even if I had to go rogue, take her and run, I'd cherish and protect this woman. I cleared my throat. "We need to meet with my grandfather."

Her eyes widened with alarm.

I took her face between my palms. "Know this. Now and forever, I *will* keep you safe."

CHAPTER TWENTY-ONE

MARIT

A dam hadn't put his phone on speaker, but the woman's angry voice carried loud and clear throughout the truck's cab.

"I'm not about to drag poor Matthew out of bed at this time of night," she huffed. "What are you thinking calling him so late?"

Adam swallowed, visibly biting back irritation. "Can't be helped. There was an incident at the park. I killed a coyote and had to leave his body behind for the police to find."

"You did what?" Her shrill voice made *me* wince, and my ear was nowhere near the speaker. "You're unbelievable. Mark my words, Adam. You'll be the death of your grandfather yet."

He jerked the phone away from his ear, inhaled a deep breath, then slowly blew it out. With a tight jaw, he put the phone once again close to his mouth. "Get the alpha, please, Olga."

"Very well," she snapped.

I squirmed in the passenger seat and shot a sympathetic glance at Adam. Olga—whoever she was—seemed to take real pleasure in chewing him out.

"She sounds... uh... fun," I whispered.

Adam rolled his eyes.

A muffled exchange of words. I couldn't stop myself; I leaned closer to Adam so I could better listen in on his conversation with the alpha. A man's voice came on the line.

"Tell me what happened, son."

I shivered. Even at a distance, I sensed his power.

Adam laid out the events of the evening for his alpha. His *alpha*—the leader of a wolf shifter pack—a concept so outlandish that part of my brain still insisted that this had to be a world-class prank. In the space of an hour, my understanding of the natural order had cracked apart. I had no idea how all the pieces would fit back together again.

"I'm calling a meeting for 8 a.m.," Adam's grandfather said. "Bring the Hagen woman."

At hearing my name on the alpha's lips, my new reality hit home. I bit back a gasp and pressed my fingers against my lips. Unless I intended to hightail it out of town, meeting the alpha was inevitable. Was I ready to come face-to-face with the leader of a wolf pack?

Adam's concerned gaze cut to me.

Now and forever, I will keep you safe.

His words echoed in my ears. The vow held weight and substance. He meant it. Down to my bones, I knew that was true. I slid closer to him. He slung an arm around my shoulders and hauled me to his side. With a small sigh, I took shelter in his arms, basking in his promise of protection.

After another minute of conversation, Adam ended the call. "You okay?" he asked.

I nodded.

"How about we drive to the lake tonight?" His broad palm rubbed reassuring circles on my shoulder. "That way, we won't have to rush in the morning."

Too fast. This was happening too fast.

I frowned. "The road through the woods isn't very good, and there are no streetlights. Shouldn't we wait till the sun's up?"

I winced. Who me? Procrastinating?

"Road might be bad, but wolves have excellent night vision." He pointed to his golden yellow eyes. "I don't need streetlights to see."

The puzzle pieces fell into place. The way his eyes sometimes changed, their unusual color, it made sense if he shared his body with a wolf.

No excuse for putting off the inevitable.

"I'm staying with Annika and Liv. If I don't come home, they'll call the cops and report me missing."

Adam lifted a massive shoulder. "So tell them you're spending the night with me."

My lungs seized at the casual way he threw out the suggestion. It was a cover story, a way to ease Annika and Liv's minds, not a proposition. Still, the thought of spending the night with Adam, of touching his rugged body, of feeling his hands caress mine... Heat suffused my face and desire coiled low in my belly.

Next to me, Adam's nostrils flared, and his back stiffened. Oh, crap. With his enhanced shifter senses, Adam must have caught the scent of my arousal. I wasn't shy. Sexual desire was nothing to be ashamed of, at least not when it was mutual. We'd already confessed to feeling some kind of connection— an intense vibe—but neither one of us had made a move to act on that attraction.

From the back seat, Loki sneezed twice. Grateful for the distraction, I glanced into the back seat at my happy and trusting dog. Nothing was going to go wrong when I met Adam's pack, but I'd feel better knowing Loki was safe with my cousins.

"The bake shop is closed on Sundays and Mondays," I said. "Annika and Liv will be home for the next two days. I'd like to leave Loki with them before we drive to the lake."

"Sounds good." Adam turned the key while I gave him the address. Five minutes later, he pulled up in front of the bungalow. Lights flickering behind the curtains hinted that Liv was still awake, or that she'd dozed off on the sofa and left the TV on.

"Wait in the truck. I'll just be a minute." Without waiting for Adam to reply, I hopped out and opened the back door for Loki.

"Hey," Adam called. "Remember, not a word to your cousins."

I jerked my head in the affirmative. I didn't like to keep things from Liv and Annika, but the existence of shifters was a secret too potentially dangerous to share. Why put my cousins on the pack's radar?

Loki and I trotted up the front walk and quietly slipped inside. Liv lay sprawled on the sofa, wide awake, the almost-empty bowl of spicy popcorn on the floor at her side. Loki dashed for the leftover popcorn.

"Nope." She whipped the bowl away from him. "Sorry, dude. No jalapenos for you." She glanced at me. "What took you so long?"

"We ran into Adam Landry." I kept my tone light, acting as if my world hadn't just tipped off its axis.

"The hot guy who punched out Bryce? Nice." Liv smiled her approval. "You going to see him again?"

"Actually, yes." I leapt at the opening Liv gave me. "I was hoping you'd be willing to watch Loki for the next couple of days, so—"

"Shut up." Liv sat bolt upright, her eyes bulging. "You're hooking up with Adam? A guy you just met? I didn't think you had it in you, cousin." Hookups were definitely more Liv's thing than mine.

"Yeah, well what did holding out for a serious relationship get me?" I made a face and spread my hands.

Liv snorted. "Bryce."

Our voices must have woken up Annika, who stumbled sleepy-eyed from her bedroom. "What's going on out here?"

"We're babysitting Loki so Marit can spend a couple of days with Adam," Liv chortled.

Annika squinted. "When?"

"Right now," I said. "He's parked out front waiting for me."

They rushed to the window and pushed the curtain aside. Annika pointed at Liv's phone on the coffee table. "Hand me your phone so I can take a picture of his license plate. Just in case."

"Just in case of what?" I asked, although I had a hunch what she'd say. Annika's tenderhearted nature balanced against a caution that sometimes bordered on timidity.

"In case you go missing," she said. "If you end up in a barrel behind his barn, the police will need to know where to look for your body."

"Fat lot of good that will do me if my body is in a barrel behind the barn," I pointed out.

Liv jabbed a finger at her sister. "No more true crime shows for you. I mean it. You're cut off."

I hugged Annika and grabbed my purse. "Adam's a good guy, and besides, you know him, and you know where he works. Even if he was a crazed killer, he'd have to be stupid to make a move on me. There's nothing to worry about." I almost winced at the small lie. My upcoming meeting with the alpha was something to worry about, but the essential part of my statement rang true. I had nothing to fear from Adam. "I left clothes and toiletries at the cabin, so I'm set. If you need me, call." With a wave, I dashed from the house.

"Everything good?" Adam asked as I fastened my seat belt.

"Yeah. Liv is thrilled that I'm spending time with you. Annika is worried that you might be a serial killer."

I meant that as a joke, but he didn't take it that way. Hand on the ignition key, he swung concerned eyes to me. "Did I say or do anything to upset her when we met?"

Jeez. I should have thought twice before I opened my mouth. "No, it isn't you," I assured him. "Annika is the kindest person I know, but she's always been a little skittish."

He cut me a sharp look. "Did something happen to make her that way?"

"What? No." The question took me aback. "I always figured that Annika's temperament was nature's way of balancing the scales. You know, Liv is scowly and fierce, and Annika is sunny and cautious."

Frowning, he turned the key and pulled the truck onto the street.

We rode in silence until we passed the city limits and turned onto the highway heading north toward Shooting Star Lake. Even in late July, few people drove through the mountains at midnight, so we had the road to ourselves. Craning my neck, I peered up through the truck's windshield. Overhead, stars bedazzled a cloudless night sky.

"Just look at that," I murmured. "When I lived in Seattle, you could barely see the stars through all the artificial city lights. I missed them." I waved my hand at the dense forest surrounding the highway and the glittering lights that filled the heavens. "I missed everything."

"What'd you do in Seattle?" Adam asked.

"Annika and I studied baking and pastry arts at a culinary school while Liv got a degree in business," I said. "We always knew we wanted to start a bakery in Belle Reve, and name it after Grandma Freya."

"You weren't tempted to stay in the big city?"

I made a face. "Not for a minute. Don't get me wrong. I like to visit the city sometimes, to go shopping or to a concert, or to eat at a fabulous restaurant. But at heart, I'm a small-town girl. I need to live close to nature."

He kept his eyes on the road but acknowledged my words with a crisp dip of his chin.

"How about you?" I played with the drawstring on my hoodie. "Have you always lived on pack land?"

"Not always. I had a job that kept me on the road for several years, but I'm back to stay now." His lips turned down; then he gave a slight shake of the head. "At least, I hope I am."

What did that mean?

"I should have asked," he continued. "Would you rather sleep in your cabin or in my room at the lodge?"

Playing coy was never my style, so instead of wondering, I got right to the point. "You want to stay together tonight?"

Adam's fingers tightened on the steering wheel. "Bryce and his alpha turned tail and ran as soon as they spotted me," he said. "In all the commotion, I have no idea if he recognized Loki or saw you, but in case he did and came looking, I'd rather not leave you alone."

A sensible response that shot a pang of disappointment through me.

"I'd rather not be alone tonight," I confessed. Because I was studying his profile, I saw the small, pleased smile that ghosted across his lips. Emboldened, I added, "Not because I'm afraid of Bryce, but because I want to get to know you better."

His small smile morphed to a full-on grin. "You do, huh?"

"I do." I waited for a beat, then added, "Don't leave me hanging here. What about you? What do you want?"

Adam eased the truck to a stop, set the brake, and unfastened his seat belt. He turned to me. Curving one hand around my nape, he slanted his big body toward mine and closed the distance between us. If I didn't welcome his touch, I could've pushed him away or shrunk back against the door. Instead, I held my ground and lifted my chin. His face mere inches from mine, he stilled.

"If you don't know what I want," he said, his voice a velvet caress, "it's past time I made it clear."

I went cross-eyed, my gaze honed in on his mouth. I held my breath, my insides quivering with anticipation. Instead of kissing me, his mouth swooped down, and his teeth gently nipped at a sensitive spot beneath my ear. His lips skated down my neck. With a flat tongue, he tasted the skin at the juncture of my neck and shoulders, leaving me shivery and weak. He nuzzled my throat and drew in a slow breath.

"Hmmm." A rumbling rose from deep inside his chest, a reverberation I felt down into my core.

Desire licked along my nerve endings. I was done waiting for our first kiss. Threading my fingers through his thick hair,

I drew his mouth to mine. One, two, three times, I delicately brushed my lips over his. A featherlight kiss, as soft as butterfly wings. An invitation.

With a groan, he took over, shaping his lips against mine. One hand still cupped my nape. The other slid down my back. He bit my lower lip, not hard enough to draw blood, but enough to sting. I gasped.

He isn't human. In the back of my mind, a small voice cautioned. *You're kissing a man who can morph into a beast.*

"Shut up," I murmured, shushing that inner voice.

Adam broke off the kiss. "What did you say?"

I chuckled, embarrassed. "I wasn't talking to you."

Confusion clouded his expression. He was considering asking me just who I *was* talking to. I saw the question form on his face. Thankfully, the desire to keep kissing me bested his curiosity. With a shrug, he reclaimed my lips.

He's a wolf-man. That pesky inner voice intruded again.

I broke the kiss this time, pulling back and studying his flushed face. With a fingertip, I traced the outline of his lips and teased them apart. I touched the edge of a pointed canine. The sharp tooth was wholly human, designed by nature to tear into food. Even as I drew my finger along its edge, I sensed its potential for change. When Adam yielded hegemony to his animal half, that tooth would elongate and grow even sharper, mutating into a weapon.

Many people possessed a shadow self. A soft heart hidden behind a brash exterior. A polite mask that concealed contempt. Greed disguised behind a cloak of piety. Many people wore two faces. For Adam—for shifters—the two faces were literal. Not masks disguising a fundamental truth, but alter egos. Within Adam beat the heart of a man and a wolf.

Bryce had ticked all the boxes. Intelligent. Well-mannered. Sense of humor. Good looking. Employed. Our relationship was a triumph of head over heart. We'd been bound together by shared interests and a measured mutual attraction. All of it bogus. I saw that now.

SECRETS OF SHOOTING STAR LAKE

There was nothing logical or measured about my attraction to Adam. Kissing Adam felt like coming home after a long absence.

This... this connection made absolutely no sense, but it was undeniable.

Tears pricked the back of my eyes.

"Marit?" Adam gently touched my cheek.

"A shifter and a human," I whispered. "How are we going to make this work? What are we going to do?"

CHAPTER TWENTY-TWO

ADAM

Marit led the way up the steps and across the porch to the cabin's front door. My eyes zeroed in on her ass. Our blistering first kiss unlocked a sexual hunger I'd been deliberately tamping down. Now free, that craving left me wanting more. Balling my fists, I silently watched her slip her key into the deadbolt, a simple act that smacked of sex. I groaned and shot a death glare at the hard-on tenting my jeans.

"What are we going to do?" Her voice had trembled and tears had sparkled in her eyes when she'd asked the question.

I'll tell you what we weren't going to do. Unless Marit jumped me, we weren't going to have sex tonight. She wanted me—thank fuck—but I wouldn't take advantage of a woman who was vulnerable and exhausted, who had to be traumatized after watching my wolf tear apart a coyote.

Claim her, the wolf urged, confused by my hesitation. His understanding of the world was more simple and straightforward than mine. Once she bore my mark, she was undeniably ours to protect. He couldn't fathom a world where the pack wouldn't accept the mating.

Not yet, brother, I soothed.

Marit unlocked the cabin door and flipped on an overhead light. "Home," she said with a happy sigh, her gaze wandering over the colorful interior. After a moment, she swung curious eyes my way. "Do you think the pack knows we're here? Do you guys watch the place?"

"Yeah." I opted for the truth. "We do. I'm sure somebody in the office saw the light come on and noted our arrival in the security log. Grandpa will know that we spent the night together."

Sooner or later, he'd have questions. If I told him I'd simply been watching out for Marit after the incident in the park, he'd smell the lie. Nobody could sneak a falsehood past an alpha. Besides, I didn't want to lie to him.

So what would I tell him? No choice but the truth. That my human mind had finally caught up with what the wolf had known from the start. Pack law notwithstanding, Marit was my mate. I wasn't in love with her—at least not yet—but I'd never heard of a wolf selecting a mate and their human half not figuring out that the wolf was right. The wolf's choice always led to love.

And what would my grandfather do with that knowledge? That was the big question.

Dire necessity had forced the pack to veto mating with a human, a law that ran contrary to our customs and history. We'd kept our distance from humans since relocating to Washington. That alone cut down on opportunities for any wolf to form a forbidden attachment with a human.

Only once during all those years had a pack member fallen in love with a human. Grandfather offered her a choice. Renounce the potential mating or be expelled from the pack. She dutifully broke things off with her human lover. In the long run, following the law didn't do a damned bit of good. Afterwards, the woman turned away every suitor, her wolf refusing to settle for a companionable marriage—like Matthew and Olga's—instead of a true mating. She never wed and never had children. How the pack benefited from sticking to the law was beyond me.

Would Grandpa give me a similar ultimatum? Marit or the pack?

I carried the blood of a potential alpha. Duty and responsibility had been drummed into me since childhood. Grandpa had groomed me for leadership. I wouldn't be surprised if he declared me his successor at the Pack Circle next week. He'd set the example of putting the pack's needs first. An alpha required a helpmeet he said, a partner to assist him in serving the people. After the death of his mate, Katia, Grandpa made a sensible union with the prickly, hardworking Olga.

He'd expect me to follow the law and make a sensible decision, too. And if I refused? He loved me. Most likely, he'd offer me the same options he'd given my pack mate: toe the line or face excommunication. My wolf would allow only one choice. If it all went sideways—if anybody threatened Marit— we'd go on the run. Grandpa would send trackers after us, most likely Zane and Remy.

Fuck.

How could a bloody shitshow be what was best for the pack?

I'd make my case before my alpha and hope he saw reason. Yeah, we needed more wolves, but procreation had *never* been the sole reason for mating—

"Earth to Adam." Marit waved her hand in front of my face. "Dude, is your brain off in never-never land?"

"Something like that." Before I could think better of it, I held out an arm.

Without hesitation, Marit came to me. She slid both arms around my waist and laid her cheek against my chest. I skimmed my hand over her hair, the honey-colored strands sliding like silk beneath my fingers. The wolf's joy bubbled up through my skin as we held on to each other.

"What a day." The words escaped her lips on a breath.

"Yeah," I agreed, glancing at the clock hanging on the kitchen wall. 1:06 a.m. Tomorrow was already beating down our door. We'd scheduled an early meeting. Marit should rest before she met the alpha and the pack. "It's late." I heard the regret in my voice. "We should turn in."

She lifted her face to mine, her expression serious. "First, I want you to do something for me, please."

My cock jumped in hopeful anticipation. I gritted my teeth and willed my voice to remain steady. "Anything you need. All you gotta do is ask."

She swallowed. "I'd like to meet your wolf when he isn't angry or about to tear someone apart."

Yes. Inside me, the wolf roared his approval. Twice Marit had witnessed him kill. If she was afraid of him—if she saw him only as a creature driven to do violence—his heart would shatter.

"All right." I pointed at the couch. "How about you sit down over there? It's better if you're outside the circle of light." Proximity to a shift wasn't dangerous for humans, but it was uncomfortable.

"Okay." She crossed the room and perched on the edge of the couch, hugging a pillow to her chest.

I pushed the coffee table out of the way, then stood in the middle of the braided rug. "Ready?"

She nodded, her fingers tightening on the pillow.

No enemy lurked nearby. No need to rush. I closed my eyes and tilted my face to the ceiling, summoning my wolf to the surface. A minute later, my lids slid open and I turned my gaze on Marit. She gasped. Already the wolf looked out through my eyes.

I unfastened my leather bracelet and held it out to Marit, entrusting her with the safekeeping of my black rock. Biting her lower lip, she clutched the bracelet in her fist.

With brisk, efficient movements, I yanked off my clothing. Boots and socks first, followed by my T-shirt. My fingers worked the buckle on my belt, and then I shoved my jeans and boxers down my thighs. Marit audibly gulped. My hands stilled and my gaze cut to her.

Nudity was no big deal in my world. A shifter typically stripped off their clothing before changing into a wolf. Good manners demanded that you don't leer at a naked packmate, but you couldn't help but get an eyeful. Like Marit was now. Her cheeks flushed a pretty pink, and she averted her eyes from my cock to the ceiling. I was one hundred percent okay with her checking me out, but if she felt embarrassed, I wouldn't make it worse by telling her that.

I finished divesting myself of my clothes, shook the tension out of my limbs, and called my wolf.

I'm ready, brother.

The air around me began to shimmer.

Pain inevitably accompanied a shift. Better to go lax and ride it out rather than to fight it. The wolf's claws burst through my fingertips. All my muscles and bones stretched and snapped into new configurations. My jaw unhinged, then elongated, reshaping into a powerful muzzle. Fur crawled up my arms and legs. I shuddered, and dropped down to the rug on four large paws.

My sharp senses took in my surroundings. I smelled the red cedar logs the cabin was built with, the ash in the fireplace hearth, the pink lilies on the kitchen table, and the leftover orange honey muffins still in a pan on the cooling rack.

I scented her, Marit, my mate. I breathed in the fragrance of vanilla and sugar she carried on her skin. She'd changed positions when I shifted, shrinking back against the sofa cushions, her knees drawn to her chest. I cocked my head, listening to the rapid thump of her heart banging against her chest.

Was she afraid of the wolf? No. Intolerable to frighten my mate. I assumed a nonthreatening position. Stretching my front legs out, I dropped my chest to the rug and raised my hindquarters into the air.

"Adam?" Her voice trembled.

The wolf whined softly and waggled his tail, inviting her to play.

After a long moment, she scooted to the edge of the couch and held out a hand. I walked forward and nosed her fingers.

"It's really you?" she whispered.

I dipped my chin, nodding my answer.

"Wow," she breathed. She carefully set my bracelet on an end table, then slipped forward onto her knees and held out both arms. "Come here." With a happy yip, my wolf nuzzled her face. Marit laughed and stroked my neck and throat. "What a beautiful, beautiful wolf," she crooned.

The wolf was beside himself with happiness, basking in her praise. He rolled onto his side, offering her his belly. With both hands, Marit scritched his fur, all the while murmuring words of admiration. She stretched her legs out and leaned against the front of the couch. The wolf laid his head across her thighs. Marit scratched around his ears. The wolf went limp with contentment.

"Adam," she said a few minutes later. I squinted up at her through eyes heavy with pleasure. "Thanks for showing me your wolf."

The wolf would happily spend the night sprawled across her lap, but I sensed she was ready to move. I sat up, and Marit clambered to her feet.

"I've been up since before six, and I'm super tired," she said. "I'm going to take a quick bath and then go to bed." She pointed to a carved wooden trunk sitting under a living room window. "There are extra blankets and pillows in the trunk. Would you mind sleeping on the sofa?"

The man hoped to share Marit's bed, but the wolf was amenable to sleeping anywhere that would allow him to watch over Marit and keep her safe. I trotted over to the cabin door and batted it with my paw.

"You want to go outside?" Marit asked.

I let out a wolf's whine. I wouldn't rest until I'd run the perimeter of the property, sniffing out any potential signs of danger.

"I'll leave the door cracked open for you," she said. "See you in the morning."

Cocking my head, I waited for the sound of the bedroom door clicking shut and water beginning to fill the tub before I took off into the dark. I circled the cabin and surrounding trees. No boogeymen lurked in the shadows. No stink from coyote intruders tickled my nose. All was well.

I loped back to the cabin. Once inside, I shifted to my human form, hitched my jeans up over my hips, and slapped the bracelet back on my wrist. I moved the fancy decorative pillows from the couch to a chair, then grabbed a blanket and bed pillow from the trunk.

Settling back against the pillow, I caught another whiff of the orange honey muffins. Shifting burned a lot of calories and always left me hungry. My stomach growled. Was it just yesterday that Marit and I had sat at the kitchen table—practically strangers—while I ate one of those muffins? So much had changed since then. Both of our worlds turned upside down. I followed my nose to the kitchen and helped myself to a muffin. It was still delicious, soft, and fresh. I savored every bite.

Wiping my fingers on my jeans, I made my way back to my bed. My legs were too long to stretch out flat. I had to prop my feet up on the armrest. No matter. I'd slept rough plenty of times. From the bedroom came the soft sound of Marit breathing. Good for her. I was glad she'd fallen asleep so easily. I wasn't as lucky. Thoughts of tomorrow's meeting raced round and round my head, holding sleep at bay.

CHAPTER TWENTY-THREE

MARIT

Annika, Liv, and I used to make up stories about the sprawling timber lodge perched on the opposite side of the lake. A hundred years ago, a rich lumber baron had built the four-story log palace. He spared no expense, creating a haven for the wealthy, a place they could indulge their gilded fantasies of life in the Old West.

Giddy newspaper articles reported on the grand opening in June of 1924. The proud owner invited Hollywood celebrities, socialites, magazine editors, and minor European royalty to the celebration. A grainy photo in the *Seattle Times* showed Rudolph Valentino standing next to a taxidermied grizzly bear in the lodge's lobby. Next to that photo, a picture of a Romanian princess admiring a painting of buffalo by the famous western artist C. M. Russell.

Even though it sat across the lake from the cabin, my cousins and I never got a good look at the place. The best we could do was to borrow Grandma's binoculars, stand on the edge of the water, and examine the back side of the lodge. Lights shone through the windows at night. Tendrils of smoke curled up from the massive stone chimneys. In summer, small figures moved about on the wide patio.

We had questions about the environmentalists who'd taken over the lodge and lake, questions Grandma steadfastly refused to entertain. Instead, she told us to mind our business and keep our distance from the conservancy folk.

I sat in silence now as Adam turned his truck onto the gravel drive leading to the lodge. Swinging my head from side to side, I took it all in. Finally, I'd get to see the entrance to the lodge and the elegant lobby. Would it still look like the photos from the grand opening?

Adam drove right past the object of my curiosity, parking instead in front of a small nondescript building. Black Rock Environmental Conservancy Administrative Offices, a sign next to the front door declared.

"Darn." I gave voice to my disappointment.

Adam shot me a look. "What?"

"Ever since I was a little girl, I've wanted to see the inside of the lodge. I've seen photos of it online, but never the real thing. I was hoping the meeting was there."

He chuckled. "I'll give you the tour later."

"I'd like that." I unfastened my seat belt but couldn't bring myself to open the door and climb from the truck. Instead, I asked, "What did you guys do with the grizzly bear? The one from the lobby."

"You mean Igor?" Humor flashed in Adam's eyes. "We put his moth-eaten carcass in the pack party hall. The teenagers like to dress him up. They put him in a diaper and a bonnet and stuck a pacifier in his mouth for the baby shower." He squinted, studying my face. "Are you stalling for time? You nervous about the meeting?"

Well, duh. I wasn't a little kid, so I wouldn't say that aloud, but acid was burning a hole in my stomach. I'd been distracting myself by thinking about the lodge. "I'm more than a little nervous," I admitted.

"My grandfather is a good man. The other sentries are all my friends. You'll like them." He paused. "My cousin Zane can be grouchy—"

"As grouchy as Olga?" I asked.

"Nobody's as grouchy as Olga," he conceded. "But don't worry. No matter what, I got you. You're safe." With that final assurance, he jumped out of the truck, jogged around to my side, and opened my door.

I'm okay, I whispered my mantra.

Hand-in-hand, we walked up the steps and into the building. A grim-faced older woman, her gray-streaked hair pulled back in a severe bun, sat behind a reception desk. She glanced disapprovingly down at our clasped hands, then lifted her gaze to Adam's face.

"The alpha wants to speak to you first, Adam." She inclined her head toward me; her lips twisted with distaste. "Without her."

My hackles rose. What had I done to piss her off?

Next to me, Adam bristled. "Olga, I'd like to introduce you to Freya Hagen's granddaughter, Marit. She's here at the invitation of the alpha."

Olga pressed her lips into a flat line.

Etiquette can be deployed as a weapon, a reproach against another person's bad behavior. I fell back on formal manners, speaking to Olga with the same politeness I'd show one of Dorrie Mittelmann's garden-club friends. "How do you do, ma'am? It's good to meet you." I couldn't bring myself to say, "nice to meet you." Good was a shade closer to the truth than nice. And it was certainly good to get the introduction out of the way.

Olga sniffed, not at all placated.

Down the hall behind the desk, a door swung open, and a tall, broad-shouldered man with blond hair stepped into the corridor. "Alpha's ready for you, Adam." He directed the words to Adam, but his curious gaze was fixed on my face.

"Be right there, Zane." Ignoring Olga, Adam dragged his knuckles over my cheek and pushed a lock of hair behind my ear, a gesture so intimate that it made me shiver. We were moving fast—faster than made sense—but it felt right. "I'll come to get you as soon as I've finished giving my report."

I nodded, then took a seat in one of the chairs across from the reception desk. Olga stared at her computer screen at first, ignoring me. Normally, when I'd find myself face-to-face with somebody as unfriendly as Olga, I did one of three things. I'd sling the attitude right back at them, kill them with kindness, or assume an air of haughty indifference.

Clearly, the woman didn't like me. Instead of resorting to one of my tried-and-true methods of dealing with hostility, I adopted a new, humiliating one. I slumped down into my chair and kept my mouth shut. The knowledge that the grim-faced biddy could morph into a wolf—complete with sharp claws and snapping teeth—made me positively meek. I trusted Adam's wolf, but I bet Olga's would cheerfully eat me for lunch.

The minutes ticked by. Every time I shifted positions in my chair, it creaked, and the sound drew the glowering Olga's eyes. She looked me up and down, taking in every element of my appearance, from my casual sneakers to my silver hoop earrings. Everything about me seemed to draw her ire. The saliva in my mouth dried up, and my throat and tongue felt parched. I ignored it as long as I could, finally walking over to a cold water dispenser on the far side of the waiting room. I guzzled down two small paper cups of water, then returned to my seat.

Half an hour later, Adam emerged from the conference room and crouched down in front of me. Rubbing my cool hands between his warm ones, he asked, "You ready?"

I wobbled to my feet, my legs unsteady. Dammit. *Get a hold of yourself. You're a grown woman—a Hagen—not a timid little bunny.* I squared my shoulders and imbued my voice with confidence. "I'm ready."

He dipped his chin and flashed a reassuring smile. We strode past Olga and down the short hallway. Head held high, I followed Adam into the meeting room. Five people sat around a long conference table. My eye was drawn to the head of the table where an elderly man—undoubtedly the alpha—sat.

Once again, my mouth went dry. There was nothing inherently menacing about the man. Unlike his wife, he didn't scowl or shoot me the evil eye. He didn't draw himself up, puff out his chest, or try to look intimidating. His expression was deceptively mild, if not downright pleasant. He looked like a kindly old uncle. An uncle who wore a shiny black rock pendant on a leather necklace. Power swirled around him so thick and potent that it clogged the air.

He patted the empty seat to his right. "Come sit by me, Marit."

With a hand on my lower back, Adam escorted me to his grandfather's side, then pulled out my chair. His old-fashioned manners felt deliberate, as if he was making some kind of statement to his pack. I sat down. Adam took the empty seat to my right.

Folding my hands in my lap, I waited for the alpha to speak first.

"I was sorry to hear of your grandmother's passing," he said. "Despite our differences, I admired and respected her."

I blinked, surprised. "Thank you, sir."

"Let me introduce you to Adam's fellow sentries." He pointed to the brawny, middle-aged man seated to his left. "Rolf, my senior sentry." I recognized the name, the man who'd ordered the cupcakes. Rolf gave a curt nod. "Next to him are Zane and Remy, Adam's cousins." I smiled at the pair, searching their faces for any family resemblance. Unlike Adam, they had blond hair and blue eyes, but something about the shape of their mouths and the set of their chins reminded me of him. Remy bobbed his head in greeting. Zane—the rumored grouch—ignored the social niceties and examined me under lowered brows. "And this is Kyra." The alpha gestured to a young woman with red hair and vivid green eyes. Finally, a genuine, openhearted smile from one of Adam's friends.

I returned her smile. "Nice to meet you all."

All of the sentries wore leather cords around their wrists, with wire-wrapped chunks of black rock, just like Adam. Interesting.

"Adam tells us that you've been drawn into our war with the coyotes." The alpha got right to the point.

Under the table, Adam reached for my hand. I twined my fingers through his, drawing comfort from his touch.

"Yes, sir—"

"Call me, Matthew," he interrupted. "We don't stand on formality around here."

"All right... Matthew..." Calling an elder by his first name felt odd, even with his permission.

"We deeply regret what you've endured at the coyotes' hands," he continued.

Endured? I shifted uncomfortably in the chair. I didn't like that word or how it painted me as a victim.

"I'm embarrassed that I allowed them to dupe me. It makes me question my judgment," I said slowly. "But mostly, I'm angry. Angry that they manipulated me. Angry that they tried to scare me into running back to Bryce. Angry that they used me to hurt your pack." I sucked in a breath, then pushed out the words before I could think better of it. "To hurt Adam."

Adam's fingers tightened on mine, and I glanced at his face. Through his glittering golden eyes, the wolf gazed at me with undisguised adoration. The world came to a standstill, as if we existed in the eye of a storm, a quiet lull before winds buffeted us once again. I swayed, my body listing toward his.

Matthew cleared his throat. "You know our secret."

I tore my eyes away from Adam and looked at his grandfather. "I do know your secret. And I promise that I'll keep it, even from my cousins."

We could've talked it over for hours, I suppose. The alpha could've reiterated all the reasons why I had to keep my mouth shut, why the existence of shifters had to remain hidden from the human world. He could've threatened me if I blabbed. Instead, he accepted my promise at face value.

"Good enough," he said in a voice that implied 'case closed.'

"Grandpa—" Scowling, Zane spoke up.

The alpha waved a hand, cutting off Zane's protests. "Marit said she'll keep our secret, and I take her at her word."

"Did Grandma Freya know that she was living next to a pack of wolf shifters?" I asked. If she did, she held the knowledge close to her chest, maybe for decades.

"No. I ordered my people not to shift within sight of the cabin. We generally kept our distance from her."

They kept their distance from her? Everything I'd learned about the pack carried the ring of truth, everything except this.

"With the coyotes breathing down your necks, I finally understand why you were so eager to buy Grandma's lease." I hesitated before continuing, but there was no avoiding the unpleasant subject. "What I don't understand is all the petty and mean-spirited vandalism. Breaking her things. Stealing her things. Locking a skunk in the cabin." I threw my hands in the air. "How can you justify that?"

"I can't justify it." Matthew leaned forward and met my bewildered gaze. "When Adam told me about the vandalism, I was shocked. I knew nothing about it. I certainly never sanctioned it. If I'd known, I would have put a stop to it and punished the perpetrators."

There was no doubting the alpha's honesty. The truth of his words reverberated in every cell in my body. Still, a question remained. "If it wasn't your people, then who? Who could sneak onto pack lands and make mischief? It wouldn't benefit the coyotes, so who did it?"

"That I can't tell you." Frustration stamped his features. "I have my sentries looking into it. If anybody in my pack tormented your grandmother, it's a stain on our honor." Again, his sincerity was undeniable.

"Okay." I nodded, making peace with the new knowledge. "Now what?"

"You're on the coyotes' radar because of the pack. We'll protect you."

"I'll protect you." Adam laid a reassuring hand on my shoulder.

Zane and Remy stirred in their seats. I glanced their way and saw them exchange raised brows. Cousins could be as protective of each other as siblings, at least in my experience. Good. I was glad Adam had people in his corner, the way I had Annika and Liv.

"Are you and Adam heading back to town today?" the alpha asked.

I turned to Adam. "I'd like for us to stay another night at the cabin, if that works for your schedule." In front of his alpha and packmates, I was asking him if he'd like to spend the night with me again. What they'd think of my proposition, I had no idea, but the room fell silent, as if everyone was holding their breaths.

The wolf resurfaced in Adam's eyes. A smile crawled across his face. "That's fine. Gives us time for that tour of the lodge I promised you. We can go back to Belle Reve tomorrow."

Sitting up straight, I turned to the alpha of the Guardians of the Black Rock pack. My pulse pounded in my throat. Grandma taught my cousins and me to do the right thing, even when it cost us. Certainty took root in my heart. I knew what I had to do.

"When Grandma was dying, I promised her that I'd *never* sell you the lease to the cabin. That's a promise that I can't break."

"I understand." Matthew inclined his head.

"But Grandma didn't know you're wolf shifters. She didn't know how many people you lost in the Great War, or why you needed to protect yourselves by controlling access to your land." I paused, summoning the strength to spit out the next words.

Adam's fingers slid across my cheek. "Marit, what are you saying?"

I gave him a tremulous smile, but directed my words to the alpha. "You trusted me when I promised to keep your secret.

I'm ready to trust you to keep your word, too. I... I *can't* sell you the lease, but if you promise to leave the cabin as it is, and to allow me to visit it whenever I want, I'll sign papers and give the lease to the pack."

CHAPTER TWENTY-FOUR

ADAM

Marit was willing to give the pack her lease, free and clear? I didn't see that coming. Shock almost knocked me off my chair.

If she sold us the lease, she'd walk away from the deal flush with cash. Instead—with one unselfish act—she honored her promise to her dead grandmother, passed up a windfall, and did right by the pack. Admiration and pride swelled in my chest.

We chose well, brother.

The wolf huffed his agreement.

Grandpa leaned forward, a puzzled expression on his face. "Why?"

Marit lifted a shoulder. "It's the right thing to do. And it gives us both what we really want."

Grandpa's gaze sharpened. "What do you really want?" Alpha power crackled in the air and filled his voice with a force—a compulsion to obey—that no shifter could resist.

"I want..." Marit swallowed. "I want to be able to spend time in my favorite place, surrounded by things that remind me of Grandma." Her eyes cut to mine. "And I want to explore whatever is happening between Adam and me."

Guess the alpha voice worked on humans, too.

Grandpa nodded once. "I agree to your terms. The lease will be ours, but the cabin is yours, and you can visit whenever you like."

The ever-practical Rolf spoke up. "My mate is the pack's attorney. She'll prepare the paperwork."

"Whenever it's ready, I'll sign," Marit said.

Grandpa rose from his chair and straightened to his full height, a triumph of willpower over the weakness that ravaged his body. Three steps brought him to Marit's side. He held out his hand.

She hopped to her feet and took the proffered hand. "It was nice to meet you, sir. I'm glad we could reach an accommodation that benefits us both."

He held on for a minute, studying her face. "It was nice to meet you, too, Marit. I see why my grandson cares about you."

Marit stood up on her tiptoes and kissed his cheek, a spontaneous act so unexpected that my breath froze. Generally, people didn't touch the alpha. What would Grandpa make of the forward human?

He smiled and his eyes twinkled. The alpha liked Marit. If Olga was here, no doubt she'd pitch a fit. Some of the tension eased in my chest. Whether he'd agree to a mating was yet to be seen, but I couldn't have asked for a better start.

"I understand that Adam promised you a tour of the lodge," he said.

"He did. I've seen photos of the grand opening of the place back in 1924. I can't wait to see what it looks like now."

Grandpa shook his head apologetically. "It looks very different now. The original owner's heirs sold all the works of art long before we purchased the place."

"But you got to keep Igor," Marit reminded him.

"Yes, indeed." With a smile, Grandpa relinquished her hand. "We got to keep Igor."

After a round of goodbyes, Marit and I decided to stretch our legs and walk over to the lodge. My curious packmates' heads were on a swivel as we passed, but they kept their distance. She squeezed my fingers as we climbed the steps and walked through the entry into the lodge lobby.

The architecture still looked grand—a vaulted ceiling, massive cross timbers, gleaming hardwood floors, and a huge stone fireplace—but the place had a cozy, lived-in appearance. Instead of western paintings, plain old bulletin and white boards hung on the lobby walls, covered with announcements about meetings and pack activities. Three big couches and overstuffed chairs formed a rough U in front of the fireplace. A corner of the lobby had been turned into a play area for kids, complete with a pint-sized table and chairs, toys, and books.

Two little girls were making something out of plastic building blocks while their babysitter sprawled, phone in hand, in a nearby chair. Spying us, the girls' faces lit up.

"Adam!" They dashed toward us. I crouched down, and the girls flung themselves on me.

With an *oof*, I fell backward, pretending that they knocked me over onto my ass. Chattering excitedly, the girls told me all about the dinosaur they were constructing. When they paused to catch their breath, I made introductions.

"Tory, Emma, say hi to my friend Marit Hagen."

"Hi," they echoed, their eyes wide. Most pack kids weren't shy, but they didn't meet many strangers.

Marit dropped down to the floor and sat cross-legged next to me. "Hi, Tory. Hi, Emma. That sounds like quite a dinosaur you're building."

"It is." Emma launched into a description of their pink-and-purple triceratops.

Tory joined in the discussion, then asked, "You wanna see?"

"Yes, please," Marit said.

Tory and Emma hopped up and held out hands for Marit, who tossed a grin over her shoulder as she took their hands and followed the little girls to the play area. Perching on a child-sized chair, she oohed and aahed over their creation.

Through my eyes, the wolf watched with rapt attention. *She likes children.*

She does, I concurred, smiling to myself as Marit laughed with delight over something Emma said.

I'd always taken it for granted that I'd be a father someday, and I'd presumed that any children I had would be wolf shifters... That we'd run together through the forest in our animal forms... That I'd teach them how to hunt, to stalk, and bring down prey.

If I mated with Marit, any children we had would remain locked forever in their human forms. Did I care? Would I regret not bonding with a fellow wolf? I watched as Tory hugged Marit, and Marit ruffled the little girl's hair with easy affection.

No.

Conviction pushed aside any doubts. Children or not, wolf pups or not, I'd never regret choosing Marit.

As if feeling my eyes on her, she glanced my way. Rising to her feet, she exchanged a few final words with the girls, then walked back to me. "They're adorable," she declared.

I took her hand. "C'mon. I want to show you the rest of the place."

I led her through an arched opening and into the dining hall, originally the lodge's fancy restaurant. Floor-to-ceiling windows gave a primo view of Shooting Star Lake. Three big chandeliers decorated with bronze horse heads hung from the high ceiling. The original carved wooden tables and chairs dotted the floor. A dozen packmates sat around eating breakfast. I stopped at a table where two women were seated, and introduced Marit to Rolf's mate and his daughter.

"You made the cupcakes for my baby shower," Bethany exclaimed. "Oh my God, they were good, especially the chocolate one with salted caramel filling." She moaned. "I wish I'd socked away a dozen for later."

Marit laughed. "If you like, I'll give you Grandma's recipe so you can make them whenever the craving strikes."

"Really?" Bethany looked surprised. "It's not a top-secret recipe?"

"Grandma didn't believe in top-secret recipes," Marit said. "Why keep a good thing all to yourself?"

Marit chose to share, an essential characteristic for a successful life in a pack. Under my skin, the wolf rumbled with satisfaction.

We said our goodbyes and continued the tour. I showed her the party room where Igor presided over our festivities, the library, the clinic, and the school.

"Where's your room?" Marit asked, bumping her shoulder against mine.

"Fourth floor." My pulse ratcheted up at the prospect of taking Marit to my quarters. "Grandpa and Olga live in the old presidential suite at one end of the top floor. The sentries have rooms on the other end."

"I'd love to see it."

"I'd love to show it to you," I said slowly. "You want to take the elevator or the stairs?"

"The stairs."

We climbed the wide wooden steps, pausing on each landing to admire the view of the lake. When we got to the top floor, we turned right and walked down a long corridor to my room. I swung open the door and gestured for Marit to go first.

She tilted her head. "You don't lock your door?"

Took me a moment to suss out where she was coming from. Of course. In the human world, only a fool would leave their place unlocked and vulnerable to thieves.

"No need. Shifters don't steal from each other, and it's bad form to come into somebody's personal space uninvited. We lock our doors only when we want privacy."

"Is that right?" she said. We stepped into my room. I followed her inside and shut the door. Reaching past me, she turned the thumb latch on the deadbolt, locking out the world.

My heart kicked against my chest. Was she saying what I thought she was saying?

While I stood stock-still next to the door, Marit strolled across the room, pausing in front of my bookcase. She traced her finger along one row of books and then another. "Classics. Thrillers. History. Sci-fi. You have eclectic tastes, Adam."

I got my feet in motion and joined her in front of the bookcase. "I've always loved to read." I pointed to the faux-leather upholstered armchair and ottoman I'd positioned next to a window. "That's my favorite reading spot. I can look out over the lake and the trees, and get lost in a good book."

Marit crossed to the window and laid a hand against the glass. "I can see the cabin from here. How many times…" Her voice faltered, and the vulnerability I sensed in her earlier returned. I closed the distance between us, the separation intolerable. Still looking out the window, she leaned back against me, molding her body to mine. I snaked one arm around her waist and held her close. Her breath hitched, then she started speaking again. "How many times were you and I right across the lake from each other, yet we never met, never knew the other existed?"

"Guess fate chose just the right time for us to finally meet," I murmured against her hair.

She jerked. "Fate?"

"Yeah, fate." I pushed her shiny hair off one shoulder, then nuzzled behind her ear and down her neck, drawing in the delectable scent of sugar, vanilla, and woman. Beneath my lips, her pulse quickened.

"You told me wolves believe fate brings soulmates together," she said slowly.

"That's right." I tasted the skin at the juncture of her neck and shoulder.

She angled her head to the side, exposing more flesh to my questing tongue and teeth. "You said a wolf mates only once, and that mating is for life."

"Mm-hmm." Her taste and scent flooded my mouth. Every nerve ending in my body sparked to life.

"Adam, wait." She pulled my hand away from her waist, turned around, and clutched at my arms. Her eyes searched my face, her expression serious. "If you believe fate brought us together, does that mean you think *I'm* your mate?"

I stilled, every muscle in my body locking tight.

Trust Marit to come right to the point.

After all the lies Bryce told Marit—how he distorted the whole notion of fate—the truth might send her running for the hills. But I couldn't withhold the truth from the woman who was my mate.

"The wolf figured it out before I did." One side of my mouth turned up in a wry smile. "That's usually how it happens. But, yeah, Marit. I believe that you're my mate."

Her fingers dug into my biceps. "I like you. A lot. God knows I'm attracted to you. I feel connected to you in a way that doesn't really make sense. But mating?" She sliced her head from side to side. "I'm not ready to sign up for a life-long commitment."

The wolf whined.

"I understand." I didn't like it, but I got where she was coming from. Fated mates was a concept totally foreign to humans. It would take time for her to wrap her head around it.

"In your world, I have a choice about mating, don't I? I can say no, right?" She held her breath, waiting for my answer.

My wolf barked a protest. I ignored him.

"Of course. Both parties enter a mating of their own free will." I couldn't resist touching her. I slid my fingers across her cheeks and over her honey-colored hair.

"How does it work?" she asked. "Do people exchange vows, like at a wedding?"

"No." I hesitated. I didn't want to frighten her with the violence inherent to every mating.

"Then what?" she persisted.

I forced the words out. "A claiming bite during sex seals the mating. Here—" I touched the spot between her shoulder and neck where I'd already tasted her skin. She shivered. "The bite would leave a scar and imprint you with my scent. It'd mark you as mine. Every shifter would understand what it means."

"A bite seals the deal, so to speak?" she asked.

"Yes."

Her brow puckered. "Would I bite you back?"

The question went straight to my cock. "I'd like nothing better."

"Can we... um... can we have sex without the bite, without mating?"

My cock almost punched a hole in my jeans. "We can. I won't claim you without your consent." Shit. Was that gravelly voice mine?

"Okay." She bit her lower lip. "Okay," she repeated as if speaking to herself, as if making up her mind about something. Her hands fell to my belt, and her fingers started to work the buckle. She paused. "Do I have your consent to do this?"

"Hell, yeah." I moaned.

She took her time pushing the metal prong through the hole in the leather and tugging the belt tip through the buckle. I held my breath, watching transfixed as she loosened the button on my fly and lowered the zipper. Her thumbs caught the waistband on my jeans and boxers and shoved them down my thighs and past my knees. My cock sprung free.

In a graceful motion, Marit sank to her knees. She brushed her lips over my happy trail, that narrow strip of hair that ran from my navel to my groin. My abdominal muscles clenched. She nipped my skin, capturing a short dark hair between her teeth. I gasped. Raising her eyes to mine, Marit laughed low in her throat.

Her head dipped. She pressed her open mouth against my groin and blew a warm breath into the dark, springy hair. She inhaled, slowly drawing in my scent. "Mmm," she hummed, as intent on tasting my musk as any shifter woman I'd been with.

Still making happy noises, she cupped my balls with one hand. With the other, she wrapped her fingers around the base of my cock. Already, the skin was stretched taut over a hard-on that bucked in her hand. From bottom to tip, Marit fluttered her tongue along the underside of the shaft, circling the tip before slowly sucking it into her mouth.

As if they had a will of their own, my fingers tunneled through her hair, cradling her skull and holding her in place.

Her cheeks hollowed out as she sucked my cock in and out, drawing it deeper into her mouth with each pull. When it was good and slippery, she made a circle out of her thumb and forefinger and slid her fingers up and down my slick cock. Sucking and sliding, the sensations built on one another till I was close to losing it.

"Fuck." Could not believe I was putting a stop to this. With a regret-filled groan, I pulled out.

Marit blinked up at me, her mouth open, her parted lips shiny and puffy. I groaned again, wanting nothing more than to shove my cock between those soft lips. Slicing my head from side to side, I got a hold of myself.

"First time I come in you," I choked out the words. "Don't want it to be in your mouth."

Marit sat back on her heels, a saucy smile on her face. "But the second time is definitely a yes? I mean, depending on how long it takes you to get ready for another round. We've got all day—"

She shrieked as I swooped down and threw her over my shoulder, pinning her in place with a hand across her ass. Turning to the king-sized bed, I took one stumbling step, then halted. I was still wearing my boots, and my jeans were bunched up below my knees. Best I could manage like this was an undignified shuffle toward the bed.

"Dammit," I muttered. Marit giggled. I toed off my boots, kicked away my jeans, then smacked her ass, once, and not hard, but it got her attention.

"Hey." Her whole body jerked.

"No?" I held still while I waited for her answer. Wolves were playful in bed, and nothing was forbidden, but Marit wasn't a wolf. I'd have to learn what she liked.

"Um… yes." To emphasize the point, she reached down my back and dragged her fingernails up my ass. The small bite of pain sent my libido into the stratosphere. My feet couldn't move fast enough. I strode across the room, pulled back the covers, and dumped her across my bed.

CHAPTER TWENTY-FIVE

MARIT

I bounced on the mattress, breathless and giddy. Excitement zinged along every nerve ending. I felt it in the pulse that hammered my throat and in the anticipation that curled my toes. My nipples ached with an almost painful sensitivity, and desire thrummed deep in my core.

Breathe.

Adam stood at the foot of the bed, undisguised hunger on his face. I gloried in his naked lust almost as much as I did in his naked—or almost naked—body. Sitting up on my elbows, I pointed to his black T-shirt.

"You have too many clothes on."

A slight, pleased smile curved his lips. He peeled the tee off over his head, baring his gloriously muscular chest, beautifully defined shoulders, and a chiseled six-pack. The man was perfection, more cut than a classical statue of a Greek god, more buff than the men on the covers of Annika's romance novels. My fingers itched to stroke his smooth skin.

"What about you?" he drawled, sweeping his gaze over my fully clothed body.

"Me? I have waaay too many clothes on." I batted my eyelashes. "If only someone could do something about it."

Moving like a blur, Adam grabbed my left ankle and hauled my body to the edge of the bed. With deft hands, he untied my shoelaces, slid the sneakers from my feet, and tossed them backward over his shoulder. My socks followed. I wiggled my liberated toes.

Adam planted one knee on the mattress. "Hmmm…"

The speculative, drawn-out syllable made my insides flutter. He fixed his predatory gaze on my face, his golden eyes glittering. He intended me no harm. I *knew* it; still, I had an unexpected deer-in-the-headlights moment, half expecting him to pounce. My body froze. My muscles locked. I struggled to draw breath. It took three tries to swallow the lump in my throat.

"Adam?" I croaked.

He smiled, and any sense of menace dissolved and disappeared, like morning fog giving way to sunshine. With slow deliberation, he reached for the waistband on my yoga pants. I lifted my hips, making it easier for him to draw the black leggings and panties down my thighs. One flick of his wrist and they sailed across the room, joining my sneakers on the floor. Adam's big hands slid up my legs, skimming over my calves, knees, thighs, and belly.

"Sit up," he demanded roughly. I obeyed without hesitation. Why fuss about him giving orders when he was doing exactly what I wanted? He caught the hem of my tee, pulled it over my head, and tossed it aside. Reaching behind me, he unfastened my bra, slid the straps down my arms, and sent it flying, too. "Much better," he murmured, his gaze caressing my nakedness. He touched the teardrop-shaped amethyst that dangled from one of my small hammered-silver hoop earrings, the only things I still wore. "Pretty."

"Thank you," I whispered. This wasn't the time to say that I'd inherited the earrings from Grandma. She loved them and wore them all the time, even in the photos that Dorrie had taken of her at Woodstock in 1969.

His thumb brushed across my jaw and over my lower lip. "That kiss—" he started.

"Wrecked me," I finished.

He lowered his chin; his eyes fixed on my mouth. "Yeah."

I'd been kissed countless times over the years by guys who hadn't a clue and by men who definitely knew what they were doing. Never before had the prospect of a kiss filled me with so much quivering anticipation, such a sense of wanton exhilaration. I angled up into a seated position, reached for him with greedy hands, and sunk my fingernails into his shoulders.

Adam gave a low, reproachful laugh. He manacled my wrists and tugged my hands away from his body. Eyes locked on mine, and moving with slow deliberation, he kissed the tip of each of my fingers. "First my ass and now my shoulders. You like to scratch, don't you, kitten?"

Kitten.

Why did the endearment make me wriggle with happiness? Bryce had insisted on calling me sweet cheeks, even after I told him I didn't like the nickname. One more sign I should have cued into. My smile faltered.

"What?" Adam tilted his head.

"I like you calling me kitten," I said. "Bryce used to call me—"

"No," he interrupted, the vehemence in his voice startling me. "When you're naked in my bed, I don't want to hear another man's name cross your lips."

"But you asked—"

"Yeah, I did." His voice gentled. "Lemme tell you about shifters. We're loyal to the core. We'd never betray or harm our mates."

Loyal to the core? Never betray or harm a mate? After Bryce, that sounded like a dream come true.

He continued. "But possessiveness is hardwired into our DNA. We don't share. And I sure as hell don't want to hear you talking about another man when we're about to fuck."

"You're bossy."

"Most shifters are. And remember, I come from the bloodline of an alpha."

Well, wasn't that convenient? "You're telling me you *inherited* a double dose of wanna-be-in-charge?"

He shrugged. "Let's just say leadership and authority are an intrinsic part of my nature."

Whoa. "Listen up, Mr. Bossy Pants; I'm not the type of woman who will jump when a man barks an order."

Adam laughed softly and pushed me backward onto the mattress. Supporting his weight on his forearms, he stretched out on top of me, his hard cock pressing against my thigh.

"Your powers of observation are failing you, kitten. I'm not wearing pants."

Reminding me that he was naked while calling me my new favorite nickname? The man was not playing fair. Still, I summoned the wherewithal to pursue my point.

"I mean it, Adam. I'm nobody's doormat."

"Don't want a doormat." He nuzzled my neck, as if drawn like a magnet to the spot where he hoped to brand me with a claiming bite. "I admire strength. I want a partner—"

"Who does what she's told," I suggested, shoving at his chest.

His head reared back, and he stared down at me, his eyes heavy with desire. "Sometimes," he conceded. "When it matters. But I meant what I said, too. I want a strong woman at my side." His head dropped. He brushed his lips over my throat, then nibbled along my jawline. "I want you, Marit Hagen."

Simple words spoken with absolute conviction. He offered affection, respect, and desire. Not a bad way to start a relationship. My resistance melted. I'd stated my position. We'd sort out the details of all this bossiness stuff later. Threading my fingers through his hair, I lifted my face to meet his.

"And I want you, Adam Landry."

His answering smile could have melted the ice caps or warmed an arctic wasteland. We locked eyes. Something ineffable passed between us, our mysterious connection weaving together even more tightly.

I could love this man.

The realization burrowed into my psyche. I blinked watery eyes.

Adam gently touched one of the tears that beaded my lashes. He raised his finger to his mouth and licked the wetness from its tip. "You're safe," he murmured. The words encompassed more than the pack's promise of protection from their coyote enemies. My heart was safe with him. If I let him in, he'd never hurt or betray me, the way Bryce did.

At least, that was what I thought he meant. And if I was wrong?

"You could really mess me up," I worried out loud.

He jerked his head in a quick no. "That'll never happen," he vowed, cupping my face between his hands. "I'm a wolf shifter. I'd die before I hurt my mate."

The black rock on his leather bracelet rested on my chin. Instead of cool—like I expected—the stone felt warm against my skin, as if possessed of an inner fire. That heat spread throughout my body, kindling a restless excitement in my core. My thighs softened, and Adam settled securely between them, his erection heavy against my sex.

"Adam," I whispered, undulating beneath him. His thick cock slid over my slick folds, the exquisite pressure feeding the flames that licked along my nerve endings.

Groaning, he lowered his head. His mouth hovered a fraction of an inch above mine, his breath skating over my lips. We lingered in a moment suspended in time while my stuttering pulse counted down the seconds before… before whatever would happen next.

Adam closed the distance between our mouths, shaping his lips against mine in a long, claiming kiss that robbed me of my breath. Pure pleasure rippled up my spine. I gasped, arching my back. A hand slid from my face to my breasts. He brushed a thumb over my nipple, the calloused pad creating a delicious friction.

Swallowing my moans, he scraped a fingernail across the super sensitive nub. I whimpered.

Dear God, what was happening to me? I was usually slow to warm up. With Bryce, for the first ten minutes I was only mildly interested. But Adam's touch instantly reduced me to a quivering mess. The need to be filled up and consumed by this shifter overwhelmed my senses.

He tore his mouth away from mine, his chest heaving. The same volcanic desire that swamped me apparently had him in its grips, too. Fighting for breath, he gazed down at me through eyes feverish with carnal craving.

"Next... time... slow?" he gritted out.

If that meant this time fast, I was one hundred percent on board. I bobbed my head, unable to find my voice.

"Say it," he commanded, his voice thick.

A tremulous smile, then my lips managed to shape a word. "Bossy."

Eyes hooded, he growled. He actually growled.

The hairs on the back of my neck sprung to attention. If anything, my lust burned brighter, white-hot, blurring the edges of my vision. Whimpering, I yielded. "Yes. Next time slow."

My compliance pleased him, if that satisfied nod was any indication. Adam's attention shifted, his raptor-like eyes honing in on the exact place where he'd bite me if we mated. Without warning, his head swooped down. His teeth grazed over my jugular vein, then his mouth latched onto the spot where neck meets shoulder. My pulse jackhammered, my heart almost punching a hole in my chest.

I panted, every nerve ending thrumming with anticipation. He'd promised that he wouldn't bite me without my consent, but if he asked right now—shit—if he asked right now, I'd say yes. It wouldn't be informed consent. Not exactly. I was in no state to think clearly about anything. A desperate, rapacious need clamored to be fed, and pushed aside all rational thought.

I waited with bated breath, half expecting sharp teeth to slice my flesh, the coppery scent of my own blood to fill my nostrils. His lips formed an O. I braced myself. Instead of biting, he sucked hard, so hard that capillaries must have exploded beneath my skin.

I gasped. "Did you... did you give me a hickey?"

Adam chuckled, drew back, and fingered the spot, a smug expression on his handsome face. "Yeah, I did. I promised not to bite—this time—but I still wanted to leave my mark."

Laughing softly, I slapped his chest.

Powerful hands banded my wrists. "Watch those claws, kitten," he warned, pressing my hands against the mattress on either side of my head.

I wriggled, testing my confinement. He held me firmly in place, a fact that filled me with unexpected glee. Jutting out my lower lip, I blew a strand of hair off my face.

"You promised fast, wolf, but it looks to me like you're taking your sweet time."

At the playful word "wolf," he arched a brow. "Is that right?" Leaning forward, he brushed his mouth over mine. The tip of his tongue traced the seam of my lips, then plunged inside. Like gasoline on a fire, the kiss stoked the passion that once again roiled throughout me.

"Please, Adam," I begged.

He nuzzled my throat, then dragged his bristly chin over the still-sensitive love bite. "I'm a man of my word," he growled into my ear. Releasing my hands, he levered himself up on one arm. He slid a hand down between our bodies and positioned the blunt head of his cock against my slick opening. My eyelids drifted shut, and I floated, weak and oh-so-ready. "Open your eyes, and look at me," he ordered.

I obeyed. The naked hunger that glittered in his golden orbs made me shiver. Raw desire ripped through me. His gaze locked on mine, then, with one powerful thrust, he slammed home. I gulped in air, and my eyes rolled back in my head. Not because it hurt. It didn't. But because I felt full to the brim, my body occupied, possessed by this man who claimed he was my mate.

He rocked backward and withdrew the hard shaft. The head of his cock bobbed against my slit.

"No." Bereft, I moaned, locking my ankles behind his back and arching against him in a brazen invitation. I needed more. More delectable friction. More heat. More of the sensation of being stretched to my limit. God. When have I ever been this insatiable? I clutched his ass, my nails gouging his skin, urging him on, reminding him that his kitten had claws.

With a grunt, he drove back into me, breaching my core. One large hand wrapped around my upper thigh, tilting my hips up to meet the thrusts, allowing him to go deep. True to his word, he rode me hard and fast. There would be plenty of time later to linger over foreplay, to explore each other's bodies, to learn what made the other sigh or tremble. Now, the rough, relentless possession was exactly what I needed. I squeezed my inner muscles, clamping down hard on his rampaging cock.

I thrashed my head from side to side as trembling took hold inside me and an impending orgasm bore down on me. "Adam," I gasped. "I'm close."

Unholy golden light flashed in his eyes. Beads of sweat trickled down his temples. Panting, he held himself above me, his beautiful body rock-hard. "Come for me." He gave a savage thrust. "Now."

I didn't want to scream—not in the pack's lodge—so I fastened my teeth on his shoulder, clamping down hard enough to leave indentations. He welcomed my mark; he'd said as much. I took him at his word, biting down as I spasmed around him.

Adam stilled. His cock grew impossibly bigger, seeming to lock into place deep inside my sex. What... what was happening? He shuddered and groaned, his back arching. A sudden flush of heat as hot jets of cum flooded my pussy. He came and came and came, spurting for almost a minute. I couldn't hold it all. Warm fluid slid onto my thighs. Supporting his weight on his arms, Adam pressed his forehead against mine. His breathing returned to normal, and the pulse beating on the side of his neck slowed down. He kissed me, a kiss that lacked the scorching heat of our first one, but was filled with a tenderness that curled my toes, a promise of what the slower *next time* would be like.

"You good?" he asked, brushing his knuckles over my cheek.

No words could adequately express how good I felt at that moment. I nodded, with what had to be a goofy smile on my face.

"Be right back." Adam rolled off the bed and strode across the room toward a closed door, his bathroom, no doubt. Turning onto my side, I admired his broad back and narrow hips, the play of muscles in his sculpted ass as he walked. Dear lord, the man was beyond gorgeous.

And not completely human, that small inner voice reminded me.

Don't care, I retorted, already wrapping my head around the notion that two spirits existed within Adam. When in human form, he was a man. When in animal form, a wolf. Simple. Mind-boggling, paradigm-altering, upending-everything-I-thought-I-knew-about-the-world, but simple.

Adam disappeared into the bathroom. Water gurgled from the tap. A minute later, he reappeared carrying a towel and a wet washcloth.

"Scoot closer."

I bounced sideways across the white sheet. Adam sat on the edge of the bed. With gentle hands, he washed my thighs and pressed the warm cloth against my still-sensitive folds.

"What are you doing?" I asked. No man had ever tended to me after sex.

Adam met my startled eyes. "Taking care of the woman who will be my mate."

An unwelcome memory intruded. *You might want to clean up.* Bryce's voice, accompanied by a yawn as he rolled over in bed. Why had I ever thought that what Bryce and I had was good enough?

I swallowed, overwhelmed by the stark difference between the two men.

"Thank you."

His hands stilled. "You don't get it, do you? A shifter's mate is the center of their universe. Keeping you safe, providing for all your needs, is both a duty and a pleasure."

"What about love?" I asked quickly. Just a few days ago, I'd wished upon a star, asking the universe for true love. Did emotion factor into the mating equation, or was it all about this cosmic connection and duty?

Adam tapped his chest. "I feel it. Right here. The seeds have been planted and have taken root. Give it a little time and love will grow." He laid his fingers over my heart. "How about you? Do you feel it, too?"

The world might call it crazy to fall so hard so fast, but there was no denying the truth. "I do. I feel—" I searched for the right word. "I feel the *potential* for love."

His smile shone like the sun emerging from behind a cloud, bright and full of warmth. "It's a good start."

He resumed his task, patting me dry with the towel, then tossing it aside. It landed on the sheet next to the damp spot I'd vacated. Wrinkling my brow, I pointed at the dark splotch. "Is that... is that common?" I stopped myself before I used the word "normal." Normal struck me as a little judgy when asking about the propensities of another species.

Adam shrugged. "It's a wolf shifter thing."

"What do you mean?"

"We come longer and harder than human men." He tilted his head and raked me with a curious gaze. "That a problem for you?"

A laugh escaped me. "Seriously? It felt amazing, although I am going to buy more towels, or maybe a few waterproof pads. I'm not sleeping on a giant wet spot."

"Fair enough. We'll go online later and order whatever you want." He climbed onto the bed, leaned against the headboard, and pulled me onto his lap.

Tucking my head beneath his chin, I settled against his chest. I sighed, perfectly content, while my fingers toyed with a strand of his dark hair.

Adam inhaled slowly. "You carry my scent." He touched the hickey on my neck. "And my mark." Satisfaction colored his voice.

"You make it sound like that's a good thing."

He nuzzled my throat. "It is."

I traced the incriminating red mark with my fingers. "Does that mean your packmates will be able to tell that we had sex?"

"Of course."

I squirmed, suddenly self-conscious. I was a grown woman. Sex was natural and nothing to be embarrassed about. Still, I'd rather not broadcast the fact that I'd slept with Adam to a bunch of strangers all possessed of a wolf's super sharp sense of smell. I heaved a sigh. This conversation was odd. Bryce would gag if I talked about wet spots, or he'd try to hustle me into the shower if he detected a whiff of post coital funk.

Adam's arms tightened around me. "What are you thinking about?"

"He whose name may not be spoken." I was skirting the rules by referring to my ex. I glanced at Adam's face, watching for his reaction. I didn't want to be on guard around him, afraid of saying or doing the wrong thing.

With one hand, he rubbed slow circles on my back. "Why are you thinking about that asshole right now?" His voice held more curiosity than heat.

"I keep mentally comparing the two of you," I admitted. "And every single time he comes up short."

Adam grunted, clearly pleased by my answer. His fingers warm, his touch soothing, he continued to caress my back. After a minute, he spoke again. "I hope that someday he'll stop butting into your thoughts."

"Me, too. I'm so ready to be done with him." I burrowed into his embrace, as boneless and relaxed as the kitten he called me.

Adam dropped a kiss onto my temple. "He'll never hurt you again. That's a—"

Thunderous pounding against the bedroom door cut off his words. Somebody tried the knob, but the deadbolt prevented the door from swinging open.

"Adam," a male voice called.

Within a heartbeat, Adam jumped to his feet and strode naked across the room. He flattened one palm against the door while he unlocked the deadbolt. He glanced back over his shoulder at me.

"Ready?" he mouthed.

I yanked the sheet up to cover my breasts. Shifters might be fine with casual nudity, but I wasn't about to flash one of his packmates.

He opened the door. The person in the hall pushed against it, but Adam held firm, allowing the door to swing open only a foot.

Zane peered over Adam's shoulder and spied me in the bed. His blond head jerked back, and his nostrils widened. Busted. Not only did I carry Adam's scent, the room positively reeked of sex. Pretending a nonchalance of the fake-it-till-you-make-it variety, I lifted a hand and waved at Adam's cousin.

He ignored me.

"What's going on?" Adam demanded.

"Phones in the administrative office are blowing up," Zane said. "We're fielding calls from the Belle Reve cops, the Washington State Police, and the Department of Fish and Wildlife."

"Fuck." Adam sighed. "The body in the park?"

"The coroner identified it as a wolf kill. The townspeople are up in arms over bloodthirsty wolves roaming the city and attacking citizens. They're making runs on the gun shops."

Adam groaned. "All we need are riled-up townspeople coming onto pack land to take potshots at wolves."

"Yeah, and get this. Fish and Wildlife wants to meet with *the conservancy*." Zane made air quotes around the name. "They want to talk about putting radio tracking collars on the native wolf pack and installing trail cameras in our forest."

"Dammit." Adam dragged a hand through his hair.

My stomach tied up in knots. This was happening because I froze, and Adam chose to carry me away from the park rather than dispose of the coyote shifter's body. I'd brought trouble to the pack.

Zane blamed me, too. Over Adam's shoulder, he shot daggers at me. "The shit has hit the fan, cousin. Alpha called a meeting in fifteen minutes."

CHAPTER TWENTY-SIX

ADAM

A few minutes before 10 a.m., I parked the truck in front of Annika and Liv's house. I glanced into the back seat, where a pissed-off Zane had wedged his tall frame. Might've made sense for the shorter Marit to ride in the back, but after the dirty look my cousin shot her, he could ride with his knees up around his ears for all I cared.

"Gonna walk Marit inside." I cut the engine, hopped out, and jogged around the truck.

As I opened the passenger door, Annika stepped onto the bungalow's porch, Loki at her side. Her smile was bright and welcoming. She waved enthusiastically at us. "Perfect timing," she cried. "I'm trying to decide between two different recipes for caramelized onion and sweet potato quiche. I made both and just took them out of the oven. I need guinea pigs to taste test them."

After what Marit told me about her cousin's tender yet cautious nature—and the fact that she worried about whether Marit would be safe with me—I didn't have the heart to say no. Under my skin, my equally protective wolf yipped his agreement.

"Sounds good," I told her. We ate leftover muffins a couple of hours ago, but I had room for more breakfast. I cocked my thumb toward the back seat. "My cousin Zane is with us."

"The more the merrier," Annika said.

While Marit dashed for the porch, I yanked open the rear door and leaned inside. "We're going into the house to eat quiche."

"We're what?" Zane grumbled.

"Marit's cousin baked two kinds of quiche. She wants us to try both and tell her which one we like best."

Zane frowned. "You expect me to hang out with humans and eat quiche?"

In wolf shifter culture, offering food to a potential mate played a big part in the courtship ritual. Clearly, the prospect of eating food a human offered him rubbed Zane the wrong way.

I jabbed a warning finger at him. "I expect you to make nice with Marit's family. Suck it up and put your game face on."

Zane rolled his eyes. "We don't have time for this shit."

The commotion that followed the discovery of the coyote shifter's body put done to my plans to spend the rest of yesterday hanging out with Marit. While I met with the alpha and my fellow sentries, she drove my truck back to her grandma's cabin. I spent hours in meetings while we worked out a course of action for dealing with the mess. Grandpa ordered Zane to come back to Belle Reve with Marit and me this morning. Once the strategy session concluded, I shifted and ran to the cabin. On the porch, I changed back, then knocked naked on Marit's door.

I grinned, remembering how we spent our evening.

Zane squinted at me, suspicious. "What?"

I ignored his question and focused on the comment. "We meet with the cops and people from Fish and Wildlife at two. We have time."

"What's up with you?" Zane demanded. "You gotta know this thing with Marit can't be more than temporary. Yeah, she's hot. Go ahead and have some fun. But don't do anything that will make it hard to walk away."

Marit was a helluva lot more than some hot hookup. A rare anger at my cousin roiled through me. "Marit is my mate," I said through gritted teeth.

Zane was my closest friend, but he was also a hard-ass and a stickler for the law. All expression slid from his face as he processed the ramifications of my statement. Not so long ago, if a pack member told you they'd found their mate, you'd celebrate the good news with them, even if their mate was human. No more. Not since the Great War.

With a heavy sigh, he dropped his head, then raised it, his expression bleak. "Fuck, man. Have you told the alpha?"

"Not yet, but I think he suspects." I lifted a shoulder. "My wolf chose her and he chose well. She is *it* for me."

"The law—" Zane started.

"The law is wrong," I declared. "No decree can change our fundamental nature." I thumped my fist against my chest. "We're shifters. We listen when our wolves choose."

Zane clenched his jaw. "Dammit, Adam. It's not that simple. What'll you do if the alpha orders you to break it off?"

That was easy. "I can't give her up, Zane. You'd understand if it happened to you."

Zane made a face. "I'd *never* allow it to happen to me."

He didn't get it. There was no point in arguing further, at least not yet. "C'mon." I stepped back, gesturing for him to get out. "And be nice."

Zane's scowl burned a hole in my back as he followed me up the front walk and onto the porch. He stomped past the rosebushes and flowers that lined the path, their sweet scent no match for his sour disposition. Marit glanced his way, then sidled over next to me. Annika either ignored or was oblivious to my cousin's bad mood.

She smiled at Zane. "I'm glad you could join us for the quiche contest."

He grunted noncommittally. His gaze swept over her from head to foot, lingering for a moment on the old-fashioned, ruffled apron that covered her tee and shorts, then moving down to the pink bunny slippers on her feet. The silly things had button eyes, pom-pom noses, and big floppy ears. Bet Emma and Tory would love them.

Marit took my hand and led us into the house. From the muted colors and modern sofa and chair, her cousins must have updated the living room once they moved in. We stepped into a kitchen that shrieked with what I recognized as Freya Hagen's taste. Color and patterns everywhere, from the blue-and-white checkerboard flooring to the wallpaper covered with birds flitting from branch to branch. This room definitely hadn't been changed since their grandma's death.

Annika watched me survey the room. "Liv and I made a deal. She could redo the living room if the kitchen could stay the way Grandma left it."

"Where is Liv?" Marit asked.

"Running errands and going to the gym."

My nose twitched. Something smelled fucking amazing. I glanced at the two quiches that sat on the kitchen table. Golden flaky crusts surrounded savory custards. My stomach rumbled. Annika took four plates from a cupboard and set them on the small kitchen table. While she rummaged for silverware in a drawer and Marit poured coffee, I took a seat. Loki curled up at my feet. After a brief hesitation, Zane pulled a chair away from the table.

Marit and Annika's heads swung our way. "No," they both shrieked.

Zane froze, one hand on the top rail.

"Not that one," Marit nodded at the chair. "It's too wobbly to sit on. It won't support your weight."

Zane turned it upside down and examined the chair legs and rungs.

"Woodworking is Zane's hobby," I explained. "You should see the furniture he builds. They're works of art." I'd benefited from his skill. For my homecoming, he surprised me with a solid maple bed, nightstand, and dresser.

"Wood shrinks as it ages," Zane said, glancing at Annika. "The joints have come loose. Need to clean out the dowel holes and reglue them."

"Okay," Annika said. "I'll watch some videos on YouTube and learn how to do it. Thanks for the advice."

Zane's eyebrows slanted down. I saw the war waging behind my cousin's eyes. He wanted nothing to do with humans, but he'd be first in line to help any packmate with a woodworking project, especially somebody as inexperienced as Annika.

"You're welcome," he finally mumbled.

"Take that chair." Annika pointed to the far side of the table. "I can sit here." She dragged an old step stool with a red vinyl seat over to the table. She placed two slices of quiche on each plate.

Zane eyed his food warily.

Amusement filled Annika's eyes. "I'm not trying to poison you, I promise."

Marit shook a finger at her cousin. "What did we tell you about watching so many true crime shows?"

"I know, I know." Annika heaved an exaggerated sigh. "I have murder and mayhem on the brain." She offered me a small, apologetic smile before turning to Zane. "I took a picture of Adam's license plate in case he turned out to be a serial killer."

"Adam?" Zane snorted. "Hell, no. In fact, if anybody has the personality of a serial killer, it would be me and not him." He shrugged. "Ask anyone. I'm a mean son of a bitch."

Annika made a skeptical face. "Nah. I don't buy that for a minute. Underneath that gruff exterior, I bet you're a real pussycat."

A pussycat. I bit my cheek to keep from laughing.

Zane's expression—half-incredulous, half-indignant—was priceless. His mouth fell open. His lips moved, but he couldn't manage a single word. Nobody had ever before rendered Zane speechless. My admiration for Marit's sunny cousin shot through the roof.

"Go on." Annika pointed at his plate. "Try it."

What looked like fir needles were sprinkled across the top of one slice. He cut off the tip off the other piece, then paused with the fork halfway to his mouth, his nostrils flaring. Slowly, he slid the triangle of quiche into his mouth, chewed, and swallowed. His expression altered.

"It's good," he said, sounding so surprised that I half expected Annika to take offense.

Instead, she laughed, her eyes dancing. "Why thank you, kind sir."

"Annika makes the best pie crust," Marit bragged.

Zane jerked his chin in agreement. He scarfed down the rest of that piece, then turned his attention to the second one. "What's that?" He pointed to the fir needle lookalikes.

"Fresh rosemary and feta cheese," Annika said.

He dug in. I followed suit. We ate in silence till we polished off the second slice.

"So, which one do you like most?" Annika asked.

Zane tapped the edge of the pan holding the rosemary and feta quiche. "That one."

"Me, too," I agreed.

"Ladies and gentlemen, we have a winner," Marit declared.

Zane's arm still rested on the table. Leaning forward, Annika touched the leather cords he wore around his wrist. "You and Adam are wearing the same kind of bracelet."

"They work for the Black Rock Environmental Conservancy," Marit said quickly. "Most of the members wear a piece of jewelry with a black rock."

"It's pretty." Annika rubbed her fingertip over the meteorite. "And it's warm. The stone must have picked up your body heat."

Zane pulled his hand back and swung his eyes to me. "We should get going."

So far, his behavior had been more civil than I'd expected. No point in pushing my luck.

"You're right." I gulped down a final swig of coffee, stood, and turned to Annika. "I'll taste test your recipes anytime. The quiche was delicious. Thanks for a great breakfast."

She hopped up and gave me a quick hug. "You're welcome at my table anytime, Adam."

Beneath my skin, the wolf wagged his tail enthusiastically. He liked Marit's kindhearted cousin.

Zane rose to his full height, his arms hanging awkwardly at his side. Bet good money he didn't want to deal with a hug from the pretty human. "Yeah. Thanks."

"You're welcome." Annika tipped her head to one side, studying him. She must have read his body language, because instead of a hug, she held out her hand.

Zane stared at the proffered hand for a good ten seconds.

"This is the part where you shake hands," I reminded him.

He slowly reached out and wrapped his big mitt around her small one. One gentle up and down motion, then he let go.

A thought occurred to me. "Can I borrow Loki for the day?"

"Of course," Marit said. "You're his favorite person. He'll be ecstatic to spend time with you. Dinner's at six." Marit stepped into my arms like it was the most natural thing in all the world, like it was exactly where she belonged. At the spontaneous gesture, my shadow brother's satisfaction coursed through me.

Our mate, he huffed, content and at peace.

"I'll be here by six," I promised, smoothing her hair back from her forehead.

She handed me the key to Bryce Toobin's house. "You guys be careful."

"No problem," I assured her. Coyotes were no match for wolves. If we had to, Zane and I could take down a whole pack of the sneaky bastards.

She stood on her toes and tilted her face up to mine. I felt Zane and Annika's eyes on us while we kissed, and tasted their reactions in the air. My cousin's wary concern mingled with Annika's pure delight.

Zane stalked toward the front door.

I broke off the kiss and gave a final nod to the women. One whistle and Loki ambled over. He stuck by my side as I grabbed a leash and jogged after Zane, catching up with him on the front walk. "That wasn't so bad, now was it?"

His gaze cut sideways, but he held his peace. The silence lasted while we climbed into the truck and Loki sprawled across the back seat. We drove across town. Deep in thought, Zane fixed vacant eyes on the horizon, idly scrubbing his palm up and down his thigh. He didn't snap out of it till I parked the truck a few blocks over from Toobin's place.

"Ready?" I asked.

"Yeah."

We exited the vehicle. Loki's presence provided our cover story. Two men walking a dog wasn't likely to arouse any neighbor's suspicions. I snapped the leash onto his collar.

My cousin's chest rumbled his displeasure. "Hate to see a canine with a collar and a leash."

"He's used to it," I said.

"Maybe. Doesn't mean it's a good thing," Zane replied.

Couldn't argue with that sentiment, could I?

We strolled along the sidewalk. A child playing in his front yard called out, "Hi Loki" as we passed.

"If anybody challenges us about going into the house, we'll tell 'em Toobin hired us to walk the dog," I said.

"Do I look like a fucking dog walker?" Zane scoffed.

Sure. If a dog walker was built like an MMA fighter, he did.

When we got to the coyote's house, I paused and pretended to scroll through messages on my phone. I snuck a look at the house. No lights on and no movement detected within. Casting out my senses, I listened for a heartbeat, a footstep, any sign of life. Nada.

"Nobody's at home. Let's go in," I said.

We headed up the front walk to the door. I stuck the key in the lock, swung the door open, and stepped inside. On familiar ground, Loki took off, running from room to room. The living room appeared undisturbed, the sofa, chairs, and tables all neatly in place. The kitchen was messier, dirty dishes abandoned on the small table and a grease-splattered frying pan in the sink.

I cocked a thumb toward the back of the house. "Marit said Toobin's office is this way."

In the digital age, it was probably too much to hope that Toobin had left some incriminating documents in his home office, but we had to check. His laptop was missing. An examination of the desk drawers and bookshelves revealed nothing of interest. Ditto the guest room at the end of the hall.

"What's that?" Zane pointed at the dark red stain on the padded headboard on the guest bed.

My wolf's chest swelled with pride. "Marit chucked curry soup at a pair of coyote shifters."

Zane gave a low, appreciative whistle. "Nice."

We made quick business of searching the rest of the house. No sign of Toobin or his coyote compatriots anywhere. The only thing that gave me pause was walking into the upstairs bedroom that Marit had shared with her ex.

I stopped in the doorway and drew in a deep, reluctant breath. The barely there scent of sex and sweat assaulted my nose. The wolf lunged forward, snarling. An irrational urge to take a piss on the bed—to mark my territory—filled me.

Get a fucking grip.

I forced myself to stride across the room and throw open the closet door. Half the closet was empty—Marit had packed up her things—but Bryce's dress shirts, slacks, and ties filled the other half. I slid open a built-in drawer and found his socks and briefs. A glance into the bathroom showed his toothbrush and an ear hair trimmer on the counter.

Was Toobin planning to come back, or had he abandoned his stuff and taken off? If he was smart—I snorted—if he was smart, he'd hightail it back to the relative safety of his pack.

I started toward the bedroom door, but the sight of a framed photograph on top of a wooden dresser stopped me in my tracks. I crossed the room and picked it up. In the photo, Marit perched on Bryce's lap. His fingers gripped her wrist as he held her hand up to show off a sparkly diamond engagement ring for the camera. In the background, restaurant patrons smiled and clapped, congratulating the newly engaged couple. Bryce's complacent smirk filled me with homicidal rage. The fucker had thought he'd won. Marit appeared shell-shocked, her lips tipped up in a facsimile of a smile that looked nothing like the unforced, spontaneous ones she'd shared with me.

My gaze fell on the fancy wedding invitation propped up next to the photo. A snarl rolled from my chest.

"I'll keep you safe from the coyotes," I vowed. My fingers itched to snatch the photo from the frame and rip it up, to crush the wedding invitation. But they weren't mine to destroy. Marit might want to keep them as a reminder of the bullet she'd dodged. I set the photo facedown on the dresser top.

Zane stuck his head inside the bedroom. "Find anything?"

"Nothing much." I gladly exited the room. "Toobin's personal belongings are still here. How about you?"

"I got zilch," he said. He took his phone from his pocket and texted a message to Remy. That done, he folded his arms across his chest and leaned against the doorframe. "We have a couple of hours before our meeting. What do you say we dump our stuff at the apartment, then walk around downtown and try to get a sense of people's mood?"

"Sounds good. Freya's Bake Shop is closed on Mondays, but we can get a cup of coffee at a diner, then sit and listen to the chatter."

We headed downstairs. I whistled and Loki came running. We exited the way we came, through the front door, like we had nothing to hide and every right to be in the place. Ten minutes later, we stowed our duffels at the two-bedroom apartment the pack rented in Belle Reve. We swung by the bungalow and dropped off Loki, then drove into the downtown district.

The atmosphere in town had changed since my last visit, when I'd had to jostle my way through sidewalks crowded with tourists and townsfolk. Fewer people were out and about.

Those whose paths we crossed wore strained expressions as they hurried about their business. A mother gripped the hand of her little boy and urged him to keep up.

On a street corner, I spied a newspaper vending machine for the *Belle Reve Gazette*. "Killer Wolf at Large," the sensational headline proclaimed.

"See that?" I pointed.

"Son of a bitch." Zane groaned. "What's next? A mob with torches and pitchforks?"

"Wolves are an endangered species," I reminded him. "Feelings might be running high, but state officials will intervene if anybody tries to organize a wolf hunt."

"What's to stop one yahoo with a gun?" Zane's voice was grim. "If anybody takes a shot at a packmate out for a run… or a pup…"

"We protect our own," I said.

"Damn straight we do," Zane agreed.

Half an hour later, we slid into a booth at a mom-and-pop diner a few blocks from Brenner Park. We ordered coffee, then settled back to eavesdrop on the conversations swirling around us. The diner looked to be ground zero for discontented hotheads ready to take action into their own hands.

"The only good wolf is a dead wolf," a man at the counter declared emphatically.

At those words, Zane—who had a death grip on his coffee cup—slowly rose to his feet. The air around him crackled with the threat of violence. The fool at the counter blathered on. Shit. How could the human not sense the predator who had him in his sights?

Nothing good could come from a confrontation now. I rapped my knuckles against the tabletop, drawing my cousin's eye.

Jerking my head, I mouthed the word, NO!

Good sense prevailed. Zane dropped back down onto the red vinyl bench, but he shot me the stink eye, like I'd spoiled his fun.

Keeping the peace between a pissed-off wolf and a loudmouth human. And the day wasn't half done. I sighed. I understood why the humans were frightened, but their fears were misplaced. No native gray wolf had wandered into town and savaged a hapless citizen. *I* stirred up this hornet's nest when my wolf killed an enemy coyote and I left the body behind. It was on me to do everything in my power to calm the situation.

We'd had enough of the conversation at the diner. Zane stewed in a foul mood as we drove to our meeting with state officials, so I took point. Grandpa had ordered us to keep our cools, to listen politely, to offer reassurances and promises of cooperation, but to delay any plan to put radio tracking collars on our gray wolves or trail cameras on our land. Striking the right balance, jumping through so many mental hoops, really kept me on my toes. By the time we called it quits, the clock read 5:40.

"I need to pick something up before the hardware store closes at six," Zane said as we crossed the parking lot. "How about I drop you off at the house then take the truck?"

"Nah, don't bother," I said. "It'll take no more than twenty minutes to walk there. After sitting for so long, I could use the exercise." I tossed him the keys.

Zane snatched them from the air and walked toward the driver's-side door.

"Zane," I called out.

He looked over his shoulder. "Yeah?"

"Why don't you come for dinner? You know you'd be welcome."

He made a face. "Don't think so. Catch you later, cousin."

Still reluctant to hang with humans, huh? Had to hope he'd eventually warm up.

I took off on foot, walking at a brisk pace so I could cover the two miles in twenty minutes. By the time I reached Annika and Liv's block, my limbs were loose and I'd exorcised my frustrations from the day. A relaxing evening in Marit's company was exactly what I needed. I jogged up the front walk and took the porch steps two at a time. A brass knocker shaped like a giant bumblebee hung on the door.

Freya Hagen strikes again.

The whimsical hardware brought a smile to my lips. I lifted the bee's body and dropped it against the strike plate. From the back of the house, Loki barked. The door swung open and a white-faced Annika stood trembling in front of me, her hands zip-tied in front of her waist.

"I'm sorry." Her eyes flooded with tears.

CHAPTER TWENTY-SEVEN

MARIT

Taken literally, the old proverb "Too many cooks spoil the broth" couldn't have been more wrong. Liv, Annika, and I worked together harmoniously in Grandma's kitchen, weaving around each other in the small space in an unchoreographed but error-free dance. Liv fried chicken. Vegetarian Annika—a scarf tied over her nose to block the chicken smell—mashed potatoes and sautéed green beans. I assembled a salad, mixed up my favorite celery seed dressing, and baked a batch of rolls. Far from spoiling the broth, when the Hagen women cooked together, we crafted a killer meal.

The doorbell rang as I was pulling the rolls from the oven. I glanced at the old cuckoo clock hanging on the kitchen wall.

5:48 p.m.

"Adam's early. I'll get it." I yanked off the oven mitts, dashed through the living room, and flung open the front door. "Hi—" The happy greeting died on my lips. I rocked back on my heels.

"Hi there yourself, sweet cheeks." Bryce smiled and held out a bouquet of red roses. "I've missed you."

My shocked brain scrambled to formulate a response. On autopilot, I reached out and took the roses. We'd parted on friendly terms, or so he thought. I'd deliberately dangled the prospect of reconciliation in front of him. Maybe he was making a move to win me back. Dammit. Talk about bad timing. I had to get rid of him before Adam showed up, and Bryce figured out I was on to him.

"Bryce—" I started.

"Something smells mighty good." He sniffed the air. "You going to invite me in?"

"This isn't a good time—"

"What the fuck?" Liv stomped into the living room. Her eyes flashed fire. She slapped both hands on her hips. "You have one helluva nerve showing up here."

Bryce pushed past me and stepped into the house. A smile stretched from one side of his face to the other as he confronted Liv.

"Shut up, bitch."

He pretended to shiver and did a little shimmy. "Ooh, that felt good."

Now I knew. Reconciliation was the last thing on Bryce's mind.

Liv sputtered. "What did you call me?"

"What's going on out here?" Wiping her hands on her apron, Annika emerged from the kitchen and crossed to her sister's side.

By calling Liv a bitch, Bryce crossed a line. No more making nice to keep him on the hook. I threw the roses at him. They struck his chest and scattered at his feet.

"You need to go. Right now."

He chucked me under the chin.

"You're adorable when you're mad."

"Get out," I ordered, pointing at the door.

"I'm calling the cops." Liv pulled her phone from her pocket.

Moving with shifter speed, he knocked the phone out of Liv's hands and crushed it beneath his expensive leather oxford. "I could use a little backup here," he called out.

Two bearded men strolled in through the front door.

I gaped.

Both were freaking huge, tall and burly, with forearms shaped like ham hocks. They reminded me of the competitors in a strong man competition I'd once watched on TV, the kind of men who could deadlift a zillion pounds or singlehandedly pull a fire truck across a parking lot.

The coyotes were in cahoots with the wolf pack's grizzly enemies. I bet these intimidating behemoths were grizzlies. Shit. An unsuspecting Adam could show up at any minute. In a showdown between a wolf and a grizzly, who would win? Wolves might be fast, but the odds had to favor the bigger, stronger grizzlies.

My heart sank. I turned to Bryce. "What do you want?"

Loki trotted out from the back of the house and pressed against my legs.

Bryce dropped down on his haunches. "Hey, Loki. Come say hi to your *daddy*." He imbued the word with a mocking inflection.

A growl vibrated in Loki's chest. I grabbed his collar and held on tight.

"You don't want to hurt Loki," I said in a quiet voice.

He considered my words, then stood. "Lock him in the laundry room, but don't get any ideas about running. You wouldn't get far."

Seriously? As if I'd save my own hide by abandoning my cousins to the tender mercies of the coyote who bamboozled me.

"Bryce, this isn't like you." Annika's brow furrowed. "What are you doing?"

Bryce swaggered over to Annika and laid a finger against her lips. "Keep your mouth shut, sweetheart."

Annika blinked, clearly taken aback by his rudeness. Gone was the polite, charming fiancé who worked so hard to ingratiate himself with my family. From his cocky strut and smug smirk, he relished showing his true colors.

Liv pushed between the two. "You keep your filthy hands off my sister."

Bryce tsk-tsked. "Mind your manners."

He glanced over his shoulder at me. "Go ahead. Put Loki in the back."

Loki was already on edge. If he lunged at Bryce, things would get ugly fast. The brave dog wouldn't stand a chance against shifters. I didn't trust them not to hurt him.

"Come on, boy," I murmured, tugging on his collar.

Loki obediently followed me to the laundry room. I shut the door, locking him in. Ignoring his whine of protest, I walked back to the living room and took up position next to my cousins.

"What do you want, Bryce?" I asked for the second time, trying to ignore how badly the probable grizzlies rattled me and how much I wanted them all gone by the time Adam arrived. I still had no idea if Bryce knew I knew he was a shifter and I was aware our whole relationship was built on a lie.

"A little birdie told me that you've already moved on, that you're shacking up with a—" He leaned toward me, his eyes sparkling. He paused for dramatic effect. "With a man from the Black Rock *Conservancy.*" Oh yeah, he knew everything. At least he didn't say *pack* in front of my cousins.

Then it struck me. "Who told you?"

He shrugged. "Doesn't matter."

"So take a hint and get lost," Liv snarled. "Showing up with a pair of hired goons won't make Marit change her mind."

"Oh, baby, it's waaay too late for that. On to plan B."

Contempt flashed in Liv's eyes. "Plan B, asshole?"

"Yeah." Bryce bobbed his head. "A sort of two-for-one deal."

Two-for-one deal? The ominous words tied my stomach into knots.

I stepped closer to Bryce, my skin crawling at his proximity, and spoke in a low, urgent voice. "Annika and Liv have nothing to do with this. There's no need to involve my cousins in our business." Liv made an unhappy noise. Ignoring her, I continued. "How about you and I, and these... um... gentlemen, take our discussion elsewhere?"

The taller of the two *gentlemen* didn't appreciate my tone, not if the growl that rumbled from his chest was any indication.

Bryce scrunched up his face. "Sorry. No." Phony regret colored his voice. "Your cousins are my business. We'll all sit tight and wait for Landry to show up."

Shit. Shit. Shit.

"How did you know Adam's coming for dinner?" Annika asked.

"Well, I didn't. Not for sure, although I suspected as much." Bryce rubbed his hands together. "Let's get this party started. Gentlemen." Emphasizing the word I used, he looked over his shoulder at the grizzlies.

The taller one—the growler—pulled a handful of zip-ties from his pocket and lumbered toward us, a cruel smile on his ruddy face.

Liv sucked in a breath and lifted her chin. I half expected her to rush forward, headbutt the big guy, and grapple him to the ground.

Or try to. If she thought it would allow Annika to get away, Liv would make a suicidal run at the giant.

No. *I'd* brought Bryce into their lives and exposed my cousins to danger. This was on me. I stepped in front of Liv and shifted my stance. If I could delay the men for even thirty seconds—shoot, even grab their legs and trip them when they ran past—Annika and Liv could dash out the back door and hop a fence into a neighbor's yard. It was a Hail Mary pass with only a slim chance for success, but I had to try something.

"Run," I shouted, lifting my knee. I pivoted and snap kicked at the grizzly's chin, delivering the same kind of roundhouse blow that had knocked over the coyote in the creek. Crap. My foot couldn't reach the brute's jaw, and I struck his chest instead.

Snorting derisively, he caught my foot in his meaty hand and shoved. I sprawled backward, landing on my ass. Pain shot up the base of my spine.

Annika dropped to her knees next to me and patted my face. "Are you okay?"

"You should've run," I muttered.

The big grizzly roughly pushed Annika aside. Grabbing my elbows, he hauled me to my feet and slammed my back against the wall.

My head thwacked hard on the surface. The air whooshed from my lungs.

He pressed his ham-hock forearm against my throat, then twisted his head around and spoke to his companion.

"Bind 'em," he ordered.

While I fought for air, I was only dimly aware of the second bear fastening the cable ties around my wrists. He tugged hard on the nylon strap, and it bit into my skin, cutting off my circulation. The first bear removed his arm from my windpipe. Drawing in a shaky breath, I looked down at fingers already starting to go numb. A sideways glance confirmed that Annika and Liv were bound, too.

"Not so tight," Liv gritted out through clenched teeth.

"One of you head outside and set up for our final party guest," Bryce ordered. "I'm going to check out what smells so good in the kitchen."

The shorter bear rolled his eyes, then slipped out the front door. Bryce followed his nose toward the fried chicken, leaving us alone with a single grizzly intruder.

Three against one. On the surface, our odds had improved, but the odds were meaningless. Three human women—our hands bound—were no match for the hulking shifter.

Shock and fear bleached Annika's face bone white. Unlike her pale twin, angry red color slashed across Liv's cheekbones. Her body hummed with helpless fury.

The clock in the kitchen chimed, and the cuckoo bird called out six times. As the sound faded away, the brass knocker struck against the door.

Chapter Twenty-Eight

Adam

Over Annika's shoulder, I saw Marit and Liv huddled together against the wall. A monster of a man loomed over them, one beefy hand wrapped around Marit's neck. My nostrils twitched.

A grizzly.

"I wouldn't," the bear warned, tightening his grip on her throat and hauling her up onto her tiptoes.

Thanks to the black rock, I could shift lightning fast, but not even I could go wolf before he snapped her neck.

Bryce wandered in from the kitchen and waved a drumstick in my direction. "Hey! Nice to see you again, buddy."

A sharp sting bit the side of my neck. I slapped at the dart protruding from my skin. Movement on my right drew my eye. I swung a head that already felt weighed down by boulders. A grizzly shifter jumped over the fence from the neighbor's yard, dart gun in hand.

The fuckers tranked me.

I staggered against the doorframe, the world going all tilt-a-whirl around me. My vision narrowed till I couldn't see worth shit. I fumbled for my phone. If I somehow could key in the emergency call numbers…

The phone slipped through clumsy fingers. Rough hands shoved me inside. My legs like rubber, I tripped over my own feet and went down hard. Tried to lift myself up, but my limbs wouldn't cooperate.

Bryce appeared at my side, making phony sympathetic noises. "Let me help you." His voice sounded like he was underwater.

"No." I barely made out Marit's shout.

Pain exploded on the side of my head.

My sense of hearing came back first. Garbled voices, *mwa-mwa-mwa*, one word indistinguishable from the next.

Smell came next, the coppery tang of my own blood mixed with the stink of coyote and grizzly… And fear… The unmistakable scent of human fear wound through the space, almost propelling me to my feet. In the nick of time, I forced myself to remain lax and still. Couldn't let the enemy know I'd regained consciousness.

I lay facedown on a hardwood floor, my bloody temple and cheek plastered against a brick hearth. Had to be the fireplace in the living room. Cool metal cuffs secured my wrists behind my back. No zip-ties for me. Any shifter would tear 'em right off.

Where was Marit?

Centering myself, I sharpened my senses to a fine point, then cast them out, searching for my mate. Annika was closest to me, less than a dozen feet away, probably sitting on the couch. Her racing heart and frightened gasps triggered all my protective instincts. Beside her, Liv sucked in quick, shallow mouthfuls of air. Anger rode her hard, the air in the room vibrating with her fury.

And Marit?

I honed my focus.

There.

On the far side of Liv. Her heart beat a steady rhythm, and her lungs expanded with slow, deep breaths. I tasted her resolve. Refusing to yield to panic or rage, my woman forced ice into her veins.

The wolf lunged against my skin, desperate to break free, to shed blood.

Not yet, brother.

A chair creaked. The unhurried *thump-thump-thump* of a grizzly's heart sounded. Standing guard over the women, no doubt.

Where were Bryce and the other grizzly? From the kitchen came the ticking of the clock and the hum of the refrigerator, nothing more. Loki's claws clicked against the floor in a back room. Hushed voices filtered in from one of the bedrooms. If I strained, I could make out words that no human ears could overhear.

"We take our orders from Medved. We're allies, not your damned puppets." The bear sounded bored.

"The deal I made was to kill Landry and the Hagen women," Bryce said with exaggerated patience.

Bryce made a deal with grizzlies to kill us all? Because Marit kicked him to the curb and thwarted his plans? Some men didn't handle rejection well.

A dismissive laugh from the grizzly. "Don't give a damn about any deal you made. My alpha wants to interrogate Landry. As soon as Medved gives the word, we're bringing him back alive. End of discussion."

"Seriously?" Bryce protested. "You're changing the game now?"

"Kill the bitches. Be my guest. But Landry lives." He paused. "Although you might wanna make your move before

Landry comes to. Never wanna underestimate a wolf shifter bent on protecting his woman."

Kill the bitches.

My blood chilled, then lava raced through my veins. I clenched my jaw so hard it almost cracked. No way. No way would I allow these bastards to harm Marit or her cousins.

Bryce was a dead man.

"We gave him enough sedative to knock a rhino on its ass," Bryce scoffed. "He won't be coming to anytime soon."

"Just sayin'." I couldn't see the grizzly shrug, but I heard it in his voice.

Already the black rock had started to weave its healing magic, the poison working its way out of my system. I was as weak as a pup, nowhere near full strength. If I tried to stand, my legs might crumple beneath me. But consciousness had returned and I had to believe my strength would follow.

No matter what, I'd do what had to be done to stop Bryce.

Without turning my head, I opened my eyes a sliver and squinted through my lashes. The grizzly sprawled in a chair facing the couch and the front door. From his posture, he wasn't anticipating trouble.

Good.

Keeping a wary eye on the bear, I tugged on the handcuffs, but they held fast. One by one, I carefully tensed my muscles, testing whether sensation had returned to my body. Hands. Arms. Shoulders. Thighs. Calves. Feet. No pins and needles. No trembling either, but my limbs still felt heavy as stone.

Marit's gaze cut sideways at me, as if she suspected I was awake. I gave a barely perceptible chin jerk. One corner of her mouth curved in an answering smile, then her eyes snapped forward. Her pulse kicked up, not from fear—I'd taste fear—but because she was readying herself for whatever came next.

"Whaddaya got there?" the grizzly in the back room asked Bryce.

I stilled, listening hard, a bad feeling percolating in my gut.

"This little beauty? It's an all-titanium, multi-caliber sound suppressor," Bryce bragged.

A silencer. He was talking about a fucking silencer. Bryce planned to shoot the Hagen women.

Without conscious intent, my Ice Man persona slipped firmly into place. I took my fear for Marit and her cousins, wrapped it up tight, and shoved it away into the darkest corner of my mind.

Anger slid away, replaced by cool calculation, a dispassionate weighing of viable options.

The sedatives hadn't burned out of my system. As long as I retained my human form, the metal cuffs rendered my hands inert. If I shifted, the shackles would fall right off. Going wolf in front of unknowing humans violated pack law. If push came to shove, I'd do it, but there had to be a better recourse.

The bedroom door slammed shut, and footsteps clumped up the hall.

Out of time.

Bryce led the way into the room, a pistol in his outstretched hand.

I rolled to my feet. Calling upon every bit of the black rock's recuperative power, I bunched my muscles and yanked on the handcuffs. With any luck, an adrenaline-fueled burst of energy might snap the chain connecting the manacles... and... and...

Nothing happened.

I stumbled on still unsteady feet—what the hell was up with that?—and threw myself between Bryce and the women. Rules be damned. Sucking in a breath, I summoned my wolf.

Hurry, brother.

I settled my stance, anticipating the sharp pleasure-pain of shifting into wolf form. I waited for claws to erupt from my fingertips. For my bones to snap. For my limbs to contort and reshape. For my teeth to elongate.

Instead of a rapid transmutation, the change crawled through me at a glacier's pace.

My muscles bunched.

My neck cracked.

My vision sharpened, although colors faded.

Two claws broke through my fingertips, the ring and pinkie fingers on my left hand.

What the fuck was wrong with me?

Bryce snorted and I turned my gaze his way. His eyebrows pulled down and his nose wrinkled in a mocking expression. He held up his left arm. "Missing something, dumb-ass?"

Wrapped around the coyote's wrist was my leather bracelet. He must have swiped it while I was unconscious. Tranked and deprived of the black rock, I was dealing with a real double whammy. No wonder my strength was slow in returning and the change was taking its own sweet time.

Painful spasms racked my entire body. Caught midshift like this, I couldn't control my limbs, couldn't fight. I was powerless to protect my mate.

Gotta stop the shift.

Help me, brother.

The wolf was desperate to break free. He hungered for blood, but he had to see that the shift was taking too damned long. With an unhappy yip, he retreated, ceding control back to me. Gritting my teeth, I rallied all my strength and willpower and put the brakes on the change.

Bryce watched me struggle to reverse the shift. He must have sensed the moment when I regained control. He lifted his arm and pointed the pistol at me.

"No," a grizzly bellowed. "Kill the women, but we want him alive."

The bear slapped the weapon out of Bryce's hand. The gun flew toward the fireplace.

Marit jumped up and scrabbled after it. She'd been biding her time, watching for an opportunity to make a move. This wasn't it. No human could outrun a shifter. As she dove past him, Bryce snatched her hair.

"Stupid bitch," he snarled. With a snap of his wrist, he threw her across the room. Her shoulder struck the television, leaving a cracked crater on the screen. She slid down to the floor.

"Ow. Dammit," she moaned, clutching at her shoulder with her bound hands.

Blind with rage, I rushed Bryce. My head plowed into his stomach like a battering ram. Air exploded from his lungs, and he went down hard, coughing. A grizzly took one step toward us. I rolled to my feet, bracing for a desperate, hands-free battle against my gargantuan enemy.

The front door burst off its hinges and crashed to the floor. A torpedo the size and shape of my cousin Zane blasted into the room.

With a face like judgment day, he stalked toward the grizzlies. Zane never backed down from a fight. One wolf stood little chance against two powerful grizzlies, but if he was fast enough, he could shift and rip out their throats before they had time to assume their bear forms.

And they knew it.

Grizzlies fought dirty and without honor. The pair bolted, dashing toward the back of the house. Couldn't be surprised they turned tail and abandoned their ally. A cautious man would call it a day and let 'em go.

Zane—all predator—gave chase.

I stumbled toward Marit. "You all right?" I asked, dropping to my knees next to her.

"Yes." Trembling, she leaned against my chest.

Behind me, Annika shrieked and Liv cried out, "What the hell?"

I whirled around. The cat—or coyote—was officially out of the bag. Bryce stood on four furry legs, breathing hard after his first rapid shift. His clothes and my black rock bracelet lay at his feet.

Annika threw herself off the couch and crawled away from the animal on her elbows.

Liv stood and confronted him.

The coyote lunged, knocking her to the floor. He straddled her chest and clamped his teeth around her neck. Slobber dripped from his pointed canines.

Growling, he locked yellow eyes on mine, his gaze daring me to move, and promising bloody murder if I so much as twitched.

Silence reigned, as if the universe held its breath.

A single gunshot shattered the unnatural quiet. The coyote slumped down on top of Liv, a bullet hole in the middle of his flat forehead.

Her face blank with shock, Annika held the gun.

With her hands zip-tied in front of her, Marit's gentle cousin had managed to pull the trigger. I shouldn't be surprised. Even the most timid prey can turn feral when fighting for their life.

Marit clutched at my chest.

Tossing her head from side to side, Liv pushed frantically at the coyote's dead weight. The body morphed. A naked Bryce sprawled across Liv. The usually tough-talking woman lost her shit, screaming and wriggling out from underneath the corpse. Marit and I lurched to her side.

"What just happened?" Liv demanded, scooting away from the body. She scrubbed her bound hands over her face, gaped in horror at the blood, then wiped her fingers on her jeans.

Marit glanced at me, uncertainty stamped across her face. She'd promised to keep our supernatural world a secret from her cousins.

Bryce had blown that secret out of the water when he shifted in front of Annika and Liv. There was no erasing that knowledge. We had to bring them into the circle.

"I'll explain everything later," I told Liv.

Marit picked up my bracelet and slipped it into her pocket.

A breathless Zane appeared in the doorway leading to the back hall. He must've abandoned his pursuit of the grizzlies once he heard gunfire. His gaze swept the room, taking in Bryce's body and Liv's hysterics, before settling on Annika's frozen figure.

Three quick steps brought him to her side.

Dropping into a squat, he gently took the gun from her trembling hands and tucked it behind his back.

He pulled a knife from his pocket and cut off the zip ties from her wrists. His brows drew together. Frowning, he massaged the circulation back into her hands.

Annika fixed wide, shocked eyes on Zane. "Bryce turned into a dog... or maybe it was a wolf."

Zane stiffened, but he didn't correct her mistake.

"He attacked my sister," she continued, unaware of the insult she'd accidentally given. "I shot him. I... I think he might be dead."

"Yeah," Zane agreed. "The fucker's most definitely dead."

Annika's face crumpled. With a sob, she threw herself at Zane, twining her arms around his neck. He reared back, his hands hanging limp at his side.

C'mon, man. Would it kill you to hug her?

The awkward moment dragged on. Finally, Zane carefully wrapped his arms around Annika's shoulders. He patted her back. Over her head, he shot me a desperate get-me-outta-here look. I rolled my eyes. It wouldn't hurt the big bad wolf to suck it up and comfort a distraught human.

In the distance, a police siren blared. A neighbor must have heard the gunfire and called it in.

"Listen up. We need a cover story for the cops." I angled my head toward Bryce's body. "When Bryce figured out that Marit wouldn't take him back and that she had moved on with me, he lost his mind. Hired a couple of goons. They took the women prisoner. Said they planned to kill us all. Waited for me to arrive for dinner, then sedated and cuffed me." The siren's wail grew louder as the police drew near. I spoke quickly. "My cousin showed up. There was a skirmish. The goons ran away. In the confusion, Annika got her hands on Bryce's gun. She shot him when he threatened to kill Liv."

Annika drew back in Zane's arms and tilted her face up to his. "Why *did* you show up? How did you know?"

"I *didn't* know. I'd gone to the hardware store to pick up some tools and wood glue." He hesitated, looking sheepish. "I was gonna fix your broken chair."

"Focus," I barked.

I glanced through the gaping hole left behind by the shattered front door. Three neighbors stood on the opposite side of the street, cell phones out and ready to record the cops' arrival. "Everybody understand the cover story?"

They all nodded.

"Are we just going to ignore the fact that Bryce turned into a wolf?" Liv's voice was shrill.

"Not a wolf." Zane threw his hands in the air. He was done with the confusion. "A coyote. He shifted into a fucking *coyote*."

Liv's mouth fell open. She stared at my cousin as if she couldn't believe he was quibbling over such trivial details.

"Wolf! Coyote! Whatever... WHO CARES? The point is, Bryce turned into an animal." Liv teetered on the edge of hysteria.

"He did." Marit said gently, clearly trying to calm down her agitated cousin. "We'll explain everything later, I promise. What you need to know now is that shifters are real. People who can turn into animals live among us. They always have. They're not all dangerous."

Not true, but this was definitely not the time to make that point.

"In fact—" She turned to me and smiled. "Some of them are downright wonderful."

We locked eyes.

For a handful of seconds, the world spun away, and I was alone with the woman who everyday claimed a bigger piece of my heart. *This* was what bone-deep contentment felt like, a connection that brought joy and meaning, no matter the shitstorm life threw your way.

I ceded a sliver of control to my wolf, allowing him to look out through my eyes, to assure him that our mate was safe and well.

Brakes squealed outside.

Car doors slammed.

Weapons drawn, four police officers cautiously approached the house.

"Please trust me," Marit urged her cousins. "Keep quiet about Bryce turning into a coyote, please."

"We will," Annika promised.

Liv's expression hardened as she fought to regain control of herself. "But we still want an explanation," she demanded.

"You'll get it," Zane growled.

The next couple hours passed in a blur of activity. The cops removed my handcuffs and cut Marit and Liv free. When no one was paying attention, Marit slipped me my black rock bracelet. As soon as I wrapped it around my wrist, I felt a jolt of energy as the last of the tranquilizer burned out of my system and my strength returned.

With Loki in tow, we all headed down to the station. I drove my truck while Zane took Marit's car. The police took our statements. Long story short, they accepted our cover story. When Annika shot Bryce, all the evidence bolstered her claim that she had a reasonable fear of imminent death. Her use of force was justified. The prosecutor was unlikely to press charges.

Even if they wanted to, Annika and Liv couldn't spend the night at their house, not while the police were still processing the scene.

While Zane called pack headquarters to fill them in on events, the rest of us gathered around our vehicles in the police station parking lot. The sun rode low in the sky, and the temperature was dropping. Marit shivered and burrowed against my side.

"I hate to suggest it, but can we close the bake shop for the week?" Annika asked Liv. "I can't imagine getting up in the morning and going to work and trying to act like nothing happened."

"Of course we can." Liv took her sister's hand. "People will understand. Nobody will expect business as usual after Bryce took us prisoner and threatened to kill us."

Annika's lips trembled. "I still can't believe any of it really happened."

"Come to the cabin," Marit suggested. "I'll sleep on the sofa and you guys can have the bed. It'll be good for you to get out of town and be someplace safe and familiar."

Bryce was dead, a fact that probably nullified any deal he'd made to kill the Hagen women and me, but I wasn't taking any chances. I'd make sure Marit and her cousins were safe at the cabin. We'd send out extra patrols, and I'd park my furry ass on the porch to stand guard over the place during the night.

"I'd like that." Annika stared off into the distance for a moment, then she shuddered. Her shoulders curled forward. Marit threw an arm around her cousin's shoulders and pulled her close for a hug.

My stomach clenched. Annika's actions had saved her sister's life, but she'd have to live with the knowledge that she'd killed a man. I saw many sleepless nights in the gentle woman's future.

Zane tucked his phone back into his pocket and sauntered over to us. "Grandpa called a meeting of the—" He hesitated. Annika and Liv had no idea that Zane and I were shifters, or that the Black Rock Environmental Conservancy was the cover for a wolf pack. No doubt that was information the alpha wanted to disclose himself. "A meeting of the board," he finished.

"When?" I asked.

"Tomorrow morning at ten." Zane dropped his chin and met my eyes. "Grandpa wants to talk to the Hagen women."

CHAPTER TWENTY-NINE

MARIT

A dam told us that he'd assigned extra patrols around the lake and promised to keep an eye on the cabin while we slept. Despite his assurances, Annika, Liv, and I passed a restless night. Liv paced anxiously from room to room, double-checking the window locks, before finally agreeing to go to bed around midnight. A little past 3 a.m., Annika cried out in her sleep. She wandered into the kitchen for a glass of water, then stood at the window looking out over Shooting Star Lake. I kept punching the pillows on the sofa, rolling from side-to-side, but I couldn't get comfortable.

By the time Adam showed up at nine, I'd given up on sleep and was drinking my third cup of coffee. Fifteen minutes before our meeting, we locked Loki in the cabin and headed toward the north shore of the lake.

I expected our meeting with the alpha to take place in the conference room of the administrative building, the same spot where I'd met with the pack leadership. Instead of pulling up outside the bland office building, Adam parked his truck in front of the grand lodge.

Liv's gaze lit with interest, her shock over yesterday's events giving way to curiosity. We'd speculated about the log edifice for years. Now she'd see it for herself. Annika—lost in her thoughts—barely lifted her eyes.

Adam reached across the console and twined his fingers through mine. "We'll be meeting with Grandpa up in his private quarters."

"Sounds good." I squeezed his hand, seeking a moment's comfort and reassurance in the warmth of his touch. We'd promised to tell Liv and Annika about the supernatural world. Far better to break the news in a homey environment—a place that affirmed the humanity shifters shared with us—rather than in a cold, barren conference room.

Zane waited for us on the porch. Together, we jogged up the stone steps and through the double-door entry into the lodge. Bypassing the stairs, we took the elevator to the fourth floor. The door slid open with a *ding*. An old brass plaque engraved with the words *Presidential Suite* and an arrow pointing to the left hung on the opposite wall. We turned left and followed a long corridor to the alpha's quarters.

A subdued looking Olga answered the door. She might not like Adam or me, but the grizzlies' attempt to kidnap the alpha's grandson silenced even *her* snark. She quietly led us to the suite's living room, where a pair of leather sofas flanked an imposing stone fireplace. Rolf, Remy, and a teenage boy sat on one sofa.

Matthew stood in front of the hearth. A relieved smile crossed his face as he stepped forward to embrace first Adam, then Zane. He held out a hand to me. "I'm glad to see you safe and well, Marit." Glancing over my shoulder, he nodded at Annika and Liv. "And your cousins, too. I'm deeply sorry that you were drawn into this mess." He introduced Olga and the others.

"When we talked to the police, we kept our mouths shut about Bryce turning into a coyote," Liv said without preamble or any attempt at pleasantries. "Adam promised you'd explain everything."

"I will." The alpha lowered himself into an upholstered armchair and gestured for us to take a seat. "Mythology sometimes contains a grain of truth," he started. For the next fifteen minutes, he told my wide-eyed cousins about the animal shifters who'd lived alongside humans since the dawn of time.

"You run the Black Rock Environmental Conservancy," Annika said. "You protect the land and the animals who live on it. Is that how you discovered the existence of shifters?"

"Not exactly." Matthew glanced at Olga. "Will you go get Kyra and Tory, please my dear?"

A minute later, Olga escorted the friendly, red-haired sentry into the living room. Kyra held the hand of the vivacious little girl I'd met days earlier.

"Marit," Tory exclaimed, dancing to my side. She climbed onto my lap and threw her arms around my neck. One bare knee poked out from under her lavender bathrobe. A small black rock dangled from a charm bracelet that jangled on her wrist.

"Hi, sweetie. It's nice to see you again," I said.

Matthew cleared his throat. "The Black Rock Environmental Conservancy is more than a nature advocacy group." He paused, his eyes moving from Liv to Annika. "We're a pack of wolf shifters. I'm the alpha. Adam, Zane, Remy, Rolf, and Kyra are my lieutenants."

Liv sat up straight. "You're wolves," she repeated. "*Adam's a wolf.*"

Frowning, her gaze dropped to where I rested my hand on Adam's thigh.

"And Marit knew?"

"Yes, I've known for a few days," I said. "I couldn't say anything to you. It wasn't my secret to tell."

"Can I show them now, Auntie Kyra?" Tory asked. She jumped from my lap and twirled around in the middle of the room.

I suddenly understood the child's presence. What better way to introduce Annika and Liv to shape-shifting than to have an adorable, nonthreatening little girl shift into a wolf in front of them?

"You sure you want to?" Kyra asked. I understood her hesitation. Shape-shifting might be as natural as breathing, but the process hurt. Nobody would want to cause a child unnecessary pain.

"I'm sure." Tory hopped in place, clearly eager to show off her ability to change.

Adam and the other sentries leaned forward, their attention focused on the child. Were they somehow able to absorb some of the pain, to ease her transformation? I'd ask him later.

"Shift, Tory," the alpha ordered.

"Okey doke." Tory glanced around the circle of adults, smiling broadly. She dropped down on all fours. Her entire body vibrated. The air surrounding the child began to sparkle. Annika and Liv gasped. Through the dense field of glittering lights, a small wolf took form. The pup pranced sideways, the lavender robe sliding to the carpet. Balancing her front paws on the alpha's knees, the wolf pup yipped.

"You did a good job, Tory." Matthew patted her head.

Quivering with excitement, Tory ran from person to person, begging for attention. When she got to me, I dropped down onto my knees. "You're so pretty," I marveled, admiring her soft gray fur and her bright golden eyes. Her tail wagged. She licked my face, then moved on to Annika.

"Hi," Annika said hesitantly. Tory nudged my cousin's hand. Annika took the hint. She stroked her sleek head, then laughed softly, thoroughly charmed by the pup.

With a wobble, the alpha rose from his chair and came to sit next to Annika and Liv. "I'm sure you have questions," he said.

"Oh, yeah. Lots," Liv agreed.

"How about some strawberry lemonade?" Olga spoke for the first time.

"That would be very nice. Thank you, sweetheart," Matthew said.

Like it or not, if I were in any kind of relationship with Adam, Olga was an inescapable fact of life. My conscience demanded that I at least try to make the best of it.

"Can I help?" I asked.

Olga frowned, clearly taken aback by the offer. After a downright awkward moment of silence—during which Matthew raised an eyebrow at his wife—Olga's lips turned up in a saccharine smile. "How lovely. I'd appreciate the help."

"My pleasure." Okay. So pleasure was an exaggeration, but there was a certain satisfaction in doing the right thing.

I followed her to a small, utilitarian kitchen that utterly lacked the whimsy and personality of Grandma Freya's favorite workspace. "Glasses are in the cupboard above the dishwasher. You can put them on that tray." Olga pointed at a plastic tray leaning against the white-tiled backsplash.

I arranged a dozen glasses on the tray. With brisk movements, Olga took a pitcher of lemonade from the refrigerator and thumped it so hard against the counter that pink liquid sloshed over the side. Muttering to herself, she wiped up the spill, then filled the glasses. Her dislike of me tainted the air, a potent cloud of barely suppressed fury.

"What's the problem?" I shoved my hair back behind my ears and jerked up my chin, sending Grandma's earrings swinging. "What did I do to make you dislike me so much?"

She pressed her lips together in a straight line, her gaze fixed on the swaying silver hoops. "Your grandmother was a troublemaker, and so are you."

"My grandma was the finest woman who ever lived." Heat rose in my cheeks.

Olga shrugged, a dismissive gesture that made me see red. *Deep breath.*

"I'm sure Grandma had her reasons for holding on to the cabin," I continued. "Whatever they were, I'll probably never know." I tossed my hands into the air. "Listen, you got what you wanted. The lease is yours. What's the point in clinging to an old grudge?"

"An old grudge?" Olga snorted. "Did Adam tell you that he's breaking pack law by being with you? That's it's forbidden for a wolf to mate with a human?"

"What?" Shock slackened the muscles in my face.

She bobbed her head, a mean-spirited smile on her face. "Adam was in the running to become alpha when Matthew retires. That can't happen now. Not that it's a bad thing. Adam doesn't have the temperament to lead."

"What's going on?" Adam appeared in the doorway to the small kitchen.

I whirled to face him. "Is it true? Is it against pack law for a wolf to mate with a human?"

God. How could Adam do this to me? How could he dangle the promise of a life-long love, of a soul-deep connection, if he knew it was impossible?

Bryce did, a small voice in the back of my head reminded me.

Adam isn't Bryce, I shot back.

"Dammit." Adam pierced Olga with a scathing look. Two steps brought him to my side. His strong fingers gently cradled my cheeks.

"The law is wrong. It tears to shreds the relationship between a shifter and their wolf, violates a trust we've held sacred for thousands of years."

He swallowed, his eyes anxiously scanning my face. "I swear by all I hold holy, you're my mate and I'll stand by you forever, no matter what the law says."

I believed him. Truth and sincerity imbued every word of his declaration. Tears welled in my eyes. We weren't quite in love… yet, but every moment in his presence brought me closer to that tipping point.

Love isn't selfish. Grandma had never been especially religious, but she liked to quote that verse from the Bible.

"Olga said you're giving up your chance to be alpha to be with me."

A small smile curved his lips. "No contest, kitten. A wolf's mate comes first. Besides, either Zane or Remy would make an outstanding alpha. The pack won't suffer if I'm not in charge."

"That's true enough." Olga sniffed. "But tell me, if the alpha declares you a rogue—an outlaw—do you plan to take your little human and go on the run? Force Zane or Remy to hunt you down and execute you?"

The words were a slap across my face. I jerked, horrified. Would the pack kill Adam if we mated?

"What are you doing, sweetheart?" The alpha stood in the doorway, his voice filled with weariness.

Adam turned to face his grandfather, a protective arm wrapped around my shoulders.

Olga jutted out her lower lip and assumed a defensive posture, folding her arms over her chest. "I'm speaking nothing but the truth, and you know it."

Matthew leaned against the doorframe, looking so defeated and demoralized that my heart sank. Would he—shit—would he really order the death of his beloved grandson?

The pain that cut through me at that prospect almost drove me to my knees.

"I'll go away and never see Adam again."

The promise tumbled out of my mouth. "Just please don't kick him out of the pack. Don't order his cousins to hunt him down and… and kill him." My voice broke on the final words.

"No." Adam protested, his voice vehement. "No way I'll let you go." His tone gentled as he pulled me closer to his side. "That's not how this works. If you leave me to keep me safe, I'll track you down and bring you back. I wouldn't know a moment's peace otherwise. Whatever happens, we'll face it together."

"You heard him," Olga told her husband. "He puts that woman—"

"My *mate*," Adam interjected.

Olga ignored him. "He puts that woman above the law and the good of the pack."

Matthew sighed. "Our mates have always come first, or at least they did until all the losses from the Great War forced me to upend tradition and change the law." Age and illness had worn the alpha down. He sagged against the doorframe. His paper-thin lids drifted shut over eyes that had lost their luster.

"Grandpa." His brow furrowed with concern, Adam laid a hand on his grandfather's arm.

The alpha's eyes snapped open. "I love you, son, but I can't ignore the fact that you're determined to break pack law."

Adam straightened his spine. "I understand, sir."

The alpha looked at me. "And I haven't forgotten what you've done for the pack by signing over your lease."

After Olga's warning that the alpha might execute Adam, I was willing to beg. "I hope you'll factor that into your decision about Adam."

He smiled sadly, then turned again to Adam. "You possess all the qualities of an exceptional alpha. You're thoughtful. You see the big picture. Of all my bloodline, you're the steadiest and most compassionate. You're also brave and willing to fight to defend your people."

Adam waited a beat. When the alpha didn't continue, he said, "Thank you, Grandpa."

Matthew raised a hand. "You were the one, you know. I was planning to select you as my successor. But you can't be alpha if you mate with a human, if your children won't be wolves. The law forbids it for a reason."

Olga heaved a happy sigh. "So Adam's out."

"What do you mean if his children won't be wolves?" I asked. Why hadn't it occurred to me to wonder if our children—if we could have children—would be wolves or fully human?

"It's simple," Matthew said. "For a person to be a shifter, they have to have more than fifty percent shifter DNA."

I swung my eyes to Adam.

"You're my mate." He cradled my face between his hands. "If we decide to have children, it doesn't matter one lick to me if they're wolf or human. We'll love them and raise them right."

"And they'll be valued members of the pack," Matthew said firmly. He turned to Adam. "I'm not banishing you or declaring you a rogue," he added. "You're still a sentry. You're still pack. But you can't be the alpha."

"That's more than fair," Adam said. "Although I should warn you, I plan to petition the next alpha to change the law."

Matthew chuckled. "You do that, son. Who knows, maybe he'll see things your way."

"That's it?" Olga sounded both stunned and offended. "Adam breaks the law and he gets off virtually scot-free?"

I couldn't keep my mouth shut. "It sounds to me like you were rooting for Adam to be kicked out of the pack." I raised both brows and waited for Olga to respond.

She harrumphed. "My husband has a kind heart, and I hate to see anyone take advantage of his generous nature."

"Enough." Matthew waved a hand, silencing our bickering. "We have guests. Adam, will you carry the tray to the living room for your grandmother?"

"Yes, sir."

When we got back to the living room, we found Annika sitting cross-legged on the floor with the wolf pup curled up on her lap. She stroked Tory's fur, murmuring soft words to the shifter child. Both Liv and Zane watched her. Annika had retreated into herself after shooting Bryce. Thanks to Tory, she was emerging from her stunned stupor. I saw the same relief reflected on Liv's face that I felt. Zane's sharp eyes studied my cousin, his face expressionless.

A sulky Olga dropped onto the upholstered chair. Matthew sat down on the sofa next to Liv and drew my cousins into a friendly conversation. Zane jerked his chin, summoning Adam to his side. With an apologetic glance to me, Adam joined his fellow sentries.

The confrontation with Olga, left me too wound up to sit still. I picked up a glass of lemonade and wandered across the room to a wall covered with framed photographs. Leaning forward, I examined them.

A grainy old black-and-white image caught my eye. Against a backdrop of tall trees, two men wearing rough work clothes and battered fedoras flanked a large boulder. Each man rested a hand on its stony surface. Was that the famous Black Rock?

Next to the picture of the rock, a photo of a pretty girl in her early teens. A young man stood at her side, one arm slung affectionately around her shoulders. Eyes bright, expression guileless, she smiled adoringly up at him. They weren't in love. Nothing about their posture or expression hinted at a romantic connection. I looked closer. Both had wavy brown hair and brown eyes. The same high cheekbones and sharp jawline. Brother and sister most likely. They almost looked familiar, like someone I should know, but I couldn't place them. I frowned, frustrated.

In the next photo, three grubby little boys—two blonds and one dark-haired—roughhoused on the ground. The dark-haired boy held one of the blonds in a hammerlock. The photographer must have called out to them. They all looked straight at the camera, big happy smiles on their faces.

I laughed softly and laid a fingertip on the glass over the dark-haired boy's face. "Hi, Adam."

"Their grandmother Katia took that picture." I jumped and glanced over my shoulder. The teenage boy stood behind me. At my startled reaction, he grimaced, looking abashed. "Sorry. I didn't mean to scare you."

"That's what I get for being lost in thought." I held out a hand. "I'm Marit."

"Xander, Adam's cousin." He shook my hand.

"You're Olga's grandson, right?" I tried to keep my voice and expression neutral, but some anxiety must have bled through.

"Yep, her one and only." Xander grinned. "Don't worry. I make up my own mind about people."

A twinge of sympathy shot through me. How hard must it have been to grow up with a grandmother as notoriously crabby as Olga? "I'm happy to meet you," I said. "Adam tells me you're one of the good guys."

He flashed another smile, pleasure at his cousin's praise written across his face. "Coming from Adam, that's a real compliment. I'm happy to meet you, too." He tilted his head toward the wall. "I saw you looking at the picture of Grandma."

"What?" I blinked, confused.

He pointed at the photo of the pretty teenaged girl. "That's Grandma and her big brother. He was killed in a car accident a few months after the picture was taken."

I gasped. Reluctant pity tied my stomach in knots. "Your poor grandma. How horrible."

He nodded. "People say she was never the same after he died. I was named after him."

I touched his arm. "That's a lovely way to honor his memory."

"Xander." Olga's voice was sharp. "I need you."

Xander sighed. "I'd better see what Grandma wants."

No doubt what his grandma wanted was to get him away from me, but I couldn't say that aloud. "I'm looking forward to getting to know you," I said instead.

"Me, too."

I turned my eyes back to the photo of Olga and her brother. It was sad to think that grief had turned the radiant, affectionate girl into a bitter old harridan.

Adam walked up behind me, slid his arms around my waist, and pulled me against his chest. "What are you doing?"

"Admiring family photos." I tapped a finger against his picture. "You were so stinking cute."

He groaned. "Don't say 'stinking cute' in front of Zane or Remy. I'd never hear the end of it."

Laughing, I turned around in his arms and tilted my face up to his. "With the right inducements, I can keep my mouth shut."

"Oh yeah? What do you want?"

"I don't know." I widened my eyes. "What are you good at?"

"Brat." He dropped a quick, hard kiss on my forehead. "We're definitely gonna continue this conversation later. Right now, we need to talk with your cousins."

I sobered and followed him back to the seating area. Adam signaled for Zane, Remy, and Kyra to join us.

"You've met Zane," he said. "This is Remy. He's in charge of security for the pack."

Remy nodded a greeting. His blue eyes coolly appraised Annika and Liv. Annika offered him a small friendly smile. Liv returned his silent scrutiny, arching one dark brow.

"You're now under the protection of the pack—" Remy started.

"Why?" Liv interrupted. "Bryce is dead and whatever beef he had with Marit and Adam died with him."

"Bryce was the coyote alpha's second-in-command," Remy said. "The coyotes will want payback."

Annika paled. "I shot Bryce. Is my sister in danger because of me?"

"No." A muscle worked in Zane's jaw. "You're in danger because the damned coyotes and grizzlies dragged you into our war."

"Not your fault, sweetheart," Adam assured her. "And don't worry. The pack will keep you safe."

Liv turned to Remy. "Define 'under the protection of the pack'."

"You'll stay with us on pack land until the situation has resolved," Remy said.

I winced. Liv was a sensible woman, but a declaration like that—one that eliminated her from the decision-making process—was sure to make her eyelids twitch.

"We own a business," Liv said. "We have employees who depend on us for their livelihood. We plan to take a week off, but we can't put our lives on hold until you finish your war with the coyotes."

Remy folded his arms over his chest. "Then what do you propose?"

"If you say the coyotes might come after us, I believe you." Liv rubbed the back of her neck. "I don't want to do anything stupid or risky, but there has to be a solution that doesn't involve abandoning the bake shop."

"The alpha ordered Zane to go to Belle Reve today to replace your broken front door and TV," Remy said. "We can beef up your security, too."

"Remy's our tech expert. He can install a top-of-the-line security system with cameras at the house and bake shop," Adam explained.

"I'll put heavy-duty steel doors in the front and back of the house. Add window bars and motion-sensor exterior lights," Remy added.

"Hold on." Liv lifted a hand. "We're not putting bars on all the bungalow's windows."

Remy tilted his head. "So a *pretty view* trumps safety in your world?"

I winced. Those were fighting words, and Liv loved a good fight.

"*Nothing* trumps my sister's safety." Liv crossed her arms over her chest, mimicking Remy's posture. "I'm saying there has to be a better solution than making us live in a jail."

"It *would* be ugly to look out at the garden through metal bars," Annika said hesitantly.

Zane shoved a hand through his hair. "How about putting alarms on all the windows instead of bars?" he suggested, taking on the role of peacemaker.

"Alarms would be fine." Liv nodded.

Remy shrugged, unhappy, but conceding the point. "Alarms it is."

"If Annika and Liv are going to stay in town, they'll need personal security," Zane said.

"You mean a bodyguard?" Annika asked slowly. "Somebody who'd live with us?"

"I can do it," Kyra volunteered. "If anybody asks, we'll tell them I'm a friend who's staying with you for a while and helping out at the bakery."

"Wouldn't work as a long-term solution, but I suspect we'll be taking the war to the coyotes sooner rather than later." Remy glanced at Liv. "Whaddaya think? It's a solution that doesn't involve abandoning the bake shop."

"I like it." I spoke up, throwing my support behind Remy's suggestion. "I'd feel better knowing that a trained soldier is watching out for you guys."

"Can't say I love the idea of having a babysitter." Liv cut Kyra a sideways glance. "Nothing personal. But if it allows us to stay safe and keep the bake shop open, I'm for it."

"I'll run it by the alpha." Remy rubbed a hand over his chin. "Our annual Pack Circle is Friday night. Every member has to attend, no exceptions. Are you willing to wait till Saturday to go back to Belle Reve, so Kyra will be free to go with you?"

"Of course," Annika said. She turned to Kyra. "Thank you for helping us."

Kyra grinned. "No problem."

Contradictory feelings coursed through me, relief that Annika and Liv had a plan and worry that I didn't. Adam would insist on staying at my side to protect me from coyote retaliation. I needed to pull my weight at the bake shop. How was this going to work?

My concerns must have shown on my face. Adam squeezed my hand. "We'll figure it out."

CHAPTER THIRTY

ADAM

Marit snored. Not a god-awful, window-rattling rumble. More like an occasional snuffle, but with my hypervigilant senses, it was the kind of unpredictable sound that jolted me awake. Mom once told me that after they mated, she had trouble falling asleep next to Dad's warm body. She'd roll against him and wake up, overheated. She got over it soon enough, and said she came to crave his solid, reassuring warmth in their bed.

I'd adjust, too, learn to filter out Marit's night sounds.

Marit.

My soon-to-be mate. I grinned, an unfamiliar contentment settling into my bones.

Claim her now, the wolf urged.

Patience, brother.

My parents would fly into Seattle this morning and arrive home sometime this afternoon, in time for tonight's Pack Circle. Both were healers—not soldiers—inseparable since they fell in love back when they were teenagers. They'd spent the last six weeks in northern Greece. The Pindus pack had lost their healer in an accident, and my parents were training a new one. I couldn't wait to introduce them to Marit.

I turned my head and looked at her. Pale, break-of-dawn light streamed through the windows of my room and touched her sleeping figure. She lay flat on her back, one hand thrown over her head. The sunlight made the highlights in her dark honey-colored hair glint. I reached out and ran a strand through my fingers. She stirred and her eyes fluttered open. Arching her back, she offered a sleepy smile.

"Morning," she mumbled.

"Good morning."

I dragged my thumb across her plump lower lip. She nipped the pad—held it for a moment between her teeth—then slowly sucked my thumb into her mouth down to the first joint. My cock, already at half-mast, jumped to attention. Rolling onto her side, she edged closer and threw her leg over my thigh. She released my thumb, then with a fingertip, outlined my bottom lip.

Turnabout was fair play. I snapped my teeth, capturing her finger.

"Hey," she protested. I snarled and her eyes grew wide. "What big teeth you have, Mr. Wolf."

Who could resist such a perfect setup? Not me.

I let her finger go, then rolled over on top of her, settling my weight between her thighs. "All the better to eat you with, my dear."

A slow smile blossomed across her face. Her eyes sparkled. "So... what's stopping you?"

I dropped my head and tasted her neck, breathing in her scent.

Sugar. Vanilla. Woman. My woman.

My already stiff cock grew harder.

"I like to savor my meals."

I nibbled on that sensitive spot beneath her ear, the one that always made her go all weak and shivery. The sweet slope at the juncture of her neck and shoulder beckoned me like a siren. Every moment spent with Marit, the call grew stronger, a hardwired compulsion to sink teeth into my mate's flesh, to make my claiming bite.

I resisted the urge. Not yet. Not until she was ready.

With a small cry, she arched beneath me and pushed at my shoulders, encouraging me to take my attentions south.

I captured one small wrist, then kissed each fingertip. "Unh-uh, kitten," I chided. "Told you I wanna take my time."

She heaved a long-suffering sigh.

I chuckled. "You don't think I'm gonna make the wait worthwhile?"

She bit her lower lip, her eyes already heavy with desire, and gave up the playacting. "I know you will."

Yeah. I would.

Humming with satisfaction, I pressed small kisses against her neck and throat and across the curves of her breasts. I captured a nipple between my teeth. My tongue flicked back and forth over the tip. Marit made a small, happy sound that grew into a moan when I turned my attention to the other side. I scraped my chin over the tip, dragging stubble across her sensitive skin.

"Adam," she cried, my name on her lips the sweetest sound I'd ever heard. She writhed beneath me. Her fingers tunneled through my hair, clenching tight as my mouth wandered the hollow between her breasts and her soft, vulnerable belly.

I nuzzled her navel, exploring the dent with my tongue. Working my way lower down her body, I brushed my lips over her curls. I blew out a slow breath, then drew the air back into my mouth, tasting her musk and the undeniable scent of her arousal.

Gentle, I reminded myself, tamping down the shifter's primal need to take, to mark, to stamp my claim on her tender flesh. I sat up, kneeling between her legs. My hands shook as I seized her thighs and urged her legs apart. I glanced at her face.

Cheeks flushed pink, she panted softly. Anticipation mixed with a whiff of anxiety drifted toward me on the air. Her rapid heartbeat echoed in my chest. My predator's gaze honed in on the pulse that tapped against the side of her neck. Prey would fall deadly still, heart thrumming, paralyzed by fear, while they waited for me to strike.

Marit was no prey. Rolling her hips in an unmistakable invitation, she rose up on her elbows. "I want you."

With a slow, triumphant smile, I pressed her back against the mattress. My fingers teased apart her pussy lips, exposing her glistening clit. I locked my eyes on hers, then slowly licked over her sex. Her head fell back against the pillow and her back bowed. I licked again, the tip of my tongue sketching circles around her clit. Marit whimpered.

"Hmmm," I growled. If her needy, desperate mewling was any indication, the vibration penetrated to her core. I found my rhythm. Like a starving man plonked down at a feast, I ate her out with unbridled gusto.

Her inhibitions dissolved and fell away, and she abandoned any attempt to keep quiet. I slipped two fingers inside her molten core. Screaming my name, she came. She was still trembling when I crawled up between her legs. Her slick heat slid against my shaft. Gripping her ass, I positioned the head of my cock at her entrance, then slammed home.

Marit made a sound—half laugh and half gasp—and clawed at my back, as fierce as any shifter. Sharp little teeth caught my earlobe, and hot breath tickled my ear. "I marked you," she whispered, triumph filling her voice.

"Just you wait," I promised. I scraped my teeth along the cords of her neck, teasing her with a hint of the pleasure and pain to come.

Twisting her head, Marit bit my shoulder. The small hurt pushed me over the edge. I abandoned myself to hedonistic sensation, pounding hard into her tight sheath. Sweat slicked our bodies and pooled beneath her breasts. Finally, her eyes rolled back in her head. She inhaled, holding her breath while her pussy spasmed around me. My balls drew up tight. The head of my cock locked in place. I shuddered. My cum flooded her pussy and spilled out across the sheet.

Lifting my head, I gazed down at my woman. I dragged a knuckle over her cheek. Her lips curved up in a lazy, satisfied smile. She turned her head and kissed my fingertips. I rolled off Marit, then tugged her to my side. Strands of damp hair clung to her forehead and neck.

"I'm hot," she said, shimmying out from under my arm and scooting a few inches away.

I deliberately misunderstood. "Yeah, you are. Hot, sexy, and beautiful."

She rolled her eyes and batted at my chest. "I'd love to fall back asleep, but we have a big day ahead of us."

"You're right." I sighed. I had a million things to do before the Pack Circle tonight.

"Race you to the shower?" she suggested, springing from the bed.

After a five second head start, I gave chase, overtaking her by the bathroom door. Without breaking stride, I bent forward and tossed her over my shoulder. She shrieked and kicked her legs.

I held her squirming body in place with one hand and turned on the water with the other. When the temperature was right, I deposited her under the spray, stepped in next to her, and shut the shower door. I squeezed shampoo onto my palm, then rubbed it into Marit's hair.

"Nice," she breathed. Her head fell forward as I massaged the shampoo into her scalp. My fingers worked their way to the base of her skull. I kneaded her neck.

"This is definitely it," she said, moaning with pleasure.

"What's it?" My fingers stilled.

She glanced over her shoulder. Her lips curved in a lazy smile. "I asked you what you're good at, remember? So you can bribe me not to tell Zane and Remy that you're stinking cute?"

"Oh, yeah." I kneaded her shoulders, my thumbs rubbing circles against skin slippery with shampoo bubbles. "I recall something about that."

Marit groaned again. "If you get tired of being a sentry and want to go into the massage business, I'll write a glowing testimonial. *Adam Landry is very good with his hands.*"

"You think so, huh?" I preened inwardly.

"Mm-hmm." Her eyelids drifted shut. She turned back and pressed her forehead against the wall, limp with pleasure. A simple act made my woman go limp.

Shit.

Soon as I had a few free minutes, I'd go online and order one of those folding massage tables. My imagination jumped forward to next winter, when I saw myself setting the table up in front of the fireplace and stripping my mate naked. She'd stretch out on the table, the firelight dancing across her skin, while I oiled up my hands and massaged every inch of her body. She'd go all weak and languid, sighing with happiness, the way she was now.

"Earth to Adam." Marit laughed low. "Something is poking into me, and it's not your fingers."

I looked down. My little fantasy had awakened the beast, so to speak.

"You know, now that I think of it," Marit continued, wriggling backward against my hard-on. "You're good with something else besides your hands."

The beast roared to life. No more than ten minutes had passed since I pulled out of her sweet pussy, but I was good to go again. I slid my hands over her sudsy body, stopping when my fingers cupped her breasts. I jerked her backward against my chest. My thumbs brushed back and forth across her slippery nipples.

Marit gasped and rocked her hips against my jutting cock.

I dragged my teeth along the corded tendon of her neck. God. The wolf's primal need to bite down hard—to make my claim—shot through me. It took every ounce of forbearance I had to resist the urge. Instead, I dropped my mouth to her ear.

"Let me show you what else I'm good with."

CHAPTER THIRTY-ONE

MARIT

From the barely concealed smiles that greeted us in the pack's dining hall, I suspected that the long shower hadn't erased every bit of evidence of our early morning romp. Er, romps. Shit. Was I blushing? Sometimes the enhanced wolf shifter sense of smell was awkward as hell. Or maybe it was the sappy grin that I couldn't keep off my face every time I glanced at Adam that gave me away. In any case, *busted*. Ignoring the knowing looks, I kept my chin high and my gaze fixed on Adam's back as I followed him to the breakfast buffet.

"Good morning, Marit," a cheerful voice called out.

I glanced to the end of the buffet. Xander stood behind the table, wearing a black chef's apron. He waved a whisk at me in greeting.

"Good morning," I returned. "What are you doing?"

"Running the omelet station," he said. "Can I make you one?"

Adam tilted his head toward mine. "Xander makes a killer western omelet. If I get our juice and coffee, will you ask him to make one for me?"

"Sure thing." I walked over to the omelet station. "Two western omelets, please."

"You got it." Xander set to work breaking and whisking eggs.

"So how did you end up running the omelet station?" I asked. The day-to-day mechanics of pack life were still a mystery to me. "Does everybody take a turn working in the kitchen, or is cooking a special interest of yours?"

"Everybody in the pack is expected to contribute in some way," he said. "But cooking is my thing. I want to go to culinary school." He glanced toward the far side of the room. "Don't tell Grandma."

My gaze followed his. Olga sat at a table near the windows, watching us over the top of her reading glasses.

"She has other plans for you?" I guessed.

Xander made a face. "She has some crazy notion that I could be alpha. I mean, I guess *technically* I could. Leadership usually follows a bloodline, but sometimes for the good of the pack somebody else steps up." He shook his head. "Adam, Zane, and Remy carry alpha blood. Any one of them would make an excellent alpha. I don't want the job. I want to feed people. I wish Grandma saw that as a worthy goal."

"You're preaching to the choir," I said, feeling a kinship with the young man. "I always knew I wanted to be a baker. Feeding people *is* a worthy, soul-satisfying goal."

Xander bobbed his head. "It's nice to talk to somebody who gets it."

"And if you ever want to talk about culinary school, come to me." An idea occurred to me. "In fact, I have some textbooks you might want to borrow."

His face lit up. He plated the two omelets, then circled the table and swept me into a bear hug. Laughing, I returned the embrace. Over his shoulder, I watched Adam approach us, one eyebrow cocked.

"You making a move on my mate?" Adam asked without heat.

"Nah." Xander turned to his cousin, one arm slung casually around my shoulders. "More like welcoming her to the family. You did good, man."

Adam inclined his head. "I think so."

"Marit is going to lend me some of her textbooks from culinary school," Xander added.

Adam gave a low whistle. "Won't Olga just love that?"

"She'll come around." Xander faltered. "She has to."

As one, we swung our eyes to the table where Olga sat alone. She harrumphed, her lips twisting in displeasure. Xander's face fell.

I squeezed his arm. "Your life, your choice. I support you one hundred percent."

"Thanks." Xander frowned as he looked at his grandma.

"Could you do me a favor?" Adam asked him.

Xander jerked his eyes away from Olga. "What?"

"I've got a shit ton of work to do getting ready for the Pack Circle. After Marit and I finish breakfast, could you show her around the kitchen, the pantry, and the greenhouses?"

"No problem," Xander said. "Once you guys mate, I imagine she'll be putting her baking skills to use here."

I stiffened, taken aback. Xander clearly presumed the mating was inevitable. Adam believed that fate had brought us together. In their eyes, it was a done deal, not a question of *if* we would mate, but of when.

I swallowed. Did *I* consider the mating a done deal? I'd known Adam for less than two weeks. A year ago, I would have said I'd be out of my mind to even think about making a commitment to a man I'd known for so short a time.

And now? Truth be told, now it felt like I'd be out of my mind to hesitate or to walk away from him. His strength, his loyalty, and his integrity all offered a powerful allure. More than that, an intangible but undeniable connection had sparked between us, that mysterious attraction that elevates a relationship from sensible to sublime. Every time I looked at him or our hands brushed, I forgot how to breathe.

Sucking in a shaky breath, I met golden eyes that glittered with a wolf's intensity. If I accepted Adam as my mate, I'd be binding myself forever to the wolf, too. A shifter's mate. I shivered, allowing the full meaning of that to sink in. In many ways, the wolf was simpler than the man, less conflicted, less subtle.

The wolf simply knew. He chose me. He'd die to keep me safe. He'd patiently—or impatiently—nudge the man to follow his lead.

Did Adam love me? What was it he had said? The seeds of love had been planted and had taken root in his heart. But had they grown? Had he crossed the tipping point? He hadn't said the words, and without the words I couldn't agree to mate. I needed the certainty of a mutual declaration, a declaration I wasn't going to get in the middle of the crowded dining hall.

"After the Pack Circle, will you come and get me at the cabin?" I asked. "We need to talk."

The planes of his face shifted subtly, as the importance of my request sunk in. His posture stiffened. His eyes locked on mine, questions swimming in their gilded depths.

I couldn't leave the man in a state of uncertainty all day, wondering if we were going to have the dreaded this-isn't-working-for-me conversation. Reaching out to him, I laid my hand over his heart. "We're good."

His expression cleared and his shoulders relaxed. "It'll be past midnight before the Circle breaks up."

"Not a problem. Annika and Liv are heading back to Belle Reve early tomorrow. They'll probably go to bed early. I'll stay up and wait for you."

"It's a plan." His voice roughened, the way it did when the wolf was close to the surface.

"It's a plan," I repeated, emotion channeling my voice to a whisper. Unmoving, we stared at each other.

Xander shuffled his feet. "Your... um... your omelets are getting cold."

Adam and I found an empty table near the windows. Through the glass, I glanced at Grandma's cabin on the opposite side of the lake. Mist swirled like smoke above the roof as bright morning sunshine burned off condensation from last night's heavy rain.

If I lived in the lodge with Adam, I could see Grandma's cabin from here every day. Whenever the mood struck, we could spend the night there, a realization that brought a smile to my face. There were still a lot of things to figure out—how I'd manage to work at the bake shop, for one—but hope found a home in my heart. Maybe, just maybe, this could work. Maybe I could build that true love I'd wished for on the shooting star.

We ate, then lingered for a while, holding hands across the table and sipping coffee. Zane appeared in the doorway and called out to Adam. He tossed his napkin onto the table and stood. He hesitated, then grabbed my elbows and pulled me to my feet. In full view of his cousin and his packmates, he kissed me. Not a chaste see-you-later peck on the cheek, but a deep kiss that left me wobbling in his arms. Somebody whooped. We broke apart.

"Later, kitten." Dark promise filled Adam's deep voice.

Without conscious thought, I lifted my fingers to my neck and touched the spot where he'd lay his claiming bite. It tingled. My entire body buzzed with anticipation.

The wolf watched me through Adam's eyes, his focus absolute, his predator's gaze unwavering. Triumph flashed in his golden orbs.

Dear God, was I actually going to let him bite me? My heart nearly leapt out of my chest. I took a step back, retreating far enough to regain my composure. My lips trembled and I had to try twice to shape the answering word.

"Later."

Chapter Thirty-Two

Adam

Good thing the preparations for the Pack Circle involved mostly grunt work, because my concentration was shot to shit. If I read the signs right, Marit was ready to say yes to our mating. Or at the very least, she was on the brink of committing to it.

She is ours, my wolf declared complacently.

Not till she says so, brother.

He snorted, smug and confident of the outcome.

The wolf may have been calm, but I went about my work with my head spinning.

The Pack Circle took place behind the lodge and sprawled out across both the wide stone patio and the ground that sloped down to Shooting Star Lake. Clouds had dumped rain across the forest last night, but tonight's forecast called for clear skies. We'd lucked out. Our celebration was always scheduled for the height of the Perseid meteor showers. Cloud cover would've meant we couldn't see a damned thing. Rain would've meant we got wet. We were wolves. We could handle wet, but dry was better.

By tradition, the sentries were in charge of logistics. The festivities started with a banquet, followed by dancing. Once the sun went down, packmates spread heavy blankets on the slope. We had portable cribs and sleeping pads ready to set up on the patio for sleepy babies and children. Close to the patio, we put a row of folding chairs for elders whose bones gave them trouble if they sat on the hard ground.

At each Pack Circle, we celebrated the past year's births and matings and commemorated the packmates who'd passed. Old-timers told stories about bygone days. New sentries were announced.

Our pack's greatest treasure—the Black Rock itself—was hauled from its hiding place and installed in the middle of the circle. Everyone would file past it and lay their hand on the rock, feel its power. In a special ceremony, the alpha broke off chips from the meteorite and presented them to new pack members.

Fireworks were a no-go in the woods. Our tech whiz Remy had planned a small drone light show to cap off the evening. Remy loved his high-tech toys, but if you asked me, no drone light show could match the magic of sitting in the dark, waiting for a shooting star to streak across the night sky.

The biggest event at this year's Pack Circle—the thing no one but Olga and the sentries knew about—was Grandpa's stepping down and the appointment of a new alpha. I'd always had a hunch that when the time came, it would be me. By choosing Marit, I made that outcome impossible. I was fine with that. I'd serve if called, but power for its own sake had never appealed to me. And my mate came first.

By midafternoon, everything was in place except the Black Rock. Zane, Remy, and I piled into Rolf's superduty pickup truck. The senior sentry drove over an old logging road deep into the forest. Bumps and ruts made for a rough ride. Four human men couldn't have wrestled the meteorite into the back of the truck. The job taxed even the strength of four wolf shifters, but we got it done. By the time we rolled it into place on the slope next to the lake, it was getting close to dinnertime.

The smell of cooking food drifted from the dining hall's kitchen.

Zane dragged an arm across his sweaty brow, then tilted back his head, sniffing the air. "Hamburgers. Ribs. Chili. Smells good."

"Yeah," I agreed. Wolves favored hearty, protein-rich, chow-down food. And desserts. We were notorious for our sweet tooth. At that thought, I looked across the lake toward the cabin, where my favorite dessert maker waited for me.

Zane's gaze followed mine. "You sure she's worth it?"

Easiest question ever. "One hundred percent."

He nodded, taking me at my word. A moment of silence, while his eyes stayed glued on the Hagen cabin, then, "Annika doesn't like to eat meat. What's up with that?"

Vegetarianism was a concept foreign to wolf shifters. Our animals were true carnivores. Marit told me that Annika had watched a video about factory farming when she was twelve. She gave up meat on the spot. A man like Zane who chased down and ate deer, elk, and rabbits in his wolf form probably couldn't relate to Annika's concerns about animal cruelty or eating a creature with a soul.

That wasn't my story to tell. Instead, I shot Zane side-eye and went on the offensive. "Why are you thinking about Annika, and what she does and doesn't like?"

His head jerked back and he frowned. "I'm not. Not really."

"Right," I drawled, then punched him on the shoulder. "Keep telling yourself that." Turning my back on my flummoxed cousin, I sauntered toward the kitchen and snagged a beer.

Drink in hand, I wandered through the lobby and up to my parents' room on the third floor. They'd sent a text when their plane landed at SeaTac and another when they pulled up to the lodge. The door to their room stood open a crack. Mom's familiar laughter rang out, followed by the deep rumble of Dad's voice, and another side-splitting guffaw.

I halted midstep, childhood memories broadsiding me. Mom's unbridled laughter. Dad's wry observations. A loud, happy home chock-full of unconditional love. That's what my parents gave me. That's the kind of home I wanted to create with Marit.

I rapped three times on the door. No way would I walk in on my parents without giving them a heads-up. I learned that lesson at seven, when I barged into their room and got an eyeful of something I'd rather not see.

"Come in," Mom called.

I stuck my head in the door. Mom was sitting on the bed, emptying a suitcase.

"My baby boy." She jumped to her feet and rushed me, arms outstretched.

Dad shot me a sympathetic grin. At twenty-eight and a strapping six-foot-three, I was hardly a boy, much less a baby. It could've been worse. When I was a kid, Mom called me her "angel bunny." Zane and Remy caught wind of the nickname and teased me mercilessly, until I reminded them that Aunt Grace called them "Peanut One" and "Peanut Two." I had a field day with those nicknames, twisting them in a way that would make any eleven-year-old proud. Fisticuffs ensued. We declared a truce. Mom retired "angel bunny" under protest, but warned me that I was and always would be her baby boy.

"Mom." I swept her off her feet and spun her around and around, then deposited her gently on the floor.

When her laughter subsided, she reached up from her five-foot-nothing height and cupped my cheeks. Concern etched her pretty features. Eyes the same gold color as mine studied me, frowning. "How are you, son?"

They'd already talked to Grandpa. Nothing else could explain that worried look.

I was a grown man, sure of my decision, and willing to accept the consequences. Still, a small part of me hated the thought of disappointing my parents. Taking a step back, I shoved a hand through my hair. My uneasy gaze darted from Mom's face to Dad's.

"You mad?"

"No. We're not mad." Three steps brought Dad to my side. He hauled me into a rough hug and thumped my back. When he let go, his hands gripped my shoulders. His eyes scanned my face with the same intensity that Mom's had shown. "Are you all right, Adam?"

Relief sucker punched me. "Better than all right. I found my mate."

The declaration hung in the air for a silent moment. I was breaking pack law and forfeiting my chance to be alpha. How many parents would accept that without complaint?

Mom took my hand and led me toward their sitting area. I dropped onto a chair while my parents sat down side-by-side on the sofa facing me.

"Tell us about Marit," Mom said.

For the next half hour, that's exactly what I did. When I wound down, Mom leaned back against the cushions. She sighed and glanced at Dad. "Sometimes fate can be—" She hesitated.

"Damned inconvenient," he finished. "I was sixteen and visiting from Wisconsin when my wolf told me Leigh was the one. Her wolf agreed. Everybody said we were too young to mate—"

"We were," Mom interrupted, picking up the familiar story. "But we knew—we *knew*—that fate got it right and we were destined to be together."

And I knew how it all played out. How Dad transferred to Grandpa's pack as soon as he turned eighteen. How two years later, my mother mated with Jason Landry. How they traveled together in their twenties, visiting other wolf packs and studying medicine with the shifter world's best healers. And how they settled down at Shooting Star Lake once I was born.

"When fate brings you your mate, you don't ignore it." Mom laid a hand on Dad's thigh and squeezed.

Was the alpha's daughter advocating defying pack rules? I cocked a brow. "What about the law?"

"Screw the law," she said. I reared back, startled by her vehemence. She lifted a hand. "Your grandpa meant well. He always does, and he's usually right. But not about this."

Dad nodded his agreement.

My parent's unqualified support unraveled the knot in my stomach. I hunched forward, sucking in a deep breath, then straightened.

"When can we meet Marit?" Dad asked.

"Tomorrow. I'm going to bring her back to the lodge after the Pack Circle. Speaking of which—" I glanced at the wall clock, winced at the time, and stood. "I need a shower. See you at the banquet. And welcome home. It's good to have you back."

After another round of hugs, I loped up the stairs to my suite. Fifteen minutes later, showered and wearing clean jeans and a fresh tee, I jogged down to a crowded dining hall. Kyra caught my attention and beckoned me over.

"So far so good," she said. "Looks like we ordered enough food."

"Xander's in his element." I watched my smiling cousin replenish a giant bowl of potato salad.

"Yeah." She bumped her shoulder against mine and lowered her voice. "I heard Marit's going to lend him some textbooks from culinary school. *That'll* make Olga's day."

I groaned. "Where did you hear about Marit and the textbooks?"

Kyra snorted. "Didn't anybody ever tell you? Wolves gossip."

No kidding.

"Great." I groaned again. My gaze traveled around the room, seeking out Olga. I'd try to keep my eye on the alpha's wife and intercede if she made a beeline toward Xander. It appeared that neither Grandpa nor Olga were here yet.

"Wolves gossip *and* we're nosy."

I swung my head toward the young sentry. Kyra's innocent expression belied the words. "Whaddaya mean nosy?"

She batted her lashes. "When are you and Marit actually going to mate? Inquiring minds want to know."

"Soon. I hope."

Kyra stood on her tiptoes and pressed a kiss against my cheek. "I hope so, too. I like Marit. She has a good heart and she makes you happy."

Word had gotten around that I hoped to mate with a human. I'd been ignoring the occasional dirty looks I was getting from some folks. It was good to know that Kyra was on my side. "I appreciate your support."

"You got it. Always." She squeezed my arm. "I'm going to go check out the dessert table. I heard rumors of huckleberry cheesecake."

"You're going to love working at Freya's Bake Shop," I said.

"I know, right?" With a little wave, Kyra skipped across the room.

I spied Dad and Mom sitting at a table with Aunt Grace. They tried to wave me over, but I shook my head and pointed toward the kitchen. I headed there to see if they needed help, and ended up hauling platters full of pork ribs, corn on the cob, and biscuits to the buffet tables. By the time I was ready to eat, the music had started up. My parents wandered outside, pausing to greet friends as they made their way to the dance floor.

I filled a plate and parked myself at a table near the window, a spot where I could watch the dancing while I ate. Kyra dragged a scowling Zane onto the dance floor. He lasted for a good three minutes before Kyra did some kind of silly pirouette that made him shake his head and stomp off. Undeterred, Kyra grabbed a new partner and continued her free-form dance.

Laughing at my fellow sentry's antics. I scrubbed barbecue sauce from my fingers and dabbed my chin with a napkin. A teenager rushed over and took my plate. I thanked him, then went looking for Remy.

"You need any help getting ready for the drone light show?" I asked when I found him. Tech was not my strong suit, but I could schlep stuff that needed moving.

"Nope." He kicked back in his chair. "The ground station is set up and the dashboard display is good to go."

I nodded as if I understood what that meant. "You seen Grandpa yet?"

"Yeah. He checked in a few minutes ago. I told him the drones were all set." Remy yawned. Bet he'd been up most of last night working on the light show. "He said he wasn't hungry, so he was gonna go take his seat by the Black Rock."

I'd moved a couple of the deck chairs from the porch to the slope, so the alpha and his wife could sit in comfort during the long evening.

"I'll go see if he needs anything." I raised a hand. "Later."

I walked outside, threading my way between the dancers. Zane stood on the edge of the patio with his arms folded across his chest. Several packmates cast wistful glances his way, as if they wanted to ask him to dance, but nobody dared. The grimace on his face guaranteed that admirers kept their distance.

Zane's bad moods never scared me off. I sidled up next to him and poked him in the ribs. "Lighten up, man. You're scaring the kids."

He tilted his head toward the Black Rock, where Grandpa sat alone on one of the chairs.

I frowned, scanning the crowd. "Where's Olga? She should be at the alpha's side during the ceremony."

Zane lifted a shoulder. "She's been in a pissy mood all day. Most likely she's pouting in her room."

"Because she finally figured out that Xander won't be the next alpha?" I asked. "She had to know that was a long shot."

"That's probably part of it." Zane lowered his voice. "I heard she confronted Xander about culinary school and the kid held his ground. Told her it was his life and his choice and she couldn't stop him."

His life and his choice? Those were Marit's words of advice to Xander. Hoped he didn't quote her to Olga. I gave a low whistle. "No wonder she's in a snit. Olga doesn't like it when she doesn't get her way."

"Yeah." Zane gave a deep sigh. "Still, you think she'd want to lord it over everybody during her last night as the alpha's wife."

"Maybe one of us should go try to talk her into making an appearance," I reluctantly suggested.

"One of us, huh?" Zane's lips quirked. "You volunteering?"

"Me? No." I glanced around the dance floor.

My gaze landed on Kyra, who was dancing something that vaguely resembled the twist. Her cheeks were flushed from the exercise, and her eyes sparkled with good humor. Would it be crappy if we exercised our seniority and sent our newest sentry to check on Olga?

Yes. Yes it would. I blew out a breath, my cheeks puffing out. "I'll go," I said reluctantly.

"You're a better man than I." Zane bowed his head.

I jabbed a finger in his direction. "And don't you forget it."

The sun had slid behind the mountain peaks. The music stopped and the dancing ended. Folks began setting up cribs on the patio and spreading bedrolls, a sure sign that the celebration was shifting gears.

I strode into the lodge and took the stairs to the top floor two at a time. A narrow strip of light shone from under the door, and classical music played from inside the alpha's quarters. I thumped on the door with my fist. "Olga, it's Adam. Let me in, please."

No response.

"The Pack Circle is starting. Grandpa needs you." There, an appeal to her vanity. If that didn't roust her, nothing would. Bouncing on my toes with impatience, I listened, but no sounds came from inside the room. I pounded on the door again. Still no response.

"Come on, Olga. You should be there." At her continued silence, I threw my hands in the air. "I give up." I turned on my heel and dashed downstairs to the patio. Zane raised his brows in a wordless question. I shook my head no.

If Olga chose to hide in her room, we'd have to start the circle without her. All five sentries formed a row behind the alpha. Rolf formally introduced Kyra—who'd joined our ranks last winter—to the assembled pack. Never one to stand on ceremony, she waved and blew a kiss to her proud parents and brothers.

Rolf regaled the group with a story about his early days as a sentry. He called on my mom and dad, who stood and talked about training a new healer for our allies in northern Greece. The oldest member of the pack held everyone's rapt attention as she recounted her memories of the Great War. Her voice broke when she described her parents' deaths at the hands of the grizzlies, how her mother hid her before facing down our enemies. More than one packmate wiped teary eyes at the conclusion of her story.

Grandpa rose to his feet and presented chips of black rock to our new pack members. One baby had been born in the past year. The tiny girl gurgled and grabbed the alpha's finger when he briefly touched the stone to her forehead. Instead of allowing the infant to hold the rock—she was likely to stick it into her mouth—he handed it to her father.

A young man had recently transferred from my dad's pack back in Wisconsin. Liam wasn't related to us by blood, but I was sure my folks would go out of their way to make him feel at home. He closed his eyes and went very still when Grandpa pressed the black rock to his brow, no doubt reeling under his first experience of the meteorite's mystical powers.

Back ramrod straight, Grandpa gingerly lowered himself onto the chair.

He cleared his throat. "Form the procession."

Everyone lined up and solemnly filed past the Black Rock. One at a time, they paused and laid their hand against its stony surface. Grandpa dipped his head and smiled at each packmate as they walked by. The effort cost him. Beads of sweat dotted his brow, and he clenched his fists, probably to hide his quivering hands.

Barely half the group had touched the rock when the crowd stirred. Murmurs and cries broke out. Folks turned their heads and lifted their arms, shock stamped on their faces as they pointed across the lake. Dread cramped my guts, and a suspicion that something was terribly wrong gripped me. I pivoted around.

"What the fuck," Zane gasped.

Flames licked along the porch of the Hagen cabin. A *whoosh*. A line of fire encircled the structure. The dancing orange flames reflected on the still surface of Shooting Star Lake.

Marit.

I broke into a run.

CHAPTER THIRTY-THREE

MARIT

L iv mixed another pitcher of margaritas and refilled my glass.

Annika sat cross-legged on the sofa next to me, hugging an orange batik pillow to her chest. The woman was a major lightweight. Her first drink had reduced her to silly giggles. A second one would probably knock her on her ass. She held up her empty glass and tilted it back and forth, begging for more.

Liv rolled her eyes. "Remember the last time you had too much tequila?"

Annika pouted, jutting out her lower lip.

"We're not doing that again, are we?" Liv asked with exaggerated patience.

Annika solemnly shook her head, then held out the thumb and forefinger of her free hand. Squinting, she brought them close together. "Just *this* much more."

Liv heaved a long-suffering sigh. "We're going back to Belle Reve early. You have to get out of bed at six a.m. No complaints, no matter how crappy you feel. Promise?"

Frowning with concentration, Annika reshaped her free hand, pinning her pinky down with her thumb and leaving the three middle fingers sticking more or less straight up into the air.

"I promise. Scout's honor."

"Okay." Liv grudgingly poured another inch of margarita into her sister's glass.

"Yum." Annika swallowed, then turned her head toward me. "Do you think Zane was ever a Boy Scout?"

I choked on my drink. Tequila and lime stung my nose, and my eyes watered.

Zane, a Boy Scout? The man was the walking-talking, living-breathing opposite of friendly, courteous, kind, and cheerful. Blinking, I cleared my throat. "Um… I don't think wolf shifters join the Scouts."

"Huh." Her expression thoughtful, Annika leaned back against the sofa cushion. She took another mouthful of her drink and glanced at me again. "What's it like?"

"What's what like?" I asked slowly.

"Sex with a shifter. You know, is it like… regular sex?"

I looked to Liv for support. My cousin waggled her eyebrows, a wicked grin on her face. "Yeah. What's it like? Does Adam go all—" She snarled and slashed the air with an imaginary claw.

I set my drink on the coffee table, bent forward, and dropped my voice to a conspiratorial whisper. "Imagine the best sex you ever had with the hottest man you ever met."

Eyes wide, Liv licked her lips. "Go on."

Lifting my shoulders, I plastered an innocent expression across my face. "Best sex. Hottest man. That's all you need to know." I picked up my margarita and took a ladylike sip.

"C'mon." Disgusted, Liz threw her hands in the air. "Give us details, woman."

I smiled like the cat that got the cream. "Nope."

"Nope?" Liv sat up straight. She pointed at Annika, then back at herself. "What if one of us decides to sleep with somebody in the pack? Don't you want us to be prepared for any of their… um… *wolfy proclivities?*"

She had me there. I sighed. "Okay. Listen up because I'm only saying this once. Shifter Sex 101." I held up a finger. "First, amazing stamina." I raised a second finger. "Second, world's shortest refractory period." A third finger went up. I hesitated, searching for the right words. "Third, and here's the biggest difference: their cock locks in place, and they come like a geyser."

I left out the part about the mating bite. My cousins might freak out if they knew I was considering it. Besides, while I could imagine a curious Liv hooking up with a pack member, making a lifetime commitment was an entirely different thing. How likely was it that either of them would fall in love with a shifter?

"Locks in place?" Annika's eyes went wide.

"Did you say 'geyser'?" Liv repeated.

"You heard me. I recommend you put down a towel."

Annika's mouth fell open. "But the sex is good? It's worth it?"

"Best. Sex. Ever." I enunciated clearly.

"Well, all right." Liv pursed her lips and flopped against the seat back. I could practically see the wheels turning in her head.

Annika held out her empty glass. "A little bit more, please."

Liv roused herself and dumped another few inches into Annika's glass, then she gulped down her own drink. They lapsed into silence. Apparently I'd rocked their world with my description of shifter sex.

Loki trotted over and nudged my leg, whining.

"You need a potty break?" I clambered off the sofa and led the way to the cabin door, pausing in the kitchen to grab Grandma's binoculars. I followed Loki outside and into the yard. While he attended to business, I walked to the edge of the lake and lifted the field glasses to my eyes.

Lights blazed from almost every window in the old lodge. A crowd milled about on the patio and slope leading down to the lake. I scanned the throng. From this distance, there was no way I could pick out Adam in the mass of people, but that didn't stop me from trying.

"Where are you?" I whispered, suddenly desperate to see the wolf shifter who'd staked a claim to my heart. Just a glimpse of his tall figure moving confidently among his people would tide me over until we were face-to-face again. I swept the binoculars back and forth, an irrational, niggling sense of disquiet ticking along my spine.

Loki barked. I jumped. Heart pounding, I lowered the binoculars and whirled around. Loki stared into a blackberry bush, his ears raised and his posture alert. He barked again and pawed at a thorny cane.

Crap. The woods near the cabin teemed with animal life, and Loki had already demonstrated an unfortunate predilection for bolting. "Don't even think about it," I warned him. "Remember what happened when you ran into a skunk?"

A skunk was bad. A raccoon would be worse. They might look cute, but their claws were vicious. Even a rabbit could prove a problem if it hopped away and Loki took off after it into the dark.

"Come on." I patted my thigh, summoning him to my side. He looked at me, considered my request, then swung his gaze back to the bush. "No you don't," I warned, locking my fingers around his collar. "Inside. Now."

Loki whined. With a final backward glance at the blackberry bush, he trotted next to me back into the cabin. I locked the door behind us and on impulse, pulled the curtain closed over its small window.

"Hey." Annika smiled, her eyes heavy from both tequila and oncoming sleep. "I'm going to head to bed."

"Good idea. You need anything?" I asked.

She yawned—a big, jaw-cracking yawn—and shook her head. "No. I'm all set."

Liv stood and stretched her arms over her head. "I think I'll take a nice long bath before I hit the sack."

"I won't be here in the morning when you guys wake up," I reminded them.

"That's right. You and Adam are going to have *the talk.*" Liv put air quotes around the phrase.

Annika shuffled over and threw her arms around me. "I hope it goes well."

I returned her hug. "I think it will."

After a round of good nights, they retired.

Through the bedroom door, came the low murmur of Liv and Annika's voices, followed a few minutes later by the sound of water filling the tub. I didn't want my cousins to wake up to a mess. I washed and dried our glasses and put the tequila and triple sec back in the cupboard.

I'd been meaning to look through Grandma's recipe box and to pull any items that might make good additions to the bakery's offerings. Sitting at the kitchen table, I thumbed through the recipes while Loki dozed at my feet. I set aside cards for Swedish apple pie and an oatmeal cake. Smiling, I took out the card for the orange honey muffins that Adam loved. That was definitely going into the muffin rotation at the shop. I turned it over and traced a fingertip over the mysterious inscription on the back. *Aleks loves these!*

"Who were you, Aleks?" I wondered out loud.

After selecting a dozen new recipes to try at Freya's Bake Shop, I ambled to the living room, plumped the pillows on the sofa, and made myself a cozy nest. I didn't want to disturb the sleeping Annika and Liv, so I slid in a pair of earbuds and curled up in my nest of pillows. A few days ago, I'd downloaded my favorite author's new audiobook. I settled down happily to listen to a story while I waited for Adam.

The narrator had an especially soothing voice. Either that, or the tequila caught up with me. My head slipped sideways onto a soft cushion. My eyelids drifted shut and sleep took me under. I woke sometime later to a cool, wet nose nuzzling my face. My lids flew open, and I met the dog's pale-blue eyes.

"Loki," I groaned. "Don't tell me you already need to pee again."

He barked, ran halfway to the door, then zoomed back to my side.

"Okay. Okay. I get it. You gotta go." I wobbled to a seated position and scrubbed my hands over my face. Loki headbutted my arm. "Dude, give me thirty seconds, will you?"

He yipped and backed up, his ears dropping. His anxious posture snapped me into wakefulness. I hopped to my feet, followed him to the door, and turned the knob. It wouldn't budge. I yanked hard, trying to twist it sideways, but it held firm.

What the hell?

Shoving the curtain aside, I pressed my face against the glass and peered into the yard. The circle of light cast by the porch lamp illuminated the bottom half of a person standing a few feet from the porch. From the chest up, they were shrouded in shadow. The figure appeared to be a stocky woman wearing what Grandma called a duster, a knee-length bathrobe favored by old ladies. Her feet were bare, a detail that gave me the willies. Who would wander through the dark, lonely woods barefoot?

In her right hand, she carried a bright-red can of gasoline.

She stepped forward. Porch light slashed across a broad face devoid of emotion. With one hand, she held up the gas can. With the other, she fumbled in the duster's pocket and pulled out something squarish and metallic. She popped its lid. A brilliant orange flame flared into life.

Olga's face split into a wide smile.

CHAPTER THIRTY-FOUR

ADAM

"Fire brigade," Rolf roared behind me, rallying pack members trained to fight a fire. They'd grab shovels, buckets, extinguishers, and fire blankets and rush to the site.

I'd get there first.

With Zane and Remy hot on my heels, I raced for my truck. We jumped inside. I shoved the key into the ignition and burned rubber out of the parking lot.

Marit. Marit. Marit.

Her name beat like a drum in my head. Blind panic shoved out every other thought.

"You think Rolf will call DNR?" Remy's question to Zane barely penetrated my mental fog.

"Dunno. Maybe." Zane's terse reply showed him to be as caught up in worry as me.

"Hope we can put it out without calling in state firefighters," Remy said. "Last thing we need is the Department of Natural Resources up our ass."

"Shut up," Zane barked, uncharacteristically harsh with his brother.

The truck shot over the road leading to the southern shore of the lake, then skidded to a stop a short distance from the cabin. Zane, Remy, and I hurtled out of the cab.

"Get the shovel and ax from the truck bed," I called over my shoulder as I ran toward the woman who would be my mate. Beneath my skin, my frantic shadow brother howled to escape.

I got this, I assured him.

At a glance, I took in the situation. Last night's heavy rain suddenly felt like a blessing. The ribbon of fire encircling the cabin was already sputtering out, whatever fuel that fed it exhausted. It hadn't spread to the trees, thank fuck. With the exception of a small blackberry bramble—Freya Hagen had loved her blackberry pies—she'd cut back the bushes and brush surrounding the cabin.

The porch was a different story. Flames crawled along the handrails and up the support posts to lick the roof. The wooden steps were ablaze.

Tipping back my head, I sniffed the air. Gasoline.

I spun my eyes to the cabin's only door, squinting through the smoke. What the hell? Somebody had looped and padlocked a chain around the doorknob, and locked the other end around an upright post. Whoever started the fire wanted to trap the women inside the cabin.

"Marit," I bellowed.

No response.

If they'd gotten out in time, if they'd crawled out a window, they'd be in the yard.

"Adam."

I turned my head and followed Remy's gaze.

Close to the lake, Olga sat on the ground, knees drawn up to her chest. She was rocking back and forth. Her lips moved as she spoke to... to nobody. She tossed back her head and laughed. Next to her, a gasoline can lay on its side.

No time for this. We'd deal with Olga later.

I snatched the ax from Remy's hands and charged the porch, leaping over the burning stairs. Two steps brought me to the door. Embers rained down on me from the roof as I lifted the ax and chopped through the chain.

Zane landed next to me. We threw our shoulders against the door and stumbled inside when it gave way.

"Marit." Coughing, I scanned the room.

Zane swung his head from side to side, then called out, "Annika."

Silence.

CHAPTER THIRTY-FIVE

MARIT

With a flick of her wrist, Olga tossed the lighter onto the porch. An orange fireball erupted on the wooden steps. I staggered backward, my mouth falling open. Panic squeezed my chest and I couldn't breathe. For a good five seconds, shock locked me in place. Loki barked, snapping me out of it. Thank God. I whipped my head to the side and gaped at him, rallying my wits.

Annika and Liv. My cousins were sound asleep, unaware that the porch was on fire, that *Olga* had somehow blocked the cabin's only door and set the freaking porch on fire. With gasoline. I shuddered. Had she thrown gas on all the outside walls, too? Was the entire cabin about to burst into flame?

"Come on, Loki. We gotta move."

Grabbing his collar, I tugged him toward the back of the cabin. I threw open the door and ran toward the bed.

"Wake up." I touched Liv's shoulder. "There's a fire."

Liv sat bolt upright, frowning with confusion. "What did you say?"

"Fire." I yanked off the quilt, seized her hands, and pulled her to her feet. "We need to get out."

"Fire?" Liv repeated, coming fully awake. "What the hell?"

I turned to Annika. After two drinks, she wasn't blackout drunk, but the tequila had done a number on a woman who rarely imbibed. Not even my shriek had roused her. Mumbling, deep in sleep, she burrowed into her pillow.

"Annika, wake up." I shook her shoulders. Her eyes fluttered open and she blinked up at me. "That's right. Keep your eyes open." I grabbed both of her hands and hauled her into a seated position.

"What's happening?" she grumped, her head lolling to one side.

"Cabin's on fire. We're getting out."

"Come on." Liv slid an arm around Annika's waist and hauled her to her feet. Annika wobbled. They took one unsteady step toward the bedroom door.

"The porch is burning," I said. "We can't get out through the front."

Liv switched course, half carrying her sister toward the bedroom's double-pane window.

I raced ahead of them, unfastened the latch, and slid the glass panel up. Glancing outside, my heart seized. Flames flickered on the ground. Dammit. Olga must have splashed gasoline around the cabin before tossing a lighter at the porch.

I looked closer. We caught a break. It wasn't a wall of fire. Apparently, Olga hadn't brought enough accelerant to leave a solid line or standing puddles around the perimeter. Already, some of the flames were dying out. Maybe we could throw a blanket on the ground and jump across to safety.

I dashed back to the bed and grabbed the quilt—the beautiful quilt hand-stitched by Grandma—then ran back to the window. "You go first," I told Liv. "Then help Annika."

Liv climbed out the window and held up her arms to catch her sister. Annika was awake, but floppy-limbed and punchy. I boosted her up onto the windowsill. She tumbled through the opening, knocking Liv to the ground. Liv scrambled to her feet, then hauled Annika up. I tossed them the quilt.

"Find a break in the flames, throw the quilt on the ground, then jump across." I groaned as something occurred to me. "If you see Olga, run. She might have a gun. I'll be right behind you."

"But—" Liv protested.

"Gotta get Loki," I said. "Now go."

She nodded and threw an arm around Annika's shoulders. Together, they lurched away from the cabin.

I wheeled around, frantically scanning the room for the dog. I'd dragged him to the bedroom. He'd been *right next* to me. Where was he now?

"Loki. Here boy." I whistled and patted my leg.

No sign of him. No answering bark. No sound of claws clicking across the floor.

Shit. Shit. Shit.

I dashed to the bathroom. Empty. I shoved aside the shower curtain, in case he'd taken it in his head to hide in the bathtub. No. Dammit. I ran back into the living room, desperately searching for my boy.

"Loki," I cried. Through the front windows, orange light from the burning porch illuminated the room. The roar and crackle of burning wood filled my ears. If the dog was whimpering, I wouldn't hear him. I stumbled across the room, checking behind the sofa and upholstered chair. I swept aside the floor-length curtains. Nothing.

Where was he?

With a sob, I ran back to the bedroom and slammed the door shut. On impulse, I dropped to my knees and looked under the old brass bed. A pair of pale-blue eyes met mine. Loki had crawled under the frame and wedged himself next to the wall. I held out my hand. "Come on, baby."

Paralyzed with fear, he didn't twitch.

Could I fit under there? It would be tight. Pressing myself flat on the wooden floor, arm stretched out in front of me, I wriggled under the bed, worming my way forward until my fingers *almost* reached the dog.

"Please, please, please," I begged. I didn't want to leave Loki behind. I couldn't abandon him to a fire. But I didn't want to die in an inferno, either.

Clarity struck like a hammer. In my mind's eye, images of the life that I wanted unwound like a thread from a spool. It was all so simple. I wanted Adam. I wanted to fall asleep every night next to him and to wake up in his arms. I wanted to tease him. To work side-by-side with him. To bake for him, and watch the expression on his face when he bit into one of my treats. I wanted it all, the drudgery and the bliss. I wanted a life with the man I loved. I definitely didn't want to die in a fire.

My chest hitched on another sob. "Come on, Loki. You have to move."

A crash from the front room.

Oh dear God. Olga wanted to kill me.

The woman was shifter-strong and unhinged. Had she broken into the cabin to finish me off? My pulse hammered in my throat. My ears rang. I tried to draw my legs all the way under the bed, but couldn't manage it in this narrow space. Footsteps thundered across the cabin, and the door to the bedroom flew open. Somebody grabbed my ankles and hauled me out from under the bed.

I screamed, struggling in their arms.

"Marit, it's me."

I froze. My head reared back and I looked into determined golden eyes. "Adam," I whispered. The fate I'd said I didn't believe in had given me a second chance. My chin trembled. No more hesitation. No more playing it safe.

"I love you, Adam Landry. I want to be your mate."

His fierce expression softened. "Love you too, kitten. I got you. Now and forever." His arms tightened around me. "Let's get you out of here." He took a step toward the open window.

"Loki is hiding under the bed," I said quickly.

I hadn't noticed Zane in the room. He grabbed the brass footboard, jerked the heavy bed away from the wall, and scooped the traumatized dog into his arms. Still holding me close, Adam climbed out the window, Zane and Loki right behind us.

Adam strode around to the front of the cabin, where at least twenty packmates fought the fire. Smoke stung my eyes. Empty extinguishers were piled on the ground. I don't imagine extinguishers did a lot of good against the spreading flames, but clearly the shifters were throwing everything they had at the blaze. Shovel after shovelfuls of dirt smothered the fire. Buckets filled with water from the lake were lined up, ready to soak every surface once the gasoline fueled flames had died down.

Olga sat on the ground, watching events unfold with a vacant expression. A frowning Kyra stood guard next to the alpha's homicidal wife. On the opposite side of the yard, Annika and Liv were speaking to a tall man and petite woman.

"Annika," Zane said under his breath. He set Loki on the ground and marched over to my cousins.

I turned in Adam's arms. "Olga—" I started.

Adam's lips tightened and he gave a curt nod. "I know."

"I told Annika and Liv to run the other way if they saw her. I stayed behind to look for Loki."

Unhappiness flitted across his face, but instead of chastising me for risking my life, he dropped a kiss on my forehead.

"When you love, you love hard."

"I do, even if sometimes it takes me a while to get there."

"Adam," a frail voice called out.

Somebody had dragged a lawn chair to the edge of the lake. The alpha sat there, looking old and unwell, as if his wife's actions had hollowed him out and robbed him of the last of his vitality.

Adam set me on my feet and led the way to his grandfather. Loki followed us, glued to Adam's side. Adam dropped into a crouch next to the chair and took the alpha's hand. "Grandpa. What can I do?"

The alpha waved both hands, clearly at a loss for words.

Xander abandoned his spot in the bucket brigade and rushed over. His expression stricken, he pulled me into a hug. "I... I can't believe this happened. I'm so damned sorry."

"Not your fault, sweetheart," I said. "Nobody died. That's what matters."

"Your grandma's cabin—"

Adam hopped up and clapped his young cousin on the shoulder. "Marit's right. Nobody died and that's what matters. As for the cabin—" He lifted one powerful shoulder. "We'll assess the damage, save what we can, and rebuild."

I turned and looked at the cabin. It had always been my happy place, a place intrinsically tied to memories of my grandma. Every nook and cranny reminded me of her. The porch was toast—*ha ha*—but the main structure appeared intact. Smoke might have permeated the upholstery and fabrics and rugs, but they could be cleaned or replaced with something similar. Many of Grandma's treasures probably survived: the Little Red Riding Hood cookie jar, her recipe box, her blue-and-white dishes, her poster from Woodstock, maybe even her collection of '60s vinyl records.

Even if we'd lost everything to the fire, the most important things remained. The things nobody could ever take away. My memories of Grandma. I imagined her standing next to me, her gray hair pulled back in its typical long braid, wearing her silver hoop earrings, dancing and singing along to Jefferson Airplane or Tom Lehrer.

"Pfft," she'd say if I told her about the smoke damage. "It's all just stuff. People matter. Stuff doesn't."

Everybody I cared about was safe. Adam loved me. I was fine.

"I better get back to work," Xander said, hugging me again.

From the corner of my eye, I saw Olga struggle to her feet. She launched toward us, Kyra at her side, holding onto her arm. Adam and Xander stepped in front of me. Zane, Remy, and Rolf rushed over and formed a ring around Matthew. Liv hustled over, bringing a still-wobbly Annika with her. The tall man and petite woman followed them. Liv planted herself next to me, forming a sort of defensive line of Hagen cousins.

"As if I'd ever hurt the alpha or the pack," Olga sniffed, then turned pleading eyes to her husband. "I did it for us. To protect us."

"What are you going on about, Olga?" Matthew asked, looking heartbroken and unbearably weary.

Olga drew herself up to her full height and jutted out her chin.

"Those women. They should never have been born. Especially her." She jabbed her finger in my direction.

I gasped, dumbfounded by the rage directed at me and my cousins. What had we ever done to hurt Olga, to warrant her attempt to kill us?

Adam bristled. A low growl rolled from his chest. His body vibrated with suppressed violence. Glancing at him, I saw the wolf in his glittering eyes.

Olga ignored both my indignation and the seething beast beside me. "She's the spitting image of that wretched woman. Freya Hagen took everything from me, everything that mattered—" Her face twisted and she laughed, a low, bitter sound devoid of humor. "And now Marit Hagen shows up and history repeats itself. She's a blight and a constant reminder of what I lost."

"What the hell are you talking about?" The question burst from my mouth. "What did Grandma take from you?"

Olga fixed steely gray eyes on me.

"Only the person I loved best. My brother. Aleksandr."

CHAPTER THIRTY-SIX

ADAM

"Aleks." Marit looked stunned. "Aleks was your brother?"

"I suppose your grandmother told you all about him?" Olga's voice was full of accusation.

"No." Marit's head sliced left and right. "Not a word. I saw his name on the back of one of Grandma's recipe cards." She touched my arm and lifted beautiful gray eyes to mine. "The one for the orange honey muffins you like. Grandma wrote 'Aleks loves these.' I had no idea who he was."

"Aleksandr was my closest friend. Like a brother to me." Grandpa spoke up. "We grew up together. Back in Alaska, his father was one of my father's sentries. They were both killed in a logging accident before the start of the Great War. When Aleks died in the summer of '69, I was gutted."

"And years later, you married me out of a sense of duty to your dead friend," Olga said. She held up a hand. "Don't bother to deny it. I know you never loved me the way you loved Katia."

Standing on one side of Annika, my mom sighed and shook her head. This wasn't the first time she heard Olga reproach Grandpa about his enduring love for her mother.

"Love can wear different faces," Grandpa said gently. "Katia was my mate. You're my wife. I care deeply about you."

Olga snorted.

"What does Aleks have to do with Grandma Freya?" Liv asked.

"They were *in love*." The warble in Olga's voice made a mockery of the word. "Her parents held the lease to the cabin, but it was only hippie-dippie Freya who visited after we closed the lake. Freya, with her loud music and peasant dresses and stupid paintings."

At this insult to her grandmother, Marit clenched her fists and inhaled a deep breath, but held her peace.

Indifferent to Marit's anger, Olga continued. "Freya had set up an easel in the woods and was painting a picture of a tree stump when Aleks came across her. A tree stump, can you believe it?" Olga shook her head. "Aleks was totally charmed and carried the easel back to the cabin for her. And that was that. He fell for her, hook, line, and sinker."

"How do you know all this?" Liv asked.

"My big brother changed almost overnight. He'd disappear for hours at a time. I followed him one day and saw them together. When I confronted him, he told me about her. He said they were in love. He said... he said they'd mated."

Grandpa frowned. "Aleks never said a word to me about Freya."

"Well, he couldn't tell you, could he?" Olga pointed out. "You weren't just his friend. You were his alpha, and you'd outlawed mating with a human. I tried to talk sense into him. I told him he was breaking the law, but he didn't care. He said I was fifteen, and I was too young to understand what it meant to find your mate."

"So what happened?" Annika asked, clearly caught up in the story of her grandmother's lost love. "How did Aleks die?"

"He was killed in a car accident." Grandpa closed his eyes, as if the simple act of shutting his lids could hide the painful memory. "It's been decades, but it feels like yesterday. The police came to the lodge and told us the brakes failed in the car he was driving." His eyes snapped open and he swung a curious gaze toward Olga.

"What is it, Grandpa?" I asked.

"The car was registered to Freya Hagen. The police said that when they informed her of the accident, they asked if her car had been stolen. She said no. She told them that a member of the conservancy had flagged her down and asked to borrow it. Told her there was an emergency and he needed to drive to Belle Reve. I didn't think too much about it at the time. Aleks's death dwarfed the question of why he was driving Freya's car."

Marit grabbed my hand, holding on for dear life. "Wait. This doesn't make sense," she said. "Aleks was no neighbor who borrowed her car. She loved him. Why did she lie to the police?"

We all looked to Olga. She wrenched her wrist free from Kyra's grasp and crossed her arms defensively over her chest. "Well, obviously, she didn't want the pack to know about their relationship. Maybe she was afraid we'd punish her for mating with Aleks. She certainly deserved it." Jaw set, Olga stared at the ground.

A sneaking suspicion sprung to life in my chest. "It was you, wasn't it? All those years. You're the one who kept sneaking over and vandalizing Freya's property. Breaking stuff. Stealing things."

Marit gasped and squeezed my hand.

Xander's shoulders drooped and he covered his face with his hands. "Dammit, Grandma."

Olga's face softened when she looked at the young man she loved, the teenage grandson she'd hoped would one day be alpha. "Xander, you don't understand. Freya deserved to suffer. It was supposed to be her, not Aleks who died."

What the fuck?

"Olga, what did you do?" Grandpa finally demanded, alpha power in his voice. I felt the irresistible pull of that power, the compulsion to obey.

"What I had to, don't you see?" She directed pleading eyes to her husband. "Freya turned Aleks against us. He told me... he told me she was pregnant. They were going to run away. He was willing to abandon the pack for the sake of a human."

Freya was pregnant with Aleks's child. My world upended. Shock robbed me of my voice. The woman I loved—my future mate—was part shifter. If we had kids, they'd be shifters. Beneath my skin, the wolf howled his joy.

Beside me, all color drained from Marit's face. Wide-eyed, she turned to me.

"My grandfather was a wolf shifter."

Annika swayed. Zane caught her arm, steadying her. Nobody said a word. Sound retreated. The crackle of the flames and the voices of those fighting the fire fell away.

"Aleks was trying to protect his pregnant mate." Mom spoke up, defending Olga's brother. Dad threw an arm across her shoulders and pulled her close.

"The law," Olga hissed. "They were breaking the law. They had no business mating or creating a child who could never shift."

"Children," Liv corrected through stiff lips. "Grandma had twins. Michael and Nicholas."

"Olga." The alpha's body might be weak, but his voice held an undeniable strength and authority. "I'll ask again. What did you do?"

Olga clasped her hands together. "I thought that if I could just get Aleks out from under Freya's spell, I'd get my big brother back. With Freya gone, everything would go back to normal." She paused. "I cut the brakes in her car. I never imagined—" Her voice broke. "In a million years, I never imagined that Aleks would take the car instead of Freya."

Olga was responsible for her brother's death. What would that kind of guilt do to a fifteen year old? Twist her into a bitter, vindictive woman, that's what.

Trembling, Marit buried her face in my chest. I wrapped both arms around her and held her close, meeting my mom's sympathy-filled gaze over her head.

"But you knew Grandma was pregnant when you cut the brakes," Annika faltered.

"With an abomination," Olga spat. "A baby who should never have been conceived."

"The babies *were* born. They're our fathers." Annika pointed at the smoldering porch. "How could you try to kill us? We share blood. We're your family."

Olga made a face. "I want no part of Freya Hagen's grandchildren. As far as I'm concerned, the coyotes and grizzlies should have killed you all."

My blood turned to ice. The deal Bryce had made to kill us back in Belle Reve, had it been with Olga? Did her hatred for me and the Hagen women run that deep? I met Zane's eyes and saw in them the same suspicion that I felt. He dipped his head. We'd get to the bottom of that later.

"I'll claim you as family," Xander said.

Marit turned in my arms and laid a hand on Xander's chest. "With all my heart, I'll claim you as family, too."

Such a sentimental sweetheart. I sent a quick thank you to fate for bringing her into my life. And Xander's. They were some sort of cousins by blood, and the young man could use the tie of family, especially now.

"No." Olga stomped her foot and jabbed a finger at Marit. "You're stealing Xander away from me, just like Freya stole Aleks." Spittle flew from Olga's mouth as she ramped up. "You show up on pack land. You wheedle your way into Adam's life. Persuade him to break pack law. It's like Aleks all over again. Then you prance around, flaunting my mother's earrings."

Marit's hands flew to her ears. "Your mother's earrings?"

Olga nodded. "Aleks told Mama about Freya and asked for her blessing. Mama gave him her silver hoop earrings to pass along to Freya. I always thought they'd come down to me, but no. Freya got them. And now you're wearing them. It's like a knife to the heart every time I see you."

Grandpa had had enough. "Rolf, will you escort my wife back to our quarters. Leave a guard at the door."

"Yes, sir." The senior sentry strode forward and offered Olga his arm. "Please come with me, ma'am." It was an order, couched as a request. She took his arm. He turned to our youngest sentry. "Kyra, you come, too." The three of them walked to his truck and drove away.

What a mess.

Grandpa scrubbed his hands over his face, then sat up straight. His gaze slowly traveled from Marit, to Liv, to Annika. "You're Aleksandr's granddaughters. I wish I'd known before now."

"It's your fault that you didn't, Daddy." My outspoken mother walked over and laid a hand on Grandpa's shoulder. "If it weren't for your no-mating-with-humans law, Aleks would probably still be alive. He would have grown old with the woman he loved. He and Freya would have raised their children in the pack."

"Mom," I protested. Grandpa felt bad enough. No need to pile on the guilt.

"No, son." Grandpa waved a hand. "Let her talk. She speaks her mind, just like my Katia did."

"I love you, Daddy. Always." Mom squeezed his shoulder. "You had the best of intentions. But the law has done far more harm than good. It cost Aleks his life. It cost Adam his chance to be alpha. And being forced to choose between his mate and his duty to the pack nearly tore my son's heart in two."

"I hear you," Grandpa said. "And now, I'd like to have a private word with Adam and Zane."

Mom walked over and kissed my cheek, then smiled at Marit and offered her hand. "I'm Leigh Landry. It's good to meet you." She tilted her head toward the other side of the yard. "Let's go get to know each other."

"I'd like that."

The group scattered, leaving Zane and me alone with Grandpa. To my surprise, Zane spoke first. "I was your second choice for alpha. If you want to give it back to Adam, you got my blessing. We both know he's the best person for the job."

"Whoa, Zane, you're jumping the gun," I said. "We have no idea what Grandpa wants."

"No, that's pretty much it," Grandpa said. "Zane would make a fine alpha, but his strengths lie elsewhere."

"Amen to that," Zane agreed. "I'd rather kick ass than play politician or diplomat any day."

"Will you accept the position, Adam?" Grandpa asked. "Allow me to step down knowing the pack is in safe hands?"

I rocked back on my heels. Everything that I thought I'd lost—Marit, wolf pups, becoming alpha—fate had thrown it all back on my lap. I felt like the richest man in the world.

"Thank you, Grandpa." I inclined my head. "I'll serve the pack to the best of my abilities."

"I know you will, son." Grandpa offered a weak smile. "And I know Marit will be a fine alpha's mate. I'm tired and want to be done for the night. I'll call a special pack meeting for Sunday, transfer the power to you, and announce that you're the new alpha." He turned to Zane. "Will you drive me back to the lodge and walk an old man to one of the guest rooms?"

"Yes, sir."

Zane didn't offer Grandpa his arm—the way Rolf had with Olga—but from his stiff and cautious gait, the alpha could have used the support. Back ramrod straight, Grandpa made his way to the car, pausing only to exchange a few words with the packmates putting out the last of the fire. That's what a good alpha did, set aside his or her own needs to offer comfort and support to their pack.

Soon, the job would be mine. I'd do my damnedest to prove myself a worthy successor to Grandpa. I looked across the yard to where Marit stood with my parents. As if feeling my eyes on her, she glanced at me and pressed her palm against her heart.

"I love you, too." She couldn't hear the words, but from the smile that crossed her face, she understood.

We'd gone through one hell of a night. She needed a soak in the tub and a good night's sleep.

Tomorrow. Tomorrow we'd mate.

CHAPTER THIRTY-SEVEN

MARIT

Hand in hand, Adam and I walked up to the front door of a blue 1930s-era bungalow. I rang the bell. Inside the house, a dog barked furiously. Footsteps tapped across a hardwood floor.

"Hush now, Buttercup," a woman's voice said. "Mama will see who it is."

The door opened. Surprise registered on the elderly woman's face, followed quickly by a bright, welcoming smile.

"Marit." Dorrie Mittelmann held out both arms and pulled me into her embrace. "You've been in my thoughts."

I returned the hug, surprised by the tears that pricked the back of my eyes. "It's good to see you, Mrs. M."

She glanced behind me. Her gaze swept over Adam from his dark hair to his boots, then back up again, lingering for a moment on his leather-and-black-rock bracelet. She tipped her lips up in a positively mischievous grin. Good lord. Was the spry septuagenarian checking out my man?

She extended a hand to him. "Dorrie Mittelmann. How do you do?"

Adam's big hand gently enclosed hers. "Adam Landry. Pleased to meet you, ma'am."

I was used to it, but the deep rumble of his voice made me shiver. It had the same effect on Mrs. M.

Apparently Buttercup didn't like a strange man getting too close to his mama. Glaring at Adam, he snarled and showed his teeth.

Adam dropped down onto his haunches and lowered his chin. "We gonna have a problem?" From my angle, I couldn't tell if he allowed the wolf to show in his eyes. Maybe he didn't have to. The Pomeranian crouched down on the floor and rolled over, exposing his belly.

Mrs. M. sighed. "I just brewed a fresh pot of coffee. Marit, dear, why don't you and your wolf shifter fellow come sit at the kitchen table with me? We can have a nice chat."

Wolf shifter fellow. That answered the question of how much she knew about Grandma and Aleks. Looked like Grandma's best friend knew everything.

Adam and I followed Mrs. M. to her sunny yellow kitchen and sat down at a table covered with a daisy-strewn oilcloth. She poured three mugs of coffee, then joined us. Buttercup curled up at Adam's feet. Like Loki, he'd gone all-in on team shifter.

She tipped her head at Adam, her brown eyes sparkling. "You've upgraded, sweet girl. I put on a happy face for your sake, but I never was particularly fond of Bryce. I was glad to hear that you canceled the wedding."

The wedding. Today was supposed to be my wedding day, and I hadn't spared Bryce a thought. My world now centered around a man I met a little more than a week ago. Adam reached across the table and took my hand, his thumb rubbing circles in the middle of my palm.

"It's only been eleven days," I murmured, my eyes seeking reassurance in his.

"Puhleeze," Mrs. M. interjected. "They say God created the world in six days. Freya fell head over heels for Aleks in less than a week and stayed in love with him until the day she died."

"When fate shows the way, eleven days is plenty of time," Adam said. "I love you with all my heart, kitten."

The world righted itself. "I love you, too."

Mrs. M. fanned her face "You're giving an old lady palpitations. This is better than one of my soap operas."

I laughed. "I hope so."

She sobered. "Are you two breaking the law? Will you get in trouble with the pack?"

"No." Adam's voice was firm. "My grandfather saw the error of his ways and abolished the law."

"And starting tomorrow, Adam will be the new alpha," I bragged. "We're safe."

"Oh, my. Congratulations are in order." Mrs. M. craned her neck, looking around the kitchen. "I have a bottle of schnapps somewhere I can break out."

"No, no." I waved a hand. "We're good, but we do have a few questions for you."

"Yes?" She tilted her head, her eyes alight with curiosity.

"Grandma and Aleks didn't have a lot of time together. Do you think they were happy?"

She nodded. "Deliriously happy, especially when they found out that she was pregnant. I got to know Aleks. He was ready to give up everything he knew to keep Freya and the baby safe. Your grandfather was a good man, and he loved your grandmother very much."

"But—" I hesitated. "Grandma let everybody believe that Dad and Uncle Mike were conceived at Woodstock. None of us knew about Aleks, or that we had shifter blood. None of us knew Grandma had lost her great love."

Mrs. Mittelmann patted my arm. "We weren't supposed to know that shifters existed. Aleks made us promise never to tell. We honored that promise. Until you showed up just now with a shifter in tow, I never admitted it to a soul, not even my late husband."

"Thank you for keeping our secret," Adam said solemnly.

Anger sparked in her eyes. "Remember, their mating broke pack law. After Aleks was killed, Freya was afraid of what the alpha might do if he discovered she was carrying an illicit half-shifter baby. Fear played a part in keeping your secret."

"Is that why you went to Woodstock? Was it a cover story to explain the pregnancy?" I asked.

"No." Mrs. M. scoffed. "We weren't thinking that far ahead." Her expression grew solemn. "Aleks's death crushed Freya. She stumbled through her days, half-alive. Woodstock was my idea. I thought a change of scenery might do her good. I thought seeing Janis and Jimi and Arlo might give her something to look forward to, so I dragged her across the country to the festival. It turned out that Woodstock made a good cover story for the pregnancy, but that was never our intention."

"You were a good friend," I said. "I'm glad she had you. It would've been a lonely burden to keep her secrets all to herself."

Tears filled her eyes and spilled down her cheeks. Buttercup whined. She picked the dog up and settled him on her lap. "I'm an old woman. One thing I've learned is that good friends are one of life's greatest gifts. Freya was my dearest friend. I was honored to help her carry the burden."

"Do you know why she was so determined to hold on to the cabin's lease?" Adam asked.

"She asked me to promise never to sell it," I added.

"That's easy." Mrs. M. smiled through her tears. "Freya told me that she felt Aleks's presence in every corner of the cabin. All of her memories of him were tied to the place. If she glanced into the bathroom, she'd imagine him in the old tub with his knees drawn up to his chest. She'd catch a glimpse of him sipping coffee on the porch at sunrise. She'd play a record and there was Aleks, dancing around the room, waving his arms in the air. At night, she'd blink and see him sprawled across their bed reaching for her."

Oh, God. Her words turned me into a soggy mess. I rose from my chair, slid onto Adam's lap, and tucked my head under his chin. "Don't you dare leave me," I whispered.

His arms tightened around me. "I'm not going anywhere."

Mrs. M. studied us for a long moment. "This might sound silly, but maybe deep down inside, Freya hoped that one of her granddaughters would fall for a wolf shifter. Find the kind of love she shared with Aleks. Maybe that's why she made you promise never to sell the lease."

"Maybe." I agreed. We'd never know for sure, but that's how things turned out, at least for me.

We chatted for another half hour, then left with a promise to visit again soon. In downtown Belle Reve, we stopped to post a new announcement on the door of Freya's Bake Shop. The shop would reopen in ten days, not three as originally planned. Annika, Liv, and I needed more time to regain our bearings after all of the recent turmoil. The pack offered to reimburse us for lost income. We refused at first, but Matthew insisted. My cousins would stay in a guest room at the lodge until they moved back to town.

Adam pulled his truck onto the highway and followed the river toward Shooting Star Lake, toward home. Half an hour from town, he turned onto the narrow private road that threaded through dense forestland.

"You picked a challenging time to become the new alpha," I observed.

He grinned. "I didn't pick the time. It picked me."

"You know what I mean," I chided. "Bryce is dead, but you still have to deal with the coyotes and the grizzlies. Olga is in custody and you have to decide what to do with her. Belle Reve is up in arms about killer wolves. Fish and Wildlife wants to install trail cameras on pack lands. And within the pack, not everybody will be happy about changing the law to allow human mates."

He gave a low whistle. "That's a daunting list. You trying to talk me out of accepting the job?"

"No." I shook my head. "I'm not. I'm one hundred percent certain that you're up to the task. You'll be an amazing alpha."

"And you'll be an amazing alpha's mate," he said. "Our lives won't be easy, but they'll be good. They'll have meaning and purpose, and we'll be surrounded by good people."

"And if we have children, they'll be shifters." I watched him closely for his reaction. Having wolf pups mattered to him. I'd be naive to think otherwise. Honestly, I couldn't begrudge him wanting to have children who shared such an important part of his life, of his identity.

"That makes me happy," he said. "But our mating never depended on it. You were always enough."

Gratitude squeezed my heart. Less than two weeks ago, I was ready to settle for a second-rate relationship with a totally unworthy man. Second-rate? More like third-rate, or whatever the absolute bottom of the barrel was called. I was beyond lucky. I was blessed.

"Hey," I said. "Pull over."

"What? Why?" He swung curious eyes my way.

"Just do it."

With a shrug, he complied, bringing the truck to a quick stop in the middle of the gravel road. We bounced against our shoulder belts. A cloud of dust particles flew into the air.

"Now what?" he asked.

"Keep your hands on the steering wheel and count to one thousand," I ordered, my unsteady breathing betraying my nerves. I squirmed, my panties dampening in anticipation.

"What happens when I get to one thousand?" His voice had already thickened, as if he suspected what I was doing, as if the wolf was creeping closer to the surface.

"When you get to one thousand, you'll chase me. And if you catch me, you can bite. Just make sure we're not within view of any of the pack's security cameras."

Adam's body shut down. The breath halted in his lungs, his broad chest unmoving. His muscles locked. If he gripped the steering wheel any harder, it might crumble beneath his hands. Good thing I saw the pulse tapping against the side of his neck. Otherwise, I would've sworn his heart had stopped beating.

In his unnatural stillness, a hungry predator stirred, sniffed the air, and turned his laser focus on me. A predator I'd invited to give chase, to sate his desire for blood and sex on my oh-so-willing flesh.

The muscles in his throat worked. "You sure?"

"Yes," I breathed.

"Who do you want to chase you? The man or the wolf?"

"Hmmm." Before my courage failed me, before caution reared its head, I answered. "Both."

"One," he counted out loud.

The word jolted me into action. Adrenaline flooded my veins, and my hands shook as I fumbled with the door handle. "Two."

The door swung open. I lurched toward the opening, but the damned seat belt held me fast.

"Good grief," I muttered in disgust. My trembling fingers struggled with the belt's latch.

"Three."

Got it. I slid awkwardly out of the truck and landed on my knees. Jumping to my feet, I sprinted toward a break in the trees.

How long would it take Adam to reach one thousand? He wouldn't cheat—his honor wouldn't allow him to cheat—but neither would he show me any mercy when he caught up with me. And his victory was inevitable. Fated, as Adam liked to say. That didn't mean I had to make it easy for him. Rather than surrendering to the inescapable, I pushed myself harder. My feet flew over the uneven ground. I'd done this before, hadn't I? Fled a predator. Only this time, I wanted him to catch me.

Low-hanging branches slapped me as I dashed through them. Pine needles caught in my hair. I tripped over a log and face-planted on the soft earth. Rolling to my feet, I brushed crumbly twigs and soil from my cheeks. I'd look like a holy mess when we got back to the lodge. I'd look like a woman who'd been chased through the woods and taken. I'd look—and to keen shifter senses—I'd smell like Adam's mate.

My breath hitched as the full import of what I was doing crashed down on me, something far beyond my human understanding. Mating with a shifter. An undying union sealed with blood and fang.

Somewhere behind me, a wolf howled.

Holding my hands up to protect my face, I plunged through a thicket and stumbled into a small clearing. I gulped in mouthfuls of air. Trees and bushes surrounded me on every side, but the thick wall of growth promised no protection. I couldn't hide from the predator pursuing me.

The back of my neck prickled, a warning from some primitive part of my brain. I whipped my head around. A huge gray wolf stalked toward me, his golden eyes glittering with dark purpose. Instinct shrieked at me to run, to save myself. I quashed the impulse. I'd asked for this. I wanted this. Lifting my chin, I held my ground.

The wolf leapt, closing the distance between us. The powerful beast took me down to the forest floor. My back slammed against the ground, and the air exploded from my lungs. He straddled my chest, his sides heaving. Deadly fangs glinted in the dappled sunlight. Hot breath tickled my face. Lowering his head, the wolf nuzzled my throat, then slowly scraped his tongue across my cheek.

Sparkling lights enveloped us, a shimmering miasma that clogged the air with so much supernatural power that it was difficult to draw breath. The lights broke apart and faded. Now a naked Adam sprawled on top of me. Panting, he supported his weight on his elbows.

Without warning, he flipped me onto my stomach. He tore my shirt off over my head and cast it aside. Nimble fingers worked the clasp of my bra. With a snap of his wrist, he flung the bra across the clearing. It landed on a blackberry bush, followed quickly by my jeans and panties.

"You good?" he growled into my ear.

"Yes." I gasped.

Calloused hands seized my hips and jerked me up and backward. Adam's knee nudged my thighs apart. Before I could catch my breath, before I could ready myself, he thrust into me, his cock piercing all the way to my core. Grunting, he set an unforgiving pace, riding me hard and fast.

My fingers scrabbled against the ground, raking through pine needles and soil and twigs. Through bleary eyes, I half noticed the dirt embedded beneath my fingernails. I'd been afraid I'd go back to the lodge looking like a holy mess? Shoot. I'd look more like I'd been dragged kicking and screaming through the woods, the most willing victim ever. The notion struck me as oddly funny. I chuckled, my shoulders shaking with barely suppressed mirth.

Adam stilled, shuddering with the effort. "You okay?"

I groaned. "Don't stop."

That was all the encouragement he needed. Banding an arm around my waist, he pounded into me. With a happy sigh, I surrendered to sensation. My vision frayed and a buzzing sound filled my ears as an orgasm inched closer.

I was only dimly aware of Adam sweeping my hair off my shoulder, of his lips caressing the spot where shoulder curved into neck. Only when his teeth scraped against my skin did I realize what was happening, and by then, it was too late. With a predator's speed and precision, he struck. Fangs split my skin, drilled through muscle and tendon, and sank into bone.

The world sheeted white. I'd asked for this, but in the face of pain, instinct overruled intent. Arching my back, I tried to shake him off, but struggling was useless. He held fast, unwilling or unable to retract a claiming bite midway. His hand slid from my waist to my sex. A fingertip circled my clit, pleasure stealing some of the sting from the bite. Recoiling from a thrust, I accepted the pain, let it wash over me, until the balance shifted and pleasure overrode any hurt.

Deep inside me, his cock swelled, the signal that he was close. I let go, tipping over the edge just as hot jets of cum filled my pussy and spilled down my thighs. I slumped forward, breathless. Adam's fangs retracted and his tongue lathed the wound.

"What're you doing?" I mumbled, too spent to speak clearly.

"Sealing the bite mark," he said against my skin. He rolled onto his side and pulled me into the curve of his body. Perfectly content, my cheek resting on his arm, I snuggled against him.

Sunlight filtered through the trees and kissed our naked bodies as we lay together on the forest floor. My fingers drifted to the bite mark on my shoulder. Instead of torn skin dripping blood, I found a raised scar. My fingers came away clean.

"Shifter magic?" I asked sleepily.

"Something like that." Adam pressed a kiss against my hair.

"We're mated." I stated the obvious.

Chuckling, he rolled on top of me and trapped my wrists above my head. "Yep. From now until forever." He cocked his head to one side, and his expression grew serious. "Were you scared? When I chased you?"

I pulled a hand free and laid my palm to his rough cheek, my eyes never leaving his. "I could never be afraid of my big bad wolf."

"Never?"

An emphatic shake of my head. "Once upon a time, I was afraid of you—after you beat up Bryce—but not anymore. Not now that I know your heart."

He pressed a kiss to my palm. "I'm sorry you almost lost the cabin."

"It doesn't matter." At his puzzled expression, I stroked his cheek. "Grandma's cabin is my happy place, but whatever was damaged can be rebuilt."

"Your happy place?" He smiled gently down at me. "That's what I'm supposed to be, kitten."

"You are. My happy place. My safe place. But more than that, you're my home."

Epilogue

Zane

Five Weeks Later

I brought the truck to a stop in front of the Hagen cabin and cut the engine.

The place looked good as new—hell, better than new. Adam promised the women that we'd restore their grandma's cabin, and he put me in charge of the project. Smart move from the new alpha. There's a right way and a wrong way to go about things. If you're gonna do a task, don't half-ass it. He knew I wouldn't take shortcuts or do a slipshod job.

Adam, Remy, and Xander helped me rebuild the porch and the porch roof. The fire-damaged front siding and the door had to be replaced. I added a pair of French doors off the bedroom. While we were at it, I figured we might as well install all-new windows with weather-resistant, triple-pane glass. Keep the cabin warm and cozy when Annika and Liv visited in the winter. I updated the wiring, too. The women were full of plans for get-togethers at the cabin, so I tripled the size of the deck overlooking the lake. With any luck, I could seal the wood before the weather changed.

Smoke had infiltrated the cabin when Adam and I busted down the front door. We ventilated and cleaned the interior, but the smoky smell clung to the fabrics. Annika, Marit, and Liv ordered new curtains, rugs, and upholstered furniture, all in what they called "Grandma Freya style."

The small party celebrating the completion of the remodel was in full swing when I pulled up. Adam, Marit, Remy, and Liv raised their beer bottles in greeting. Grandpa nodded from one of the two Adirondack chairs in the yard. Xander was in his element, flipping burgers at the big new propane grill on the deck. Grinning, he waved a spatula at me.

The cabin door opened and Annika skipped down the porch steps, a quilt in her arms. The sun would set soon, and the temperature was dropping. She draped the quilt across Grandpa's lap, then took the chair next to him. In the dying sunlight, her hair glowed like polished maple. She spied me, smiled, and gestured for me to join the party.

I glanced over my shoulder at a cargo bed piled high with my secret project. I don't often second-guess myself, but now I wondered if I'd gone overboard. Too late to do anything about it if I had. With a sigh, I climbed out of the truck, put down the tailgate, and lifted out the first of two teak double-wide porch rockers.

"Whaddaya got there?" my brother called out.

"Outdoor furniture," I grunted.

Remy set down his beer bottle and jogged over to the truck, Adam, Marit, and Liv on his heels. Annika hopped up and ran over, too.

Hands on his hips, Adam looked over the contents of the truck bed. He gave a low whistle, and the asshole actually smirked. "You've been busy."

I was tempted to knock the smug expression off his face, but it wasn't right to hit the alpha. Instead, I lifted a noncommittal shoulder.

Annika touched a curved seat slat, then lifted her brown eyes to meet mine. "You made all this?"

I shifted my weight from one foot to the other. "I did."

She ran her hand slowly across the rocker's back rail. "It's absolutely beautiful. The wood's so smooth."

Well, yeah. Nothing could compare with handcrafted, solid-wood furniture.

Adam elbowed me. "Say thank you to the nice lady."

For fuck's sake. I glared at my exasperating cousin. My eyes fell on the black stone he wore on a leather cord around his neck. Lucky for him he was alpha.

"Thank you," I muttered. Shit. Why were they all staring at me?

"What all did you make?" Marit craned her neck, peering into the packed truck bed.

"Two double rockers, a couple of end tables, and a chaise lounge with an adjustable backrest." Annika had mentioned that she liked to lie out by the lake and read a book. I figured a lounge chair would be a good addition to the new deck.

"Holy shit," Liv exclaimed. "When did you find time to do all that? Did you give up sleeping?"

I shrugged. Woodworking relaxed me. I welcomed the time alone with my thoughts.

Annika bounced on her toes, excitement on her face. "I love it all. Thank you so much, Zane."

"Yes, thank you," Marit and Liv echoed.

"You're welcome," I replied quickly, before Adam could remind me of my manners again.

"What are those box things?" Marit pointed to the back of the truck bed.

"Cedar window planters." I turned to Annika. "You said you wanted window boxes for flowers."

She blinked. "You remember that?"

"Yeah," I said, not adding that I remembered everything she told me. Most of the time, too much conversation frayed my nerves and wore me out. But for some reason, Annika's happy chattering was different.

Annika turned to Liv and Marit. "Let's plant a bunch of hyacinth and tulip bulbs for next spring. Tulips were Grandma's favorite flower."

"I hate to be a buzzkill, but what about deer?" Liv said. "Grandma called flowers deer candy."

"Shoot. You're right." Annika looked crestfallen. "Maybe we could research deer-resistant flowers."

"Got a better idea." I surprised myself by speaking up.

All eyes swung my way.

"What?" Annika asked.

"Deer are afraid of predators," I said. "One whiff of wolf urine and they'll hightail it outta here."

A moment of silence, then Marit held up her hand. She shot an amused sideways glance at her mate. "Hold on. Are you suggesting that you guys pee on the flowers?"

Liv snorted. "A urine-soaked hyacinth. Wouldn't that smell nice?"

"Not *on* the flowers." Dammit. Why did I suddenly feel self-conscious and awkward? "We could—you know—mark the territory around the cabin."

"Make a sort of pee perimeter?" Annika suggested.

"That's right."

A furrow appeared between her eyes while she thought about it. Her brow smoothed out and she touched my arm. "I appreciate everything you do for us. You're a good man."

This kind of openhearted, sincere declaration pushed me way out of my comfort zone. "Ditto," I mumbled.

Ah, fuck. Did I just call Annika a good man?

Adam took pity on me and clapped me on the shoulder. "How about we move the furniture to the deck?"

Grateful for the change of topic, I nodded. We hauled the furniture to the deck, then left the women to arrange it how they liked best. I grabbed a beer and sat down next to my grandfather.

"How are you doing, Grandpa?" I asked.

He offered a weak smile. I'd hoped that retirement would lift a burden from his shoulders, take some of the stress off his ailing heart, but no. He looked worn out and worn down. Olga's lies and secrets weighed heavy on the old man. Adam was close to making a decision about her final fate—exile, continued incarceration, or death. I know which one I'd choose if I were alpha, but Adam was a more forgiving man than me. Maybe once the new alpha made up his mind, the old one could move on.

"I'm fine, son. Glad I lived long enough to see Adam happily mated and to meet Aleksandr's grandchildren."

I laid a hand on his shoulder. "We're counting on you to stick around for a good many more years."

"I'd like that. I'd like to live long enough to see all of my grandsons mated and happy."

"Don't hold your breath waiting for me to settle down," I warned. "Can't imagine any woman who'd put up with me."

"Is that right?" he said mildly. "Fetch your grandpa a beer, will you?"

I hopped up, grabbed a bottle of beer from the cooler, then sat down next to Grandpa again.

He took a long pull on his beer, then sighed with satisfaction. "Some things never get old." We clinked bottles. After a long moment, he said, "Adam asked me to talk to you about spending some time in Belle Reve."

"What? Why?" I frowned. Why would Adam send me to the city?

Grandpa patted my hand. "Kyra's been pulling bodyguard duty, working at Freya's Bake Shop during the day and sleeping on Annika and Liv's couch at night."

"That's right." From what I heard, Kyra was having a grand old time with the Hagen women.

"Kyra's aunt mated into a pack in Minnesota. The aunt is pregnant and the baby is due any day. She asked Kyra to come stay with her for a couple of weeks. Adam gave permission. He wants you to take Kyra's place in Belle Reve. Temporarily, of course."

I slumped back in my chair. Me? Working in a damned bakery? Making nice with human customers? Going home at night with Annika and Liv? There had to be some pack member with a better temperament for the job.

I turned suspicious eyes toward my cousin and his mate. Adam flashed me a shit-eating grin. Marit smiled with satisfaction, then blew me a kiss.

My eyes narrowed. What was my cousin up to?

Thank you for reading *Secrets of Shooting Star Lake*. I hope you enjoyed it. If you have the time and inclination, please visit the site where you purchased it and leave a rating or a brief review.

Want more Susanna Strom?

Sign up for Susanna's newsletter for book news, sales announcements, and exclusive content. When you subscribe, you'll receive a free short story set in the World Fallen world.
http://eepurl.com/h6WRRb

Join my readers group, Susanna's Stormers:
http://www.facebook.com/groups/1572291033136914

Follow me on Facebook:
http://www.facebook.com/susannastromauthor

Follow me on TikTok:
http://www.tiktok.com/@susannastrom_writer

Follow me on Instagram:
http://www.instagram.com/susannastrom.author

Acknowledgments

I'm grateful to the many people who offered support and assistance while I wrote *Secrets of Shooting Star Lake*.

Many thanks to my wonderful developmental editor, Christina Trevaskis, aka the Book Matchmaker. Tina brings decades of experience and expertise to our collaboration. With endless enthusiasm, she teaches me how to craft better stories and encourages me to write fearlessly.

Raven Dark—my writing BFF—is the first person to read everything I write. Raven is my go-to person for brainstorming, advice, and the occasional pep talk.

My proofreader, Brittany Meyer-Strom, is persnickety in the best possible way. She's saved me from some truly boneheaded errors.

I owe a debt of gratitude to editor Julia Fortune. Julia has a gift for identifying plot holes and potential problems in a story. Her suggestions helped me to write a better book.

Lori Jackson designed the gorgeous cover for *Secrets of Shooting Star Lake*. Lori is one of the best cover designers in the business and is a dream to work with.

Thanks to the brilliant photographer, Wander Aguiar, for providing the perfect cover image. A special shout-out to his associate, Andrey Bahia, who offers a truly exemplary level of customer service.

Author Michael Aspen—one of the wisest and most generous people I know—always offers help and advice when I come to him with a problem.

Additional thanks to everybody who has helped me along the way: Harry Shook, Sharon Shook, and Debbie Morley.

And finally, a big thank you to my husband, John Hoefer, who always encourages me to follow my dreams.

OTHER BOOKS BY
SUSANNA STROM

THE WORLD FALLEN SERIES

Pandemonium

Maelstrom

Bedlam

Cataclysm

Requiem